WILD GEESE

L. FAIRALL

WILD GEESE

By MARTHA OSTENSO

NEW YORK
DODD, MEAD AND COMPANY
1925

Published, October, 1925
Second Printing, October, 1925
Third printing, November, 1925
Fourth printing, November, 1925
Fifth printing, November, 1925
Sixth printing, November, 1925
Seventh printing, December, 1925
Eighth printing, December, 1925

PRINTED IN U. S. A.

THE VAIL-BALLOU PRESS
BINGHAMTON AND NEW YORK

Ex Libris

Edna J. LaFollette

WILD GEESE

CHAPTER I

1

It was not openly spoken of, but the family was waiting for Caleb Gare. Even Lind Archer, the new school teacher, who had come late that afternoon all the way from Yellow Post with the Indian mail carrier and must therefore be hungry, was waiting. Amelia Gare, Caleb's wife, with all her cheerful bustling about the kitchen as if everything weren't quite ready, could not break the suspense. Judith and Charlie had milked several of the cows, and had come in and out of the house repeatedly for no reason whatever. Martin, slow and clumsy of feeling as he was, had cleaned the entire stable so thoroughly that it looked unnatural. Ellen, Martin's twin, was playing the organ, but appeared to have forgotten even the more familiar parts of her repertoire, such as *Red Wing* and the less recent *Ben Bolt*. Ellen played, harmoniously enough, "by ear."

The Teacher sat quietly in the low red plush rocker, listening to the springs of it exclaim as she rocked to and fro. She reflected, with some misgivings, on the noncommittal opinions that had been expressed at Yellow Post the day before in reply to her delicately asked questions about the Gares. She remembered also, with increasing dis-

1

comfort, the short, scornful grunt of John Tobacco, the mail carrier, when she had sought from him what manner of being she might expect in Caleb Gare. Now, the squeaking rocker kept her mind off her hunger. The rocker seemed to say, "Caleb! Caleb! Caleb!" It amused the Teacher, rather wanly.

Presently the outer door swung open. Judith had come in again. Lind Archer saw her against the dim light of the lantern that hung by the kitchen door. She had a great, defiant body, her chest high and broad as a boy's; her hair was wild-locked and black and shone on top of her head with a bluish luster; her eyes were in sullen repose now, long and narrow; her lips were rich and drooped at the corners. She wore overalls and a heavy sweater, and stood squarely on her feet, as if prepared to take or give a blow.

Judith approached Lind with a heavy, swinging stride. Lind thought she had never before seen such vigorous beauty.

"Are you hungry?" the girl asked her abruptly.

"A little," Lind admitted.

Ellen's hands paused in mid-air over the organ keys. Her eyes held a reproach as she looked at Judith. But the younger girl, ignoring her sister, took a few long steps and disappeared into the pantry. She emerged with a plate on which were two slices of bread well-buttered, and a glass of milk.

Ellen's reproach grew. She stood up before the organ.

"Jude, you know father doesn't——"

"This won't spoil your supper any—if you're ever goin' to get it," said Jude to the Teacher, breaking in upon

Ellen's speech. Lind took the proffered food, too embarrassed to refuse it.

Ellen rose erectly and without a word walked into the kitchen. Lind felt that she was conferring in a whisper with her mother. The Teacher nibbled uncomfortably at her bread and took a sip of the milk.

Jude, who had been winding a bit of twine about a stick, threw herself on the floor at Lind's feet.

"You might as well know that he'll try to bully you," she said matter-of-factly. "He's starting by keeping supper waiting. He always does the same thing when a new teacher comes. He expects you to be a man. All the teachers have been men. He's in for a jolt. But you stick up for yourself, Miss Archer. Don't you let him bully you."

Amelia spoke from the doorway.

"Judith!"

"Never mind, Ma. I'm only tellin' her the truth."

Ellen came back into the room and placed a pitcher of water heavily on the table, as if she had miscalculated the distance between the table and her hand. A pucker of anxiety drew her brows together. Ellen wore silver rimmed glasses that were not originally prescribed for her. As a result the pupils of her eyes were always dilated and strained, the lids reddish and moist. She stood before the table for a moment and shot a bitter glance in the direction of Judith. Then she passed quickly out of the room.

Lind Archer finished her bread and butter in silence. There was a raw feeling in the air that no superficial remark could dispel.

Judith, apparently bent on tormenting her sister Ellen, whistled to her dog where he lay in the niche under the staircase. The dog looked up.

"Caleb!" she said sharply. The dog started, pricking up his ears.

Jude smiled maliciously toward Ellen, who moved about the kitchen as though she had not heard.

"You see—" said Judith, then began on another line. "He loves to ride around in the cart to show the Icelanders how much spare time he has during the busy season, while the rest of us slave around in the muck all day."

A feeling of apprehension was growing upon Lind. The high romance which had attended her setting out for this isolated spot in the north country was woefully deserting her. She had never before looked upon the naked image of hate. Here it was, in the eyes of a seventeen-year-old girl.

The light, gritting sound of wheels came from outside. Ellen returned to the organ stool, her face, for all its youth, bearing the hard serenity of a strong woman in a crisis. Lind wondered why the occasion should call for such fortitude.

"Judith, you had better call Martin," Ellen said in a thin voice. "Father has come."

Judith got to her feet without a word.

In the kitchen, Amelia hastily cleared the sink and placed in it a clean basin of hot water. She whipped the towel from its roller and put a fresh one in its place. Untying her apron, she straightened her dress and combed her hair briskly back before the cracked mirror on the wall.

Then the door opened. At first, Caleb seemed to be a huge man. As he drew into the center of the kitchen, Lind could see that he was, if anything, below medium height, but that his tremendous shoulders and massive head, which loomed forward from the rest of his body like a rough projection of rock from the edge of a cliff, gave him a towering appearance. When attention was directed to the lower half of his body, he seemed visibly to dwindle. He had harsh gray hair that hung in pointed locks about his head, a weedy, tobacco-stained mustache, and startling black brows that straggled together across the bridge of a heavy, bony nose. His eyes were little beads of light that sought Lind out where she sat in the lamp glow of the other room. He did not speak until he had hung his coat and hat on a peg, and had washed himself at the sink.

Lind saw that with Caleb was a frowsy-looking farmer in a red mackinaw. He also relieved himself of his outer garments and sat down without a word on a chair in the kitchen. Mrs Gare spoke to him but he answered only in broken monosyllables which Lind could not distinguish. The Teacher noticed, however, that Amelia addressed him with the same calm deference that had been in her attitude when Lind first met her in the barnyard that afternoon, upon her arrival with John Tobacco.

Caleb did not speak until he had finished washing. He did not so much as touch a comb to his ragged hair.

"Skuli will stay the night," he announced finally to Amelia. His voice surprised Lind. It was remarkably soft, almost like a purr.

"But I have no extra bed. The teacher has come," Mrs Gare protested mildly.

"The teacher—yes, of course—the teacher. Skuli stays the night," he repeated, with no more emphasis in his voice than when he had first spoken.

He called Skuli and proceeded, with a sort of hulking shuffle into the dining room, which constituted the other part of the ground floor of the log house, and also served as a living room.

"You are the teacher, I suppose," he said, seating himself near the iron stove with his back half turned from Lind. There was nothing in the expression of his face to indicate that he was surprised to find the new teacher a girl. She rose and extended her hand, which he ignored. Lind flushed helplessly.

"This is the other trustee of your school, Skuli Erickson," said Caleb, with an elaborate sweep of his hand toward the Icelander.

Lind gave Skuli her hand and he shook it heavily.

"There should by rights be three of us," Caleb went on in a wearied tone, as though he was giving perfunctory and tiresome information that might as well be dispensed with, "but there ain't been another appointed since old Josh Curtis died. Out here in this unorganized territory things go on much as the weather sees fit. And I don't know but what it ain't just as good with the two of us. Eh, Skuli?"

Skuli uttered a grunt which might have been an affirmation or a denial. He was slightly deaf, spoke very little English and understood little more.

In a few minutes they were all seated for supper, Lind between Ellen and Martin, Skuli directly at the other end of the long table from Caleb Gare.

"Looks like an early spring, eh, Skuli?" Caleb called to the Icelander.

Skuli nodded. "Ya," he agreed, helping himself well to potatoes and gravy.

There was a silence, during which the food was passed around the table. The children, all except Judith, sat with their eyes lowered to their plates, shame-facedly self-conscious in the unused presence of one so pretty and dainty as the new Teacher.

"Much rain down your way lately?" Caleb asked Skuli, calling the length of the table. Amelia glanced with faint dismay from her husband to Lind.

"Naat muts," Skuli replied. "Soom last veek. Purty dry."

Throughout the meal Caleb exchanged observations with the brief-spoken Skuli. You would have thought Skuli the honored guest of the evening. Lind looked across at Jude, whose eyes were smoldering. The Teacher smiled. Caleb's evident obliviousness of her was not half so humiliating to her as it was to Judith.

After supper the situation remained unchanged. Caleb ignored the Teacher as cleanly as if she were air. She withdrew to the horsehair couch in a corner and opened a book. Martin and Charlie, the youngest of the family, went out to finish milking, while Judith scraped and piled the dishes and removed them to the kitchen.

"Play us a piece, Ellen, play us a piece," Caleb requested. He and Skuli had drawn their chairs up to the stove in the center of the room and had taken out their pipes. A feeler of blue smoke curled up and around Caleb's head. Lind was reminded of a painting she had once seen of the fixed, sardonic face of a fakir, lifting his eyes upward to catch the demoniacal image of his conjuring.

While Judith helped in the kitchen, Ellen obediently went to the organ. She sat erect and prim in her washed-out gingham dress, that had apparently shrunk and grown too small even for her narrow shoulders and uncertain breast. Her fine brown hair, that was lighter in color and much less luxuriant than Judith's, was drawn back without a relenting wave from her rather prominent, austerely white brow. Her eyebrows were exquisitely shaped and black as ink-lines. Behind the magnifying glass of her spectacles her dark blue eyes swam liquid and vague. Her raw-looking, thin fingers sought out the keys.

"Yes, Bjarnasson's got the best fishing sites, no doubt about it—no doubt about it," Caleb declared in a loud voice, while Ellen played *Lead, Kindly Light*. "But he'd better not get to thinkin' he's goin' to hog the whole lake. Not by a damned sight—not by a damned sight. I'm goin' to send Martin over there one of these days with some new nets—too far to do anything during the freeze-up. What do you think about it, Erickson? Is he showin' you any fight?"

"Na-aow," Skuli grunted. "He geev me v'at I vant, de dirty djevil. I tak it first."

Caleb and Skuli both broke into stormy laughter at the Icelander's joke. Ellen faltered over the keys. Caleb glanced sharply at her and she hurriedly picked up the thread of the song. Judith came in from the kitchen and sat down on a fur rug on the floor. Her dog followed and snuggled his head in her lap. The girl sighed and leaned wearily against the wall. Lind noted again how strangely beautiful she was. Like some fabled animal—a centauress, perhaps.

Caleb launched upon an account of an involved sale of timber, at times almost shouting into Skuli's ear to make clear to him the technicalities. The strains of the hymn mourned lamely to an end. Ellen hastened into a patriotic march, stumbled over the keys, shifted to a lullaby and then to a waltz. A spot of red showed on either cheekbone. Her mouth was tightly drawn, her chin flat and long so that in profile she looked like an old, tired woman.

Amelia came and stood by the table. She turned up the wick of the lamp slightly. As she did so, the light picked out the shadows under her eyes, the rigid lines about her mouth, the pale sandy hair whitening about her temples. Amelia was fifty and was beginning to put on flesh, but she bore herself with a dignified reserve that seemed almost a part of her physical being, so that the grace which was hers in youth still clung to her. She seemed preposterously ill-fitted to her environment. Lind was filled with pity as she watched her move about the room, picking up a paper, straightening a doily, or, from a habit Lind realized must have been formed in another life, pulling down the shades before the windows. Amelia must surely have been worthy of a better lot.

"That reminds me," Caleb Gare began again. "How did you make out with those furs you sent to the Siding? Grini buy 'em up?"

"Ya-a. Gode monney." Skuli said, sucking comfortably at his pipe. "Fur-rrs—naow gode. Grini, he's fool himself. Hee! Hee!"

"Did I show you that wolf pelt Martin got east of here? Big beast he was too, eh, Martin? Where's the pelt? Find the pelt, Martin. Made a rug out of it, Skuli—you ought to do that with some of yours. Here —Jude—show Skuli the rug!"

Martin had crossed the floor to take the rug from Jude. The girl got up slowly. Her resentment flooded in a dark wave across her face.

"Skuli has seen it three times already," she muttered, snatching up the rug. Martin took it from her, a half grin on his face at her anger. Martin had long since learned the futility of indignation. He was twenty, past.

Caleb smiled blandly.

"Skuli forgets what a rug it is. Heh, heh!" His laugh was genial.

The Icelander examined it again, to please his host. He commented upon its quality, then handed it back to Caleb, who sat holding it while he resumed his talk.

Judith called Pete, the dog, and strode out of the room.

Amelia sighed and sat down with a lapful of worn stockings and a handleless cup over which to mend them.

Presently Judith returned, without the dog, and seated herself beside Lind. Caleb still held the rug.

Charlie was playing solitaire at the table.

"Here, Charlie," Caleb said to him. "Bought ye a new deck of cards at Yellow Post to-day. Couldn't think of anything to buy the girls—they have everything."

Judith thrust her shoes out before her. The toe-cap was off one of them. Amelia glanced at her quickly and shook her head in protest behind Caleb's back.

Ellen yawned behind her hand.

"Cheer up, Ellen my dear, we'll all be goin' to bed soon," Caleb said. "Skuli and I are both tired. Had a hard day, eh, Skuli?"

Judith sprang up.

"Well, I'm goin' anyway!" she asserted.

Caleb looked gently at Amelia, pointing with his pipe at Jude.

"Mother, Jude had better be lookin' to her manners, eh?" he suggested in his softest voice.

Amelia's eyes darted to Judith.

"Judie—remember——"

The girl reseated herself carelessly enough beside Lind, but the Teacher saw that her hands were clenched. Lind felt then that, like the other members of the household, she would come to hate and fear Caleb Gare.

2

It was so arranged that Judith slept with Lind that night. Amelia begged the Teacher to overlook the irregularity—Skuli, the Icelander, must be accommodated.

The great loft was curtained off into three compartments— the bed rooms of all the children and such infrequent guests as chanced to come. In the room below Caleb and Amelia slept; their bed was a cabinet during the day, folded up against the wall.

The floor of the loft was composed of pine boards scrubbed white and smooth. You could look down through a knothole and see the stove glowing red in the darkness of the room below. Above, the rough, cobweb-hung rafters leaned down upon you; and on a wild night a jet of wind would ripple over your cheek if you lay with your face to the wall. In a winter dawn even tiny siftings of snow might be found in the crease of your pillow.

Judith undressed. When she came to her undergarments she put her nightgown on with her arms free beneath it, so that she might finish disrobing in this manner.

She watched Lind taking off her trim outer clothing. When she saw that she wore dainty silk underthings she glanced at her more covertly. She made no comment.

After both girls had undressed, Judith picked up a string of amber beads Lind had placed on the stand near the bed. There was also a pair of ear rings of the same limpid yellow substance.

"Wild honey! Drops of wild honey!" Judith exclaimed in a whisper. "Just the color of you!"

Lind looked at her curiously. "You may have the beads, Judith," she said on an impulse.

Judith laughed. It was a rich laugh, from her deep young lungs. "My, wouldn't I look funny with them on! Specially, cleaning the stables. No, thanks. They were made for you, Miss Archer."

When the girl was asleep beside her, Lind, restless in her new surroundings, knelt at her window and looked out into the night. There was still a pale glow from the sunset, and the land stretched out black and remote under it.

3

Far out across the prairie a lantern was swinging low along the earth, and dimly visible was the squat, top-heavy form of a man. It was Caleb Gare. He walked like a man leaning forward against a strong wind. He frequently went out alone so, with a lantern; no one knew where, nor why; no one asked. Judith had once told Amelia scornfully that it was to assure himself that his land was still all there. . . .

Caleb pressed on through the half-dark, leaning forward as if against some invisible obstacle. Presently he came to a ridge from which he could look east and west, north and south, upon the land that was his; the two tame hayfields, separated from each other by a neck of timber belonging to Fusi Aronson (it would be well to own that timber, a fine stand it was); the dark, newly plowed furrows where in another five months the oats would again be stirring like a tawny sea under the sun; the acres where barley and rye would be sown for cattle feed, vanishing into the blue night toward the south; the small rectangle of wheat that he raised for chicken feed; the acres of narrow woodland stretching northward like a dark mane upon the earth; and the good, flat grazing land with two bluffs, that might have extended farther westward had it not encountered the holdings of that miser, Thorvald Thorvaldson; and, beyond the muskeg and a dried lake-bottom, his cherished field of flax.

Southeast, under the ridge, bottomless and foul, lay the muskeg, the sore to Caleb's eye. In the heat of summer it gave up sickly vapors in which clouds of mosquitoes rose. Cattle and horses, breaking through the pasture fence and heading for the hayfield, had disappeared beneath its spongy surface. South of it lay his flax field, the most precious part of all his land. To get rid of the useless land and buy in its place the neck of timber held by Fusi Aronson: that was an honest ambition and one to be achieved. That Fusi Aronson would part with his right hand rather than sell him a square inch of ground, Caleb knew all too well. But many a better man had been glad to part with a right hand in certain exigencies. There was the little matter of Bjorn Aronson's slight dishonesty, for instance, that was not generally known in the community—that little discrepancy in Bjorn's moral balance that hurt Fusi more than any other thing on earth. What a comfort it was to Fusi that Bjorn was now one of the trustees of the Yellow Post church fund, a connection that would surely brace his manhood and beat into him a true metal. Caleb smiled as he thought of the trusting Fusi. Something might come up that could be used to good advantage. Somehow he would use brother against brother . . . he would wait.

Caleb felt a glow of satisfaction as he stood there on the ridge peering out over his land until the last light had gone. He could hold all this, and more—add to it year after year—add to his herd of pure bred Holsteins and his drove of horses—raise more sheep—experiment with turkey and goose for the winter markets in the south—all this as long as he held the whip-hand over Amelia. Amelia's word would start the children, then it would be all over—the results of his labor would be swept from these fields like chaff from a barn floor. He was too old to carry on alone. Hired help was worse than none— lazy, treacherous, rapacious. As long as he kept track of the outcome of that little folly of hers. . . . And, so far, he had managed very well. True, he might at any time lose that little contact—the boy, good Lord, he must be a man now—might even die. He had come out of the war safely, in spite of Amelia's praying . . . oh, no doubt the woman had prayed that he would die! But it was an uncertain world. Amelia, she was a soft fool, thank God! Not many women would be so conveniently sentimental and self-sacrificing for the sake of a son born out of wedlock—and that son a man grown, and a stranger to his own mother. Well, if she was loth to have Mark Jordan learn of his parentage, Caleb Gare would not reveal it to him—providing that Amelia kept her place and did not force him to. . . . Mark Jordan was a fine young fellow, too, according to Bart Nugent. Bart had kept track of him very well, in the town where Caleb was unable to do his own spying. The good fathers in the mission had taken Amelia's story for truth, and Mark had grown up with the solid idea that he was the last of a family of saints. There was a joke for you!

The war had saved the boy from the priesthood, Bart Nugent had thought, and it had also radically altered his philosophy. He had always been interested in architecture, and had gone into it seriously after the war. Bart had written that a nervous disorder had lately developed in Mark Jordan from over-work, and that he might take to farming for a spell. Perhaps—the coincidence was not beyond thought. . . . It might not be well, however. . . . Amelia might weaken if she saw him. There was no guessing what a woman's reactions might be. Amelia had loved the boy's father, that he knew. The knowledge had eaten bitterly into his being when he was a younger man and had sought to possess Amelia in a manner different from the way in which he possessed her now. In that earlier passion of the blood he had found himself eternally frustrated. The man who had been gored to death by a bull on his own farm in the distant south had taken Amelia's soul with him, and had unwittingly left her bearing in her body the weapon which Caleb now so adroitly used against her. His control over her, being one of the brain only, although it achieved his ends, also at moments galled him with the reminder that the spirit of her had ever eluded him.

Caleb lifted the lantern and examined the wick. Things would turn out to his liking. He would hold the whip hand. Judith, yes, she was a problem. She had some of his own will, and she hated the soil . . . was beginning to think she was meant for other things . . . getting high notions, was Judith. She would have to be broken. She owed him something . . . owed the soil something. The twins, they would stay—no fear of their deserting. Martin and Ellen would not dare to leave; there was no other place for them. And Amelia, she was easy . . . yes, yes, she was easy, Amelia was!

Caleb glanced again at the coveted bit of woodland, and crossed the ridge toward home. After he had crawled through the barbed wire fence that surrounded the second hayfield he turned down the wick and blew out the flame in the lantern. No need of wasting oil. . . .

4.

Lind woke to the comfortable drowsiness of farmhouse lofts and piece quilts, and the inarticulate outdoor sounds of early spring mornings. Something had wakened her. She did not know then that it was the three knocks of the broom handle upon the ceiling of the room below, which was nothing else but the planks of the loft floor.

She lifted herself upon her elbow and looked down upon the dusky rose cheek of the girl beside her. Judith was more than three years younger than Lind, but somehow there was a wisdom that Lind did not share in the bountiful, relaxed beauty of her body as she lay asleep. An intangible fragrance rose from her, like warmth. Like the warmth of milk, or newly mown hay. Lind touched her lightly to waken her. Jude's eyes slowly opened, veiled like a waking child's. She yawned and stretched her round, strong arms above her head. Then she turned over on her stomach and lay for a few moments without speaking. Lind got out of bed and prepared to wash.

"I hate to get up," Jude declared from the pillows. "Some day I'm going to have a silk bed and lie in it forever, and hear cows bellowing right at my elbow and know I don't have to get up to water 'em."

Lind laughed at the absurd picture, while she saw the pathos in it. Three more knocks sounded peremptorily against the floor, and the Teacher turned questioningly toward Jude.

Judith drew herself lazily out of bed and began to pull on her stockings under her nightgown.

"You'd better hurry," she said to Lind. "There goes Ellen down."

Lind wrinkled her brows. "You don't mean that *I* must hurry?"

"He won't let breakfast be kept for anybody," Jude told her briefly.

Lind was thoroughly amazed. "But it must be only five o'clock! Whatever shall I do every morning until nine?" she exclaimed.

"Hm-p!" Jude retorted, relishing the perverse contempt she felt for the Teacher together with her admiration and envy. "You might milk a cow or two, or chase skunks. There's lots of 'em in the bush. That's Pete after one now. Hear him barkin'? The smell ain't bad —*isn't* bad—when you get used to it."

The Teacher shook herself free from the annoyance she felt at Caleb's rigor, and resolved to make the best of it. After all, it was rather amusing.

Breakfast, it turned out, was a meal eaten in almost complete silence. It was a fixed duty discharged without zest. Except Jude, the children did not seem half awake. The toil of the day before hung about them still like a tedious dream.

"Guess we'll plow up that fallow field over east, after all, Martin," Caleb said, settling back in his chair while he wiped his mustache with his hand. "Jude can start it all right this morning, eh, Martin?"

Martin continued eating his porridge. He was a slow eater, as he was a thinker. He could not quite appraise the meaning of his father's words. It was folly to seed the worn-out east field this spring. And as for Jude's plowing it—it was a heavy field, full of stones, difficult enough for a man. And hadn't there been talk of Jude continuing morning school as she had done last year, so that she might write her entrance examinations?

"Well—" Martin began solemnly. His face reddened as he found himself unable to protest. "Guess I could do it. Kind o' tough for Jude."

"Tough for Jude? Pshaw! Hear that, Jude? He says you can't do it! Guess there ain't a field that 'd stump you, eh, Jude? Some girl, that, Miss Archer. Look at the arm on her! Bigger'n mine. Heh! Heh!"

It was the first time he had addressed Lind that morning. The Teacher shrank from the tyranny so thinly veiled behind his jocularity. She ventured to smile at Judith, who appeared not to have heard her father's sally.

After breakfast, Judith went out to milk, and Lind accompanied her. The cow pen was overhung at one end by weeping willows, which were putting forth tiny buds. Judith led her cow to that extremity of the pen.

"It's a little prettier over here," she explained.

The cattle sheds and the shelters for the other animals were all of gray logs, the low roofs sodded and showing faintly green now, although it was still cold and raw. The ruts of the cow pen, since there had been no rain or snow for weeks, were hard as cement, and reminded Lind of the relief maps children made at school. The deep tracks of the cattle were almost indistinguishable from the human tracks intermingled with them. The cold of winter had fixed them there and only the rains of spring would wash them away.

"When did you stop school, Judie?" Lind asked. She had seated herself on a stone near the girl, and was watching the straight white stream of milk striking the bottom of the pail with a thin churring sound. The cow's flanks were satiny, her tail clotted with manure. The animal looked over her shoulder with a round, vague inquiry, and went on chewing her cud.

"Went half a day last year—every morning. Guess I won't go at all this year. He hasn't said, lately. He talked some about it during the freeze-up, and it sort of cheered me up then. But I guess he didn't mean anything by it."

Lind felt her indignation mounting once more against Caleb. This was criminal, denying the girl what education was at hand.

"Oh, my dear, hasn't your mother a thing to say about it? Do you *want* to go?"

"Wantin' and goin' is two different things," she replied, looking into the pail between her knees.

"But Judith," Lind said earnestly, bending toward her, "is there no way to arrange for your going—can he not do without you here?"

"He *can*, but he won't. There's no use talkin'." Judith shifted her great body on the milk stool. She seemed to have grown suddenly shy, with this talk that lay so close to her inmost desires.

Lind rose and touched Jude's shoulder. As she did so Caleb appeared from the end of the barn. He glanced sharply toward the girls once, then looked studiously away.

"You'd best go. He ain't likin' you being here," said Judith.

Feeling helplessly a culprit, Lind picked her way back across the rutted ground. She decided to go early to the school house and air the place thoroughly before the children came. It would give her something to do.

5

There stood the school house, across the trail from the Gare farm. It was low and square, and built of uneven logs: the white paint of it had peeled and fallen off here and there in large flakes. There it stood, in unashamed relief against the gray green haze of spruce and tamarac.

Lind would have liked Judith's company that first day at school. A teacher who had formerly taught at Oeland had told her of how he had actually been trampled in a stampede that had broken out among the young ruffians from beyond Latt's Slough.

By nine o'clock, the school room, the porch outside, and the playground were over-run by the sturdy demons who had gathered from miles around for what was an acknowledged holiday. Lind rose from her desk and

rang a small bell, which instantly brought order out
of chaos. There was a general scamper indoors, and
a hurried selection of the best and most remote seats by
the stronger of the small band. Lind looked down upon
the children, and saw that every seat was occupied; a
condition that would never prevail again throughout the
term. The children, some of them six feet tall and well
on in their 'teens, had come from every direction, even
from other districts—half of them with the sole purpose
of conveying to their elders their impressions of the
Teacher of Oeland, and with no intention of coming a
second day.

Lind sat at her desk and introduced herself. There
was dead quiet while she spoke. Every eye was fixed
upon her face.

"We are going to have a very nice time together here,
I know," said Lind. "You will keep the seats you have
for to-day, and to-morrow I shall move you about according to your grades. Don't you think that will be best?"
She smiled down at two of the ruddy cheeked girls who
sat together at one desk, and because their opinion was
thus sought, they nodded their heads energetically, and
afterwards whispered to each other how pretty the new
teacher was.

Lind opened a large black record book and began to
take their names, up one row and down another.

"Thorvaldson—Sophia, Anna, Una," Lind repeated
after three little girls in the foreground with pigtails as
white as snow. Behind them sat two boys from Yellow
Post, half-Cree, who did not know their last names and

looked back in great fright to their elder brother who sat in the rear.

And so on down the line. The Sandbos, who lived two miles to the east of the Gares, and five of whom attended school. The black-eyed Hungarian Klovacz children, whose father had a homestead several miles east of the Sandbos. The Bjarnassons, who came from the great lake on the west, and drove seven miles to school. Swarthy faced young tartars from north of Latt's Slough, momentarily impressed and suppressed, most of whom were too old to go to school and would probably not appear on the second day at all.

Lind saw with relief that she had captivated the children. There would be no trouble. She looked around at the dingy whitewashed walls.

"We shall have to have some pictures," she said. "How would you like to do a little painting this morning?"

There was vigorous assent. A little apple-cheeked Icelandic boy from the Narrows and a half-breed girl from Yellow Post importantly passed around the paint boxes and the coarse paper Lind had found in the store closet.

And so the first day of school began at Oeland.

6

It was April and the little buds were opening stickily on the elms, and tingeing their boughs with purple and brown. The cottonwoods were festooned with ragged catkins. A softness was unfurling like silk ribbons in the pale air, and the earth was breaking into tiny warm rifts from which stole a new green.

The children came to school in the mornings with their arms loaded with the long green catkins of the gray birch, which Lind told them was the *Betula Lutea;* which they promptly forgot. The ditches along the wood road became a gray blur of pussy willows; and one day Lind heard the first robin. It was a time of intense wonder in the north, after the long, harsh months when the heart is shut out from communion with the earth.

Lind frequently walked alone through the green filter of light in the woods that led away from the Gare farm northward to the acres of Fusi Aronson.

She thought of Caleb Gare and Amelia, and wondered how a human soul could keep from breaking utterly. Lind had wakened early one morning and had looked out from her window to see Amelia staring with transfixed eyes at the dawn—at something beyond the dawn, it seemed. It was not like a farm woman to do that. There must be some reason for Amelia's endurance. Was it a hope of compensation of some kind? The children? No, there was not enough affection among them—after the precious flame had been sucked into the very earth upon which and by which they lived—to make the sacrifice worth while. There must be something else. . . .

On a Friday evening, Lind prepared to leave for the Sandbos', whose homestead was in sight down the wood road from the Gares'. Caleb and Martin were repairing the chicken house, removing the winter sod from the roof and sparingly inserting shingles wherever there was a leak.

Judith came out of the house with the Teacher, who had with her a small bundle. Mrs Sandbo would expect her to stay the night, at least.

"I'm going to ride down with you—the cattle are down that way," said Judith, glancing toward the chicken house, where Martin was standing on a ladder swinging a hammer upon the damp shingles. Judith turned toward the log barn that crouched like an old moss-backed turtle between the wagon-shed and the granary.

Except for the blows of Martin's hammer on the soggy shingles there was not a sound abroad. The air and the earth seemed to be held together in a glass bowl. There was that thin luster over everything that comes only on a clear April evening. The dank, clinging smell of newly turned soil rose like a presence.

Lind was glad that Judith was to accompany her. They would have many things to talk about. Even at her age, Judith had a certain fineness of mind which came to an extent, perhaps, from the seasonal contact with the teachers of Oeland, but more from a deep native consciousness drawn from Amelia. Lind delighted in the rich spontaneity of the girl, in her naïve reactions. She saw much less of her than she might wish to. Caleb saw to it that Judith was busy about the place or in the fields during the day, and at night she wished for sleep more than for the comfort of friendship.

The Teacher stood below Martin and talked to him while she waited for Judith. Caleb had gone into the tool shed near the barn.

"Martin, it must be wonderful to make things—and mend them, with your hands," she ventured. Martin talked so little. He had not yet voluntarily addressed her.

He looked down at her and half grinned, drawing in his under lip bashfully.

" 'Tain't so wonderful—got to do it in any kind o' weather," he managed to say. His long, dull face became suffused; he intently inspected another shingle.

Poor Martin! At twenty he understood only one thing: work.

Caleb came out of the shed. With his left hand he brushed the right side of his weedy mustache: a gesture that had become familiar to Lind. He did not look at the Teacher. She was rather glad that he had adopted the policy of ignoring her. It gave her more opportunity to watch him.

Judith, mounted on the mare, Lady, beckoned to Lind. Caleb turned and saw her.

"Too early to go for the cattle," he said, lifting the bank of his eyebrows toward her meaningly. "That old seeder has to be fetched from Thorvaldsons'. Charlie can bring in the cattle."

"Charlie can get the seeder," Judith said in a clear voice. She sat straight and formidable in her saddle, facing Caleb coldly. Of the two, Lind felt that the girl was the more to be feared, for sheer physical power.

"Did you hear what I said, Jude?" Caleb asked, handing a box of nails up to Martin. His voice was gentle, casual.

In answer, Judith wheeled the mare toward the gate

and started down the wood road. Lind mounted the pony that the Sandbo children had left for her. On the road she met Jude, her face dark with anger.

"I'm through putting up with it!" Jude flared. "He's got to quit thinkin' we're animals he can drive around."

They rode along together for a short distance. Then Judith turned to go back.

"It's no use—he'll take it out on Ma. He knows I'm goin' to the Sandbos'. Find out if Sven is really comin' home, will you, Lind?"

The Teacher had asked her to call her Lind.

She nodded in response to the girl's request and rode on down the shimmering wood trail. In the shallow ravine on either side lay a mist of flowering dogwood trees. Behind her, growing fainter now, came the thudding sound of Martin's hammer on the rotten shingles of the chicken house.

7

The Sandbos boasted a frame house, and a wire fence around their buildings, not a sagging wooden one such as the Gares did with. The entire place was so overgrown with chokecherry and wild plum trees that in a short time now the house and barn and cowshed would be hidden in a white nebula. This beauty was more by accident than by design, for Mrs Sandbo would have preferred the frame house to be in full view to passers-by the whole year round. Frame houses were rare at this distance from the Siding of Nykerk.

In a remote time, which Mrs Sandbo liked to speak of

as a year or two ago, the family had lived in a small
village where a locomotive and passenger coaches were
seen three times a week and where a freight train was a
daily sight and nothing to be marveled at. The Gare
children, never having been beyond a radius of ten miles
from home (save perhaps Martin and Ellen on their
trips with the cattle to Nykerk), had never seen one of
these wonders of modern times, and as for having ridden
in one—! Well, the Sandbos, all of them except little
Lars, who was born at Oeland, *had* ridden on the rail-
way. So, although they were friendly enough from Mrs
Sandbo's point of view, there was a gulf between the two
families that could not be spanned.

Mrs Sandbo, having lived in a village, awaited Lind in
the parlor. Emma, a ponderous girl of fifteen who still
attended school half days, was stiff and sober in a clean
dress which had been donned for the occasion.
She ushered Lind into the presence of her mother without
a word. She suffered, in fact, the sensation of strangling
until the Teacher was out of her sight behind the parlor
door.

All the blinds, except one, were closely drawn in the
room where Mrs Sandbo sat. There was a dry smell
of wall paper, as if the windows had been nailed down
since the day the room was decorated. Mrs Sandbo herself looked like wall paper, as if she had no sizable depth
but a crisp, flat surface, the back of which would be
gritty. On each of the four walls of the room, in geo-
metrically precise relation, hung an enlarged photograph
of one or more of the Sandbo family. The photographs
bore the rainy-day look of all enlargements. That

which first met the eye was an enormous likeness of the late Ludvig Sandbo himself, Mrs Sandbo's husband.

Lind entered and greeted Mrs Sandbo in her warm manner. Her hostess had been sitting on an upright settee of pale brown imitation leather and elaborately carved and scrolled oak.

"I em glad to see you, Mees Archer," Mrs Sandbo beamed with a square, Norwegian intonation. "Seet down. I vill get coffee. The girls say you like it at Gares. Iss that so? You are the first then, much so I hate to say it. But vait—the coffee cooks." She rustled out of the room without waiting for a word from Lind.

The Teacher sat down before the frame of Ludvig Sandbo. He had eyes like black shoe buttons. They chilled Lind. She moved to a chair near the lighted window.

Mrs Sandbo returned with steaming coffee and little round pink-frosted cakes.

She assailed Lind at once with questions, not so much to get an answer as to reveal to the Teacher her familiarity with objects of the world beyond Oeland.

"Oh, yess, my husband, Ludvig, he vass there, many, many times," she interrupted when Lind mentioned the city she had come from. "It iss him, up on the vall. And a stinker he vass, too. .Good land, I say, t'ousand times a day, I em heppy he iss gone. Vhat he could drink, that von! Never vonce sober in six years!" She smacked her lips over her coffee cup and wiped her eyes with the corner of her apron.

"Was he not kind to you?" Lind asked gently.

"Kind? Him? Good land, I vass a dog under him. Now I live good, not much money, but no dirt from him, t'ank God!" She lifted her eyes up to the photograph, and Lind saw unmistakably a look of wistfulness in them.

"Hess Mrs Gare in her new teet' yet?" she asked presently, her pale eyebrows lifting eagerly above her glasses.

"I don't believe she has," said Lind, hesitating. "I think she expects to get them."

"Expects?" Mrs Sandbo almost snorted. "Her? She don't expect not'ing—not from *him*. She been getting these teet' now four five years while I get these two sets, and vhat have I got to buy vit' teet'? Old Gare—he got money to buy teet' for hundred head cattle. My man, he vass a devil, but he vass easy vit the money. He say, long before my teet' vass all gone, he say, 'Sigri, you tak couple dollar and go to dentist.' He vass alvays easy—*for* easy, I told him. Much for easy!" She looked fondly up at the photograph and sighed. This time there was certainly no doubt as to the wistfulness.

Lind was impressed. Mrs Sandbo hitched her chair more closely to Lind's and puckered her brows. She lowered her voice.

"Tell me—how goes it there? Iss he crenky vit you, too?"

"No, he hasn't bothered me," Lind told her.

"He's a rascal, Caleb Gare," Mrs Sandbo lamented with a shake of her head. "I feel sorry for the poor woman. To be merried to such a man!"

"Why does she stand it?"

"Vell—" Mrs Sandbo hesitated mysteriously, "I vould not say it again, but they say who knows it, that he bragged vonce to von of the Icelanders that he hess it *on* her. Vhat more, I can not say. Vhat *you* t'ink, Mees Archer? She iss scared purty near cresy of him, I t'ink."

Lind could venture no opinion. Mrs Sandbo drifted into other subjects, then rose ceremoniously to show Lind about the place and to offer her the freedom of the entire farm.

Lind liked the Sandbos. There had been ten of them, but there were only eight left at home. They were big-boned children, solemn and hard working. The eldest daughter, Dora, had married and lived on a homestead north of Latt's Slough. Sven, of whom Mrs Sandbo spoke proudly, had gone to work in town. He was expected home in May.

Emma, the eldest daughter at home, spent much time thinking. At least her eyes were always downcast, her full, healthy face inscrutable. Lind watched her come up the path leading Rosabelle, the Jersey. She clumped along, a great hulk of a girl, in step with the cow.

"What are you dreaming about, Emma dear?" Lind called to her from where she sat on the stone step of the milk shed.

Emma looked up, confused.

Lind drew her down beside her on the step.

"What are you thinking of, Emma?" she asked again.

But Emma blushed more furiously than ever, and Lind concluded that if she had really been thinking of anything, it was just as well left unsaid. Emma kept her silence and got up to milk Rosabelle. Her thoughts were, indeed, too profound for utterance.

When Lind was out of sight, Emma burst into tears of emotion. The Teacher was too beautiful and too sweet. She could not endure familiarity with her.

Such was the effect of Lind's coming to Oeland.

8

On Saturday evening, Lind walked home through a fine mist drifting down from the swamps that lay to the northward.

Against the strange pearly distance she saw the giant figure of a man beside a horse. As she walked across the field he came toward her, and she saw that it was Fusi Aronson, the great Icelander. Lind had spoken to him only once before, when she and Jude had found the cattle over on his land.

He doffed his hat when she spoke to him, and returned her greeting in the quaint English that seemed odd in a man of his size. There was a vast, rough charm about the man. He was grand in his demeanor, and somehow lonely, as a towering mountain is lonely, or as a solitary oak on the prairie.

Fusi walked back with her along the margin of a stand of spruce that pointed up blackly above the mist.

"I was just thinking how lucky you people are up here to have spring so close to you," Lind said, glancing up at him.

"Yes, we are very, very lucky," he responded slowly, carefully. "But few of us know it."

"Don't you think most of the farmers realize it—in one way or other?"

"No," he said. "Here the spirit feels only what the land can bring to the mouth. In the spring we know only that there is coming a winter. There is too much of selfishness here—like everywhere."

His voice was deep, sonorous, the tone almost oracular, as if his statement were made as much to the air as to Lind. She looked at him furtively.

"I wondered just what Caleb Gare was feeling about this—this mist," she ventured.

"Caleb Gare—he does not feel. I shall kill him one day. But even that he will not feel." There was no anger in Fusi's voice. Only deep, prescient certainty.

Lind started.

"Why?" she murmured.

"He took the lives of two of my brothers. There was epidemic here with the Indians some years back. It was a snowstorm and my brothers asked in at his door. They were blind from the storm. They were not sick —my brothers. But Caleb Gare feared the sickness— it was the devil sickness—he feared for himself. And he closed the door in their faces. One I found dead a mile from Caleb Gare's farm, two day after the storm. He was frozen so stiff we could not put on him his Sunday clothes and he was buried just so he was. The other died from the cold. I could not get the cold out of him, how long I worked. But first he told me about Caleb Gare."

There was iron in Fusi's voice. His face against the

darkening air was like iron.   Lind was silent.   Fear had
come to her.   Fear of this harsh land.

Far overhead sounded a voluminous prolonged cry,
like a great trumpet call.   Wild geese flying still farther
north, to a region beyond human warmth . . . beyond
even human isolation. . . .

CHAPTER II

1

LIND stayed in the school house working over the children's lessons usually until the light faded and she knew the Gares would be sitting down to supper. Although they were crowded with work, these were lonely hours, when the last sunlight streamed in across the deserted desks and blurred with a vague gold the dusty blackboards, so that you could not make out the awkward figures that had been written upon them.

Lind would often take out from her desk drawer the letters she had received from home in the twice-weekly mail, and, ashamed and impatient with herself as she would feel afterwards, she could not check the tears that rose to her eyes. And then, strangely enough, she would wipe her eyes and suddenly realize that it was not herself that she had been thinking of at all, but the Gares—Amelia, with her inviolable reserve and quiet graciousness, behind which she lived who knew what life; Ellen, prim to a point of agony; Martin, the stumbling dreamer, forever silent in his dream; the boy, Charlie, whom Caleb pampered and played against the others; Judith, vivid and terrible, who seemed the embryonic ecstasy of all life; and Caleb, who could not be characterized in the terms of human virtue or human vice—a spiritual counterpart of the land, as harsh, as demanding, as tyrannical as the very soil from which he drew his existence.

The Teacher was lonely, and even more conscious of the stark loneliness of Amelia, of Judith, of Ellen and Martin, each within himself. Work did not destroy the loneliness; work was only a fog in which they moved so that they might not see the loneliness of each other.

Days came when the loam was black and rich with rain. Judith and Martin, being the strongest of the workers under Caleb Gare, carried the soil's heaviest burden. Judith mounted the seeder and wove like a great dumb shuttle back and forth, up and down, across the rough tapestry of the land. In the adjacent field Martin worked with the bowed, unquestioning resignation of an old unfruitful man. Occasionally Judith threw a glance at him. Then she would scowl and exclaim profanely to the plodding horse.

What with the work in the fields and the occasional trips with ax and saw into the bush there was not much time for play. And in the evening the body and the brain would be heavy with sleep, and there was nothing to do but throw one's self down like a spent animal, and seek oblivion from thought and feeling.

Lind felt that the rigid routine of the farm was imposed by Caleb to keep anything out of the ordinary from happening. And nothing happened; nothing happened. Day in and day out, not a soul came to the Gare farm; not a soul left it, not even to visit the Sandbos, two miles or less away. And Caleb went about with the fixed, unreadable face of an old satyr, superficially indifferent to what went on, unconscious of those about him; underneath, holding taut the reins of power, alert, jealous of every gesture in the life within which he moved and governed.

2

Sunday formed a sort of interval. Caleb was the only one of the family who attended church at Yellow Post, but since the minister preached there only every third Sunday, coming all the way from the Nykerk parish, the amount of spiritual guidance the others missed was not so great as it might have been.

It happened that the second Sunday after Lind's coming was Easter Sunday, and a new minister was expected to hold services. Amelia rose as early as on week days, although usually an hour's grace was allowed on Sunday, to prepare Caleb's breakfast and lay out his white collar and black broadcloth suit with the greenish velvet lapels. His shoulders were not so square as they had been the decade or so before when the suit had been bought, and the back of the coat hunched up and made a little groove just below the collar, which Amelia could not remove with any amount of pressing. Each time he put the coat on, she was afraid he would notice it and complain of her careless treatment of it. Amelia had had to wash the stiff collar he had bought through the mail order catalogue, and its wings had lost some of their contour in the starching. So that by the time Caleb rose and knocked on the ceiling to waken the children, and then came into the kitchen to wash, Amelia was thoroughly worried about how the day would go.

"Martin washed the gig over yesterday—after work. It looks real nice," she said to him cheerfully as he spread the shaving soap over his jaw. Ever since they were first married, Caleb had looked most human and likeable when he was lathering his face preparatory to shaving, and she had often approached him at such times with requests or confessions that she dared not make before or after his toilet had been completed.

Caleb stropped his razor blade to his satisfaction before he replied. He always took his time in answering Amelia. It gave him leisure to weigh his words and to create a certain uneasiness in the woman concerning his reply, that was flattering to him even when the matter under discussion was a trivial one. This morning he was in a generous mood.

"Martin did well. I'm half a mind to take him with me. He's a way of doin' things without bein' driven to it," he chuckled, as though there were some underlying humor in the observation.

"Martin would like to go," said Amelia, careful not to make her voice too eager. She set the coffee on to boil. Then she went to the door and stood for a moment looking down toward the wood road where the willows were drooping in early bud as delicate as a green rain.

It would be sweet going to church this Easter morning, she thought. It was a long time now since this had been a reverent custom with her. Amelia had been Roman Catholic before her marriage to Caleb Gare. There had been one Easter more blessed and more joyous than all the others, when she had ridden across country to church with Mark Jordan's father. She had been a girl then—such a girl—not like her own daughters, but like Lind Archer. Her heart caught her suddenly, and her cheek warmed at the little disloyalty to her own flesh and blood. No reason why Judith or Ellen should not be like Lind. Was there none? A strange little jealousy crept into her breast. Lind had undoubtedly gone to church of an Easter Sunday, just as she had done—perhaps even sung in a choir, just as she had done. Jude and Ellen knew nothing of such things. Caleb did not see fit to permit them to go to Yellow Post services, where the lusty young swains of the entire country-side gathered to worship in good weather. He had once remarked pointedly to Amelia that, as she well knew, little good could come of their mixing in with that lot, and their salvation might easily prove their damnation. Amelia had seen through his pretenses very clearly. And she had come to regard with a bitter humor the sermons he brought home each Sunday after he had been to Yellow Post, genially reading the text from the Bible and giving a résumé of the minister's words as nearly as he remembered them, all before dinner. She forgot the sweetness of the willows and went back to the kitchen stove with the faint tightening about the lips that was all that was ever visible of Amelia's impatience with her lot.

There was no sound in the kitchen save the crackling of the wood in the stove and the little scraping of Caleb's razor. In the loft above, she could hear the children stirring, and she hoped they would not delay in coming down. When Caleb saw his collar it would be enough to set him off, without further vexation.

Lind was the first to come down. Amelia glanced at her quickly and saw how pretty she was in a blue silk gown that seemed to make her hair even more lustrous and her skin more delicate.

"Let me set the table for you, Mrs Gare," Lind offered.

"No—don't bother," said Amelia, in an abrupt tone that made Lind look at her in surprise. A slight flush came into Amelia's cheek. She could not understand herself for hating the girl at the moment. "You go out and see how nice it is," she hastened to add, "and Jude'll be down and set the table."

Wondering a little, Lind went out to the corral where a pair of yearlings came up to the wooden bar and reached out their muzzles to her for stroking.

Caleb finished shaving and pulled on his starched white shirt. Then he picked up the collar Amelia had laid out for him. He looked at it once and laid it down again, without a word. Amelia, stirring the porridge on the stove, prepared herself for his usual sneering comment. She was thankful Lind had gone out. But no remark came from Caleb. He left the collar where it was and passed softly into the other room.

Jude and Ellen and the boys came down one after the other and breakfast was on the table in a few minutes. Lind entered from the front doorway that looked out on the horse corral, and her silk gown billowed softly in the little breeze that came in behind her. She carried an armful of pussy willows that she had gathered in the ditch near the school house, and placed them in a basket beside the organ. Ellen gave them a glance and went into the kitchen abruptly.

"Cluttering up the house like that," she sniffed to Amelia, "Father will have something to say about her taking it on herself."

Amelia sighed. "Let him say it, then, Ellen," she replied. "Go and eat your breakfast. Tell the others to sit in. He'll not get to church if we don't eat right away."

On Sundays Caleb said grace. Meals on the other days were taken up with discussions of things on the farm. Lind and the others bowed their heads, but Judith sat upright and looked straight ahead of her. She forced herself to think of something else until Caleb had said "Amen." The thing that actually came into her mind was that he had not the Lord to thank for what they were about to receive, but *her*, and Martin, and Ellen, Amelia, and even Charlie, whose downcast face was hiding a grin.

"I'd like to take you with me this morning, Martin," said Caleb. "It'd do you a heap o' good, gettin' out among young people for a change. But I don't want you to be ashamed o' your own father, Martin."

Martin's long countenance lifted questioningly. He did not understand Caleb's remark, and before the Teacher he dared not ask. So he fell to eating his porridge again, slowly so that he should make no uncouth sound in Lind's presence.

Every one ate in silence. An expression of pained regret had come over Caleb's face when he spoke. Amelia knew what that meant. What he was about to say was designed to mortify her, she knew.

"No, Martin, you'll have to wait until some time when I have a clean collar to wear," he said slowly, mildly, almost humorously.

Amelia's face flamed. Her eyes darted to Lind to see if she had heard. But the Teacher went on serenely eating her breakfast.

Judith spoke up, in spite of Amelia's quick frown. "Well—I guess you'd have plenty of clean collars if you'd buy more than one a year," she snapped. "And send the stiff ones to Nykerk instead of expecting Ma to do 'em up."

"You're right, Jude. You're right," Caleb chuckled. "Guess I'm a little careless." He pushed his chair back and rose from the table. "Mind hitchin' up Lady, Charlie? You and me'll go to church anyway, collar or no collar." He turned his stooped back upon them and moved into the kitchen. Amelia followed him.

"Caleb—you're not going to church without a collar on?" she said in dismay.

He turned slowly and looked at her. "Think the Icelanders'll see what a fine wife you are, eh?" he asked softly. "Well—you go talk to Jude. See she looks to her manners. That young one is gettin' a sight too smart. Understand?" The sour grimace appeared on his face that Amelia was so used to seeing there. He ran his hand over his mustache as if to wipe the expression away. He put on his coat and went out of the house. Amelia was thankful he had not noticed the hump behind his coat collar.

She hurriedly set about clearing the table, and spoke to Judith in a low tone. "You must not cross him or be cheeky to him, Jude. You know he's getting old and can't stand it," she murmured, so that Lind should not hear.

"He's no older now than he ever was. He's always been as bad, and I'm through standin' for it," Jude replied promptly and in no low tone. "Seems to me I've just started growin' a brain enough to know how I hate him!"

"Judith!" cried Ellen, aghast. "Your own father!"

"He's not! I don't care if he is! I don't give a damn for him, and you shut up with your talk!" Jude cried, wheeling upon Ellen.

"Be quiet, Jude!" Amelia said calmly. "You're crazy to go on so! Before strangers!"

Lind had discreetly slipped out the front door.

"She's been that way ever since the Teacher came. As if nothing here is good enough for her any more," Ellen said tartly.

"That's not so! The Teacher has nothing to do with it. I've stood enough of his bullying of all of us. If he doesn't get a man here soon I'm going to leave!"

"Don't talk nonsense, Judith. You have no place to go," Amelia told her.

"Haven't I? You'll see!" She went on drying the dishes then without another word. Ellen's face was a study.

Lind crept under the fence of the sheep pasture and set out across the field. The scene was painful enough without Lind's further agonizing Amelia with her presence. Distressing conflicts of this kind had become increasingly common. She felt vaguely that her coming had incited Jude to greater rebellion. Lind wondered, as she had wondered time and again since her coming to Oeland, if there were any means in her power by which she might bring a little happiness into the lives of the Gares. And then in a moment, she was overwhelmed by her helplessness against the intangible thing that held them there, slaves to the land. It extended farther back than Caleb, this power, although it worked through him. Lind found herself longing for some one of her own world to talk with, some one to whom she might escape from the oppression of the Gares.

Judith surlily attended to the milking and helped Amelia with the separator, then took out Turk, one of the colts, and proceeded to break him into the saddle. The outraged animal threw her twice, while Martin looked on with a dry smile.

"I don't need to be thrown, Martin," Jude protested when she heard his rare laugh, "but I kind o' like it."

"Aw—yes you do," Martin grinned. "So does Turk."

"Well—you see if he does it again," she retorted, jumping into the saddle once more.

Lind, who had returned from her walk, came and sat on the ground beside Martin. He moved over for her deferentially, and blushed. It was a beautiful morning, full of sunshine, and with Caleb away the atmosphere on the farmstead was almost radiant. Although there was not much change in their conduct, Lind felt a releasing of reserve among the children, and delighted in being with them. She stared at Judith on the plunging horse, her amazement at the girl's dexterity increasing every moment.

The animal reared and snorted, pawed the air with his forelegs and tossed his mane like a black cloud. He was a handsome colt, slender and glossy as black satin, with a fine blazing eye. For a half hour Jude wrestled with him, careening in mad circles about the corral, taking near somersaults as the horse's forelegs straightened under him and his rear hoofs shot into the air time after time. Her laugh rang out in peals, her eyes were full of mockery. When she came close to the bar of the corral, Lind could see that her wrists, about which the rein was tightly wound, were bleeding.

"Don't you think she ought to stop, Martin?" Lind asked anxiously.

"She wouldn't," said Martin shortly. "He's near done."

When it was over, Jude unsaddled the panting, froth-covered animal, and threw herself down beside Lind and Martin.

"Nothing like a little exercise to make you feel good," she said, wiping her wrists. Her cheeks were deep red, and little beads of moisture shone on her tilted upper lip.

"You're marvelous, Judie," Lind said admiringly, "but you did frighten me once or twice."

"Gee, it's a great day, Mart," Judith observed lightly, "Couldn't you manage to sneak the spring wagon after dinner and take us up to the Slough? I'd like to get some crocuses. The air smells full of 'em."

"He'd say you was gaddin', like as not," Martin returned dubiously, but his eyes were unwontedly bright as he leaned back on his elbows and looked on the distant horizon. "I might try, though."

Lind looked with mixed feelings from one to the other of these two Gares. The height of their desire this precious April Sunday was to go gathering crocuses, and simple as the wish was, they took it for granted that somehow it would be denied.

"He'll be back from church about now. Sorry you couldn't go, Mart?" Judith's eyes twinkled with mischief, and Martin in appreciation smiled his twisted smile. Lind sat quietly watching the two while they talked with random happiness about momentous small things.

A half hour later the rattle of a cart sounded down the road, and Martin rose quickly to unbar the gate. Presently Caleb drove in with Charlie sitting very straight and important beside him. It was the first time in his life that Charlie had gone to church, and the experience had left its mark on his face and bearing much as a physical shock might have done. Martin, in his quiet, perceiving way, looked at the boy as he got out of the gig. Caleb went on to the house, leaving the two boys to unharness.

"How'd ye like it?" Martin asked.

"I liked the singin' all right, but the rest—I dunno as it was wuth goin' for," he said with a noncommittal swagger, hands thrust in pockets. "But the singin'—

yeah, it was pretty good. Everybody sung. I sung."
He looked down sheepishly and kicked a pebble along
the ground. "You better go next time, Mart. There
was a lot o' guys there from up north way. An' some
girls. I didn't talk to 'em, though—I mean the guys.
Pa said not. Said they was Swedes and like to beat a
little fella like me up—huh!—I could o' licked any of
'em!"

Martin led the horse to the corral. He saw that Lind
and Jude had gone indoors. He was glad. Lind's presence was disturbing to him, he did not know why.
Charlie walked thoughtfully beside him.

"Say, Mart—does Pa think he's goin' to make us all
stay here after we get big?" he asked, frowning. He was
an undersized lad and looked up to his brother with some
respect because of his superior height. As Caleb had
always made a favorite of him, and was amused by his
heedlessness, he had nothing but contempt for his sisters
who had been trained never to disobey their father or
to speak impudently to him.

"Well, I'm big, Charlie, ain't I? I guess like as not
we'll all stay," Martin replied soberly. So now Charlie
was beginning to wonder, too, he thought.

Charlie was silent as they went to the house. He was
only fifteen, it was true. But to-day he had heard singing, and had found he liked to sing, with a lot of young
folks like himself or a little older. There was one boy
there he would have liked to talk to. The boy had a red
tie, and put collection in the plate from his own pocket.

Before dinner on Sunday it was the custom for the
family to assemble in the sitting room and hear Caleb

recite the sermon that had been delivered at Yellow Post church. Although for reasons of his own he did not think it well to permit the family to go to the service, he felt that it was unbefitting a Christian to keep them from the grace of God's word.

"Will you join us in hearing the sermon, Miss Archer?" Caleb asked the Teacher when Amelia was drawing the chairs into a semicircle in the middle of the room. His manner was his best, suave, gentle and benevolent. He had taken the Bible down from its place on the shelf above the organ, and held it a little distance away from him as he had seen the new preacher do, as if not to desecrate the book by contact with his sinfully mortal person.

Lind could not well refuse. She sat down with the others, and Ellen at the organ played *Lead, Kindly Light*. Then Caleb held up a hand and intoned the Lord's prayer. His voice was miraculously soft. Suddenly Lind found herself wanting to cry out against the farce, and confront Caleb with the monstrousness of his act. But she sat silent.

Caleb opened the Bible and read:

"Again, I considered all travail, and every right work, that for this a man is envied of his neighbor. This is also vanity and vexation of spirit.

"The fool foldeth his hands together, and eateth his own flesh.

"Better is an handful in quietness, than both the hands full with travail and vexation of spirit.

"Then I returned, and I saw vanity under the sun."

Caleb paused, cleared his throat, and looked signifi-
cantly at each member of the family, dwelling last upon
Lind. The Teacher stirred with discomfort under the
steely condemnation in the old man's eyes. His voice
went on, rising to a grand sonorousness:

*"There is one alone, and there is not a second; yea,
he has neither child nor brother: yet is there no end
of all his labor; neither is his eye satisfied with riches;
neither saith he, For whom do I labor, and bereave my
soul of good? This is vanity, yea, it is a sore travail.*

*"Two are better than one; because they have a good
reward for their labor.*

*"For if they fall, the one will lift his fellow: but woe
to him that is alone when he falleth; for he hath not
another to help him up.*

*"Again, if two lie together, then they have heat: but
how can one be warm alone?*

*"And if one prevail against him, two shall withstand
him; and a threefold cord is not quickly broken."*

Caleb sternly closed the book. "So endeth the lesson," he said huskily.

The children, waiting for the end of the ordeal, had
only half heard the words. But Amelia, naturally pious,
had drunk them in. One phrase stuck in her mind.
"The fool foldeth his hands together, and eateth his own
flesh." That was what he was doing. That was what
she was helping him do. Eating his own flesh, here on
the land. But for her there was no alternative, no choice
save which of her flesh she should eat. O God, it was

unendurable!　Caleb was going on—and on—the sermon —the new preacher's sermon . . .

"So must we, who dwell in this lonely land and strive to live Christian lives on the acres the Lord hath given us, cling together for warmth and for good reward for our labor. 'Better is an handful with quietness, than both the hands full with travail and vexation of spirit.' Better live here like we are, poor but content, than to seek the world and all its vices for enlargement of our worldly wealth. That, Jude, is for you to think of, careful, and for you, Ellen and Martin, and like as not, for you, Charlie. 'For if they fall, the one will lift up his fellow: but *woe*'—hear me—'*woe* to him that is alone when he falleth.' Do they understand the lesson, Amelia?"

Amelia murmured, "Yes, I think they all understand it." She could have shouted aloud, beaten his face for his hypocrisy. She could have risen and belabored him with all her strength for his bland misappropriation of a noble passage from the book that had given her many an hour's comfort. But she did nothing but sit and listen attentively until he had, in a hushed voice, given the last blessing.

"This was not strictly an Easter Sunday sermon, you understand. But Reverend Blossom thought it more like for us to have a sermon that would fit in with the season, so he said. What do you think, Amelia?"

"I think it was a well chosen sermon," said Amelia quietly.

Then they all rose and sat down at the table, while Mrs Gare brought the food from the kitchen, and Judith, yawning with boredom, helped her.

3

On the following Friday, Gertrude Bjarnasson, who had been friendly toward Ellen the time or two that she had talked with her at Yellow Post, invited Ellen and the Teacher for a visit, sending the message to them through the younger children who went to school. Ellen made so bold as to ask Caleb for permission to accompany Lind to the great stone house of the Icelanders on the lake.

Caleb regarded her with pained surprise.

"Do you want them to show you their fine house, and their fishing nets, and their boats, and their windmill, when your own father is too poor to have such things? You know how much better they think they are than us," he said gently, wagging his head, "but if you *must* go . . ."

Ellen sighed. She had never been at the great stone house. She would never, perhaps, be permitted to go. But it was of no use to protest—Amelia would be seen weeping a short time afterward if she did. There was nothing to do but bear with things. And wonder if Malcolm would ever be coming back again. He had said— ah, yes, he had said that he would, in the spring.

It was just a year since Malcolm had left to work in the lumber mills to the south. And before that there had been only a week or two of incomprehensible, guilty rapture. Malcolm had kissed Ellen but once when they were alone in the barn after milking. An unromantic place it was save for the witching flood of light from a full moon. It had been a moment of unforgettable bliss. Had Malcolm been less diffident that evening, had he seized the opportunity and taken her away before she had time to reflect, everything would have been different. But Ellen, sustained by her habitual loyalty to Caleb and by the fact that Malcolm had Indian blood in his veins, regained overnight her unbendable control, and Malcolm, wounded and perplexed, went away soon afterward. It was only the pain in her eyes that prompted him to tell her that he would be coming back again. And here it was spring—after the long winter. . . .

So, without Ellen, Lind went home that Friday evening with the children of the Bjarnassons, the great clan who lived to the westward.

The air was soft and vibrant with the whir of migratory wild fowl. Rain pools filled the ditches along the road, and lay like stained glass in the low sun; the overhanging willows were in full leaf now, the sedges vividly green and as yet unbowed by a single wind. Such a new, ecstatic world of growth! Behind the Bjarnasson children in the cart, Lind held out her hands as if to gather in the beauty of it from the wide air.

In the great stone house on the lake, dwelt four generations of Bjarnassons. Old Erik, who was among the first of the Icelanders to settle at Oeland, had seen his land pass in turn from his son to his son's son. Erik was well into his eighties now, a time for dreaming much, and fishing a little when the sun was warm on the white rocks in the cove. Young Erik, his grandson, had married long since and now sent his children to Oeland School. It was young Erik's father, Mathias, who had built the stone house.

Mathias was a massive man, sixty now, but eternal in endurance, eternal in warmth and hospitality of nature. The house he had built with his own hands was like him, was a square stone image of him. He had excavated the earth and built its rugged, lasting foundation; had hauled stones in slow wagon-loads, and with the care and fineness of a woman patterning lace, had fitted them together in the mortar and had built four broad walls to the blue.

In all that region, there was not another house like it.

Like a welcome, its western windows were aflame with light from a red sun, when Andres and Helga drove up the road with the Teacher. Below the house lay the lake, wrought through and through with silver and rose.

Helga escorted Lind into the house.

The immaculate kitchen had a warm, good smell, like cinnamon. The floor was white as bread. On it were round, braided rag mats of bright, clear colors.

Helga's mother had never been in Iceland, but her English was so little used that it halted here and there. Such was the isolation of the place.

"You will like coffee, now, maybe," she said to Lind, half shyly. "Bring the teacher a chair, Helga."

She hurried about, a round little figure of a woman with a round, unchanging face. From an immense wooden cupboard with red glass doors she brought out cups and saucers, and certain thin wafers rolled up tightly in sugar. And while Lind ate and drank, she sat with her hands clasped in her lap, saying never a word.

From an inner room, Lind heard a steady, muffled sound, between a hum and a purr.

"It is grandmother, spinning," said Mrs Bjarnasson. "She is blind, but she spins. She spins all of our wool."

"She speaks no English, of course," said Lind.

She spoke none. But when Lind went in and shook hands with her, the ancient lady raised her face to hers as if she were looking at her with recognition. She was so stooped that as she sat at the spinning wheel, her head was almost level with the distaff.

She murmured something in Icelandic.

"She means that you are good to look on," said Mrs Bjarnasson the younger. "She always says she can see people's faces when they speak the first time to her. She will tell your fortune if you ask her."

Lind was eager to hear the old lady, who drew aside from her spinning and took both of the Teacher's hands in her own withered ones. She held them and turned her knotted, brown face, that had something of the sheen of a cocoon, upward to the light, her eyes sealed.

She spoke rapidly, in a queer, lilting voice. The younger Mrs Bjarnasson interpreted as she went along.

"She says you will have a lover very soon," Lind was told. "There is a shadow over him. You will never know the secret of him. But you will be happy. That is all—that is enough, she has told you."

Lind laughed, but a ripple crossed her heart.

"Does she always tell the truth?" the Teacher asked.

"Wait and see," said Mrs Bjarnasson, nodding her head.

Superstition here lay along life in a broad vein.

The men came in to supper from work in the fields and along the shore: young Erik's brothers, Peter and Valdemar, and his cousin, Johan; Mathias, laughing mightily at some joke he had turned on one of them.

They spoke in the Icelandic, simple and rough, not thinking to change in deference to the Teacher. They spoke no ill: why should they affect a strange tongue to prove it? Each greeted Lind with an awkward politeness. The women of the family they each kissed in turn. It was the custom.

There were other women in the family as well: Gertrude and Althea, sisters of young Erik, and Althea, his maiden aunt. The women were in constant attendance upon Lind, to see that she was at ease. While supper was being prepared the elder Althea, who was somewhat intellectual, brought her a book of Icelandic sagas translated into English, and placed a stool under her feet to insure her comfort: then she moved as quietly away as a wraith.

The supper was a vast affair of fish that had been brought from the "great" river, dried meats, potatoes, and many kinds of crisp sugared cakes, and many cups of coffee. The men ate heartily of the fish, greatly of the potatoes. To Lind it was a revelation.

A wind rose suddenly before the meal was over, and in a surprisingly short time the lake was breaking in a long shudder against the rocky shore. Quiet descended upon the family group, as though from some unseen force outside.

"Baldur will not rest to-night," the elder Althea murmured in the language. Her eyes were bright and strangely young, although she was fifty and had never married.

"Baldur was a fool to defy the lake that night. He will be a long time on the bottom," grunted the younger Erik. But he started as a door slammed shut in the upper part of the house.

"Tell the Teacher," Gertrude said. She was round-eyed and pretty. She had stared uninterruptedly at Lind throughout the meal. Now there was a detached look in her face.

"The Teacher has heard, like as not," began young Erik, in the uneven vowel tones of the Icelander. "The Gares know, I think."

"No," said Lind. "I have not heard anything."

"The lake has two of our family. One, my brother, Gisli, one my sister Althea's promised husband. They were friends, and they quarreled. They carried their quarrel into the lake in two boats. It was a storm—the lake took them. We have not yet found any of them—not a small sign. Until so, we do not let others fish in the lake. Caleb Gare, he says, yes, he shall fish. We say no. We are a family, Mees Archer—a great family. We shall not let others in to fish where our dead is buried." Young Erik ended sternly.

The wind and water screamed against the shore. Lind trembled, and thrilled.

"No, they will not rest until we find them," said the elder Althea. Her niece and namesake sat still with her eyes downcast.

There followed tales of supernatural events, of visions and omens, and of disaster that befell the unheeding. The great, grizzled Mathias told solemnly of the ancient pride of the Bjarnassons in Iceland, and of the dire fate of one who was disloyal to that pride, to that great bond. Told of how the curse of the ancients fell upon him, and of how his days were a torment and his nights a madness, so that even death could not bring forgetfulness. There was a weird poetry in Mathias' telling, a great rhythm of melancholy romance. He had lived much in communion with solitude, and had come to know that there is an unmeasurable Alone surrounding each soul, and that nameless and undreamed are the forms that drift within that region. So that it was well for the members of a great family to cleave together and so ward off the menaces and the dreads of the great Alone.

When the Teacher went to bed finally, the storm had abated. High above the soughing of the wind under the great eaves of the stone house, Lind heard the trailing clangor of the wild geese. Their cry smote upon the heart like the loneliness of the universe . . . a magnificent seeking through solitude—an endless quest.

4

The farm of Thorvald Thorvaldson lay half-way between the Gares' and the Bjarnassons'.

Thorvald had nine girls, and no boys. Consequently his farm was a fragment of neglect, a ragged piece of land of no value save as a hindrance to Caleb Gare's ambition to extend his pastures farther westward. Which hindrance, Thorvald maintained, was gratifying in itself.

Lind stopped there on her way home from the Bjarnassons' to speak to Mrs Thorvaldson about the condition of the scalps of her younger daughters.   She would bring the matter up delicately.

From the seat of the Bjarnasson children's cart, Lind saw Mrs Thorvaldson struggling with the cattle in the milk yard—saw her pushed and jostled about by the unmanageable animals, which she was trying to separate. Lind saw also that she was heavy with child.

Somehow, Lind could not bring herself to mention the heads. She waved good morning to the woman and then told Andres to drive back to the road. She herself would use kerosene on the young ones.

From the top of the sharp ridge that looked down upon the forks where three roads met, from the north, the east and the west, Lind saw a man on horseback. His head was bare, his hat slung across the pommel of his saddle. His clothes, the contour of his well-groomed head, even the way he sat astride his horse signified to Lind that he was from the world beyond Nykerk Siding, from the direction of which he had come. For some reason she felt shy about encountering him, and asked Andres to rein in and let the stranger pass ahead of them on the forks. Andres stopped the horse, and Lind was confident that the man on horseback rode on without having seen them.

5

Mark Jordan smiled to himself as he jogged along the road on the Indian pony he had hired at the Siding to take him to the farm of the Hungarian, Anton Klovacz. His greenish, ironical eyes, that could in an instant take on the shadow of a dream, searched the dust in the road ahead of him, and saw never the track or trace of human passage. For a day, then, fully, the road had been empty save, perhaps, for the foraging sparrows. What an ideal place to come to, away from Arbuthnot and his wife and their eternal friends, who would leave their tracks on pavement, if self-importance counted for anything. But then—perhaps he was unfair. Arbuthnot wasn't such a rotter in some ways. But he did get on the nerves of a man whose nerves were raw to begin with—with his ever-lasting talk on art and the City Beautiful of To-morrow. A good architect, in his way, but an unbearable ass. No better as an architect than Mark himself, if it came to that, for all his name and fame. Well, he was free of it all for a half year, thanks to good old Doc Brisbane! There was a medico with perception! One who could tell what the soul of a man wanted long before the body tumbled to it, fret about as it might in the quest.

God, how good this air was! It smelt like the young lilac leaves you used to suck against your lips and break with a snap when you were a kid, or like the slippery elm bark you used to chew and make a viscous cud of!

Dwelling on his childhood, Mark thought of the kindly old priests in the mission who had given him everything in the way of training and education in the hope that his mind would develop along religious lines. If they had harbored any resentment, they had concealed it well, and had encouraged him when he took early to archi-tecture. He would have to go back and visit them when this "jump cure" as old Brisbane called it, was effected.

Mark paused in the road and looked out over the prairie, flat and new looking, as though hills had not yet been dreamt of by its Creator. On the north side of the road there was stiff timber, scantily green as yet, springing up from ground that was black and scarred from an old fire. Mark dismounted and stepped in among the charred stumps of the old trees. At the base of one, leaning against it as if for shelter, grew a tiny wood violet, almost colorless. He looked at it but did not pluck it as he was first tempted to do. He laughed at himself for his compassion and walked back to his horse.

"We all do that—lean up against burnt stumps—somehow or other," he mused. And then he wondered, rather relevantly, he thought, "What would have happened to me if mother and father had lived?"

As he rode along, a mood of loneliness overtook him— the same cold feeling of belonging nowhere that he had had at night when he was a little boy, after the priest had put the light out and he lay listening to the rain on the glass of the window. He shook himself impatiently. Time he was getting over that morose habit now, nearing thirty. He looked over his shoulder and saw that the sun made only a fillip of gold on the rim of the horizon. A steady blue was creeping over the prairie in place of the magnificent light that had been there the moment before. The churr of the frogs had begun in the ditches along the road, and the small leaves on the willows hung with a faint indolence. Suddenly Mark stopped his horse to listen. He lifted his face up to catch the strange sound that was passing over him, a great summoning trumpet-call, that seemed to hollow out the heavens.

"Wild geese," he said aloud. "They sound as if they know something about it—something about being alone."

CHAPTER III

1

ON a morning ringing with bird-song, Ellen and Martin took the wagon into the "bush" for wood. It was before school time, an hour after sunrise, and the Teacher, who always breakfasted, of course, with the family, rode with them.

When the horse came to a stand, Lind asked Ellen and Martin to listen. In the stillness among the dogwood trees the first sunlight lay like a faint yellow dust. Suddenly a cat-bird called. Lind trilled, whistled. The cat-bird returned the salute on the identical note. Lind laughed. There was a birdish laugh from the trees.

"We used to do that when we were kids," said Ellen. "A long time ago——"

"Remember that blue-jay we saw, Ellen? That one that was mad at the cat-birds," Martin put in. There was something almost eager in his voice.

Ellen laughed her half-startled laugh. She did everything suddenly, nervously, after a period of slow considering.

Lind followed them into the timber, where Martin fell to with the ax, cleaving with sloping blows into the bole of a dry birch. The swing and shock of the ax broke into the cool morning and woke a chorus of echoes. While Martin chopped, Lind helped Ellen drag the trees, which were small, into a clearing. Then Ellen, with a hatchet, trimmed them down to the trunk. Afterward they piled them into the wagon, and saw that the sun was now free of the bush and that it must be well on toward nine o'clock. Before Ellen returned to the wagon the last time she ran a thorn through her shoe and into her foot. But she said nothing about it. Ellen had come to pride herself on her stoic endurance of physical pain, and no matter how small or great it was, pain was no longer distinguished for her by its degree.

Martin was happy this morning. Lind saw that he was, and would have liked to engage him in conversation about himself, but knew his shyness.

It always made him happy to feel his strength where results were immediate. He did not know, however, that this was the cause of his mood. He would have whistled, or even stamped with both feet on the floor of the wagon had the Teacher not been there.

Caleb Gare was inspecting a number of cattle in the barn-yard when Martin and Ellen returned. They had left the Teacher at the school.

Caleb called to Martin.

"These steers go in to the Siding to-morrow. Take Ellen with you."

Martin wondered to himself what object there was in selling steers just now, but he said nothing. Then he noticed that one of the animals was a favorite of Judith's, which she had raised and planned to sell in the fall in order to purchase a winter coat. Still he made no comment. It was Judith's steer. . . .

That day Ellen applied poultices of hot soaked bread to her foot. Amelia was concerned about it, but, as was her way, made no mention of it to Caleb when he came in for the noon meal.

Charlie had given Amelia further cause for distress that morning. He had ridden the mare so hard that she had come home in a white froth: and Charlie knew it was forbidden to spend the animal in such a way. The mare was still quivering in the stable when Caleb examined her. It happened that Judith had just returned from the muskeg where, mounted on Prince, she had roped out a calf that had broken from the pasture with a number of cows.

Caleb entered the house. Amelia, busily taking biscuits from the oven for dinner, saw his face and knew that something had happened. Ellen's foot and now trouble over the mare. Amelia pushed her hair back from her hot forehead.

"Where is Judith?" Caleb demanded, the points of his eyes fixed.

Ellen, who was setting the table, straightened her narrow back and listened. So Judith, thoughtless of Amelia, had done something again.

"She's putting ointment on her hands," Amelia said.

"And well she might! Ointment! T—t—ch! Bring her here!"

"What is it, Caleb? What has she done?"

"Done! Bring her here, I say!" The veins in his neck swelled to livid welts. Amelia hurried past him to call Jude from the loft, but the girl had heard the conversation where she stood upstairs.

She came into the kitchen, her hands hanging before her and covered with yellow salve where the rope with which she had rescued the calf had burned into the flesh. She regarded Caleb coldly.

"Well?" she asked.

Caleb approached her, his head jutting forward from his shoulders.

"Don't you 'well' me! What have you done with the mare? What have you done with her, I say?" His voice rose from a sort of husky whisper to a thin peal.

"I wasn't riding the mare!"

"Then who had her? Who had her but you—tell me that."

"Charlie rode the mare, Caleb! I told him before he took her out to be easy with her," Amelia put in hurriedly.

Caleb threw back his head with a jerk. He laughed. *"You* did! Well, well!"

Laughing softly, he shuffled into the other room and sat down to the table. Presently the others came in and quietly took their places. When Lind entered and threw her wide lacy hat upon the hair sofa, Amelia winced at the incongruity of her presence in the room. The Teacher smiled at them all and sat down in her chair.

"It's the most beautiful day we have had yet this spring," she remarked. "I have never seen the sky so blue or the trees so green. The rain last night seems to have cleared the whole world. It must have been fine for the crops, Mr Gare?"

"Hm—yes, yes indeed. So she threw you, eh, Charlie?" Caleb asked the boy, scarcely glancing at Lind in reply to her question. He winked at Charlie and Charlie grinned broadly. The youngest of the Gares had an

habitual snuffle which Amelia had tried in vain to correct.
He was an anæmic looking boy, and cared little for
anything except that which was forbidden. This trait
appealed to Caleb, and he chose to humor it, to the annoyance and indignation of the others, especially Judith.
Charlie had always taken advantage of his father's len-
iency.

"Nix," said Charlie. "She smelt a bear. The Klovaczs shot at two last night—one got away with a pig."

"Bears, eh? That means trouble," Caleb observed,
to switch the subject. "Have to look out on the way to
Nykerk to-morrow, Martin. Keep Ellen under cover.
She's nice and plump. Eh, Ellen?" He leaned over
and playfully tweaked Ellen's arm. She smiled, dutifully. Judith made a grimace which she did not try to
hide.

To the end of the meal Caleb was genial, jovial, in
fact. No further mention was made of the mare. Judith had not ridden her, after all.

2

For the rest of that day, Judith's hands were of no
use to her, so she slipped away with her dog, Pete,
through the bush to a little ravine where a pool had
gathered below the thread of a spring. Pete caught a
scent and was off, and Judith was left alone.

It was clingingly warm, as before rain. Not knowing fully what she was doing, Judith took off all her
clothing and lay flat on the damp ground with the waxy
feeling of new, sunless vegetation under her. She needed

to escape, to fly from something—she knew not what. Caleb . . . Ellen . . . the farm, the hot reek of manure in the stable when it was close as to-day. Life was smothering, overwhelming her, like a pillow pressed against her face, like a feather tick pinning down her body.

She would have struck Caleb to-day had it not been for Amelia. Always pity stood in the way of the tide of violence she felt could break from her. Pity for Amelia, who would get what Caleb did not dare mete out to her, Judith.

Oh, how knowing the bare earth was, as if it might have a heart and a mind hidden here in the woods. The fields that Caleb had tilled had no tenderness, she knew. But here was something forbiddenly beautiful, secret as one's own body. And there was something beyond this. She could feel it in the freeness of the air, in the depth of the earth. Under her body there were, she had been taught, eight thousand miles of earth. On the other side, what? Above her body there were leagues and leagues of air, leading like wings—to what? The marvelous confusion and complexity of all the world had singled her out from the rest of the Gares. She was no longer one of them. Lind Archer had come and her delicate fingers had sprung a secret lock in Jude's being. She had opened like a tight bud. There was no going back now into the darkness.

Sven Sandbo, he would be home in May, so they said. Was it Sven she wanted, now that she was so strangely free? Judith looked straight above her through the network of white birch and saw the bulbous white country

that a cloud made against the blue. Something beyond
Sven, perhaps . . . Freedom, freedom. She dipped her
blistered hands down into the clear topaz of the pool,
lifted them and dipped them and lifted them, letting
the drops slip off the tips of her fingers each time like
tiny cups of light. She thought of the Teacher, of her
dainty hands and her soft, laughing eyes . . . she came
from another life, another world. She would go back
there again. Her hands would never be maps of blisters
as Jude's were now, from tugging a calf out of a mud-
hole. Jude hid her hands behind her and pressed her
breast against the cold ground. Hard, senseless sobs
rose in her throat, and her eyes smarted with tears. She
was ugly beyond all bearing, and all her life was ugly.
Suddenly she was bursting with hatred of Caleb. Her
large, strong body lay rigid on the ground, and was
suddenly unnatural in that earthy place. Then she relaxed and wept like a woman. . . .

3

Judith dressed, whistled to Pete, and when he came
bounding joyously toward her, walked slowly back home.
On the way she passed the north cow-pasture where Caleb
kept a few bull-calves among the milch cows. She
leaned against the fence and looked in at two of the
plump young bulls who were dancing about and playfully
skulling each other, having apparently just discovered
their sprouting horns. She saw how they had developed
since she had last observed them. Their grizzled, stupid
faces had become more surly, their flanks heavier, their

dewlaps smoother and whiter and thicker. Caleb would soon be ringing their noses, and they would become spiritlessly ugly, with all this madcap frenzy suppressed. They were beautiful bulls, and would bring a nice sum from one of the Icelanders, perhaps. Judith felt an inner excitement in watching them. She turned to go, feeling dismayed that she should be so attracted by the young beasts. But a curiosity over which she had no control held her there for many minutes. Ah, how violent they were becoming in their play. . . .

Judith heard Charlie crashing through the timber on his horse, calling the cattle. With the dog at her heels she fled home.

Ellen was examining her foot when Jude came into the house.

"I can take the cattle with Martin to-morrow, Ellen," Jude said sympathetically. "Your foot looks like it's spavined."

"It'll be all right in the morning, I hope," Ellen replied. "Father wants me to go."

"Huh!" Judith retorted. "And you'd go, too,—on crutches!"

"Hush, girls!" Amelia pleaded. "Let's not have any more trouble to-night. The mare's enough for one day."

However, when Caleb came in from the stable, Judith took pains to mention to Ellen again her willingness to go in her place. The Teacher, working at her desk at the other end of the room, watched Caleb out of the corner of her eye. She made a little wager with herself that he would appear not to have heard Judith. She won the wager.

After a moment, Caleb, looking up from his agriculture journal, called loudly to Amelia who was in the kitchen.

"Heard to-day that Sven Sandbo's comin' up from the Siding to-morrow," he said.

Jude's color rose at once. Ellen glanced at her. Both knew, as did the Teacher, that he had not been off the farm all day and could not possibly have heard such a thing, no one having stopped in.

A little later, after he had talked casually on other things, he turned to Judith and said, "You can use the new harrow on the east garden to-morrow, Jude."

"Ellen can't go with Martin the way her foot is," Judith observed.

"You mean, Jude, not if Sven Sandbo is coming up from Nykerk. Hah! Hah! Caught you that time!" He laughed heartily, passing his hand across his mustache. His eyes gleamed with open-hearted mischief. How he loved to have sport with the girls on the subject of beaux! "You're too young to be moonin', Jude. I notice it in you lately. Haven't you, Miss Archer?"

Lind smiled at Judith, who sprang up, furious. Caleb regarded her with amusement.

"Mother, I'm afraid Jude is forgetting herself." He turned and chuckling almost inaudibly went out once more on one of his mysterious inspections about the place.

"Oh, Jude, you know what that always means!" Ellen whispered so Lind should not hear. "Why on earth can't you control yourself?"

But Judith was sitting dumb and somber at the window, looking out into the twilight. In a few minutes she got up and began to help Amelia with the supper.

"I wish we could stop eating once in a while," Amelia sighed. "It gets tiresome."

Caleb did not come in at all for supper. Everyone, even Lind, knew the significance of that. After the children had gone to bed he would be heard talking in a low tone to Amelia, and in the morning her eyes would be ringed with shadows. During the meal, Ellen looked across the table at Judith with the rebuke that the younger girl had come to hate. Judith bolted her food and went upstairs.

When Caleb returned indoors it was to announce bed time. He did so pleasantly, but Amelia saw below his pleasantness. The children and Lind went to the loft. Caleb was the clock by which the family slept, woke, ate and moved.

"Five in the morning, everybody. Ellen and Martin are going to take the steers in to Nykerk, remember," he called after them.

4

Everyone, including Lind, to whom the tyranny was rather novel, was at breakfast at half past five.

There was this to be said about the enforced early rising: you saw the unbelievable dawn whether you wished to or not. It unfolded like a vast flower over the edge of the horizon. The earth was clear and dark under it, as if seen through blue glass. One was aware for the first time of standing on a sphere that moved rhythmically through space. It was an hour of crystal-clear perceptions.

But breakfast was a bleak affair. Ellen was pale from the pain in her foot, and Amelia torn between mother solicitude and the submission she had learned through her trying wifehood. Caleb and Martin talked about the sale of the cattle; no mention was made of Judith's steer, although Martin resolved to see that she was given one in its place.

Judith sullenly hurried out after she had had a cup of coffee, and began to pitch manure into the cart. Her hands were still swollen and sore, but pride kept her from complaining. If Ellen could stand it for Amelia's sake, she could.

Ellen and Martin drove away with the steers before the Teacher could say good-by to them.

She ran out and watched them disappear down the road, Martin stooped over on the wagon seat like an old, tired man, Ellen sitting rather too stiff to be natural.

And Caleb Gare left to attend a business meeting of the church at Yellow Post. Although it took time from his own affairs, it pleased him to be one of the trustees of the church, as he was of the school. The pleasure came mainly from seeing that none of the other guardians of the church funds abused the trust placed in them.

It was because he had a little suspicion concerning Bjorn Aronson, who was treasurer of the church funds, that he went to the meeting that particular day.

He watched the younger brother of Fusi Aronson narrowly throughout the meeting, in which it was taken for granted that the money Bjorn was entrusted with lay safely in the strong box at the Aronson farm. Caleb saw no reason why Bjorn, at this time of the year, should have been able to buy three head of pure bred Jersey cattle from that infidel, Klovacz, who did not even belong to the church. Caleb had singled out the new cattle in the herd, and had recognized them at once.

After the meeting he stepped up behind Bjorn, who was untying his horses from the hitching post.

"See you have some Jerseys," he said, tapping the young man on the shoulder. Bjorn started. Caleb smiled.

"Ya–a, sure," said Bjorn.

"Get 'em at the Siding?"

"Naa–ow. Bought from Klovacz. He needed the money, before he goes avay," Bjorn said. His eyes traveled down the road. Caleb smiled again, balancing back on his heels thoughtfully. Bjorn got into his wagon and drove down toward Yellow Post proper, giving his horses the whip.

Bjorn was not the man his brother was, but because Fusi was honest Oeland took it that good blood ran all the way through the family. There they made their little mistake, Caleb thought, congratulating himself upon having discovered a stain upon the Aronson escutcheon which he might with ease lay his finger on. No, he had long known that Bjorn was not the boy his brother was. Bjorn had not even troubled to learn English with the pains that Fusi had given to it. Caleb would pay a little visit to Fusi on the way home, he decided.

There was another little matter that Caleb thought it would be advantageous to attend to. He got into his cart, clucked to the horse and headed him in the direction of the Klovacz homestead. The day was pleasant and Caleb was in an exceedingly good humor. By turning his head westward he could look upon his own fields, already green and promising. On the east lay the straggling, stony land of Anton Klovacz, with his few acres of miserable timothy. He laughed at the irony that lay in Mark Jordan's coming to this morose patch of land, all that Anton Klovacz, with rarest good luck pending upon the granting of the government title, would leave in his will a few short months hence!

Caleb turned into the narrow, infrequently-used wood road that led past Anton Klovacz's outbuildings. He drove slowly, and let the wheels run on the grass alongside, so that there should be as little sound as possible from them. He craned his neck to see all that he could of the Klovacz place.

It was months since he had talked with Anton, but he had heard at Yellow Post that the man was failing fast and was leaving very soon for the city where a great specialist was to examine him. But that news only corroborated the statement of Bart Nugent, who in his last letter had told Caleb that Mark Jordan was leaving at once to tend to Klovacz's homestead during his absence. Bart was a clever man, and he had done Caleb a life-long service, never suspecting to what purpose. Bart had fondly thought that Caleb had Mark's interest at heart because of Amelia. A veterinary surgeon and a keeper of stables, Bart had managed to continue his acquaintance with Mark Jordan in a friendly fashion even after the war, and had faithfully reported every move that the young man made. Caleb chuckled to himself when he reviewed the situation. Bart had been a good sort. But now——

Caleb removed his last letter from his vest pocket, together with the one from the hospital which had forwarded it to him. He shook his head, and a look came into his eyes that was seldom seen there. It was the look of the old when they hear of the passing of the old. Amelia must never learn that Bart Nugent was gone. For it was Bart and his assiduous reporting on Mark that she feared. Bart was Caleb's only connection with the outer world. Even if Amelia did learn of Mark's presence on the Klovacz farm, she must never know that Bart Nugent was dead. Mark Jordan would return to the city, and Caleb would lose all trace of him, but that Amelia must never know. For that would mean an end to Amelia's fear.

Caleb skulked along in the cart, close to the alder bushes that were flowering like creamy curds between the road and the Klovacz farm. He heard the voices of two men who were approaching on the opposite side of the fence. One voice was reedy and high as a child's, almost with the thin wail of wind in a chimney; the other was rich and controlled, full of another kind of youth. Caleb at once hated the deep assurance in the second voice. He knew by instinct that it was Mark Jordan's. The other was that of Anton Klovacz, dying of consumption with his feet on government soil.

Through the thick weave of the bushes, Caleb caught a glimpse of the two men. Jordan was tall and broad, Anton Klovacz still taller and as narrow as a pine board. His shoulders were scoop-shaped, his face all gone to cheek bones and hollows. "God, how he looks!" said

Caleb to himself. Disease—destruction—things that he feared—things out of man's control.

As the men passed, Caleb turned his head and followed the form of Mark Jordan until his eyes ached from the strain. Pah, how like his father he was—walking like he was God Almighty! The furious jealousy of Caleb's earlier years came into his heart again like a ravaging disease long checked and now broken out more violently than ever. Bareheaded, he sat in the cart with his long arms stretched rigid down between his knees, his hands clasped together. The reins hung loose, the horse pawed impatiently at the ground. A cat-bird in the nearest alder-bush made a querying little sound. But Caleb sat on, oblivious to all about him. Not his son, not his son, that handsome lad! The son of Amelia and big Del Jordan, who was gored by a bull. Caleb's sons —Caleb's children, what were they? Well born, it was true, and not out of wedlock. But twisted and gnarled and stunted as the growth on the bush land he owned, and barren as had been his acres before he had put his own life's blood into them for a meager yield. Caleb's head slipped down until his chin touched his chest. The soft wind moved in his scrag of hair, and in the invisible touch was a gesture of infinite pity.

5

Caleb turned into the farmyard of Fusi Aronson. His face was lined with hard mirth. He had come upon a choice errand. The great Icelander strode down to meet him, and bade him a stiff good day.

"I hear Bjorn has bought some cattle from Klovacz," Caleb began smoothly, dismounting from the cart. "He must be well off this spring."

"It was in settlement of a debt Klovacz owed him," Fusi replied shortly.

Caleb laughed. "Oh, no, it wasn't, Fusi. Klovacz got good money in return for those same Jerseys."

Fusi started. "What do you mean, Mr Gare?"

Caleb stepped closer to the Icelander and lifted his eyebrows meaningly.

"Of course he'll put the money back in the strong box, Fusi. The church needs it, you know," he said gently, laying his finger on the bib of the big man's overalls. He turned to go.

"Of course," he added, "you needn't fear that *I'm* goin' to squeal."

Fusi, in his heavy way, was looking at him uncertainly, not quite grasping the thing. Then the slow red surged up into his face. He knotted his huge fists and plunged toward Caleb.

"Take your time, Fusi, take your time," Caleb mocked. "Look in the strong box first. And by the way, when you are ready to deal with me about that timber down there between my hayfields, let me know. The sooner the better for me."

He mounted the cart and drove away.

CHAPTER IV

1

THE three black-eyed Klovacz children no longer brought crocuses and violets to Lind on the May mornings. Their father, Anton Klovacz, was seriously ill, Lind was told. And because there was no mother in the family, all the children left with him in the covered wagon for the city in the south, where a great physician would be called into attendance. Anton's savings would go, of course.

He had hired a man to look after his live-stock during his absence, the children informed Lind on their last day at school. He was a very nice, strong man, they said, who had brought them candy from the city and had let them search his pockets and keep all the silver they found there. On the very first day they had got so well acquainted with him that the younger of them had scrambled all over him in a free-for-all tumble, until they finally got him on his back on the ground, where he lay laughing heartily.

A few days later he had gone to Yellow Post and had brought back a box that sang and made music. It had been sent to him from the city from which he had come. A number of books with shiny leather covers had come, too, but the children couldn't make out a word of them, or at least not a whole line anywhere. Whoever the

78

man was, it was plain that the children had been won over by him completely.

The evenings were now so marvelously tender that Lind could not tolerate the imprisoned feeling on the Gare farm. She made a habit of going on long cross-country tramps alone, after school, returning barely in time for supper. She rarely met anyone, either driving or on foot, to detract from the lonely charm of her jaunts. Wondering a little about the man from the city who had come to the Klovacz place, she had several times been tempted to walk over that way. Of course he would be only a laborer, and would doubtless not be bothered with talking to her, but merely a glimpse of him would restore her confidence that the world she had come from was still in existence.

One day the Sandbo children left their pony for her to ride. The evening set in with a fine gray web of rain, and Lind dressed in rough clothes, mounted the pony and rode southeast, toward the Klovacz homestead. She took the narrow, winding trail that Caleb had driven on not long before. She passed the alder bushes and came to a stretch where the chokecherry trees on either side bowed toward each other and almost shut out the sky.

On the road Lind met a man, walking bareheaded with his hat in his hand in the gray half-light. She recognized him as the man she had seen from the top of the ridge on her way from the Thorvaldsons'.

He was tall and rangy, and dressed in the conventional "camp" outfit of the outsider: breeches and leggings, brown shirt open at the throat, mackinaw and slouch hat. When Lind saw him approaching she smiled faintly at his ostentatiously appropriate clothes. She knew immediately that he was Klovacz's "hired man."

As they passed each other, they exchanged the furtive survey of strangers meeting in lonely parts. Lind saw that he was rugged and brown, with an odd over-casting of paleness, delicateness; that his eyes were thoughtful and well set. Mark Jordan saw only that here was a girl who was riding in the rain as if she was enjoying it.

Then they passed on.

But Lind could not continue. She was overcome with a desire to turn back and stop in at the Klovacz place, to make some pretext. He was not an ordinary laborer, after all. She held the horse on the road for fully a minute trying to decide on what to do. Then it began to rain in earnest.

The little "sod" house of the Klovaczs, and the few straggling out-buildings that the recent settlers had erected, stood in the downpour like huddling outcast things. Until two weeks ago this place had been home— a place to come to from the field, from the bush, from school. Lind's eyes grew misty as she thought of the Klovaczs, that plucky Hungarian family.

The pony trotted up to the "stoop" before the house, and Lind in a moment was knocking at the door.

Mark Jordan opened it.

"May I come in out of the wet?" Lind smiled, winking the rain off her eyelashes. "I am Lind Archer, the teacher at Oeland."

Mark stepped back and threw the door wider, checking the exclamation that came to his lips. His keen eye took in his unexpected guest in a quick sweep, and left him a bit bewildered.

"Hello!" he said. "You're out in bad weather, I'd say. Come right in!"

Lind looked hesitatingly toward the pony, and Mark stepped quickly out of the door. "I'll tend to the horse, Miss Archer. You go in and make yourself comfortable." Standing on the narrow stoop, they looked at each other for a moment rather awkwardly, and then for no reason whatever, both laughed outright. Mark turned away to the pony and Lind went indoors.

She looked about the kitchen into which she had stepped. It already bore that masculine orderliness, where bits of rubbish were brushed out of the way and invisible unless one stooped and looked under stove or cupboard.

Something was cooking on the stove. The oilcloth-covered table was set for one. The rain pattered with myriad fingertips on the pane. Lind pulled down the blind.

Mark Jordan came back into the house. The rain clustered in his dark hair like beads and streamed down his cheeks.

"It's a bad night to be out in," he offered by way of conversation, and then remembered that he had said something like that before. To tell the truth, the coming of Lind when he had given himself up to friendless solitude for an indefinite period had somewhat disconcerted him.

"Oh, I love it," said Lind, happy and at ease. "I love riding or walking in the rain. If you turn me out

I won't be a bit concerned." She laughed up at him from the chair she had taken near the stove.

"Then why did you come at all?" he countered, regaining himself.

"Why—oh, I don't know. I was lonely, I guess," Lind said slowly. "You looked like a human being out there on the road, and I haven't seen a real one for over a month."

"H–m. Well, I hope you won't be disappointed," Mark smiled. Lind saw that he had good white teeth, and a very attractive mouth. "I was just making a little supper. A hermit doesn't eat much for the reason that it's a lot of fuss preparing food for one person. Nearly always make too much or too little."

He had put his foot up on one of the kitchen chairs in front of the fire, and rested his elbow on his knee, while he watched the coffee come to a boil on the stove. Lind removed her soft hat and her jacket. She wore corduroy knickerbockers that were almost waterproof, and stout shoes.

"This is really a cozy little house," she observed.

"Yes," said Mark, glancing about it with her, "not bad at all considering what Klovacz had to go on. Poor devil. I don't expect to see him come back at all." He reached across the stove to a row of pans that hung behind it and took down a small skillet. This he placed on the open fire, dropping into it a spoonful of lard from a can. The lard began to snap and smoke, and he deftly broke two eggs into the skillet. Lind watched him as though she had known him for a long time. He turned toward her.

"Will you set in with me, as they say hereabouts, Miss Archer?" he asked. "Or have you a dinner engagement?"

Lind laughed and said, "Well, if you'll let me do the dishes afterward. I'm afraid there won't be anything left when I get home now, anyway, and Mr Gare doesn't approve of feeding the tardy." She watched Mark comfortably while he went about setting the food on the table. His hands were fine and capable. Lind wondered about him, but asked no questions.

When everything was ready, Mark beckoned her to come to the table. He saw for the first time that she had taken off her hat, and that her hair glowed, smooth and lucent, away from her flushed cheeks. She moved to the chair at the table across from him. They looked at each other. Mark felt suddenly that he could not take his eyes off her.

He pushed his chair back and squatted forward, leaning toward her. His eyes were dark and intent, with a regard that was almost impersonal. Damn it, he thought, it wasn't fair for anyone so lovely to come and take a man unawares!

"I wonder where you came from just now?" he asked curiously.

Lind returned his gaze without smiling. For a moment she seemed to be in a spell of abstraction, unable to answer. Fine whips of rain lashed about the little house, and the wind whistled in the birch trees outside, bleak as a lost bird. These sounds defined the feeling of enclosed warmth and safety in the kitchen of the Klovaczs'. But they did also the opposed thing.

They stirred the fear of loneliness, the ancient dread of abandonment in the wilderness in the profounder natures of these two who found shelter here. For an imponderable moment they sought beyond each other's eyes, sought for understanding, for communion under the vast terrestrial influence that bound them, an inevitable part and form of the earth, inseparable one from the other. The moment was like a warm handclasp.

Lind's eyes dropped to the table. She lifted a fork, and put it down precisely in the same place. Mark Jordan sat with his chin resting on his hand, watching her.

"Down," said Lind, pointing upward with her finger.

"I believe it," he replied seriously. "I think I shall love you."

Lind laughed nervously. He frightened her, with his intent look. He had said that almost as if he wanted to hear how it would sound.

"Do you? Will you tell me what your name is, first?" she said in a light tone, so that she might keep her voice casual. She picked up her fork.

Mark was suddenly astounded at himself. Whatever had come over him to-night? He had probably driven her away.

"Forgive me—I didn't mean to startle you. But I'm quite sure of it. I want you to know that no one ever came to me as you have to-night—as if it were fated. I've been God-forsakenly lonely."

A wave of incredible feeling came over Lind as he spoke. Her impulse was to rush over to him and touch this strange man's hair, run her fingers through it so that he should no longer be a stranger to her.

"Oh!" she cried, "I know that—so well!" She stretched her hand out suddenly on the table and leaned toward him. He put his own over it with a light pressure, and they smiled at each other.

"But you haven't yet told me your name?" she reminded him.

He straightened in his chair. "Oh, lord no—I haven't! It's Jordan—Mark Jordan. Now let's eat. You must be hungry." He passed her the bread.

"How's the coffee?" he asked brusquely after a moment.

"Very, *very* good," she assured him. "I think you're a surprisingly good cook."

The tension was for the moment broken, and they seemed to become fast friends in a few minutes. So they ate together, eggs and fried potatoes, bread and preserved wild plums that the Klovaczs had left, and coffee. They talked of the life at Oeland and of the harsh charm of it that each had felt upon arrival. Mark had not yet had time to get acquainted with the settlers. Lind sketched them to him in brief, sharp outlines. He was amused by her observations.

"The Sandbos are your nearest neighbors," she informed him. "Mrs Sandbo thinks she is happy in the death of her husband, but in reality he is more alive now than he ever was."

She told him of the Gares and the leaden spell that seemed to hang over them all.

"Judith is a beautiful creature. She's like a—a wild horse, more than anything I know of. But Caleb doesn't give her a moment to herself even to think in. I seldom get near her, much as I should like to know her better."

"Hm—you could do a lot for the girl, I should think, if you got the chance," said Mark.

He told her a little of himself, of his upbringing among the priests in whose care he had been left upon the death of his father, whom he did not remember; the little he knew of his mother, an English gentlewoman who had died while he was still an infant; of his profession, and his hope of returning to the city at the end of six months with renewed eagerness to work. And Lind in turn told him of how she had happened to come here, and of her resolve to stay in spite of the rancor of Caleb Gare and the terrible oppression in his household.

Lind finally whisked the dishes off the table and washed them, while Mark dried and set them in a neat row in the cupboard. Then Lind looked out the window and observed that the rain had nearly stopped.

"Mrs Gare will think I am at the Sandbos', and will not worry. But I must be getting home," she said. Mark took his cap and coat off the wall and they went out together. There was still a thin rain and the trees were great watery blots against the darkening sky.

Mark fed and watered Lind's pony, then saddled a horse for himself. Lind stood in the dark stable while he got ready. There was a snug intimacy about the low-ceilinged log barn with the drip of the rain faintly audible on the roof, that made her doubly aware of Mark's nearness.

He did not bother to light a lantern for the saddling of his horse. He worked hastily in the darkness lest the feeling he had toward this unaccountable girl should sweep him off his feet completely. When he was ready he walked the horse out, brushing against Lind who did not at once see him. The brief contact made his heart beat unreasonably.

With the sensitive rain on their faces, they rode down the wood trail, the horses side by side.

Although he had intended turning back long before, Mark rode with Lind well over the miles that led to the Gare farm. The rain stopped and finally overhead a great billow of hurrying cloud broke and revealed a misty star. From the northern swamps came a solitary hollow call, as if it was blown by a wind. It was the honking of a belated wild goose, the last to fly over the land to the half frozen marshes of the remoter north. Lind and Mark listened, standing still, then looked at each other. Suddenly, it seemed, the air had cleared, and the night stood over them, wide, infinite, transparent as a strange dream. . . .

2

Amelia was getting a pail of water from the well when Lind returned.

"Have you had supper, Miss Archer?" she asked as Lind came up to her. There was an almost anxious note in Amelia's voice.

"Yes, thanks, I have," Lind replied rather breathlessly.

She was flushed and preoccupied after taking leave of Mark Jordan.

Amelia looked after her keenly. Lind turned sud-denly and came back to give the woman a hand with the pail.

"I've had an adventure to-night, Mrs Gare," Lind confided. "I've been riding with a most interesting man, and a handsome one, too."

Amelia smiled. She thought Lind was joking. "Who is he? He must have dropped down with the rain."

"He is Klovacz's hired man—just for a while. Out here for his health, or his nerves, rather. He's not a farm hand by nature, of course," Lind told her, and then could have bitten her tongue through for her thoughtless words. Intuitively she felt Amelia wince.

"What is his name?"

"Oh, what is it, anyway? Jordan—Mark Jordan," Lind said.

"Wh–what?"

"Mark Jordan," Lind repeated, pulling at the pail which seemed suddenly to have thrown all its weight into her hand. Amelia paused for a moment as if she were staring at something in the dark pasture beyond the fence.

"What is it?" Lind asked, looking in the same direc-tion.

For a moment Amelia stood dumb. Her hand on the pail was limp.

"Do you see anything, Mrs Gare?" Lind urged, glanc-ing at her.

The woman's face in the indefinite light was expressionless, stony. When Lind spoke the second time, she started, and jerked at the handle of the pail.

"No—no . . . I thought I saw something. Bears around," she murmured. "Martin must tend to those sheep pens."

They went indoors and Lind released the pail.

Caleb was reading his weekly agriculture journal in the light of the lamp in the sitting room. After she had removed her outer clothing Lind came and sat at the table also, laying out her work for the morrow. Caleb did not glance up or speak to her. Lind had the feeling that he disapproved of her being absent from meals. She smiled to herself.

Amelia entered the room and changed the chimney of the lamp, polishing the one she had taken off with a woolen cloth. During the momentary flickering of the light Caleb hitched his shoulders impatiently.

Amelia spoke to Caleb lightly about the good amount of rain that had fallen, and casually mentioned the fact that she would soon have to be sending to the "mail order" for garden seed. Caleb made no response but shifted his position finally so that his back was almost directly toward her. Amelia smiled at the Teacher, almost mischievously. Lind had never seen her in this lively, self-possessed mood. She wondered what had caused it.

The others, after an unusually heavy day, had gone to bed early. In a little while Lind also went up to the loft. Caleb and Amelia were left alone.

"You didn't tell me he had come here," Amelia darted out. Her eyes shone above white cheeks. She stood at the side of the table and began with both hands to roll up the edge of the table cloth into a tight little furl.

Caleb turned slowly. "Heh!" he sneered. "You found out, didn't you?"

"Yes, I found out," Amelia repeated, holding each word as if she were trying to memorize it. "The Teacher has talked to him."

Caleb raised his eyebrows, and drew his left hand across his mustache. So the Teacher had done her little part, had she? He might have known that soft eyed chit would not keep her place.

"Well? Are you going to fall on his neck? He'll thank ye for it," he said. He turned the pages of the journal, and Amelia heard his short clucking laugh. Her hands tightened on the rolled cloth.

"No . . . I won't do anything," she said.

Caleb got up, looked into the stove, spat into it, and started to take off his shoes.

Without another remark he went to bed.

For the first time in his life, it was uncertainty that kept him silent, not the confidence that his will was understood without the utterance of his word.

CHAPTER V

1

ANTON KLOVACZ had left a five acre plot of scrub brush for Mark Jordan to clear. On the day after Lind's visit he began "slashing," going down into the bush with his ax after he had tended to the animals. The air was cool and clear, admirable for hard labor. He swung the ax with rapid, clean sweeps, enjoying the feel of the smooth wood handle on his palms.

He thought of Lind Archer. Late the night before he had lain awake thinking of her. She had made him feel for the first time in his life that he was not hopelessly locked within himself. Her physical radiance alone carried him beyond himself, but that might have been simply explained away since she was the only woman he had seen or was likely to see during his sojourn here. Unreasonable and out of keeping with his conceptions as it seemed, the deepest pulse of his being had leaped in recognition of her as he had looked across the table into her eyes the night before. The whole circumstance made him feel very humble and diffident now as he reviewed it. He must see her again, at once, and yet he feared to meet her lest he should disclose his feelings and find them unwelcome to her. And yet, he could not persuade himself that she had not responded to him in part, at least. He knew his own impetuous, strong desires so well, and he realized that to see much of Lind here would be a torment to him, especially if he should learn, for instance,

that there was some one else in her life. He would have
to see her again in a day or two, call at the school perhaps, and ask permission to see her at the Gares. That
would be the proper procedure. The modest country
swain courting . . . he grinned as he thought of himself
in the new rôle. And yet how different life seemed to-day.
He rested one hand on the end of the ax and loosened
his shirt about the throat. His eyes drifted down the
stretch of Klovacz's land where the homesteader's elder
sons had planted fodder grains before their departure.
The landscape seemed to have a gentler look than it had
yesterday.

Lind . . . Lind Archer—what a pretty name it was!
There had never been any one so suddenly complete, so
gratifying to the complex and dubious thing that was
himself—the self that had come out of nowhere and had
always seemed to belong nowhere in spite of his advan-
tages of education and natural endowment. Mark
found himself wanting her again beside him, wanting
her terribly as some one from whom he had never in his
life been separated.

He struggled to reason with himself. He had no
right to dream about her this way. The next time he
saw her he would keep himself well in check. He began
again energetically slashing the ranks of choked birch
trees right and left.

2

Fusi Aronson, on foot, came to deal with Caleb Gare
in regard to a bit of timber land. He came with great

strides across the country, like some giant defender of a forgotten race.

To fortify himself against killing Caleb Gare outright, he stopped to talk with the Teacher in her school.

"I would do it now, but you say it would be no good. That is true: somehow his time will come," Fusi agreed.

He shook hands with Lind soberly and she admonished him once more against using violence on Caleb. Fusi, the great Icelander, proceeded across the road to make a sale of a certain piece of wood land.

3

Days flow on, even after the coming of an event of great purport. Even after great sorrow and great gladness, days flow on, and all things become the shining woof and the shadowed warp of the tapestry of the past. So went the day of Lind's finding Mark Jordan, and Amelia's learning of it.

The Teacher came into the house after school on the day following the rain, to find Amelia bending over a half-completed piece-quilt which she had stretched out on the floor. She kept her eyes lowered to the bright squares and triangles of the quilt. A bar of sunlight, falling from the window across her sandy hair, cut the quilt diagonally.

"What a gay comforter that's going to be!" Lind exclaimed, stooping to touch a bit of yellow satin. "How long did it take you to collect enough pieces?"

Amelia did not answer at once, and when she did it was without raising her eyes. Lind divined that she had been crying. Her impulse was to kneel beside Amelia and ask her what the trouble was, but she had come in a short time to know that sympathy would only embarrass her. Whatever her grief, she jealously kept it to herself as if it were too intimate for unburdening. The gaudy pieces of the quilt shimmered and blazed.

"These are odds and ends I've been saving since the twins were born," Amelia said at last. "We don't have much use for silks here you know. I thought I'd save up until the girls grew old enough to appreciate a nice cover."

Lind knelt and fingered one of the larger pieces of silk. "That's pretty—a kind of brocade, isn't it? Was it a dress?"

"Yes—one that I had a long time before I was married."

"It must have been beautiful."

Amelia made no reply, and Lind, with a dozen fancies about the dress and where and how it had been worn, got to her feet and went out of doors. Before what was called the front of the log house, Ellen was planting sweet peas under a window.

"There must be something—something over-ruling—greater than life, even," Lind thought about Amelia.

Ellen looked up, blinking.

"Oh, I thought you were mother," she laughed as Lind stopped beside her. "This light gets me all mixed up."

Lind knew it was not the light.

"Ellen, when are you going to get new glasses?"

Ellen glanced down at the flower bed.

"Oh, these will do till the doctor comes to the Siding again."

Lind knew that they had already done too long—perhaps forever too long.

"Ellen," began Lind, squatting on the ground beside the girl. "Would your father let me buy glasses for you?"

"Oh, dear, don't say anything like that to him!" Ellen cried. "He intends to get them for me—only he forgets. It isn't the money."

Ellen's discomfort was so apparent that Lind could say nothing more. Her defense of her father was a pitiful thing. There was nothing she could do—no help she could give that would be accepted. Even Judith was proud and distant when it came to gifts. She would not take Lind's amber beads, for instance—insisted that they did not become her at all.

"Ellen, are you going to stay here all your life?" Lind asked quietly.

Ellen tore a corner off a package of seed and poured some of the contents into her hand.

"What else is there for me to do?" she returned, a slightly hostile line appearing at either side of her mouth. "There's nothing the matter with this place, is there? I've lived here long enough to like it if you don't." Lind had never before heard her speak with such emotion. Her head was thrown back defiantly, her flat cheeks faintly pink.

"Oh, Ellen, you know what I mean! You are bright, intelligent—with a little education you could make a great deal of yourself. You are wasted here. Have you never asked your father to let you go away for a while?"

"No," she answered indifferently. "I don't want to go." Along the little trench she had dug she sifted the seeds.

"Don't tell me that, Ellen," Lind persevered. "You do. I don't want to turn you against your own home, or anything like that, dear. But I see such fine things in you—your love of music, for instance. Your father could afford to do without you for a few months every year, I'm sure. Why don't you ask him?"

"It's no use for you to talk, Miss Archer," Ellen returned calmly. She sometimes called Lind "teacher," but never used her first name. "I know just how hard he has to work to give us this home, and I know he can't do without any of us. It's not for you to say."

Lind got to her feet, hurt in spite of herself at Ellen's attitude. She knew very well that the girl did not really believe what she said. But the contorted sense of loyalty that had been inbred in Ellen had overrun every other instinct like a choking tangle of weeds. She reasoned only as Caleb had taught her to reason, in terms of advantage to the land and to him.

Lind went into the house and got a favorite book of verse which she took with her down the wood road past the school house to a little green mound overlooking a marsh full of marigolds. Here she seated herself and tried to see the words on the page before her. But somehow her eyes would lift and lose themselves in the clear distance, where the long reeds stood like etchings of green and gold in the sun. She found herself wondering about Mark Jordan, and, ridiculously enough connecting him with the auguring of the ancient grandmother of the Bjarnassons. She had not invited him to call on her at the Gares'. It did not seem fitting somehow, although she knew he had wanted her to suggest it. So there seemed to be nothing for it but to make an errand to the Klovacz place. . . .

With her long, smooth fingers she dug a half black, half white, stone loose from the earth at her side.

"If the other side is mostly white, old Grandma Bjarnasson's tale is true. If black, not true," she whimsied. The other side of the little stone was all white. Lind smiled to herself.

4

Every evening that Jude went for the cattle her eye roved in the direction of the Sandbos'. Any day now, Sven would come home. She knew that he would be looking for her, although he would not venture actually to the Gare farm. Caleb had, in the past, made it clear that young Sven Sandbo was not welcome on the place. His smile and the easy swagger of his shoulders were a little too impudent.

At sunset one evening in the middle of May, Judith rode the colt, Turk, north across the grazing land like some dark young goddess, her hair low against the horse's mane, her blood avid for speed. She was conscious of the picture she made, magnificently riding. And she was conscious of being watched. She reined in suddenly and threw up her head. Her cheeks, already crimson, grew hot with color, her eyelids dropped.

Then, with a sweeping flourish of her whip, she rode forward to meet Sven Sandbo.

Sven was walking across the open stretch between his own home and the brush that belonged to Fusi Aronson on the north. From here one could not be seen by any one at the Gares'. Sven came up to her and rested his arms across the damp neck of the horse.

"You look great, Jude," he said, looking at her deliberately from head to foot. His hand ran over her overalled thigh. She drew her foot back in the stirrup with a jerk. Sven laughed and thrust his hands into his pockets. He threw his weight on one foot and crossed the other lazily in front of it. "How's everything to home?" he asked.

Judith returned his searching glance with equal deliberateness; took in coolly the city cut of his clothes, his flaming tie, his long shining shoes that had no bumps on the toes such as Martin's yellow Sunday shoes had; and she made no comment upon his appearance. She knew that Sven expected her to.

Sven was no fool. He laughed, and when he laughed there was no woman could withstand him, he had found. He had the most engagingly male smile in the world.

"Aw, come on, Jude, you ain't sore on me," he coaxed, shaking her foot. "How are *you*, that's what I'd like to know."

"I'm all right," she replied coldly. "How are *you?*"

"Fine. Couldn't wait till I got back. Thought about you all the time, and I would o' written, too, if I thought the old man wouldn't get hold of it. Gosh, you're prettier 'n ever, Jude. Girls in town can't hold a candle to you. I've seen 'em all."

He whipped out a sterling silver cigarette case and held it so that it flashed in the sun. It seemed that he kept it out unnecessarily long to draw a cigarette from it. Judith looked away to the horizon, and her horse stamped an impatient hoof. Sven put a hand on the horse's bridle, snapped the case together and slipped it back in his pocket.

"Come riding with me some night? I'll rot here if I don't do something—or see somebody," said he, indolently blowing the smoke upward into the air and flipping off the ash of his cigarette with his forefinger. He had not done that before he went away. Do something —see somebody, that was what he wanted to do, was it? Not something or somebody in particular.

Judith sat silent, her eyes moodily on the distance.

"Oh, that reminds me," he went on, "here's something I got you. All the girls are carryin' 'em." He drew a little package out of his pocket and unwrapped it. From the tissue paper he took out a gold plated vanity case which he held up to Judith, looking at her face for the smile of surprise he fully expected to see there.

Judith gave the thing a quick glance.

Then with a swift twist of her body she forced the horse to rear upright on his hind legs, his mouth wide, nostrils distended, eyes swimming. She dropped her head against his mane, wheeled him about and was off in an instant on an animal that had gone mad.

Sven, completely dazed, stared after her, saw the horse

jerk from the road and take the fence that enclosed a hay-field at a fine long sweep, like a slender boat rising on a wave.

"Well—I'll be—" he marveled. "By gosh, she's a live one. Worse'n ever. What did she get sore at, anyway?"

But Sven felt uneasily that he knew. She thought he had been showing off.

Galloping away on the horse, Judith gave way to tears.

5

The days grew steadily warmer and longer, the distance over field and brush took on a deeper green. Caleb's herds on the prairie westward sought shelter from the noonday sun under the trees on the bluffs, and the milch cows in the north pasture gave up nibbling sweet-grass for long moments to stand knee-deep in the tepid swamps already a-drone with insects that ricocheted like sparks across the surface of the water. The season of cold morning dews changed to that of fireflies and evening mist. The yield of the earth passed from timorous seedling to rugged stalk and stem.

But in the life in the Gare household there was no apparent change, no growth or maturing of dreams or fears, no evidence of crises in personal struggle, no peak of achievement rapturously reached. There was no outward emotion or expressed thought save that which led as a great tributary to the flow of Caleb's ambition. He talked now day and night of nothing but the livestock, circled the fields by day in the cart or walked abroad with his lantern alone at night, and compared the strength of his hay and his flax with that of Skuli Erickson or Joel Brund, the husband of Mrs Sandbo's daughter Dora. The early summer season was to him a terrific, prolonged hour of passion during which he was blind and deaf and dumb to everything save the impulse that bound him to the land.

His flax was growing in such a way that he scarcely dared look at it lest it should vanish like a vision. He would put off examining it for a week at a time for fear that in a twinkling something dire had happened to it.

But smoothly as affairs seemed to run on the surface of life at the Gares', there had been a subtle diverting of the undercurrent. Lind Archer perceived it and was troubled.

Sven Sandbo had come home. And Judith's behavior was incomprehensible. Lind had tried to talk to her about him, but she had walked rudely away. And when Lind had offered Judith a book to read which had been sent her from the city, the girl's manner had been much more like Ellen's than her own. She had no time for the book, she had said. Amelia was preoccupied these days, and her attitude toward Caleb had become almost one of indulgence. There had been a letting down of the familiar tension on Amelia's part, and a tightening of restraint on the part of Judith. Caleb for a time was too engrossed in the affairs of the farm to notice any one. Unlike himself, he went puttering about haphazard trifles, constantly looking for something to do rather than, as usual, for something that Martin or Judith might do.

Lind felt that something momentous had happened, and then realized how impossible it was for anything at all to happen here save the monotonous round of duty.

It was Lind alone who noticed these nuances in the life at the Gares. She had much time to herself in the evenings when she sat at her desk after the children were gone, and fell often to thinking about the Gares. But since the evening of the rain she had thought more of Mark Jordan.

On the third day after her visit at the Klovacz place, Lind sat at her desk in the school house. The children had been dismissed. The room was heavy with the smell of chalk and plum blossoms. Lind felt tired and rather depressed. She closed her eyes and leaned her head against the palms of her hands. She went in detail again over the frightening and delicious night of the rain.

The door opened slowly. Mark Jordan stood framed against the light, smiling, bareheaded, his hat in his hand. Lind clapped her hands to her cheeks. Then she laughed.

"You look guilty," said Mark. He came slowly down the aisle in the center of the room, looking at her happily.

"I confess I am," Lind said shyly. "I was thinking of inviting myself to dinner again at your house." She got up from her desk and stretched her hand out to him. He held it, looked at it, pointed to the chalk and ink stains.

"Salt of the earth: a school teacher. I was one myself for about a month. Got fired for encouraging the kids to play hookey," he laughed. He dropped her hand and strode around the room examining the drawings and knick-knacks the children had made and hung on the walls. Taking a piece of chalk he drew on the blackboard a ridiculous figure with knock-knees and turned-in eyes, and under it wrote in a childish scrawl. "Teacher." Then he stepped back ten paces and took aim with the chalk, succeeding in tossing it on the ledge of the blackboard. This he did several times, stepping back a few paces farther each time.

Lind watched the game for a while half-amusedly. Then she was conscious of a faint irritation. He apparently had forgotten she was there. His restlessness shut her out. Irrelevantly she recalled the words of the ancient grandmother of the Bjarnassons: she would never know the secret of him. As he stood in profile to her, her eyes outlined the well-bred shape of his head and shoulders. He turned to her so suddenly that she started.

"Let's walk," he said. "What's the matter?"

"Nothing," she answered. She would have to try to understand him. "I really don't want to walk now that you have decided upon it for me so peremptorily. But I'll use you as a means to control my temper, and go with you. You are terribly used to having your own way, I can see that. As if you were the only person on earth."

"I always was—until you came, Lind. I just have to get used to the idea of your presence," he said, so seriously that she had to smile.

"Did any of the Gares see you come in here?" she asked uneasily.

"The Gares? Oh, those people? Don't know. I didn't see anybody except a robin in the road, and he didn't even turn a feather," he told her, going to the window while she cleared her desk. "Why? Are you afraid of them?"

"Oh, by no means," she said hastily. "It's just that I don't want them to—oh, I want to know you separately from them—in another world, so to speak. If you go there, or talk with them, I'll feel that the *idea* of you has mingled with them. See? I don't want you to see them or them to see you, except, perhaps, Judith—" She glanced at him thoughtfully, as if to make up her mind as to the good judgment that lay in the reservation.

"You walked?" she asked, after they had slipped out and had taken a little path that insinuated itself through the thick growth of fir trees behind the school house.

"No, I came on an elephant. It evaporated at your door," he said, and they both laughed.

"But curiosity impels me to see this Gare family," Mark declared a little later. "Especially Caleb Gare. They told me at Yellow Post that he's the devil himself."

"No, he's too cowardly to be the devil. He's too cowardly even for a man to want to kill him. That's why Fusi Aronson hasn't done it long ago."

She told him about Fusi.

"I'd like to meet him," Mark said.

They talked of the strange unity between the nature of man and earth here in the north, and of the spareness of both physical and spiritual life.

"There's no waste—that's it," Mark observed, "either in human relationships or in plant growth. There's no incontinency anywhere. I've made trips around Yellow

Post since I've been here, and I haven't talked with a single farmer who wasn't looking forward to the time when he wouldn't have a grain of any kind in his bins if he didn't rake and scrape for all he's worth now. They seem to have no confidence in the soil—no confidence in anything save their own labor. Think of the difference there would be in the outward characters of these people if the land didn't sap up all their passion and sentiment."

Lind nodded. "That's what's wrong with the Gares. They all have a monstrously exaggerated conception of their duty to the land—or rather to Caleb, who is nothing but a symbol of the land."

They sat down upon a flat rock near the trail.

"I spent some time farther north—went up to a mission when I was only a kid with one of the priests, and later after I had grown up," Mark told her. "That's a country for you. If there's a God, I imagine that's where he sits and does his thinking. The silence is awful. You feel immense things going on, invisibly. There is that eternal sky—light and darkness—the endless plains of snow—a few fir-trees, maybe a hill or a frozen stream. And the human beings are like totems—figures of wood with mysterious legends upon them that you can never make out. The austerity of nature reduces the outward expression in life, simply, I think, because there is not such an abundance of natural objects for the spirit to react to. We are, after all, only the mirror of our environment. Life here at Oeland, even, may seem a negation but it's only a reflection from so few exterior natural objects that it has the semblance of negation. These people are thrown inward upon themselves, their passions stored up, they are intensified figures of life with no outward expression—no releasing gesture."

"Yes, I think perhaps human life, or at least human contact, is just as barren here as farther north," Lind remarked. "The struggle against conditions must have the same effect as passivity would have, ultimately. It seems to me that one would be as dulling as the other— one would extort as much from human capacity for expression as the other. There's no feeling left after the soil and the live stock have taken their share."

They talked about books and disagreed spiritedly here and there. Mark urged her to let him come to see her at the Gares' and bring with him two or three of his treasured volumes, and she consented to speak to Mrs Gare about it.

To Lind it was miraculous that she should have found him here. To Mark it seemed the most natural thing in the world that he should have found her.

"I may come to the school house then any evening?" Mark asked almost timidly. It was time for him to go, and it amazed him that he hated so to leave her. She put out her hand to him simply.

"Yes, do," she said warmly. They had come within sight of the gate at the Gares'.

He looked at her oddly, then turned and walked rapidly down the road. He looked back once, and saw her standing where he had left her. Raising his slouch hat he waved his arm in a wide arc. Lind walked on into

the barnyard of the Gares'.   Her heart was beating boisterously.

6

Shearing time was at hand.   Thirty-odd sheep, so heavily coated that they looked clumsy in their own wool,
were herded into the pen where Judith, Martin, Amelia
and Ellen proceeded with the work of shearing.   The
smell of the wool always nauseated Ellen, so Amelia
contrived to have her indoors with the housework a large
part of the time.   Judith moved among the sheep, sin-
gling out her own to see that justice was done in regard
to the disposition of the wool.   It had been a point with
Caleb since the children were little to let them have a few
animals of their own to bring up and sell, and in this manner pay for their own clothing.   He contended that it
gave them an active interest in the business of the farm
and instilled in them early a feeling of independence.
Amelia had long since seen through this mock generosity.

Caleb, although he did not materially assist in the
task, paused before the pen where the three were at work,
after Ellen had gone indoors.   Beside him stood Thorvald Thorvaldson, the Icelander, who prided himself
upon being a Master.   Caleb rested his elbows on the
board fence and gave arbitrary instructions in regard to
the shearing.   It gave him the gratifying feeling of over-
seer.

"Here, Jude!   That's no way to clip!   Get the shears
under it more—come along!   Come along!   Can't take

all day with a sheep, you know. Little closer there! Fine wool, eh, Thorvald? How many pounds do you reckon I'll get off that sheep?"

Judith turned her back directly on the two men and kept at her work. The sheep was one of her pets, a ewe who always bore well. Judith hated the Icelander, who stood glowering above her. She had glanced sideways up at him and had found his piggish little eyes surveying her limbs and the backs of her thighs as she bent over, the overalls she wore tightening across her body. She dug down into the ewe's chest and clenched a fistful of the thick wool. There were limits to endurance, even for Amelia's sake.

Amelia did not glance up. Her serenity troubled Caleb. It was a change in her he could not fathom. It had come with her discovery that Mark Jordan was on the Klovacz homestead. You could never rely on how any woman would react to a thing, not even Amelia.

"Come, come, Amelia! Thorvald is thirsty. Plenty of time to finish that before dark," he said to her. His tone was like a sudden prod in the back. Amelia straightened quickly, brushed a wisp of dun colored hair out of her eyes. The homely gesture gave her an uncouth look for an instant, a pitiful gaucheness.

"I thought you said Mr Thorvaldson had no time for coffee?"

Caleb stared at her. "Mr Thorvaldson will have coffee. He has changed his mind," he said finally, turning with the glum-faced, inscrutable Icelander to the house. No mention of coffee had been made to Thorvaldson. He grinned flatteringly at Caleb. Here indeed was control that was at once subtle and sure! The trouble was that Thorvaldson's women folk had not the intelligence to understand and properly respect such ruling. More obvious tactics had to be used with them. . . .

"How is your wife coming?" Amelia asked Thorvald when she had served him with coffee.

"She's coming long purty good," he responded, emptying the contents of his saucer down his throat. "Coming in soon, I t'ink, haa! haa! Vun after another—such a voman!"

Amelia turned away from the man. He had grotesque, overhanging mustaches that trailed in the saucer he held to his mouth. Caleb was filling his pipe. He saw Amelia turn away. He saw the tightening about her lips.

Caleb smiled cunningly. "Sit down, my dear," he said, placing a chair for her directly in front of Thorvald. "The shearing can wait. Have a chat with Thorvald. Heh, heh! My wife gets sick of seein' only her husband around, Thorvaldson. A woman should have a change, eh?" Both men laughed heartily, Caleb tilting back his head and letting his eyes rest casually on Amelia, who had without a word sat down into the chair he indicated.

Amelia's eyes wandered to the window. They were not timid, submissive, as they had been a week ago. They were nervous, alert. Caleb was disturbed.

Thorvald swallowed great fistfuls of bread and butter and cold meat that Amelia had set out for him, swallowed with an eager noise. Amelia sat before him, uttering not a word.

Yes, Caleb was disturbed. He made up his mind once more that Amelia must not set eyes on Mark Jordan.

After the departure of Thorvald Thorvaldson, Caleb approached his wife. His voice was smooth, easy.

"The Teacher has talked with that son of yours again. If she asks to have him come here, remember it isn't best. For one thing, Amelia, it would only remind you of things you want to forget. For another, he's not the kind I want to have round my children." He lit his pipe again leisurely, as if he had spoken of the most commonplace of things, and went out the door scarcely lifting his feet off the ground, his head thrust forward, his hands clasped behind him. He had been satisfied with Amelia's pallor. Whatever her state of mind, he must assure himself that he could in a moment change it. That was control.

7

The shearing completed, and the wool packed into flour sacks ready to be taken to the Siding of Nykerk, the round of more usual work began again.

While Ellen worked in the vegetable garden, weeding and hoeing, until her narrow back was numb from the strain, Judith made a number of trips to Yellow Post in the dog cart for provisions.

"Yes!" she burst out at Ellen who finally reproached her for her selfishness. "Why do you stick? I'm not sorry for you. I'm not sorry for any of us! We're all old enough to get out. Why do you stick, if you don't like it? I don't like it and I'm going to get out—soon. I'm not going through another winter up to my knees in manure—not much! I've handled enough calves for him! What do I get for it? What do you get for it?

It was different when we were small and she couldn't help herself. I tell you—I'm quitting!" Her voice rose to an uncontrollable pitch, her full breasts shook.

Ellen adjusted her glasses over her nose, a thing she always did when under excitement of any kind.

"Judith," she said solemnly. "It isn't only that. There's something else. He has some kind of threat he always makes to her—you've heard him—I've heard him. I don't know what it is, but she's afraid—afraid of what he'll do. We can't let him do it. You know we can't. It would kill her. I have given up a lot more than you ever will to stay——"

"Oh . . ." Judith gave vent to a word that made Ellen start.

"Judith, you're dreadful!"

"I'm worse than you think! A lot worse!" said Jude, driving off in the cart.

Lind was awaiting her at the school house.

"You look angry, Judie, what's the matter now?" Lind asked her when they were on their way.

"Nothing, but Ellen makes me sick with her whining. She loves to suffer. And loves to see everybody else doing it. But just because she isn't quite as strong as I am she gets it only half as bad."

"I don't think she loves it at all, Judie. I think she is giving up a great deal to stay on here, and she knows it. Has there ever been anybody that she cared for very much—who wanted to marry her?"

"I guess old Goat-eyes liked her all right. But he's been gone a year, and she never talks about him. Anyway, he's a halfbreed, or nearly."

"Of course, if Ellen loved him, that wouldn't have mattered, do you think?"

"No, I s'pose not. He was too good for her, anyway." Judith's eyes were full of intolerant contempt. She slapped the horse's rump with the reins, and the rattle of the cart soon made conversation difficult. They did not stop at Sandbos', as Jude knew that Caleb would be spying from the slight rise on which the Gare farm was built to see that the horse emerged from around the bend in due time.

Yellow Post lay in a little valley shaped like the palm of a hand, a narrow creek curving across it like a life line. Jude drove briskly up to the store of Johanneson, the Swede trader, and Lind went into the store to make a few purchases of her own while Judith tied up the horse. A few halfbreeds ventured into the store after her, to skulk about with furtive glances.

Leaning against the counter in the store and smoking his pipe, stood Mark Jordan. He came toward her with a quick stride, looking down at her almost querulously.

"You didn't come," he said in a low tone, glancing with annoyance at the open stares about them.

"Come—where—when?" Lind asked innocently.

"Let's go outside and talk," he said. He picked up his box of groceries and steered Lind out of the door before she had an opportunity to make her own purchases. Judith passed them at the doorway.

"Come on out after you've got your things, Judie," Lind called back to her. The girl went on into the store, showing none of the curiosity she felt about the stranger who was with Lind.

Mark placed his provisions in the bottom of the buggy in which he had driven to Yellow Post, and walked with Lind to the creek. They sat down on the grassy bank and watched the tiny minnows dart down with the gentle current in silver schools, and turning, snub their way quiveringly back up stream with no more provocation, perhaps, than the shadow of a sailing leaf on the water.

"I've missed you. It rained last night, and I was sure you'd come," Mark told her. "I listened until midnight."

"Oh, how ridiculous! You did not!"

"I swear it!"

"But it would be a little—irregular."

Mark frowned at her. "It wasn't the night you did come. You do the thing you want to here, anyway. I need you, Lind, more than you know. I've been plugging away clearing Klovacz's land, or I would have been over at the school yesterday. Has Mrs Gare given you permission to have me call on you?"

"I've not asked her yet. It's terribly hard. But I'll come over and cook you a dinner—" she said impulsively. "May I bring Judith? That's Jude back in the store."

Mark gave her a searching look.

"Oh, just to make it jollier," she hastened to add.

"Bring her, by all means, and any one else you like."

They walked back toward the store. As Jude did not come out, Lind decided that she felt shy about meeting Mark, and did not go in for her. She said good-by to him, and Mark climbed into the buggy and drove off.

It was the day on which mail arrived with John Tobacco, and when Lind returned alone to the store, Sven

Sandbo was there talking with Judith. Sven had dis-
carded his city clothes and most of his braggadocio air.
His heavy shoulders stood out from his narrow hips, the
calves of his legs were slightly bowed from the saddle.
The mobility of his mouth and nostrils, the lazy droop
of his eyes at the corners, the careless gesture of the hand
that held his cigarette, his frank maleness, made him at
once attractive and exasperating.

Judith, hostile-eyed and withdrawn, was trying hard
not to smile at his advances.

"Tell me," he was saying, "do you like me better without my tenderfoot get-up?"

"A little," she admitted. "But you think you're too
smart."

Sven laughed teasingly. "Wouldn't notice my clothes
the other day at all, would you? And me comin' all the
way from town just to show you 'em. You hurt my
feelin's, Jude, terrible!" She looked sternly away and
he moved closer to her. "Have you forgot all about the
picnic last summer, Judie? Remember what you said?
I ain't forgot." His voice was so low that the pitch
of it alone made Judith blush.

Lind, followed by the nudges and leering eyes of the
halfbreeds who hung about, came up to Jude, who introduced her to Sven. Sven, quite at ease, talked with
the Teacher while Judith argued with Johanneson over
the merits of a certain dried codfish.

"What's the matter?" Johanneson demanded. "That's
good fish, and double worth the money. Guess yer paw
give ye only ten cents to buy for, ha?"

Judith tossed her head angrily. "You keep still, you

flat-faced Swede! If there was another store here we'd not give our good money for your bum stuff. Give me a dollar's worth of the fish, and be quick about it!" She stamped her foot and all the men in the store looked toward her appreciatively. She had been told to get only fifty cents worth of the fish. She would have to explain to Amelia, who would understand well enough, but perhaps not approve.

Johanneson turned sheepishly about and wrapped up the package of cod. He could not afford, on second thought, to lose Gare as a customer. But this big girl's insolent quibbling over prices always annoyed him. No doubt she had been prompted by those at home.

Still somewhat ruffled, Judith went out with Sven, followed immediately by Lind when she had made her purchases. The two girls got into their own cart and Sven drove slowly away alone behind them.

"Lind," said Judith, when they were out of sight of Yellow Post, "Sven asked me to ride with him. Will you take the cart home? And I'll get out and wait for him."

"But your father——"

"I don't care. I get hell anyway."

Lind obligingly, though with some misgivings, took the cart home, and Judith rode with Sven.

"Judie," Sven began, putting an arm around her shoulders. "I want you to marry me."

Judith was silent. She thought of Amelia. Ellen would never forgive her. . . .

"Don't you love me any more, Judie? You used to," said Sven, almost humbly.

Judith's head was high, her eyes half-closed. The buggy rumbled down the hollow over a little bridge that led through a dense growth of spruce and cedar. Sven drew her suddenly into his arms, letting the reins fall slack over his knees.

"Damn—you're beautiful, Judie!"

Judith smiled. Her body softened toward him. It rippled with strength. She was peculiarly aware of her strength. It seemed to flow upward from her spine in a powerful current and issue from her breast and her fingertips and all the sensitive surface of her body. A strange desire seized her. She could not free herself from the obsession . . . it had come upon her first the day she had seen Sven after his return.

"I wonder if I can throw you," she said suddenly.

Sven laughed aloud.

"I'll bet I can," she asserted. "Let me try."

"All right, some time," he agreed, laughing still.

"No, right now," Judith insisted, her eyes roving over the muscles that moved under his shirt sleeve.

It was warm and neither wore a coat.

Sven glanced at her and saw that she was in earnest. They got down from the buggy, tying the horse to a tree at the side of the road. Then they crawled through the fence into a little clearing among the cedars, where the sunlight lay in a warm pool on the ground.

"Kiss me first," said Sven.

"No—after," Judith said steadily.

So they wrestled. Judith was almost as tall as Sven. Her limbs were long, sinewy, her body quick and lithe as a wild-cat's. Sven, who started the tussle laughing, could get no lasting grip on her. She slid through his arms and wound herself about his body, bringing them both to the earth. As their movements increased in swiftness and strength, Sven forgot to laugh and became as serious as Judith. It did not occur to him that he might have to use his real energy in defending himself until he saw that the girl's face was set and hard, her eyes burning. He realized suddenly that she was trying to get a head lock on him that he himself had taught her. He caught both her hands, twisting her right arm backward. She threw herself upon him violently, almost somersaulting over his shoulder, freeing her arm with a terrific jerk. Sven turned quickly, caught her about the waist with one arm and pressed the other against her throat, so that she was bent almost double and unable to breathe. He looked at her, saw that her eyes were closed and her face almost scarlet and dripping with perspiration.

"Had enough?" he asked, slightly loosening his hold.

Judith took advantage of the moment, and with a twist of her head was out of his grip like an eel. Her eyes were blazing, her breath coming in short gasps. She lashed out with her arm, striking him full across the face. While Sven, half stunned from the weight of the blow, was trying to understand the change in the issue, she hurled herself against him and he fell to the earth under her. Then something leaped in Sven. They were no longer unevenly matched, different in sex. They were two stark elements, striving for mastery over each other.

Sven crushed the girl's limbs between his own, bruised her throat, pulled her arms ruthlessly together behind her until the skin over the curve of her shoulders was white and taut, her clothing torn away. Her panting body heaved against his as they lay full length on the ground locked in furious embrace. Judith buried her nails in the flesh over his breast, beat her knees into his loins, set her teeth in the more tender skin over the veins at his wrists. She fought with insane abandon to any hurt he might inflict, or he would have mastered her at once. The faces, throats and chests of both were shining with sweat. Sven's breath fell in hot gusts on Judith's face. Suddenly her hand, that was fastened like steel on his throat, relaxed and fell away. Her eyelids quivered and a tear trickled down and mingled with the beads of perspiration on her temple. Sven released the arm that he had bent to breaking point. He was trembling.

"Judie," he muttered, "Judie—look at me."

Judith raised her eyelids slowly.

"Kiss me—now," she said in a breath.

CHAPTER VI

1

THERE was a thick hedge of dwarf firs at the end of the garden which lay toward the main trail. Amelia was on her knees spraying the tomato vines that grew there. The night before had been cold, and from long habit the tomatoes were last in her thoughts before she had gone to sleep, and first when she had wakened, although her heart was heavy with other things.

She got to her feet, and hearing the approach of a horse, stepped into the shadow of the fir hedge to see who might be riding by. It was a break in the day's routine even to see the passing face of a stranger. The horse came into view at a walk, the rider sitting lazily in the saddle, looking ahead of him toward the school house. He presently turned from the road and cut across the school lot, where the horse stopped and the rider dismounted.

Amelia's heart sickened her with its beating. The hedge gave way slightly behind her as she leaned against it, but her eyes held the face of the man riding as if they were physically fastened to it. The man passed and the back of his head and shoulders were all that she could see of him. Then she turned and knelt before the blanket that had covered the tomato plants the night before. He was his father over again . . . but not so simple. She wondered if it would be necessary to blanket the tomatoes

to-night again . . . a man of the world . . . education
lay on his brow like a light. He wore his clothes with
such an air, sat in the saddle like a soldier. . . .
And his father had been gored by a bull . . . after
everything. . . .

Amelia knelt on the ground above the tomato vines.
She felt cold and exhausted and exposed, as she had
years ago after being up all night with one of the children during sickness. It was as if she had been dragged
terrified out upon a stage to play the leading rôle in a
tragedy at which the audience would laugh. The unbelievable drama of her whole life flashed before her.
She shrank from the spectacle as she might have from
a hanging, or a brutal and unfamiliar scene of crime, in
which she had no part. Her body trembled with actual
cold. She had been so unfitted for the rôle that life had
chosen for her—no more fitted than Lind. She had been
so unshaped for the burden that had never known a
moment's easing. In her heart she cried out for eternal
release from the still crueller consequence of her impulse, the punishment that Caleb had in store—the
carrying out of his threat that fell upon her mind like an
awful gong sounded at regular intervals.

After a few minutes, her mind became clearer. She
had seen Mark Jordan. He was a man of the world,
perhaps his friends were people who commanded respect
and looked upon him with respect. Who was she, a common farm woman, to know what his life was or what it
demanded of him? His face was proud, sensitive. He
must never know. She would break under Caleb rather

than have him know, Caleb's children could wither and fall like rotten plants after frost—everything could fall into dissolution. He was his father's son, Mark Jordan, the son of the only man she had ever loved. Ellen, Martin, Judith and Charlie, they were only the offspring of Caleb Gare, they could be the sacrifice. She would bend and inure them to the land like implements, just as Caleb wished her to do. She would not intercede in their behalf hereafter. She would see them dry and fade into fruitlessness and grow old long before their time, but her heart would keep within itself and there would be no pity in her for the destruction of their youth. Amelia's face grew pale and hard as she knelt in the garden. A distinct change had come over her.

She carried the blanket indoors, thinking that it would be unnecessary to cover the tomatoes that night. The air seemed visible and intimate, as before rain. Her eyes wandered to the fields of tame hay and rye-grass that lay beyond the sheep pasture. There would be a tremendous yield this year. Always before, the sight of growth had somehow thrilled her, had struck a vital, creative chord within her that was otherwise left unsounded in this barren life. Now her mind was dulled by the sight of it. Growth—with death in its wake. She felt that in an instant her life had reached finality, that all the years behind her had been spent in a chrysalis, in a beginning. There had been no development in between—only a beginning and an end.

She went indoors and began energetically to polish the stove with a blackened cloth.

2

Before long Amelia returned to her old pale manner of self-effacement and submission, and the atmosphere on the Gare farm became normal once more to Lind's perception. The place was holding its breath again after a quiet exhalation.

Feeling that what had disturbed Amelia was at least for the present lulled, Lind approached her one day with a question. Mrs Gare was gathering eggs in the barn mangers, and, since it was Saturday morning, the Teacher had undertaken to help her.

"Mrs Gare, Mark Jordan would like very much to come here to see me, and to meet you people as well. Do you think Mr Gare would like to have him call?"

Amelia was prepared for just such a question. She smiled at Lind, and shook her head.

"I'm afraid it would only excite the children, Miss Archer, and stir up trouble. Mr Jordan would talk about things that we can't afford to think about."

"Well, then," said Lind, "will you permit Judie to come with me to see him? He is living there all alone and I think it would be kind to cook a good meal for him, now and then."

Amelia glanced at her, and looked away quickly.

"Judith might make an errand over that way, but don't speak of it before her father." Mark Jordan should have what he wanted, she resolved.

"I'll be careful not to, Mrs Gare," Lind said gratefully. She groped about in the hay and came upon another brown egg, which she placed carefully in the pan with the others. The feeling of conspiracy against Caleb was rather enjoyable.

She took the eggs to the house, and then went to the potato patch where Judith was absently hoeing between the rows. The sun was beating down upon the girl's bare head and on the strong honey-brown nape of her neck. A hot, dusty wind was stirring the tops of the dry potato plants. A little groove of dust had formed on either side of Judith's nose, and there were gray filaments of dust on the hair of her forearms. She crossed her arms and leaned forward on the hoe as Lind came up to her.

"A little romance, Judie," Lind said softly. "We're going to have supper to-morrow night with Mark Jordan —the man you saw me with at Yellow Post."

Judith frowned. To-morrow was Sunday. On Sundays Caleb usually went to the farm of one of the Icelanders in the afternoon, and did not return until late in the evening.

"Ma say I could go?"

Lind told her what Amelia had said. Judith was silent for a moment and then decided to confide in the Teacher to an extent.

"Will you let Sven come?"

"Why, that would be fine! We'll have a real party. If only Ellen and Martin could get away too. They never have any fun."

"No," said Jude with conviction. "They wouldn't enjoy themselves. Anyway, they mustn't know that Sven is going to be there—at least Ellen mustn't. Sven wants me to marry him, Lind, and go away to town."

Lind looked at her quietly for a moment. A change had come over the girl during the past few days. She was not so boisterous in her care of the animals, nor so defiant toward the human beings on the farm as she had been.

"And shall you?"

"Yes—before long. Don't let the others know."

Lind slipped away and Judith went on with her hoeing. She cast a resentful eye over the long rows of potatoes. Food for another winter—another winter of stumbling about in the bleak, icy dawn and tugging at stubborn calves and hauling icicle-rimmed buckets full of water through manure and frozen mud. Another winter of inhibition and growing restiveness, and hopeless dreaming of a better time to come. Another winter under Caleb Gare . . . no, anything else was preferable.

As the work on the farm grew and grew, Judith was struggling to see her way clear to liberty. Covertly she watched Ellen and Amelia and Martin, even Charlie now that he was learning to take his place, and saw them all bowing without a question under the stupefying load. And she recognized in herself an alien spirit, a violent being of dark impulses, in no way related to the life about her. She was alternately seized with an agony of pity for Amelia, whose reticence she could not fathom, and futile rage at Ellen and Martin for their endurance. And beneath it all her passion for Sven pressed through her being like an undercurrent of fire. She lay awake at night with hot cheeks, thinking of him . . . of the day in the clearing among the cedars . . . running her fingers over the muscles of his throat. Caleb had not found out that Lind had brought the cart home that day. She had not seen Sven since they had fought, had not wished to see him. She had need of an interim in which to think.

After another hour's work, Judith, looking up, saw Martin entering the gate from the pasture with three cows that were about to calve. More money for Caleb Gare, more toil for the workers under him. He had nearly twice as many cattle this year as three years ago: and no hired man now to help with their care, because Martin and Judith were old enough to do it together, and Judith strong enough to do it alone when Martin was otherwise occupied. In a hollow in the pasture she saw the sheep grazing, all of them shorn now, shorn of dollars and dollars worth of wool that would go toward the acquisition of more sheep . . . and more sheep . . . but not more freedom for the workers under Caleb Gare, not more joy in living. She remembered suddenly that the bag of wool she had got from her own sheep was still stowed away under the rafters in the loft. She must dispose of it some way before Caleb found it.

The hoe over her shoulder, Judith went to the barn where she found Martin, hammering new planks into the rotten floor.

"Martin," she began with difficulty. "Do you suppose he figures on getting a man for the haying?"

Martin looked at her dryly.

"Not with threshers askin' what they're goin' to. We'll be lucky if he hires a full crew. What you ask for?"

Judith threw herself down upon the threshold of the

barn door and leaned her head against the worn log frame. "Oh, nothing, but I was just thinkin' Ellen isn't really strong enough to help. Remember how she ran the fork into her foot last year 'cause she couldn't see it."

"Well—" Martin said slowly, "I'll ask him again."

Judith looked sideways at Martin where he was on his hands and knees fitting the new boards into the floor. She felt a sudden fullness of heart as she looked at him, and wished that somehow she might talk with him about things. She had always felt more kinship with Martin than with any of the others. How stooped already his shoulders were, how pitifully scrawny his neck! She watched him drive nails into the boards after he had fitted them, and saw how gentle his face was in the doing of the mean task. Why had she never seen these things in Martin before? Tears came into her eyes as they dwelt on him, and she could have rushed to him and thrown her arms about him from a sudden sheer realization of what he was. Martin would have been certain that she had gone out of her mind. She rose hastily and left him, before she should do the unaccountable thing.

Martin looked after her. In his uncertain way, he felt that it was not so much Ellen that Judith was concerned about. Jude was not adept at dissimulation.

His job in the barn done, Martin went to the pile of long, straight poplar logs he had cut, planed and measured for the new wagon shed. Martin was always building in his spare time. Caleb often chided him for the material and time he wasted on what he considered purely decorative and unnecessary outhouses, but since building was the thing that lay nearest Martin's heart, he was not so readily deterred.

Martin marked off with pegs which he drove in the ground, the area which the wagon shed was to cover. Now and then his eye wandered to the rough, unpainted log house that had been his home all his life, and in his heart he conceived a dream. The dream grew to a desire that crept into his hands. His hands grasped the good, enduring lumber, the plaster, the fine laths, the shingles, the panes of glass, the stones for the foundation and the chimney of the New House. It would be painted brown, a rich, dark brown . . . gallons of paint and turpentine that you could smell all over the place. There would be a veranda facing the main road such as he had seen on the houses pictured in the mail order catalogue. And there would be a tall iron fence across the driveway, and the road would be cleared of the ruts made by the cattle . . . and he would plant an acorn on either side of the road that in years to come would be a great spreading oak tree. . . .

That evening Martin's face wore an almost rapt look as he sat planing smooth a board that was to be a shelf for Amelia's preserves.

Caleb had come in after a tour of the fields. He hung his lantern on the wall, shaking it first to see whether it needed oil. Finding that it did, he handed it to Amelia to fill.

"Goin' to be a bumper crop if it keeps up like this, Martin," he remarked, ignoring Judith and Amelia, who were washing the parts of the separator.

"How's the wagon shed comin'?" he asked pleasantly, sitting down to take off his heavy boots. He had asked Martin the same question during supper, but it was the first subject that occurred to him which would obliquely shut the women out of the conversation. It was not exactly to show an interest in Martin's work that he asked it.

"Pretty good," Martin told him again. The thing that was on his mind gathered courage for utterance when he heard Caleb speak optimistically of the crops.

Slowly shaving at the wood, he said, "I was thinkin' we might build next spring if we have a good harvest."

Judith and Amelia half turned to hear what he was saying. Caleb saw their looks of interest.

"Yeah, the barn does look as if it was saggin' in the middle," he said softly, moving into the other room.

Martin and Judith and Amelia exchanged involuntary glances.

"Hm," said Judith. "Then we'll live in the barn, Martin."

Amelia said nothing, although she saw that Martin felt the rebuff keenly.

But Martin was a builder born, and the dream reared itself in his mind and would not down. He resolved to approach Caleb when the women were not around. He would wait until he saw what the end of the summer brought. Even if the crops failed the cattle should bring something, and Caleb was keeping far too many horses in pasture now. He could well afford to build in the spring.

3

As it happened, the next day was a "church" day, and Caleb at the Yellow Post service was invited to dinner at Thorvaldson's. He drove back home with Thorvald, and told Amelia that he was going on west and would not be back until dark. In the afternoon Judith and the Teacher, with Amelia's deliberate sanction, took two of the horses and rode to the Sandbos'.

Lind felt excitedly happy.

"Judie," she said. "Have you told your mother about Sven?"

"No," she replied. "She would only worry. And *he* would find out, and then it would be all over."

"Why all over?"

"He would kill me rather than let me marry Sven, or anybody. He knows that would mean a change on the farm. He'd have to get a man—he couldn't save so much money—it would start Ellen and Martin and Charlie wanting to go away."

"But, Judie—you can't all stay here forever?"

"Oh, yes, we can. We can stay here until Ellen goes blind and I go crazy and the others die. That's the way people live up here. But I'm not goin' to stick. Wait until the haying is over."

They rode along in silence then, the afternoon warm upon them. Lind glanced down at the drying pools that lined the road, and saw the countless "lucky bugs" darting about on the water like crazy sparks of light. The reeds stood up straight and brittle. It must rain soon. Lind could not bear the dry dust on the reeds. Then she suddenly realized that it was not the reeds that she was thinking of, but the Gares. . . .

At the Sandbos', Sven joined them eagerly. He came running up the road when he saw them, and caught hold of the pummel of Judith's saddle. He would have kissed her, but she drew back and looked at Lind.

"We're goin' over to Klovacz's. Come along?" Jude asked him casually. He lifted his healthy, eager face to her and she thrilled through and through at the sight of him again.

"You bet I will! I talked with Jordan one day on the road. He's not a bad sort, for a city guy," Sven commented generously. "I'll be along. Comin' in to talk to ma?"

Mrs Sandbo and the girls came out to the road and Lind and Judith dismounted while Sven got his own horse out.

Mrs Sandbo, who had not talked with Judith Gare for some time, eyed her inquisitively. She congratulated herself upon getting a look at one of the Gares again at such close range. Jude did not yet have her new shoes, she noticed. Emma, who had seen her one day near the school house, had reported that her toes were sticking out. It was almost true. And her dress! What a faded calico it was for a Sunday! Mrs Sandbo would have a choice bit of news for Dora. What a man Caleb Gare was! What a father! Ludvig had had his faults, but he had not been stingy—a spender, in fact.

"Your mother, then—how goes it vit' her?" Mrs

Sandbo asked Judith. "She had so bad toot'ache last I see her."

Lind forebore from smiling. Mrs Sandbo always seemed intent on learning the latest concerning Mrs Gare's teeth.

"She's well, thank you," Jude said stiffly. The ferreting gaze of Mrs Sandbo and her plump young daughters in their pink lawn dresses did not please her. She wished Sven would hurry.

He was with them at last, and they took leave of Mrs Sandbo and Emma and Dena. Sven was full of talk about the improvements he had made on the place since he came home.

"Can't stand having nothing to do," he told them. "Farming is my idea of nothing to do, on a place like ours, anyway. Had a real job in town—brick layin'. Good money. I'll just get ma to sell the place and go back, soon's the summer's over."

They rode gaily over the miles to the Klovaczs'. Judith scarcely looked at Sven in the presence of Lind, but when the Teacher rode ahead to announce their coming to Mark Jordan, she leaned over in her saddle and kissed him quickly.

Mark laughed with boyish pleasure when Lind swung the screen door of the kitchen open and walked in upon him. He was stretched out upon a couch in the sitting room, reading a magazine which had come from the city. He sprang up and lifted Lind by her elbows. She disengaged herself demurely.

"I've brought Paul and Virginia," she smiled. "May they come in?"

Mark went out with her and beheld the two jumping easily off their horses. "What a pair they make, eh?" he murmured. Lind nodded.

Jude shook hands a little bashfully with Mark when Lind introduced them. It was not long before Mark's good humor put them both at their ease. They all went into the house, Judith glancing about the kitchen a little fearfully as if she expected it to fall upon her, so unused was she to being in other people's houses.

They sat about in the sitting room for an hour listening to Mark's phonograph. Judith had heard one in the home of an Icelander, but it had had a horn and had not produced the alluring music that she listened to now. Her eyes grew dark and absent as she let her emotions drift with the spirit of the dance. A waltz was played, and she feared that she would cry before it came to an end.

Lind and Mark danced a little, and Jude watched them enraptured. It was all so new to her, and yet it seemed part of the thing to which she belonged. Sven, knowing that she could not dance as Lind and Mark danced, did not ask her, and she was grateful to him.

The supper, which Mark called a "banquet," was a merry occasion. Judith and Lind concocted many savory dishes while the men smoked and talked about things which Sven had heard of and some which he had seen. When they finally sat down to the table, gay humor prevailed. Judith was peculiarly alert and bright eyed, as if to seize every moment of happiness in the evening.

They went home soon after supper, Judith fearing the

return of Caleb. The horses of Lind and Mark loitered, while Judith and Sven hurried ahead of them. The air in the wood road was redolent of tree gums. Occasionally a swallow dipped across the light and vanished like the wraith of a bird. As they reached the summit of a ridge half way between Klovacz's and Sandbo's, Mark and Lind noticed that the sun was just sinking beyond Latt's Slough, drawing a bar of crimson across the long, motionless water. The sprawling shadows of the horses purpled; it seemed as if their hoof beats in the gray dust became softer. Silence had come over the world like a wing—like a brooding thought.

After a while Mark spoke.

"It changes you—this life. You won't come out of it quite the same, Lind."

CHAPTER VII

1

CALEB did not learn of Judith's trip with the Teacher to the farm of the Klovaczs'. But Ellen, absorbing the knowledge in his stead and reacting to it as she knew he would have done, vented her disapproval upon Amelia. She and her mother were frying doughnuts, of which Caleb was very fond, when she brought the matter up.

"It don't seem just decent to me—Jude going off that way on a Sunday to visit a strange man with no older person along," she began with a censorious press of the cutter into the dough she had rolled out on the table. "And father not home. It seems straight deceitful."

"The Teacher was along, and she *is older*, Ellen," Amelia said mildly. "Surely no harm could come of it, their going off for an afternoon. Judie has so little pleasure, and she works so hard." Amelia bent over the pan of sizzling lard on the stove and felt hypocritically happy. Lind had told her of how Mark Jordan had enjoyed having his visitors there.

"Well," Ellen retorted, drawing a deep, injured breath, "it seems we all work hard."

"Of course we do, Ellen, and you ought to have a holiday now and then as well as Jude," Mrs Gare hastened to say. "There's no reason why you shouldn't. And you do get out more than Jude, you know. Jude has never been with Martin to Nykerk, and you have."

134

"Yes—with the cattle," Ellen fretted. "But I wouldn't sneak around getting fun. What if he had found out where she was yesterday? What if he hears about it somehow? Jude is getting more and more selfish every day. She doesn't care about any of the rest of us. She doesn't give a pin for anybody but herself."

"Now, Ellen," Amelia said conciliatorily. "Don't take on so. There's no deceiving about it. Jude and the Teacher just went over to cook supper for that poor young man who's living all alone there. There can't be anything so wrong in that, can there?"

"Hm," sniffed Ellen. "You'd think he was some relation or something! There's enough bachelors living alone on homesteads around here to keep Jude busy all week at that rate."

Amelia smiled and turned the doughnuts over in their pan with a fork. Ellen, out of her high tower of self-righteousness, if she learned the truth, would be the first to condemn her mother.

The days were growing longer and more full. Caleb was sending cream and some butter to the Siding again, and there was the separating and the churning to be done. The garden cost Amelia no end of work and worry; she tended the delicate tomato vines as though they were new born infants, and suffered momentary sinking of the heart whenever she detected signs of weakness in any of the hardier vegetables. She was grateful for the toil in which she could dwell as a sort of refuge from deeper thought. Caleb spent much time away from the farm dealing with breeders and horse traders, returning heavy with importance and news from other parts which he did not divulge to those at home. The care of the animals fell largely to the children.

Following the eventful Sunday, Judith walked about in a strange dream, not quite realizing what had happened to her. That she had been for a brief space in another world, she knew—a world marvelously familiar in spite of its strangeness. But the music—it enveloped her. She herded cattle, cleaned the stable, or hoed the potatoes to the strains of a waltz or the melody of a popular song as though it had been a symphony concert that had lodged in her heart. And then, waking, she found Amelia, Ellen, Martin and Charlie going about in the same dumb way, weeding the garden, tending mares in foal, carrying water, leading horses to the trough, searching the sky for rain. And above all, reporting to Caleb Gare by their wordless code the fact that all was serene over the land he owned.

Observing the increasing confidence with which Caleb conducted affairs on the farm, and the meek resignation of the others, Judith began to fear that there was a sinisterly passive influence in the soil tying her to it hand and foot even while she was planning to escape. Sven, on the two occasions when she had seen him during her circling of the north pasture after the cattle, had urged her to speak to her mother of their plan to be married. But Judith had put off doing so, hoping that some change in Caleb's running of the farm would make it easier for Amelia to look kindly upon the announcement.

She went again to Martin and asked him if Caleb intended to hire a man for the haying.

"I'll ask him," Martin said dubiously.

He approached Caleb in the barn, where he was unwrapping a package of patent horse-medicine newly arrived through the mail order.

"That hay is sure comin' up," Martin began. "There'll be half as much again as last year."

Caleb peered at him. He drew the cork out of one of the bottles of medicine and smelt it. Then he replaced the cork and arranged the bottles on the shelf of the barn wall.

As he made no remark, Martin was forced to go on with what he had to say without any encouragement.

"I was thinkin' it mightn't be a bad idea to get one of the halfbreeds up. They're cheap, and we could get it in quicker than with the girls."

"Can't do it, Martin—can't do it this year. Wool went down ten per cent, you know," Caleb said gently. "The girls will have to be shown how to hurry."

What anger Martin was capable of feeling came to the surface now like a squall on smooth water. "I don't see what difference a little wool makes," he broke out. "I call it poor economy, figgerin' like that."

Caleb turned slowly. "It doesn't make much difference what you call it, my boy," he said in the same even tone. "This farm is goin' to be run like I want it run. When you're old enough to do it better, then I'll ask ye how." He slapped the dust from the shelves off his hands and shuffled out of the barn. Martin, red of face and humiliated, went off to find Judith.

She was mixing chicken feed in the hen house.

"Well, Jude, you might as well stop worryin' about

Ellen. There ain't goin' to be any man for the hayin'," he remarked.

"There ain't?" Jude repeated dully after him. Her eyes hardened but she made no further comment. After she had prepared the feed, she went into the house and faced Amelia.

Judith stood before her mother with her hands in her pockets, much in the attitude of a laborer demanding his wages. There was nothing soft or confiding in the girl's manner. She had an announcement to make, and she made it.

"Sven Sandbo wants me to marry him," she stated.

Amelia looked at her dazedly. "And will you?" she asked in a faint voice. One of the things she had feared had come, then.

"As soon's I know *he* won't kill everybody if I do," was her reply. "You best tell him he'll need another man for the haying, and see what he says. I can't stay after that, anyway—I just can't."

She turned abruptly on her heel and went upstairs. It had surprised her that Amelia was not at once opposed to the idea. She would go straight ahead now, and agree to any plan Sven suggested.

As the girl went out, Amelia lifted her eyes and looked long at the rough plaster of the wall before her. It was coming, in spite of all that she could do. She could not expect the girls to sacrifice all their youth for her— she could not achieve that sacrifice for all her concentrating. Caleb would be obdurate if Jude went away with Sven. He would carry out his threat concerning Mark Jordan in order to keep the others on the farm. The disgrace would fasten them all within these log walls forever. No one would want to marry into the family after the truth was out about the mother. Caleb would ruin Mark Jordan to insure himself against the desertion of the others. She knew him so well. Would it make any difference to Mark? To Lind Archer? That was the question. And she had no way of finding the answer to it.

That night, after the others had gone to the loft, Amelia spoke hurriedly to Caleb. He was in an unusually mellow mood, having transacted profitably during the day in regard to a second-hand hayrack.

"Caleb, Sven Sandbo wants to marry Jude," she began in a low tone, lest those in the loft should hear.

Caleb glanced up irritably. "Speak out, woman, speak out. There's nothing you're ashamed of, is there?"

Amelia drew her lips in, a flush gathered on her cheeks.

"I think she ought to marry him *now*, before Bart Nugent comes up here, if he does. He might—he might not be so careful what he says when he has had something to drink," she said nervously.

Caleb had been hinting lately that Bart Nugent might take a trip up from the city during the summer. Amelia did not know whether to believe him or not.

Caleb began to enjoy the situation. "*You* think, do you? Hah! Scared Bart might tell the truth, eh? Rather have Sven taken in, eh? Have him think he's marryin' into fine stuff?"

"You know—you know nobody around here would marry the girls—if—if they knew."

"No," he agreed softly, "the people around here are careful of their morals. But that's no reason why you should take advantage of them. Wouldn't it be better to wait and find out what Jude is going to be before you turn her over to an honest man?"

Amelia sprang to her feet, her face white.

"I've had enough from you, you hypocrite!" she said, her voice breaking. "It isn't Jude you're thinking of. It's your filthy greed—and the work you can get out of her. If you even told the truth—I might—I might respect your bullying. But this—this I won't bear it—you—you sneak!"

She heard her own voice without recognizing it. As he descended upon her, his eyes burning into her face, she stood rigid, all feeling gone out of her body. Then suddenly the old fear of him swept upon her like a torrent of icy water, beads of sweat broke out about her lips, her hands shook.

Caleb laughed under his breath. He spoke now almost in a whisper, as he always did when frenzy had its way with him.

"Getting independent suddenly, are you? Mark Jordan isn't so far away but what I could reach him to-night, before I go to bed."

Amelia shook her head, her lips moving silently. If she did not end the scene the children would know that something was happening below. Lind would hear. Caleb looked at her. She was a poor thing, after all, scarcely worth the trouble.

Calmly taking off his shoes, he barred the door for the night, blew out the lamp, and went to bed. In the kitchen Amelia sat for a long time in the light of the lantern, shelling tiny new peas, for something to do.

2

Judith, who had heard fragments of the talk from the thinly partitioned staircase, noiselessly crept back to bed. But she lay all that night without being able to sleep. She felt that she had learned something too terrible to frame in words. Something that kept her eternally from Sven. Monstrous conjectures as to what it might be fled through her mind like a waking nightmare. Whatever the disaster that hung over Amelia, she knew now that it threatened her as well.

The next day the thing gnawed at her mind like a pain. She could not unburden her knowledge to any one. She watched Amelia and her pity grew, an intangible thing. There was no demonstration of affection between them, no mother and daughter sentiment. Indeed, the feeling Judith had in regard to Amelia was rather a deeper thing, springing from the broad stratum of human sympathy.

When she went for the cattle she took the wood road on the opposite side of the timber out of sight of the Sandbos', to avoid meeting Sven. The evening was so clear that the trees in the brush seemed to be standing in a glaze. She heard him calling across the swamps to his own cattle, and knew that it was to make her hear. It made her bitterly lonely. But there was no romance of desire in her loneliness. What she had heard had made her feel soiled and mysteriously unworthy. "Nobody would marry her if they knew," Amelia had said.

She shut herself in from the Teacher completely. Here was something raw, inexorable, that Lind, who had soft fingers and belonged to that other world of dance and magic music, could never understand.

A horse dropped dead one day in the pasture, and Caleb sent Martin and Charlie out to skin it. Before the carcass had been taken away, Judith came upon it, red and horrible in the burning sunlight. After that, the hurt in her mind seemed to take on the image of the horse.

She worked like a tireless machine from morning till night, and Caleb almost admitted his pleasure in her industry.

"I'll be goin' in to town one of these days, Jude. Perhaps there's something you'd like me to bring you—a pair of shoes, or something like that," he suggested, as though he did not know that she was wearing Charlie's boots for want of shoes.

"H–mp!" Judith muttered. "I don't want anything."

Amelia noticed Judith's stolid indifference to everything about her, and she reproached herself even while she was reminded of the vow she had made to herself in the garden the day she had seen Mark Jordan. "She is too proud to ask me whether I have spoken to him about the man for the haying," she guessed, "and it's worrying her." But long custom kept her silent. They were separate workers under Caleb Gare, each with her own concerns.

Caleb's acres of delicate flax became a tissue of pale silver under the sky. Caleb watched it daily now,

measured its height, noticed the moisture in the soil.
The flax was his pride—his great hope. He had planted
twice as much this year as last. Articles on its cultivation had become to him the Word of God. The rye
grass would grow abundantly without a thought, and he
would sell it well, but the flax was a thing to pray over.

On the day following his little difference, as he called
it, with Amelia, he walked with increasing satisfaction,
through and through the timber he had "bought" of Fusi
Aronson. To the south lay the muskeg and the dried
lake bottom that he had disposed of in exchange for the
timber. Fusi would no doubt be able to put it to good
use—the Icelanders were a thrifty lot. . . . He smiled
to himself as he saw how things were shaping up. It
was all a matter of resolve and one got what one wanted.
True, it might be a little difficult to persuade the pig-
headed Thorvaldson to sell the grazing land adjacent to
his own on the west. It was a shameful waste of land,
given up to a few head of moth-eaten scrub horses. He
would have to get around Thorvaldson.

Caleb felt secure and mellow after his encounter with
Amelia. She had betrayed by her attitude that she
would not abet Judith in any scheming. And, thorough
egoist that he was, he could not conceive of Jude's cross-
ing him without the support of at least one other member
of the family. Caleb had no special desire to bring
matters to a climax in regard to Mark Jordan. As it
stood now, the thing savored of intrigue and the per-
vasive, subterranean control of a Master. In a sense,
it had lost its serious significance and had become a sort
of game by which he amused himself. A dénouement,

while it would perhaps tighten the screws on the fixtures on the farm, would make him less an heroic figure in a mystery. For Caleb, although he had known of Amelia's moral defection before he had married her, had always looked upon himself as the betrayed and cheated victim in a triangle. It was perhaps this which prevented him from ever feeling pangs of remorse for his acts. His sensibilities were crystallized in the belief that life had done him an eternal wrong, which no deed of his own could over-avenge.

3

On the last day of June Caleb went to the city in the south. It was a semi-annual journey which occupied only three or four days, and was made solely for the purpose of laying in such provisions as could not be obtained at Yellow Post or at Nykerk, but it was attended always by a show of solemn importance. And there was never a releasing of tension after Caleb's departure: he always took pains to set tasks which would remain behind like stern images of himself.

Judith was free to go where she liked without discovery for four days. But she did not try to find Sven Sandbo.

CHAPTER VIII

1

CALEB was away, but things went on with the same unbroken monotony: Martin finished the wagon shed, and dreamed his dream of the New House; Amelia and Ellen worked in the garden, milked, churned, and sent the remainder of the cream to the Siding with Skuli Erickson, from whom the cans were borrowed for the purpose. Caleb did not believe in buying them for so short a season. Judith and Charlie tended the livestock.

The Teacher, free of her school duties for two weeks in the month of July, watched the Gares out of the pity of her heart, and came no closer to any of them. Ellen harbored a scarcely concealed resentment for everything about Lind Archer, from the dainty underwear she hung on the line to dry, to the manner in which she taught the children at school to look for beauty in every living thing. She pointedly refrained from remembering whether Lind took sugar in her tea or not, so little did the Teacher and her tastes mean to her. Martin avoided her out of sheer shyness and awe. Charlie was more unbending, and offered to play "catch" with her now and again, but the boy, old as he was, was peevish, and sulked when he did not get his own way, and Lind could draw nothing from him that was not a reflection of Caleb.

Lind was nonplussed by Judith. Whenever the girl spoke to her it was in a brusque, almost offensive tone. The Teacher had gone to the Sandbos' one evening, where she frequently met Mark Jordan, and Sven had asked her why Judith went out of her way not to meet him when she brought in the cattle. But she could get no response from Judith when she approached her in Sven's behalf. It hurt and surprised her, especially after the pleasant Sunday when the girl's restraint had been so completely broken.

On a drowsy afternoon during Caleb's absence, Lind took the little pony of the Sandbo children and rode to the homestead of Dora Brund, Mrs Sandbo's married daughter, who, according to her mother, lived a life of misery under a brutal husband. "The poor girl," Mrs Sandbo had lamented. "She vill be so glad vhen you come."

The trail led several miles along a swamp mottled with clumps of floating moss and rank, hair-like grass. The landscape had a suave bleakness, as if it were complacent in its poverty.

Lind wished that Mark Jordan were with her. She got so much from him of warm ease and contemplative companionship. There was an impersonal glow in him. He offered her always a deliciously casual intimacy that never once had bordered upon a redeclaration of the feeling he had expressed on the night when she had come in upon him out of the rain. It piqued her to know, however, that the thought dwelt just behind his eyes whenever he looked at her, and that there had been times

when she had not dared to meet his eyes for fear of precip-
itating the moment that each knew lay ahead.

Lind was wisely aware that she could not see much of
Mark without causing comment of a malicious nature
among the settlers. The intolerance of the earth seemed
to have crept into their very souls. And the school
teacher above all was looked to as a model of propriety.
But there were moments when Lind could have thrown
her concern to the winds and fled from the overhanging
chill of the Gares to the shelter of the Klovacz homestead and buried her face in Mark Jordan's shoulder
from utter loneliness.

She looked out now upon the level monotony of the
prairie with its low, ragged woodland on the west, north
of the Gares', and wondered how she would live through
the summer. Were it not for Mark, who, she knew,
would miss her keenly, she would have gone back to the
city for the short vacation.

Back among a few lean shreds of birch trees, stood the
"shack" of the Brunds. It was covered with tar paper
and perpendicular laths. It looked like a flat pan up-
side down on the ground. In the only window at the
front of the house hung a lace curtain with frayed
edges. The slanting barn and the two ungainly looking
outhouses that could be looked straight through, so
large were the crevices in them, stood below a slope near
the margin of Latt's Slough. Joel Brund's cattle stood
knee deep in the water, all staring absently at Lind.

Dora Brund opened the door and looked at Lind with
round china-blue eyes. Her face was emptily pretty, her

full small mouth had a sulky droop. She wore a pink wrapper that was sticky with food, and on her round breast dangled four linked safety pins. An odor of cheap talcum powder hung about her heavily.

"I am Lind Archer," the Teacher smiled at her. "Your mother told me where you live and I thought I'd like to call on you."

"Oh—yes, you're the Teacher," Dora said. "Sit down, please, and I'll get my clothes on. I been working round all day. You got no idea how it is in a place like this. No time to clean up decent, even." Her voice was reedy and petulant as a child's.

While she was gone, Lind looked around the room, one of the two in the house.

The linoleum on the floor had been washed in streaks. A little iron stove in the corner had spilt its ashes from the grate. On the oil cloth of the table were little clots that looked like dark gum. A smell of old rags filled the place.

Dora came back presently from the other room, the door of which was closed. She had put on a pale blue figured cotton dress ornamented with rosettes of black velvet, and looked listlessly pretty.

She sat down in a chair by the table and rested her cheek on her hand.

"My, it's getting warm, ain't it?" she said with a sigh. "How do you like it up here?"

"I like it very well. I find the people most interesting," Lind told her. "You and your husband have been back only a short time, your mother tells me?"

"Yes—and long enough. I'm near dead, I'm so lone-some," she fretted. "This is the slowest place on earth. Nothin' ever happens except the weather, and it's rotten most of the year."

"Does your husband expect to stay here long?"

"Expect? He never thinks of anything else. Never been anywhere else, except the six months we was away in Nykerk. I wouldn't care if we had a little pleasure once in a while, or if I could get some decent clothes, or somebody to look at 'em. But he don't care whether I've got anything or not. Don't know the difference between a coat and a hat." Her eyes traveled discontentedly out the window.

"You have no children, Mrs Brund?"

"No—thank God, and I'm not goin' to," Dora asserted. "That's a pretty waist you got on, Miss Archer. Get it in the city?" She scrutinized it avidly, biting her under lip with her small white teeth.

"Yes. But you could make one very easily."

Dora shrugged.

"I ain't got any sewing machine, and if he got me one he'd expect me to do all my own sewing." She surveyed Lind from head to foot with a sort of grudging admiration and envy. Then she rose and went to the stove from which she took a small granite-ware coffee pot. She emptied the grounds out of it into a pail that stood near the sink, rinsed it out briefly with cold water, filled it again and replaced it on the stove. With limp hands she measured out two large spoonfuls of coffee and put them into the pot. All of this without a word.

She sat down again by the window to wait for the coffee to boil. Lind asked her how long she had been in Loyola, where she had been employed. She brightened.

"I was there nearly six months, on the lunch counter. Before I was married, that was. Blundell's place— maybe you been there?"

Lind had not been there, and Dora went on to tell her about the town. Then a smell of coffee rose in the air, and the Teacher was served with a cup of it—wan stuff with grounds floating on the top. While they sat at the table Dora told her of the "guys" who used to come to Blundell's lunch counter, and of how all of them were "stuck" on her. She was sighing over the romances of her past when the door opened and Joel Brund stepped in. He was ponderous as an ox, nearly as tall as Fusi Aronson. He looked abashed when he saw the Teacher, and half turned as if to go out again.

Dora called him languidly. He came forward and took Lind's hand in his own huge hairy one. Without a word he turned away and opened a tool chest that stood under the window. Dora glanced at him sideways and shrugged her pretty shoulders. Lind pitied the man— so like a great, kindly ox.

When he left the house he barely looked at the Teacher, and nodded. Dora did not say a word to him.

In a short time Lind took leave of Dora Brund, promising to call again. When she got outside the house she breathed with deep relief. Down near the thatched barn she saw Joel moving about, as though he were as heavy in spirit as in body: an ox, dimly, uneasily aware of a man's pride.

2

Riding home, Lind met Mark Jordan, who was on foot. He had been at the Sandbos'. She felt that she had known all along that she would meet him—she needed him to-day. A fleet wonder passed through her mind that they had not acknowledged each other long ago—what was keeping them apart? When the thought was gone she would not believe that she had harbored it. It was not for her to make overtures, after what he had said.

"Lind," Mark said softly, his arm across the pommel of her saddle, "you always come at the right moment—like hope."

Lind looked down into his eyes. "It's ages since I saw you last. I've been so busy promoting the children. What have you been doing?" She strove to keep her voice even.

"Well, I have most of that brush cut down. I'm starting to burn it now, before the leaves get too dry. I don't want to start a bush fire." Mark stroked the muzzle of the horse.

As she was silent, he said, "Come home with me. I need scientific nourishment. I'll walk slowly beside you while you gallop your horse." Lind laughed at his nonsense. Impulsively she reached down with her hand and tugged at his hair.

"Are you so vain that you have to show your hair off to the birds?" she teased. "Better be careful or they'll be wanting it for their nests."

She consented to ride to the Klovaczs'. On the way

she told him of Dora Brund and her husband, and of the absence of Caleb Gare.

"I've heard more of that man Gare," Mark commented. "One of the Icelanders was saying that he has something on his wife and is blackmailing the whole family into staying on the farm. He must be quite a character. Are you still against my calling on him?"

"No. But Mrs Gare hasn't changed her mind about your coming. She is afraid it would rouse the children to revolt, it seems."

"Poor kids! That girl Judith has fine stuff in her. Sven Sandbo was telling me a little about her to-day. He's thinking of carrying her off bodily out of the clutches of the old man. Sven is a decent chap, too. Funny how you see interest in classes up here that you would ordinarily not think about. Too much civilization is a stifling thing."

They went easily along through the aisle of shadow formed by the rough spruce trees, down the hollow that led to a clearing, and beyond that to another hollow filled with clustering dogwood bushes. There wasn't the lifting of a leaf; the air hung in a leaden haze. The palms of Lind's hands were moist on the reins; a spoken word seemed scarcely to leave one's lips.

"I am afraid it's going to rain," Lind said, looking up at the sky. "I really ought not to come."

"Oh, but that's just what you ought," Mark corrected her.

At the Klovacz place, Lind made a custard, and set it away on a shelf. Then she spread a white cloth on the table, and went about preparing the meal. Mark was outside feeding the chickens. She thought about him, in spite of herself, and finally gave up trying not to. She saw his other pair of shoes standing under a chair and thought how familiar, how friendly, they looked.

After the supper, they sauntered out to the chicken house, where Mark showed her twelve newly hatched chicks. They looked at the sky and found it heavy with rain. Lind decided it would be better not to start for home until it had gone over, and they returned indoors with great round drops falling about them.

Lind played the phonograph while Mark smoked his pipe. He looked more remote than ever when he smoked, as if he found in the blue spirals an irresistible mystery. Suddenly Lind went over to him and snatched his pipe away. He looked up in boyish surprise. Lind thrust the pipe between her lips and puffed violently.

"Nothing much to that," she said, handing it back to him.

"Most satisfying thing in the world."

"Must be, the way you devote yourself to it."

"I thought you were listening to the music. I'll get you a pipe if you like." He got up as if to find a pipe. She smiled and went to the window to look at the rain. It came down in great curves, and with it came the dark.

Mark lit the lamp, and while he plucked at the wick, Lind held the chimney. He took it from her and their hands touched briefly. Mark's lips almost touched her hair. He drew away quickly and Lind clasped her hands together and began to hum a little tune.

When the rain had gone, the evening was as soundless and clear as if it stood over a newly created earth. Lind and Mark walked down the wood road, leading their horses. Above the darkening cedars the moon rose, and the night opened upon them like a tender, gloomed flower. They moved together involuntarily. Lind looked up and saw his face clear and intent upon her in the ashy light. His absorption was gone now. He was all human and very near to her. They stood still in the road and looked at each other. The moonlight seemed to form a globe over them, locking out every alien sound. Without a word Lind went to him. His arms, his breast and his lips possessed her. She yielded herself to the dark, warm entirety of him, knowing the full moment.

"Lind . . . Lind . . ." he whispered her name, over and over.

The horses walked on ahead, keeping to the road.

CHAPTER IX

1

On the day that Caleb was expected home, Mrs Sandbo became suddenly aware that life was tedious. True, Mrs Thorvaldson over westward was "expecting," and she, Mrs Sandbo, would be present at her confinement, but that was at least two weeks off. No wind of gossip had blown her way for a long time, no choice morsel of scandal had fallen into her hands to knead and reshape. The Teacher, who must surely hear things, was not the one to recount them generously. On the day that Caleb was expected home, then, Mrs Sandbo's curiosity won her over to its side completely.

Sven having gone to Yellow Post, she maneuvered the cattle into the Gares' hayfield, and proceeded in an elaborately unscientific manner to herd them out. Lind, watching her flying across the east field, wondered what her purpose was in driving them toward the Gares'. Presently the scheme behind it became obvious to her, and she smiled to herself.

When Mrs Sandbo had finally cornered the beasts up against the fence, Martin came to her rescue and opened the gate into the yard, through which she drove the cattle, heading them toward the road. Then she turned, panting, with a hand on her chest, to see who was about. Lind, who had been looking at Ellen's sweet-pea vines, came toward her and smiled a greeting.

155

Mrs Sandbo responded absently, apparently over-come at finding herself at last on the spot where she had craved to be. She looked past the Teacher toward the house with eyes greedy for revelations.

"And where is Mrs Gare—and the girls?" she asked, her words stumbling over each other with eagerness. While she talked, she noticed the garden with its clean, straight rows, the new wagon shed, and the plump white leghorns tilting tail as they pecked and scratched in the screened yard. Her cows had ambled out into the road, but they could wait.

"Ellen is working indoors, Mrs Sandbo," Lind told her. "Judith is at Yellow Post, and Mrs Gare is busy at something." She knew Amelia would be embarrassed at finding the woman here.

"Vell—issn't—vell!" Mrs Sandbo found no expression for her feelings at the moment. She was too disconcerted at seeing no one rush to meet her, as she would have done had a caller approached her home under such circumstances, that it did not occur to her at once to turn to the house.

Before she could say any more, Mrs Gare came into sight among the outbuildings, her white apron gathered up in front of her and bulging roundly. Amelia shielded her eyes with her free hand as she approached them.

"Vell—vell—Mrs Gare," said Mrs Sandbo, in the manner she used in her own parlor among the bright brown leather furniture and the looming photographs of all the Sandbos. "You look just like you alvays vass! My, vhat eggs! Do you get so many every—ver day!"

Her eyes traveled quickly over Amelia's dress, her shoes, the look of her face.

Amelia smiled, glancing with amusement at Lind. She had never cared particularly for Mrs Sandbo on the two or three occasions when she had met her before, but she would nevertheless have liked to ask her in, were it not for her old fear of Caleb's criticism. "Not every day," she replied. "And how are you keeping, Mrs Sandbo?"

"Oh, me, I'm not vell lately. Since he vent it's been purty hard. A farm goes up—phoo!—vit'out a man. Sven, he's got no use for the place after he been to town. He vill back—and vhat can a poor voman do?" She glanced disconsolately toward the house. Was not Amelia going to ask her in?

"Yes, it must be hard for you," Amelia said. She looked toward Mrs Sandbo's cattle scattering in the road.

"I had such a time to get those lubbers out of your field, Mrs Gare! They vill after sveet hay. I have Sven fix the fence vhere they got through. And vhere is the girls?" she asked, sweeping the place with a sharp look. She had heard Lind's reply to that question well enough.

Amelia told her.

"Oh, Ellen iss sewing? New summer dresses, now, maybe?"

"Well—not exactly. How is Dora?"

"Oh, that one," Mrs Sandbo composed herself with her hands across her waist, glad of an inexhaustible subject. She had a feeling that was nettling and at the

same time gratifying because of its implication, that
Amelia was trying to get rid of her. "Vhat a life she
hess! Vit' such a man! I alvays says to her, I says,
you have no bissness to marry him. But she hess her
vay, and now you see vhat it iss! She vass a purty girl,
Dora, and a good girl. Everybody vass after her, in
Loyola vhere she vaited on table. But vhat can you say
to them—the young ones! Sven—he vill run off and
marry some dirt, too, maybe. If Judith" (she pronounced it *Yudit*) "vill not look on him. Hee, hee!
Vhat you t'ink of dose two, Mrs Gare?" She tittered
at Lind, and looked again toward the house. Surely now
that this much had been said, Mrs Gare could do
nothing but ask her in. A cup of coffee, anyway.

"I don't think Dora is so badly off, Mrs Sandbo,"
Lind said, "now that I've seen her. I think her husband
looks like a good man."

"Hm! You don't yet know him."

Amelia took a securer grip on the eggs in her apron.
Lind touched Mrs Sandbo's arm. "Let me help you
drive the cows home, Mrs Sandbo. They'll be all over
the place in a minute."

"I hope you get them in safe," Mrs Gare smiled.
"Good-by, Mrs Sandbo."

On the way down the road, Mrs Sandbo could not
contain her chagrin and amazement at the fact that she
had not been invited into the Gare household.

"Iss it him? Iss she so scared of him that she can't
ask a neighbor in to coffee?" she demanded of Lind.

"I think it's because he's away," said Lind, clearing
her throat.

"Vell—so I vill come one day vhen he iss home. The stinker!" she said emphatically.

Mrs Sandbo was well acquainted with the situation on the Gare farm, but occasionally when life hung dully about her, she liked to regale herself by freshening her knowledge of the state of affairs. So that now she was doubly shaken, first by her renewed awe at the tyranny of Caleb Gare, secondly by the personal affront she had suffered.

2

Judith had not counted on finding Sven at Yellow Post. Somehow he had gone out of her mind, to give place to that dark thing that had agonized her thoughts ever since she had overheard the conversation between Amelia and Caleb. For some reason unknown to herself she was wretchedly unworthy, even to live.

Sven was hiring a halfbreed for the haying time when Judith first saw him. Out of the corner of her eye she watched his dominating gestures, watched him flip a match out of the open window with a male grace that tantalized her. It was only necessary to see him, then . . . She hated herself suddenly.

He turned and saw her, leaning against the enormous vinegar barrel near the counter. The corners of her lips tightened, and she looked away. Sven dismissed the halfbreed with a word and sauntered lazily toward her.

"So that was all you wanted me for, eh?" he mocked. He strove to look indifferent, but his lips worked nervously. "Well—it's all right with me. I just want to know where I stand."

Judith raised her eyes but could not keep them on his face.

"Listen, Jude. I mean what I say. You make up your mind one way or the other, and meet me at the water hole in the bush. I'm not throwing myself around like a fool for anybody. Be there for the cattle, to-night."

"Not to-night—to-morrow night," Judith said shortly, and turned to Johanneson.

Perplexed, Sven went away. He could swear in his heart that Judith loved him. But she was strange. What on earth had he done to make her avoid him? Nothing that she herself had not provoked. He was half tempted to force her to ride home with him, to frighten her into submission, as he had done. . . . The morning was pure and mobile with a soft wind. It would be sweet riding together. He would tell her again of the town where he had worked, and where he would take her when they were married. He would—oh, what was the use? She, likely as not, would lash him across the face with her whip if he spoke to her again that day.

Judith rode home in a flux of emotions. To demand of Amelia what there was to prevent her marrying Sven might perhaps lead to the unfolding of secrets that would forever bind her to the life on the farm. And yet, this agitation of the spirit would not cease until she knew.

As she jogged along in the cart, her eyes idled across the flat, unsurprising earth that went on and on into the north with scarcely a perceptible undulation. Here was the bush land, without magnificence, without primitive redundance of growth: here was the prairie, spare as an empty platter—no, there was the solitary figure of a man upon it, like a meager offering of earth to heaven. Here were the little wood trails and prairie trails that a few men had made on lonely journeyings, and here the crossings where they had met to exchange a word or two. The sky above it all was blue and tremendous, a vast country for proud birds that were ever on the wing, seeking, seeking. And a little delicate wind that was like a woman, Jude thought to herself, but could in a moment become a male giant violating the earth.

She could find the sky and the wind in a more profuse place, where life was like silk, and she belonged there. She would have to ask Amelia what that was. . . .

Amelia was spraying lice powder on the interior of the chicken coop when Judith returned. The girl stood at the door and watched her for a while in silence, then told her there was no mail. Amelia had not expected any. There never was any mail with any meaning for her. She went on with her task without comment.

"What were you talking about with him that night you told him about Sven?" Judith asked abruptly.

Amelia had her back to her and did not turn.

"Why—I can't remember anything special," she replied slowly. "He wouldn't listen to it, of course."

"There's something else—I heard you. I have to know right now what it is," Judith kept on.

Amelia faced her. "I guess you heard what he said about my family," she began haltingly. "He's always reminding me that he came from better people than I did.

He makes my parents out a lot worse than they were—
they were only poor, nothing worse. You know how he
is, Judie. That was all."

The chicken coop smelt pungently of lime. It was suf-
focating. But Amelia apparently did not notice it. Judith looked at her hard for a moment. Amelia's face
was blank. She turned again and continued spraying
the roosts.

Judith turned doubtfully away. It was like Caleb to
make a great to-do over so little, but——

In the chicken coop Amelia's hands were inert. She
set the spray down. Judith had not heard Caleb's reference to Mark Jordan, then. She would have to submit
to anything hereafter rather than create a scene that
would lead to disaster.

The next day Caleb returned. He had shoes for Judith, stout leather things with room for heavy woolen
stockings. There would be another winter.

CHAPTER X

1

AT the spring where weeks before she had lain on the ground with her clothing in a heap beside her, Judith met Sven. They sat down together beside the water-hole and listened to the insects in the air humming of rain. Judith placed her hand over Sven's mouth when he started to speak.

"Don't!" she whispered. "You can hear the clouds move!"

They sat in silence and listened to the close, foreboding stir above and around them. The air became gray under the trees, and from the clearing the cattle lowed uneasily.

Judith moved close to Sven and studied his face. He kissed her almost fearfully on the lips and at the base of the throat. It seemed that he had never known how beautiful she was.

"I will go with you after the haying," she told him.

2

True to her word, a week later Mrs Sandbo came to visit the Gares. She came dressed in her finest, bringing with her a fruit cake. Surely such a token of neighborliness would offset any rebuff.

When Ellen met her at the door, Mrs Sandbo stepped

hastily inside. Amelia, who was working in the garden, did not come in at once although she had seen Mrs Sandbo drive into the yard. She stood for a while with her eyes out toward the bluffs on the prairie, where Caleb had gone to look over some cattle.

Lind was sewing in the sitting room when Mrs Sandbo stepped in. It was the Teacher who placed a chair for her. Ellen stood back uncertainly.

"Vell—" Mrs Sandbo began, settling herself. She looked critically about the room before she went on. "Vell—it's getting varm, Mees Archer. My! Ellen, I vould not know you again! How thin you are. Vhat you doing vit' yourself, now? Somet'ing the matter?"

Ellen smiled stiffly. "No—nothing. I feel good," she responded.

"You are a real big girl, now, though. Perhaps you vill be getting married von of these days, ya? And Mees Archer, you are yourself looking for a husband now, I hear?"

"I?"

"Oh," Mrs Sandbo supplemented elaborately, "maybe it's a mees-take. But I vass t'inking it vassn't for not'ing that Fusi Aronson vent over to Thorvaldson. Of course, they say so much at the Siding."

"What do you mean, Mrs Sandbo?" Lind asked uneasily.

"Oh—not'ing—not'ing to say again. It vass only at the Siding the story vent that Fusi Aronson knocked Thorvaldson crezy on his own farm for saying about the teacher and this hired man on Klovacz place. Not'ing to say again."

Lind sat aghast. How on earth—did the very wind carry spite here? It had been, perhaps, unwise to go there at all.

Amelia came in at that moment and greeted Mrs Sandbo quietly. Ellen, who had heard the latter's story, gave Lind a sidelong glance and went out. She had her own opinion of such downright and flagrant indiscretion.

"And how is Mr Gare, back from the city?" Mrs Sandbo asked mildly. Amelia told her he was well.

"He brings many nice t'ings for the girls, now, maybe?"

"We can't afford anything that isn't useful, Mrs Sandbo. I want to thank you for that fruitcake. I haven't had time to make a cake for quite a while. The garden keeps me busy."

"Yess—" sighed Mrs Sandbo. "And it takes money too, to bake and cook fancy."

"Ellen," Amelia called toward the kitchen. "Make some tea for Mrs Sandbo, please."

"Mrs Thorvaldson, she iss the unlucky von," Mrs Sandbo said profoundly, folding her hands in her lap.

"What's the matter with her?" Amelia asked, seeing that her visitor wished to be prompted.

"She had a young von last veek, and it vass born dead—a boy, too. It vass too soon for me to get over," she said regretfully. "Thorvaldson vass so mad he almost bust—nine girls already, and this the first boy. But I t'ink it vass a mercy it died."

"Why, was anything wrong?"

"Wrong? And haven't you heard?" she exclaimed, prolonging the mystery with relish. Of course the Gares hadn't heard. How could they have?

"No."

"Well—" she cleared her throat, settling back in her chair. "I vouldn't say it again—but the baby vass born with the head of a calf." Having launched her information she watched bright-eyed for the effect.

"Gracious!" Lind cried.

"You mean it wasn't right?" Amelia asked calmly.

"It vass a fright. Mrs Lindahl, she helped, and she told me all. It came before they could let me know. The voman vass stepped on vit' a cow just a month before. It serves him good—that man—to make a voman vork like that just before."

"That's dreadful," Lind murmured. She saw that Mrs Sandbo actually believed that the child's head was shaped like a calf's.

Ellen brought Mrs Sandbo tea, and some of her own cake.

Caleb came in after a while and glanced at Mrs Sandbo. He did not speak to any one in the room, but rummaged around in a drawer for a letter which he took to the table.

"Fusi Aronson hass sold you his timber, I hear, Mr Gare? It vass more than he vould sell me, and I offered him a good price for it, too."

Caleb scarcely glanced up. "Yes," he said absently, peering at the paper before him.

"That vass a terrible t'ing that happened to the Aronson boys, four five years ago. Fusi iss not the same since."

"It was sad," Amelia remarked.

"Nobody seems to know much of it," she went on.

"Funny t'ing nobody vass around to pick them up, or take them in for the night. It wassn't so far from people vhere they froze."

"Of course the storm would keep people from going out, Mrs Sandbo," Amelia said hurriedly.

"Yess, and the epidemic vass around, too."

"I'm afraid I'll have to go to the garden, again, Mrs Sandbo," Amelia told her, glancing at Caleb. "I'm picking beans for supper, and it's after four now."

"Good land, I stop so long already! Vell—good-by, Miss Archer. And don't t'ink not'ing of that Thorvaldson. He's a mean von. Good-by, Mr Gare. Good luck vit' the hay." She rustled out, her skirts making almost the rattling sound of paper. Amelia followed her gratefully.

After she had gone, Caleb coughed softly and replaced the letter in the drawer of the secretary. He had actually not looked at a word of it. He closed the drawer and turned the key in the lock of it, placing the key in his vest pocket where he kept his large silver watch. The drawer of the secretary reserved for Caleb's correspondence and papers was never touched by the rest of the family.

Amelia, in the garden, worried about what he would say when she returned to the house. She knew that he had come in only to torment her with his knowledge that Mrs Sandbo was there.

Lind hurried to her room and wondered just how far the news had gone that she had been seen with Mark Jordan. No one could have known that she had eaten with him at the Klovaczs', so that any report of this kind must be nothing but malicious conjecture. But she must give them nothing to talk about while she was teaching at Oeland. It occurred to her that Amelia was justified in fearing Caleb if he held any damaging knowledge about her. Once the countryside got hold of it her name would be bandied about mercilessly.

3

"If I see her here again I'll put her off the place," Caleb added, after giving Amelia a dressing down for entertaining Mrs Sandbo. "We'll have no mixin' in with that lot. The Teacher's settin' her cap for Mark Jordan, eh? The Siding knows about it. She'll not want to find out the truth about that handsome young man, eh?" He chuckled under his breath and went out to the cattle yard. Amelia stood still and thought. The Teacher was so fine, so generous—it would not matter to her. But it would matter to him—yes, it would matter a great deal to Mark Jordan. A sudden impulse came to her. Caleb was well out of hearing, and Ellen had gone to bring in water.

She called up stairs to the Teacher. Lind came and looked down at her.

"I'm going to bake two chickens—would you like to take one over to that young man at the Klovaczs'?" Amelia asked. "Keep it a secret, of course."

Lind smiled at her, hiding her surprise. "What will the Icelanders say if they see me going there?"

"Well—do as you like. They will talk anyway, here."

It followed that Lind took the chicken, full of savory

dressing, to the Klovacz homestead. On the way she wondered at Amelia's sudden bold generosity, and wondered also what the woman's real self was.

Mark Jordan was repairing a binder when Lind rode up to him. His hair clung in damp little curls to his forehead, his bare arms were sunburnt and the muscles stood out on them. She laughed aloud with delight as she looked at him. He came and put his arms around her where she sat in the saddle.

"Do you know, I think you're an awful fraud. There isn't a thing wrong with you, and it's not necessary for you to be here at all," she told him.

"Well—it wasn't, but it is now," he smiled at her. "At least until the end of October."

He helped her down from the saddle and took the parcel she gave him.

"There's a scandal about us," she said. "The prairies have seen me riding with you."

"Well—then we'll have to be married right away. And Oeland will lose a first class school teacher," he declared.

"No—just for spite we'll wait," she laughed. "But that's delicious chicken. Mrs Gare is a dear. I could kill the old man ten times a day. There must be something terrific keeping her there."

Mark caught her about the shoulders and kissed her repeatedly, taking off her hat so that he could bury his face in her hair.

"You are too lovely to be alive," he whispered. "I think sometimes that I've just dreamt you."

She kissed his hands, that were becoming tough in the palms with callouses. "Wonderful, isn't it?" she said, examining the callouses. "The doctor won't know his trembling patient."

They walked together to the house with their arms about each other, since from that point no one on the road could see them. When they were seated at the table for supper, Mark told her that he had had a letter from Anton Klovacz and that he was returning home in a few weeks. The letter had been dispirited, and Mark feared that the great doctor had not given him much hope. Anton had been spending the summer in a sanitarium, but his money was dwindling, and additional improvements would have to be made on the homestead before the government granted it to him.

"I'll stay on here until the winter work begins, Lind, to help the poor devil out. So that means that we shall be leaving together."

Lind looked at him thoughtfully. It would be at the time of the wild goose flight. Suddenly she clasped her hands about his own and held them to her breast. "Dearest dear—I love you," she said. Mark drew her into his arms and they sat for a long time saying nothing.

She left early, after they had arranged to meet again the following day at Yellow Post.

4

Caleb made daily tours of the fields now and took careful note of the weather. Every evening for a week he went out with his lantern while the others were milking, coming back with it unlit after dark. He spoke to no one except to give directions about the work on the farm, and at mealtime he was absolutely silent. He was absorbed with the process of growth on the land he owned, lending to it his own spirit like physical nourishment.

While he was raptly considering the tender field of flax—now in blue flower—Amelia did not exist to him There was a transcendent power in this blue field of flax that lifted a man above the petty artifices of birth, life, and death. It was more exacting, even, than an invisible God. It demanded not only the good in him, but the evil, and the indifference.

Caleb would stand for long moments outside the fence beside the flax. Then he would turn quickly to see that no one was looking. He would creep between the wires and run his hand across the flowering, gentle tops of the growth. A stealthy caress—more intimate than any he had ever given to woman.

The tame hay and the rye grass were coming up as if there were hands at their roots pushing them. The fodder grains too, were heavy headed, straight and yellowing. And the cattle and horses in pasture were growing sleek and round.

Martin, dutifully going about his daily chores, knew that the signs were good.

"Thinkin' of buildin' in the spring?" he asked Caleb. The New House stood large and beautiful in his mind.

"Buildin'? Buildin' what?" Caleb said absently. He was peering westward, where he thought he saw some of his cattle in Thorvaldson's summer fallow.

"A house."

"A house? Heh, heh! Well, well, Martin, the women must be gettin' you. What on earth do you want to

build a house for, when we have one? Heh, heh!" He
went off chuckling to himself at Martin's vagaries.

Martin split a log with a tremendous swing of his ax.
Well, he had dreamt a little vainly, then. That was all.
But Caleb couldn't live forever.

Caleb watched the market and decided it was time
to sell a number of head of cattle. The roads to Nykerk
Siding were dry and hard, it would be easy to herd them
in. Martin and Ellen were summoned before Caleb in
the sitting room and told to prepare to leave on the morrow. Then Martin went out with Caleb and selected
fifteen steers and cows from the herd. Among them
were the two steers that Judith had assumed were her
own in place of the two that had been sold in the spring.

"These are Judith's steers," Martin said this time.

"Eh? Judith's—oh, yes, yes," Caleb agreed. "She'll
get the money for 'em." He prided himself upon his
fairness.

"But she doesn't want to sell until the fall."

"Nonsense—nonsense. Beef is going down."

Judith, who was at Yellow Post with Lind, did not see
the steers turned into the pen. The next morning Ellen
and Martin left before daybreak, while Judith was helping Amelia indoors with the morning work. So she did
not see the herd of cattle mottling the early gray air with
their swinging flanks of red and white and black and
white. It was not until after Ellen and Martin had gone
that it occurred to her that she should have looked for
her steers.

At Yellow Post the day before, Judith had disposed of
the wool she had been hiding under the beam of the loft.

She had scorned to ask Johanneson not to mention the sale of the wool to Caleb. He had paid her for it and she had sent the money at once to the city for material for a dress that Lind had promised to make for her.

Judith soon discovered that her steers were gone. She vowed to demand payment for them. Caleb had gone to Yellow Post, and she waited for his return to bring up the subject.

At Yellow Post Johanneson spitefully asked Caleb if he had any more of the same wool that Judith had brought in. Caleb smiled blandly and said that he had not.

When he returned home he came slowly upon Amelia in the kitchen. She stepped back.

"So—she's showing the streak, eh? It'd come out somehow—somehow, yes! And you encouragin' her in it, too, like as not, eh?" His voice was a soft purr, his lower lip thrust forward. Amelia whitened.

"What—what is it?" she stammered.

"What *is* it? You know well enough what it is. You know she kept that wool—you know she sold it, you——"

"I didn't—what wool—she had wool coming to her from her ewes——"

"T-ch! She has no ewes—from now on. Hear me!" He spat between his teeth as he went out. Amelia, fearing a thousand things worse that might have happened, pushed her hair back from her brow. It was beginning to tire her spirit, this constant anticipation.

Judith met Caleb on the path. Over an arm-load of kindling wood which she just chopped, she said to him,

"I'll be wanting the money for those two steers you sent in."

"Tch—you! Go in and talk to your mother. She'll show you it pays to be honest."

Judith expected to find Amelia in tears. Instead she was coldly composed. "He's found out about the wool," she said, her fingers working quickly over the yellow beans she was stringing.

"What about it? Is he kicking?" Judith dropped the wood noisily into the box beside the stove.

"You should have told him you had it."

"Told him—hell! I'm not going to tell him anything from now on. And when the haying is over I'm leaving."

"No, Judith, you are not."

Judith turned on her. "Why not? Who's going to stop me? Him?" She flung a long brown arm toward the door.

"No. If you go it's against my will, and you won't be let back." Amelia had straightened her shoulders against the chair, and her voice came hard and even.

"You? What—when—" Judith was for a moment speechless.

"I don't want you to go away, Judie, until you are old enough to take care of yourself," Amelia said in a softer voice. "You have never been off this farm, really, and you would only be miserable."

Judith narrowed her eyes at her. Then her face flamed.

"You're lying! That's not the reason at all. You're afraid—afraid to let me go because of what he'll do to you! You'd keep us all here to protect yourself, be-

cause you're scared green of him! You're a coward!"
Her voice rose to a bitter pitch, the tears trembled in
her eyes. Amelia recoiled as though she feared she
would strike her. Then Judith suddenly plunged out of
the door, caught Prince who was in the corral, and in
another moment was racing the wind down the wood
road.

Judith beat the horse furiously, goaded him with her
heels. She raged at him, because he was not in a mood
with her. Then, as if he wanted no more of her on his
bare back, he curved and danced like an overbalanced
see-saw, kicking his hoofs in the air behind him. Judith
laughed and cried. The horse proceeded into a terrific
gallop, turning finally off the road into a clearing beyond
which he saw a fence. The clearing was full of low
stumps, and the animal's legs buckled under him, throwing Jude over his head. She fell on her side, a sharp
splinter of a stump tearing open the flesh of her arm.
She lay there motionless for a few minutes in a sort of
ecstasy, her eyes closed. Then she looked at her arm,
and glanced about for the horse. He had risen, unhurt,
and was standing on the road.

She turned her sleeve around so that the torn part
would not show, first stopping the bleeding of the wound
with some dry moss. Then she mounted Prince and
rode home. She said nothing about her adventure, binding up her arm so that no one saw there was anything the
matter with it.

CHAPTER XI

1

At Oeland no game laws were taken into account except those which the settlers agreed among themselves were good. Fishing in the lakes of those who were fortunate enough to have them on their land was open to those who did not have them, most of the year round. It had become such an old custom that the owner's right in the matter had been lost sight of. So that Caleb saw no reason why he should humor the sentimental Bjarnasson to the extent of doing without fish, when this food saved him dollars' worth of meat. He resolved that during the coming autumn there should be no lack of fish at his table, whether the bodies of the two that had been drowned were recovered or not. It was well to fix this idea in the mind of Bjarnasson at once, although there would be little time for fishing during the summer, and no way of keeping the fish more than a day.

On a morning before haying began, he sent Martin to the lake. Martin was dubious, and as reluctant as he had ever been to carry out any order of Caleb's. Nevertheless, he went, fish pole and tackle in the cart behind him, as well as a small net which Caleb had borrowed from one of the halfbreeds at Yellow Post. Martin realized the significance of that net. It was that which he balked against particularly, though he said nothing.

It meant that Caleb intended selling what fish he could not use, probably to Johanneson at Yellow Post.

Martin's long face lengthened as he drove down the road westward. There were ruthless things a man might do honorably, such as violating another's property to secure needed food for those dependent upon him. But what he had been sent out to do was neither honorable nor necessary.

As he struck the open road, his eyes turned toward the prairie lying on the south. This was Caleb's cattle land, broad and flat, with two good bluffs for shade. The great herd was scattered over it with an intermingling of horses. The milch cows were kept separate, in the richer grass near the marshes to the north. Dull anger surged through Martin as he regarded this manifestation of his father's cupidity. The great herd meant the sacrifice of one dream after another. There would be no new house in the spring, but the year following the herd would have doubled in size—and perhaps the flax lying to the east would have stretched still farther, like a greedy hand gathering the earth.

Martin loved the land, but there was something else in him that craved expression. It had been represented by the dream of the new house, the dream of the thing that was to be made by his own hands, guided by his own will. Now that, too, was gone. Nothing to do now but toil on without a dream. It might have been kinder of Caleb to have deceived him until the end of the harvest —there would then have been a vision to ease the burden. A false vision was better than none.

There was no rebellion in Martin's soul—only a sort

of passive resentment that did not often rise above the hard, surrounding shell of endurance in which he had grown. Had he been asked he could not have told why he endured—the fact was that he did not even recognize the state in which he lived as endurance. And yet he understood Judith better than he did Ellen. The subjected manhood in him admired Judith, although it never found expression toward her.

Judith had not known he was going to the lake. He half hoped that she would not find it out, if he came back without fish. Her eyes had of late held a contempt that one had to turn away from.

At the Bjarnassons', Martin decided to go against Caleb's instructions. Instead of taking the road that led around to the opposite side of the lake, he drove into the farm yard, where young Erik was unharnessing his horses.

"Doin' any fishing yet?" he asked Erik, who had come up to shake hands with him.

Erik shook his head soberly. "Not a sign of one of them," he said in reply. "We do not fish ourselves, yet. Soon we shall drag the whole bottom again, and maybe we shall find. Until so—no."

"Not after freeze-up, either?"

"If we find, yes. If not—no."

"Lots of fish goin' to waste, don't you think?"

Erik shrugged. "Caleb Gare—he should not want for fish. The poor homesteader round, maybe so. Caleb Gare, he have beef, pork, sheep, chicken—he should not want for the fish, too."

Martin looked away. "No," he said slowly, "only for a change."

"You go up to the house," Erik went on heartily. "They give you coffee."

"No, thanks," Martin answered, clucking at the horse. "Got to go along." Erik's hospitality shamed him doubly.

He drove out of the farm yard, and Erik looked after him, seeing the fish pole and net in the back of the cart. The Icelander's face screwed into a half pitying, half ironical smile. But he did not wait to see whether Martin would take the main road or branch off below the willows to the road that went around the lake. There was in this Icelandic family, a sort of grand faith in the honor of human kind.

Martin did not take the lake road. He thought with self-scathing of his original plan in coming here—to slip down below the willows and around the bend to the cove where he would not be seen by the Bjarnassons. Such had been Caleb's instructions—given in full belief that they would be obeyed. He would have to tell his father the truth when he arrived home. Caleb would be in a towering rage, which would express itself in a gentle sarcasm and later in a strange and sinisterly effective abuse of Amelia, that Martin never understood.

But he was glad that he had followed his own instincts not to violate the sentiment of the Icelanders. He had felt the hidden scorn of Caleb Gare in Erik's words. Now, perhaps, the Icelanders would have reason to think better of a Gare.

Amelia came out of the house as he was unharnessing the horse. Her face bore a shade of distress, and Martin guessed what she was looking forward to. There would be trouble somewhere—all under the surface. It would gather like a storm when the children were not around.

"You didn't get the fish?" she asked, looking into the back of the wagon.

"No," Martin answered shortly. "They're not fishing yet."

Amelia left him and went to the garden, where she counted the new tomatoes on the vines. They would not be ripe until late in August. The vines were still delicate and needed careful propping. Amelia stood with one hand on her hip, the other on her chin, trying to think of something for supper to take the place of fish. Caleb had planned on having fish. Anything else, no matter how good, would not be fish. She would have to prepare something especially savory to lessen his disappointment. She would have new carrots and chicken—no, they had had chicken the Sunday before, and Caleb disapproved of killing them while they were laying so well that the eggs were preserved for the fall market—something else would have to do. Amelia pulled an apronful of new carrots, and went into the house to consider.

Caleb came home late that evening from the farm of an Icelander with whom he had arranged for a threshing crew. He had not intimated that he would be late and supper was held over an hour. The omelet and bacon was cold, the potatoes soggy from being heated over.

Judith had seized some food off the stove and had gone out. She had not returned.

In silence everybody sat down to the table. Caleb's eye fell on the dishes before him. Without a word he began to serve the food.

"Did you get the crew for the first of September?" Amelia asked, after a long silence.

Caleb helped himself to butter and passed it to Lind before he answered. "Yes—yes," he said then, as if he had just recollected that she had spoken.

Characteristically, he made no reference to the absence of fish. Suddenly he threw a sharp glance around the table.

"Where's Jude?" he asked.

"One of her calves is missing," Ellen put in for the sake of Amelia.

"No doubt—no doubt," he mumbled, and went on eating as though there was no one else present.

After the meal, Lind went out and walked down the road to look for Judith. Ellen and Charlie had the milking to do.

"Got cold feet, eh? 'Fraid of a couple of dead ones like the rest of 'em," Caleb sneered at Martin. "You'll bring back another story before freeze-up, or—we'll do without meat. Think I've been keepin' the lot of ye for nothin' all these years, while I've been breakin' my back to make a living out of this soil? A pack of good for nothings I've got for it!"

"The Bjarnassons ain't fishin' themselves, yet," Martin said in a low voice. "And I won't until they let us."

"Eh? You won't, eh? We'll see if you won't! Hm!"

He went out with his lantern chuckling to himself. As he moved along the cow path into the pasture and across it to the flax field, he speculated upon some way of compelling Martin to fish when the cooler weather came. It was not altogether that he wanted the satisfaction of taking fish from the obdurate Bjarnasson; it was also that he must quell any rising independence in Martin. If he started at twenty to show a will of his own, at twenty-five there would be no holding him. He must think of something. . . .

Caleb walked in the approaching dusk like a thing that belonged infinitely to the earth, his broad, squat body leaning low over it. Presently his mind was far from the annoying trifles that symbolized his family. Before him glimmered the silver gray sheet of the flax—rich, beautiful, strong. All unto itself, complete, demanding everything, and in turn yielding everything—growth of the earth, the only thing on the earth worthy of respect, of homage.

North of it lay the muskeg, black and evil and potted with water-holes. Aronson ought to fence the rotten land now that it was his.

2

Mark and Lind agreed to meet at the Sandbos' until the return of the Klovaczs.

"School-ma'ams must toe the line," she laughed at Mark, "and I just couldn't stand a scene. That would finish me as far as earning my own living for the rest of the season is concerned."

"I would like that," Mark urged. "I really have a little money of my own, somewhere."

But Lind would not listen to him. She would stay conscientiously to the end of the term.

At the Sandbos' the chokecherry trees were bending over in wine-red arches. Sven picked Lind a tin-canful of them, and she and Mark ate them until their mouths were puckered and dry. Mrs Sandbo enjoyed having the Teacher and her "boy" as she called Mark, around, and often served them with coffee and some trifle. At heart Mrs Sandbo was sound, and as she became more used to Lind's visits, she did not ply her usual busy questions.

The Teacher walked with Mark to the edge of Latt's Slough, where they knelt and picked tiny, black snails off the reeds. Lind found little waxy water lilies growing there, but the mud was too soft at the edge of the swamp for her to reach out and get them.

"They would die right away after I got them, anyway," she said to Mark, stepping back to firm ground.

"Yes, and they would be mostly long slimy roots," he consoled her.

They walked half a mile or so to a little sunny knoll at the edge of Gare's timber. Here they sat down, Lind spreading her pale, billowy dress out about her. In a little while Mark stretched himself out full length, shading his eyes with his hand and nibbling at a straw.

The grass below them leaned up the hill, like the smoothly combed hair of a person's head. Lind regarded it curiously. The air was strung with humming insects, poised like little black periods in the light. Occasionally a blue-bottle sailed majestically past, the tissue of its wings gathering the sun. A droning bee blundered into a swarm of tiny, jigging gnats, disentangled itself and soared lazily on to a distant flower, unconscious of the excitement it had caused. Below them, a few feet away, stood the gray, pocked cone of an ant hill; up and down its slope the ants twinkled, providently absorbed. A tiny world of intense life.

"Mark," Lind said softly. "Every second something is going—going."

"And coming, Lind," he told her.

"I don't know. We can't stop the going—that's beyond our control. But we can stop the coming—we have the power to stop everything, in ourselves."

Mark would not be serious. He rolled over and put both his arms about her tightly, holding his head against her breast. "Don't, Lindy—don't. You saved me from all those gloomy contemplations. If anything happened now to take you away from me I don't know what I'd do. I was always so alone, Lind—beached on a desert island. You don't know how it was. I wasn't even sure of my own identity, sometimes." She kissed his hair and drew her fingers across the tanned skin at the back of his neck.

"It's never going to be like that any more," she whispered. She dropped her head against his and clung to him. "We are one entity now, my dearest."

CHAPTER XII

1

On a late afternoon in July, before the haying began, the cattle on the swamp land to the north came hurrying home, bawling out their warning of the approaching storm. The herd farther away sought shelter with the horses under the bluffs. Close to the earth there was a pale, unnatural glow, like the reflection from a white fire. Higher up the air was slag-gray, hanging in sultry folds. The hot voice of the grasshoppers was the only sound abroad; it cut like little scissors in the grass.

Amelia, hoeing in the garden, drew the back of her hand across her wet forehead. The gray heat was overwhelming. She looked westward to the drab bank of cloud that had been building up for ten minutes or more. Now it was a gigantic unraveling of soot, widening out to the south and the north. It broke with lightning as Amelia looked at it.

Suddenly a greenish light shot up as if from below the horizon. It had the effect of hollowing out a luminous void between heaven and earth.

"Hail," said Caleb almost under his breath as he came out of the barn. He would not admit it aloud. It might pass over.

"Hail," said Amelia to herself, her hand going instinctively to her breast.

She looked around and saw Caleb approaching. He

passed her without speaking, as if nothing unusual was about to happen.

Martin, who was building an extra pigpen for two new sows, threw his leg over the bar and herded all of the pigs into the shed. Then he turned the milch cows that had come home and were drinking at the trough, into the cattle yard.

Lind, who had been reading, put aside her book at the sound of thunder. It had grown suddenly dark, and then suddenly light again. She spoke to Ellen, who was baking bread in the kitchen.

"Looks like a storm, doesn't it?" She stood in the doorway and looked out. Judith was running about in the sheep pasture, getting her sheep into the pen. Pete was circling about them, helping her.

Lind thought how wildly beautiful she looked in the unnatural glamour: the able grace of her tall young body; her defiant shoulders over which her black hair now fell; the proud slope of her throat and breast.

Then Lind saw Judith suddenly stop, standing erect. Caleb had come to the fence of the pasture, and was shouting to her. Jude called Pete off, and he ran at her heels back to the barn yard, leaving the sheep in the pasture. Lind saw the girl throw her arm out characteristically in argument with Caleb, then toss her head and leave him abruptly.

Judith came to the house, her eyes blazing. She hurried past Lind at the doorway without a word.

"What's the matter now?" Ellen asked, looking up from the oven before which she knelt.

"Huh! What do *you* ask for? You'll only say he's

right, anyway.   A lot you care, any more than *he* cares, what happens to the sheep," she declared, throwing herself into a chair in the kitchen.   "There's goin' to be either a cyclone or hail, or both—and he thinks that by his not letting it come, it won't come.   So he leaves the lambs in the pasture.   Besides being the devil himself, he's crazy."

There was a heavy rumble of thunder.   Martin and Charlie came indoors, and a moment later, Amelia.   The strange green light darkened to purple and gray.   A few large drops of rain struck the window.   Amelia closed the kitchen door, first letting in Pete, the dog.   Caleb had not come in.   From the window he could be seen moving quietly about the barnyard, not even glancing at the sky.

A crash of thunder split the dome of the world.   Lind covered her ears with her hands.   The dog whined, and crept under the hair sofa in the sitting room.   Then the wind came.   It strained at the roots of the old house, rattled the window panes like cracking bones, rushed in a great tide of sound through the poplars beyond the garden.   The poplars and the fir hedge would protect the garden—maybe.   The sheep were in the pasture, the lambs cowering under them.   The rain came in colossal gusts.   Now the outer world was black, except for the livid flares of lightning.   The thunder was almost incessant, shattering.   Martin lit the lantern in the kitchen, and they all sat about, waiting.   Caleb did not come in.

"The hail must have gone over," said Ellen presently, from the window.

"And it wasn't a cyclone—I thought I made out a funnel in the clouds, but it was getting too dark to see," Jude remarked.

A deafening crash of thunder sounded immediately outside the barn. The house rocked.

"The barn!" Ellen cried. They all flocked terrified to the window. They could see nothing.

Martin opened the door and stumbled out. In a moment he returned, drenched to the skin. "It was the pump," he said, and they all breathed once more. Jude giggled nervously, and Ellen looked her rebuke.

"That's bad enough," said Charlie, squatting on the floor.

Amelia, in a trice, had an image of Caleb lying dead on the barn floor. She was trembling now.

The storm kept up with pitched violence for over a half hour, and then yielded as suddenly as it had begun. The air became pellucid and cool, the low, ragged clouds hurried to the east before a wind that did not touch the earth. Pete crawled out from beneath the sofa.

No one had mentioned Caleb. After it was all over, he came quietly into the house.

"Well, well! Some little storm we had, eh? The hail passed right over—they're gettin' it over east," he said.

Judith went out immediately, a hard light in her eyes. She went to the sheep pasture, where she saw the ewes huddling, wet to the skin under their cropped wool. She picked up one of the lambs and hugged it to her. Then she glanced up and saw a man on an Indian pony riding in at the gate. She recognized the pony.

"Goat-eyes!" she exclaimed to herself.

2

Ellen came out of doors. When she saw the man on the horse she stopped stock-still, her hands darting together before her.

He got down from the saddle, and quietly fastened the bridle to the post. Then with long, slow steps he approached Ellen, removing his wide brimmed felt hat as he did so.

"I've come back, Ellen, like I said," he told her in a low voice. "You look surprised." She had given him her hand dazedly.

"I—I wasn't sure," she murmured.

"All the folks here?"

Ellen nodded, adjusting her glasses over her nose. "Won't you come in? Where were you during the storm?"

"Where was I?" he laughed, walking beside her toward the house. "My pony and I find a place in any storm."

He told her that he had been camping out all the way from the southern lakes, and that he intended to do so for the rest of the distance to the most northern outpost on the great river.

"Will you come?" he whispered, just before she opened the door of the house.

Ellen dropped her eyes before his dark face. His eyes were peculiarly drawn back, and a yellow olive in color, like the eyes of a goat. He was Scotch, with Cree blood two generations back, and had been Caleb Gare's hired man for three years until a year ago.

They went indoors and Caleb saw him.

"Well—" he declared, stepping forward to seize Malcolm's hand, "if here ain't Malcolm back again! How are ye—how are ye, boy?"

Malcolm grinned and shook hands with Amelia and Martin in turn. By his heartiness, Caleb made it appear that there was no embarrassment felt at his coming —although each member of the family privately suspected that it meant more to Ellen than she had any right to permit it to mean. Ellen stayed in the background and buttered the crusts of the biscuits she had taken from the oven, while Malcolm replied to Caleb's questions about his trip.

"We can put Malcolm up for a couple of days, eh, mother?" Caleb suggested, turning to Amelia. "Better rest before you start on the next lap."

Malcolm thanked him, but said that he had arranged at Yellow Post to do some boat building for Erik Bjarnasson, and that he would be leaving again that very evening, westward.

Malcolm went out to the barn with Martin and Caleb. Ellen began to prepare supper, while Amelia hurried to see whether damage had been done to her tomato vines. While Ellen was alone, in spite of herself the thing that was young in her heart cried out for recognition. She had only one little memory—before he went away Malcolm had kissed her in the half darkness when they were milking, and later he had in a breath asked her to wait until his return. Then it had been all over, and she had gone about her work as if her day was not just one great loneliness. For no one must know. No one must know.

The tears rose in her eyes and she brushed them hastily aside, starting as the screen door creaked.

It was only Lind, coming in quietly as she always did. She stepped up and put an arm around Ellen's waist.

"Who is that dark man with your father, Ellen?" she asked.

"Oh—just an old hired man of his," she responded. Lind noticed that she said, "his." Everything about the place was "his," even the hired man, it appeared. She wondered if he were the one Judith had spoken of. He seemed to have come out of nowhere, like the storm.

Lind looked out of the window to the west where the evening was setting in a cloudless rose. It would be beautiful down the wood road now, the trees washed and shining.

"I wish you had time to come for a little walk with me," she said to Ellen. "It's so peaceful out now after the storm."

"Have to get supper," said Ellen.

"Well, then I think I'll go alone."

When Lind had left, Ellen stepped softly to the door and glanced in the direction of the barn. On the cattle trail that led along the pasture, she saw Malcolm with Caleb, who was sweeping his arm toward the south in an inclusive gesture. Her mind tried to follow them, to learn what Malcolm was being told. There was something behind this cordiality of Caleb's. Its motive would be clear before long. It was pride of a strangely severe kind that kept Ellen from rebelling against her father. Rebellion would be the open admission of the consciousness of a wrong. Caleb was her father, and any wrong that he had committed must, necessarily, reflect upon herself. Hence she strove to vindicate in her own mind Caleb's conduct of the lives and the affairs on the farm. In her struggle to do this she was driven farther and farther within herself. The coming of Malcolm into her life again was like the scene in a mirage which she hoped with her whole heart were solid land, even while she knew it to be only a vision. It could not materialize. Nothing ever did.

She stood in the doorway, a shallow-bodied little girl with red hands and a flat chin. Her large, dilated eyes that somehow gave her an appearance of beauty, watched the two men until they turned and went southeast in the direction of the flax field. She wondered if Malcolm would not look back and see her standing there—then she remembered that she would not at that distance be able to see whether he did or not. Presently the figures of Caleb and Malcolm merged into one, and the distant pallor of the flax field swallowed them. Ellen pressed her hands to her eyes and turned from the door.

3

"Pretty fine stuff, that, eh?" Caleb demanded of Malcolm, who stooped to examine the texture of the flax. "That'll mean a new house in the spring, if it keeps on the way it's goin'. Got to build, you know, Malcolm. The girls—they deserve a decent home. Ellen's gettin' old enough now to have beaux and the like, and they'll be comin' round—young fellows with farms of their own, like as not. I want to show 'em the girls *come* from as

good stuff as they're *goin'* to. Have to build—have to
build. The girls 've got to have something good to catch
something good, see? Heh, heh. No slouchin' round in
mean homesteads for them—you ought to hear 'em talk.
Ah—no, indeed!"

Malcolm was silent. His eyes roved admiringly over
the rich flax, and around northward to the acres of
luxuriant tame hay and rye grass. Caleb Gare was a
prosperous man. A mean man, he knew, but his children
would live after him—his children would be established
in comfort for the rest of their lives on this land—and
he, Malcolm, was a wanderer, hearing ever a call in the
wind, a summons to far lakes and lonely forests.

They went back by way of the dried lake bottom,
skirted the edge of the swamps, and crossed the hayfield
that lay farthest south. Malcolm brushed his fingers
through the long silky hay, breathed deep of its rich,
sweet smell that rose in the air. It was good, the hay,
good to lie down in under the stars. . . .

"Yes—yes, no way out of it—have to build—Ellen and
Martin both want a good house to live in—save on other
things, maybe."

Caleb spoke almost to himself, it seemed. But beside him, Malcolm, who was simple as a tree, and wise
only as a tree is wise in directness and free living, heard
every word he said.

At supper that evening Caleb confined the conversation
to himself and Malcolm: talked with him about the condition of the crops around Oeland and asked him what
the prospects were farther south; discussed the epidemic
of foot and mouth disease that had broken out among the

cattle in the west, and observed that this ought to mean a rise in the price of beef; told him of his plan to raise turkey and goose next year; occupied many minutes with the details of a story of a trade in horses, in which he had got badly swindled.

"Yes—yes," Caleb chuckled. "We all get fooled sometime or other, eh, Malcolm? All get fooled sometime! Heh, heh!"

There seemed to be some special ironical significance in his laughter.

"By the way," he continued after a moment. "There's a bit of building goin' on at Yellow Post, ain't there? Talk with any of 'em down there on the way up? Somebody was askin' about you just the other day—John Tobacco's daughter, if I'm not mistaken. Fine girl, for an Indian. Been goin' to school over in the mission. Goin' to teach at Yellow Post soon's they get the school built, old John was tellin' me."

"I didn't stop but a few minutes there," said Malcolm, glancing across at Ellen. "Come right through from Shell Lake."

"Didn't, eh? Well—you sort o' lose interest in your old friends when you've been away a while. I know how it goes—I know how it goes," Caleb mused.

Ellen kept her eyes on her plate. Her cheeks were warm. She struggled against the shame that rose in her heart toward Caleb's unfairness—tried to tell herself that it was a just advantage that he took, that Malcolm was, after all, of mixed blood and should be shown his place. That he was all she had ever known of romance did not matter.

Judith watched Caleb and her lips curled. Not for long—not for long would she stand the spectacle of his tyranny. Only until after the haying.

Amelia, in her place, sat still, unflinching. If this was to be Ellen's part of the cost, let her pay it. She was a child of Caleb Gare. Amelia had determined to isolate herself wholly from Caleb's children, so that she might not weaken in her resolve. She would be as hard with them as he had been, lest they dare break for freedom and so bring ruin on Mark Jordan. With this thought she looked at Ellen's lowered face as if she were a stranger to her.

4

It happened that Skuli Erickson drove in at the Gares' just after dusk and sought conference with Caleb in regard to the new shingles for the school house roof. Where Ellen was milking she saw him drive up, and her heart stopped for a moment. He would take Caleb's attention away from Malcolm for a while. Ellen got up and moved her stool to a cow that stood in a corner between two sheds in the milk yard, out of sight of Judith and Charlie, who were milking farther down the yard.

Presently Malcolm came, from behind the shed as he used to do, in a roundabout way so that the others should not see him.

"Ellen," he muttered, standing erect close beside her. "I'm not goin' to coax you away from all you've got. But if you'll come without, I want you. I'm not much, but I'll be good to you. I used to think you liked me."

Ellen glanced aside and saw his strong legs encased in their old leather leggings. She wanted suddenly to throw her arms about them, and hold on tight, tight; to cry and laugh, and look up at him and say, yes, she would go with him. But she did none of these things. She went on milking, the white stream entering the pail with a thin, purling sound, the warm smell of the milk coming up into her face.

"I'd buy a horse for you—we'd go slow, and sleep out nights all summer under the stars, Ellen, and in my silk tent when it rains. I've got an old cabin up north— make lots of money on furs—you wouldn't be needin' for nothin'." Furtively he touched her soft brown hair, the thing he had remembered as lovely about Ellen.

The touch thrilled her unbearably. Her back straightened, her hands dropped before her. Her heart beat like a gong sounding a brief hour. Why didn't he snatch her up and carry her bodily away before she had time to make up her mind? But he wouldn't—things didn't happen that way, for her.

"I can't, Malcolm. I can't leave them," she said tonelessly.

He was silent for a while.

"Well—you don't want to go, then. No use my stayin' round. I'll be gettin' out to-night, for Bjarnassons'. When I'm through with the boat over there—I'll be thinkin' of you all the time, Ellen. After that—the trail north."

Ellen's body was a great tight knot. She could neither move nor speak, but sat staring at the still heavy udder of the cow.

"So long, then, Ellen girl, and good luck," Malcolm said, putting out his hand. She placed her own in it nervelessly, without looking up into his face. His eyes above her were dark and sad, with the despair of humility, since he thought it was because he was unworthy that she would not go with him. But she did not see his eyes.

Then he vaulted easily over the board fence of the milk yard and was gone.

Ellen sat and stared at the downy udder of the cow, a rich and unfailing supply of nourishment for the human body, that would go on living in spite of pain and grief.

That evening Malcolm, the Scotch halfbreed, as he was incorrectly called, took leave of the Gares, thanking them for their hospitality. Ellen was present, only one of the Gares now.

"Better get yourself a wife for that trip, Malcolm," Caleb grinned, nudging Skuli Erickson in the ribs. "The Bible says it is not good for man to live alone."

On his Indian pony, Malcolm, whom Jude called "Goat-eyes," made a low, graceful sweep of his broad brimmed hat that was full of mockery. Ellen's heart contracted, for she saw that he did not understand.

5

The hay and the rye grass ripened into great wide curves under the sun. Martin overhauled the hay racks and oiled the mower. Judith prayed that it would not rain and so delay the cutting. Caleb went about rubbing his hands together with pleasure at the beauty of his land.

The days went on and Ellen wondered how long it took to build a boat.

The price of beef went up two cents, and Caleb sent Ellen and Martin to the Siding with another lot of cattle.

They left at the sound of the first bird, to escape the bare heat of the day upon the prairie. Ellen rode until sunrise half asleep in her saddle, wishing that Judith were more trustworthy so that Caleb would occasionally send her instead. She heard Martin's voice and the snap of his long whip, and the sound of the cattle brushing one another's flanks. Catbirds and jays darted to and fro across the trail, and every feathered throat in the bush was awake and singing. But Ellen found herself in a heavy world, outside of song.

They went along the northeast shore of Bjarnasson's Lake, but from that point they could not see the farm, which was hidden by a long stand of spruce. Ellen did not glance back southward, lest Martin should see her do so. Out on the middle of the lake they could see two boats and a flat-bottomed scow.

"Guess Bjarnasson's draggin' the lake again," Martin observed.

Ellen made no comment. But she thought what a restful place the lake would be. It was glassy and lay in white and blue patches in the clear light. There would be no sound under its surface, only a luculent, gloamy peace.

They returned home in the evening, as usual, when the frogs were croaking for miles and miles in the swamps on the north. The frogs would croak at the stars, no matter who came or went.

Then, one blistering hot day, Caleb's prize sow gave birth to a litter of twelve and unaccountably died. Caleb was at Yellow Post when the tragedy occurred, and the family held their breath like one man while they waited for his return.

Caleb's face was a study when he saw the dead sow, a poor bloated thing lying in the small new pen. Martin had divided the sucklings among three other animals who had smaller litters.

Without a word Caleb went to the trough and inspected the dregs of the feed the animal had last been given. Then he felt her body over for bruises or possible kicks in the abdomen.

"Who fed her last?" he demanded of Martin.

"I did," Martin told him.

"Uh." Caleb grunted. "Thought perhaps it was Jude."

He went off to see how the young pigs were faring, and found them busily tugging at their foster mothers. Then he returned to Martin and instructed him to dispose of the remains of the sow.

"Cart it into the pasture and bury it," he said shortly. As if Martin wasn't well aware of what was to be done!

For three days after that Caleb spoke to no one, and was addressed only when it was absolutely necessary. His replies were less than monosyllables, and often he did not hear at all.

"Do you think you let her lie in the sun too long, Martin?" Amelia asked by way of relief.

"She wasn't in the sun all day until she came out and died," Martin said.

Amelia sighed and went about her work.

Each evening, after milking, Ellen trimmed her flower bed, which was under the west window. By casually turning, she could see the bend in the road beyond the poplar grove and the fir hedge—the open road where a man on a horse would be outlined black against the sunset. A rider coming from the Bjarnassons' would be seen on that road—there would be no other way that he could come. Ellen's flower bed was so carefully weeded that the blooms began to look self-conscious.

At the supper table one evening, Charlie announced the news that Ellen had been waiting to receive in one form or other. He had been at Yellow Post that day.

"Malcolm has finished the work for Bjarnasson, and is starting north to-night. He's taking the road past the swamps—up past Brund's. He'll be comin' past here. Goat-eyes'll have another look at you, Ellen," the boy grinned at her.

Caleb made no comment for some time. Then he said, "I'll be goin' up to Erickson's to-night. Have the cart ready, Charlie. Leavin' early."

"I saw some of the children over at the school to-day, Teacher. I think it was some from north of Latt's Slough. They're like as not to break in and do some damage," Ellen said to Lind. Lind made some answer, but Ellen did not hear her. Perhaps Caleb would be gone before Malcolm came past—he would assume that his very absence was powerful enough to stay her from doing anything that he would disapprove of—that was his way of reasoning.

She helped Amelia with the dishes and then went out

to the milk yard. From her stool beside the cow she watched Caleb with straining eyes, watched him putter about to and fro from the house to the barn, from the barn to the granary, from the granary to the tool shed, with his preoccupied, slow shuffle. Prince was hitched to the dog cart, waiting. But Caleb did not look toward the horse. He vanished into the barn and had not come out when the sun was a flaming globe through the poplars. Had he changed his mind, and was not going? Ellen tried to see beyond the grove to the turn in the trail, but the poplars danced together crazily before her eyes. She bowed her head once more and pulled at the cow's teats. Then she heard, still quite far away, the sound of a horse's hoofs coming through the still evening.

At that moment Caleb came out of the barn and untied Prince, mounting the cart. Ellen hoped desperately that the rider coming from the west would rein in. Then Caleb got down from the cart and went into the house, emerging in a few moments with his duster on his arm.

But the horse's hoofs were passing the curve now, behind the poplars. Caleb climbed into the cart again and drove hurriedly toward the outer gate.

Ellen heard Malcolm's greeting to Caleb, but from where she sat she could not see him. She sprang up, and ran to the wooden fence of the milk yard, leaning out over it. Then she hastily glanced about to see if any one were watching her. She could see Malcolm on his pony, sitting straight and dark, with a sifting of light falling upon his shoulders through the poplar grove. Now he was riding away, Caleb driving beside him in the cart. Skuli Erickson lived just beyond the homestead of the Brunds, on the road that Malcolm would take north.

Lind and Mark, who after supper had ridden by way of the wood road to visit Fusi Aronson, took another trail coming back, one that led eastward and met the other road on which the Brunds and the Ericksons lived. They rode slowly, for the evening was one to be enjoyed slowly. They were now on a dry ridge north of the swamps, and could look down upon the stagnant water lying in the sunset like ragged ribbons of rose and gold. On the margin, Lind saw a few delicate purple orchis flowers growing, and fern so fragile that it seemed to bend under the light.

Mark was looking eastward.

"A lone horseman," he said.

Lind followed his eyes. "Oh, that's an Indian pony— I think it's the man that was at Gares' for supper not long ago," she exclaimed, trying to make out the figure on the horse. "I believe Ellen was in love with him, once."

The glow from the west seemed to envelop horse and rider in a golden luster, so that they blended into one.

CHAPTER XIII

1

Now came ideal haying weather, dry with only a slight wind. The sky was as clear as a shell day after day. Caleb hoped that it would last only until the hay had been stacked. There were rumors of bush fires to the north as a result of drought, and Yellow Post was full of bad omens. But the Indians were always ready to predict evil for the white settlers. It meant nothing. Crops in these parts grew slowly and there would be need of more rain, and more rain would come—it would have to come.

Caleb knocked on the ceiling under the loft at five o'clock of the morning that was to begin the haying. Amelia was already in the kitchen starting the fire. Her shoulders ached from the stooping that she had done the day before when she had taken up a large quantity of vegetables for preserving. Her heart misgave her as she thought of Ellen, who had helped in the garden. Ellen would have to work on the rake to-day.

"It's not too late to get a man for the haying, Caleb," she ventured.

Caleb put on his boots, stamping heavily on the floor after drawing on each one. This was a signal for those in the loft above to hurry. After he had laced his boots he went to the sink to wash.

"You'll do well not to put high ideas into their heads,"

he finally replied. "Who's goin' to pay for an extra man, do y'think? Might get Mark Jordan for nothin', of course. Heh, heh! You amuse me, Amelia—you amuse me!"

Amelia fried eggs and strips of salt pork, and heated over the oatmeal that had been cooked the night before. She set the table with the red and white checked cloth, and put in precise position the cracked plates and the old forks with the bent prongs, and the half-black knives. Then at each place she laid a carefully ironed, worn napkin. It was one of the little observances she had carried over from a somewhat gentler life. Caleb had always ignored the napkin beside his plate because it symbolized something in his wife's life that he had tried to obliterate—a certain fineness that was uneconomical and pretentious. Amelia had known better in the last five years than ever to ask for money for new napkins.

The food was on the table when the children came down, Lind with them. All, except the Teacher, were heavy-eyed and scarcely conscious of one another.

"Come, come now—no time to waste. Lot of stuff down there. We work better in the morning, y'know," Caleb admonished them. He ate leisurely himself, and the others were away from the table long before he was through.

Protest meant only the expenditure of extra effort— the work would have to be done anyway. Ellen and Charlie hitched the horses to the two rakes, and Judith and Martin went ahead with the mowing machines. It was deadening work, so that after a while the spirit forgot to follow the body behind the horses up and down, up and down, in the bright heat that rose from the earth and fell from the bare, cloudless sky. The nostrils began to ache from the sweet, hot, dusty smell of the hay. The hands grew dry and swollen from the reins, the sun lay like a hot iron on the shoulders, no matter which way one turned. But presently it was only the body that was there, enduring; the spirit seemed to have gone somewhere else, and left an absence of thought, an absence of everything except attention to the task at hand.

Judith mowed the field west of the neck of timber that had been bought of Fusi Aronson, Charlie following behind with the rake. Martin was working in the east field, the hay falling behind him in a smooth aisle. Ellen worked with difficulty because of her eyes, and frequently had to close them to ease their smarting. The hay dust bit at her lids so that they became bright red.

Lifting her eyes from the sweating flanks of the horses, Judith saw Caleb mounting the cart near the barn. He would be coming down now to see how things were going. He would call directions from the edge of the field, or he might even take the trouble to walk in and inspect the cutting, to see that an extra inch of hay did not escape with the roots. Well, it would not be long now till it was over. All the more reason to hurry the horses.

Martin looked back and saw that Ellen was faring none too well. It would have been cheaper in the end to have hired a man. Caleb must have had some other reason for not taking on extra help. It was his idea, apparently, to blind them all with work—an extra man would give them time for thinking, and dreaming.

Dreaming of a new house and the like, perhaps. What Ellen would dream of Martin could not guess. Ellen was like a pea pod that had ripened brittle, but could not burst open. Then he realized that he, too, was a closed pea pod—they were all closed pea pods, not daring to open. The idea fascinated Martin. He felt as though he had just learned to think, that he had just found his mind with a unique idea in it. Then one of the horses stumbled, and in pulling at the reins Martin lost his idea. His mind closed again, except to the heat that jigged visibly in the air, and to the heavy, pungent-dull smell of the hay.

He glanced back at Ellen, who was piling at uneven intervals. Then he saw Caleb drive up to the fence in the opposite field, where Judith had just come into sight south of the bush. Judith stopped her horses. She was evidently listening to something Caleb was calling to her. Martin looked uneasily toward Ellen, and at the slovenly piles.

Presently Caleb drove around the west field to the southern border of the one in which Martin worked. Martin was close enough to the fence to talk with him.

"Hardly a thistle in the whole thing," he told Caleb. "Got last year's beat, all right."

"H–m," Caleb muttered, striving to conceal his pleasure. "Ellen's draggin' it there, I see. Ellen!" He beckoned to her, and she got down from the seat and came toward him.

"What's the matter with you? Day dreamin', or something? Look at that stuff there—all over the place.

Go over it again from the end of the strip—'way back,"
he said gently, as if with extreme patience.

Ellen went back to the rake and turned the horses
around. She toiled over the whole strip again, picking
up the strewn piles and measuring the distance between
the new ones that she made, trying not to feel the pain
in her eyes and in her back.

The sun moved toward the noon mark, and the two
fields were nearly a quarter mown. Amelia waved a
towel at them from the end of the garden, and Judith,
who was the first to see the signal, called to Martin.
The four teams were unhitched and turned in toward
the road, and the first half day's work was done. Ellen,
Charlie and Martin went ahead of Jude, who lingered
behind looking in the direction of the Sandbos', just
across the road. She knew that Sven must have seen
them at work in the field, and that he would be watching
for them to return home for dinner. She waited in the
shadow of some willows.

Then Sven came. He stepped down into the enclosure
of the willows and drew her after him.

"I've got to see you more than this," he said. "Charlie
was out for the cattle last night. Why didn't you come?"

"Can't let him get suspectin' things, Sven," Judith reminded him. "No use spoilin' our chances. He'd lock
me up if he knew."

"Well—be there to-night, anyway. Just for a little
while," Sven urged. She promised and then drew away.
He stood and watched her while she strode away behind the horses. Her head was high and fine as that of

a thoroughbred horse, Sven thought. She did not look back at him.

At the noon meal Judith, Martin and Charlie ate like young animals. Amelia glanced uneasily at Ellen, who scarcely touched her food.

"What's the matter, Ellen?" she asked.

"Nothing—it's a little too warm to eat much," Ellen replied.

Caleb laughed softly. "Tut—tut, Ellen. Another day or two of healthy work and you won't think of the heat. Wish I wasn't too old to pitch in and get an appetite, too. Nothin' like it—nothin' like it, eh, Charlie? Charlie's gettin' to be a first class raker, too, I see. Have to promote you to the cutter next year, eh?"

Caleb was in good spirits, loquacious, optimistic. He had met one of the Icelanders from beyond the lake, and reports from that direction were good. Then, too, he had bought from Erickson, at a ridiculous bargain, two fine young sows in place of the one that had died. So things were working out very well—very well indeed.

He left the table adjuring the others to get back to the field again without delay. Then he hitched the mare to the dog cart and drove to the Bjarnassons'.

2

As the little cart rattled along the dry road, Caleb let his eye embrace the holdings of Thorvaldson, lying indefinitely westward. Excellent cattle land going to waste in the hands of a lot of women—Thorvaldson himself being one of them, in Caleb's opinion. A man who could do no better than raise nine girls should not be farming. And yet Thorvaldson, somehow, was on friendly terms with the great Bjarnasson—had, it was known, received generous loans from him on occasion when things went badly with him and his ten women. There should be some way of forcing Thorvaldson to loosen his hold on at least part of that excellent land. . . .

Caleb's thoughts turned to Amelia. She had behaved well of late. Perhaps she was even beginning to realize that no good would come of it if the children rebelled— apart from the consideration of Mark Jordan. And yet, it was well to keep her reminded of that little mistake of hers—that little mistake. Also, it might be well to pay a visit to the young man, before the return of the Klovaczs. To sound him out, as it were, and to report to Amelia on his parts as a gentleman. Good idea, that. Amelia would break her heart rather than let a gentleman know the truth about himself. He might not even want to marry the Teacher if he knew that he had no name to offer her. Amelia would seize upon that little thought. Yes, it would be well, indeed, to pay a visit to Mark Jordan.

But here was the ramshackle farm of Thorvald Thorvaldson. And Thorvald's mower standing in the yard. He had not started cutting, then. Perhaps one of his daughters had a toothache and the hay had to wait. Although, true enough, Thorvald usually brooked no delays. He prided himself upon being a master, but he used too little foresight. He had no right to be a farmer, no right to own a fine tract of land—a tract of grazing land.

The surly bulk of Thorvald Thorvaldson appeared in
the doorway of the house. He wiped his hand across his
mustaches to indicate that he had just eaten. Then he
extended his hand to Caleb, who greeted him blandly.
On Thorvald's vest front Caleb saw unmistakably a fish
bone and the scale of a fish. H–mm.

Caleb stepped in front of Thorvald, and put his hand
on the latch of the screen door. An uneasy flash crossed
Thorvald's face.

"Come on in where I can talk to you, Thorvald," Caleb
grinned at him. "I'd be waitin' here all day for you to
ask me." His mood was facetious. Thorvald's face
grew red, but he said nothing as Caleb opened the door.

In the kitchen the women were still eating dinner.
Caleb's eye swept the table, then indifferently he passed
on to the sitting room beyond, Thorvald close behind
him. Neither of the men troubled to speak to the
women.

Caleb had seen what he wished to see. The Thorvaldson family had fish for dinner. There was only one
place where Thorvald could have got that fish—in the
sacred lake of the Bjarnassons, his respected friends, to
whom he was obliged for many favors in the past. And
to whom, if rumor was correct, he was looking for another favor in the near future. Thorvald had no money
to pay threshers, and would not be able to get his grain
threshed without the help of Bjarnasson. Bjarnasson
had his own threshing machine, and his own crew, and he
would help a neighbor. He was a kind man, was young
Erik, but a hard man when it came to a matter of honor.
Fishing in his lake would not be readily forgiven,

especially if the offender were a trusted and indebted friend. It would surely mean an end to favors, and loans. . . .

Thorvald sat down with a heavy sigh and Caleb took a seat near him.

"Hain't started your hayin' yet, I see?" Caleb observed casually.

"Na–ow. Too much to do 'round the ples," he grunted.

"Think you'll be threshin' on the first of September?"

Thorvald looked at him heavily, his little eyes glinting uncertainly.

"Yaa—sure. Got crew already."

"Yeah? Who're ye gettin'? Thought things was kind o' tied up," Caleb said mildly.

Thorvald coughed in his throat.

"Gang from across the lake—halfbreeds," he said with a vague wave of his hand.

Caleb smiled. Thorvald was a poor liar, although he lied often enough to be skillful at it.

"Wish you'd let me know how to reach 'em," he said. "I can't get a machine until the end of September. And if they come here, they'd like as not be willin' to come on over and thrash for me."

Thorvald crossed one leg over the other.

"Wa–al," he said. "That outfit have too much already."

"I'm goin' over to Bjarnasson's this afternoon. Pretty far, but I've got to see if I can hire their crew." Caleb's eyes played idly over Thorvald's face. The Icelander's great bulk moved gloomily.

"Wa–al, I vould not like you to say it to Yellow Post, but Bjarnasson vill let me hire his thrasher," he said slowly.

"*Hire* it?　He let you have it free last year, didn't he?"

Caleb was inwardly amused at Thorvald's lame efforts to dignify his position.

"And you'd tell me a story like that, Thorvald?" he laughed comfortably.　"Shame on you."

"Wa–al, I vill not have it round, or everybody t'ink I can't pay him.　I can pay—after harvest."

Again Caleb smiled to himself.　He knew Thorvald would never pay what Bjarnasson did not expect him to.

"He's been pretty decent to you, though, h'ain't he? Let's see—how much is it you owe him now, for implements?　Must be quite a little sum, with interest, Thorvald?"

Thorvald's big feet moved across each other.　He did not answer.　He was busy listening to the women removing the dishes from the table in the kitchen.

"Well—let's go out and look at your potatoes, Thorvald.　Quite some time since I was here now, ain't it?"

Thorvald muttered a reply and the two men went out together.　Thorvald saw to his relief that the table was clear, and hoped that Caleb had not noticed the fish on the table as he had come in.　He became at once talkative and cheerful.

They went out through the sun to the potato field, that stood tall and dusty over two entire acres.　This was Thorvald's chief produce for sale purposes, and the only thing that ever grew successfully on his farm.　He had no instinct for raising cattle or horses, and his grains were indifferent.

"Fine crop, that, Thorvald. Ought to bring a nice little sum," Caleb said almost in a whisper, as if he spoke to himself. "And it's work the women can do, too. With a big herd it's different. You've got to have a man. You're lucky not to have a lot of animals, Thorvald. They need lookin' after."

Thorvald stooped and picked off a bug from a potato plant.

"Nat many, you see," he said proudly, indicating the clean plants.

"Potatoes you can eat when you got nothing else," Caleb remarked. "Good investment—good investment. By the way, that reminds me—Bjarnasson's fishin' again, ain't he?"

"Uh? Na–aw, not vhat I know," Thorvald said hurriedly.

Caleb waited for a moment, enjoying Thorvald's discomfiture.

"Well, well, didn't I see fish on your table? That couldn't have come from any other place except Bjarnassons' this side of the river, and sure you didn't go way up there to fish?"

"You see fish? Na–ow—na–ow——"

"Don't lie to me, Thorvald. You had fish for dinner and you stole it—stole it out of Bjarnasson's lake. By night, like as not. And you know what Bjarnasson would do if he found out. But I'm not goin' to tell him, Thorvald. Don't think it—don't think it. I'd rather see you get your thrashin' done. Nobody knows but me, and nobody's goin' to know, but it was a mean trick, Thorvald, a mean trick."

Thorvaldson's face was livid. His large hands fumbled about in his pockets, his shoulders slumped. Caleb's left hand moved across his mustache caressingly.

"By the way, Thorvald, we talked once about that half section of yours layin' next to my land. You didn't feel like sellin' it then. And yet it's no good to you. How do you feel about it now?"

Thorvald's eyes grew sullen. Caleb Gare was getting him, then. "Na—ow! Not von acre!" 'he rasped.

Caleb shrugged his shoulders and turned to go. "All right, but don't blame me if Bjarnasson don't come across with the crew," he said.

Thorvaldson strode quickly into step with him as he walked toward the cart. Better than to lose Bjarnasson's support . . .

"Vhen you vant it?" He almost sniveled.

"Oh, any time, the sooner the better for me. I'll pay you cash, Thorvald, that's the way I do business. Perhaps it'll help just now, eh?"

They arranged to meet at the store of Johanneson, who was a notary public, and close the deal on the following day.

"Well—s'long, Thorvald," said Caleb, climbing into the cart. "It's been a good day for us both, eh?"

He drove off, leaving Thorvaldson cursing behind him.

The day was brilliantly blue. A good part of the mowing ought to be completed by evening. Ellen was falling down a little on the job, and Amelia was mollycoddling her, Caleb had noticed at dinner. Amelia would have to be reminded of her position. Caleb wondered just what the occasion would be, if it came to that, which would finally force him to play his trump card, as he liked to call it. He never doubted that it would make any difference on the farm except to bind the members of the family more closely to it. He firmly believed that knowledge of Amelia's shame would keep the children indefinitely to the land, and knew that he would not hesitate to reveal the truth to Mark Jordan if he were compelled to do so. But he drew a sort of satisfaction out of the suspense, and particularly out of seeing its effect on Amelia. He would save the revelation for the eminently opportune moment.

3

When she came in from the field at the end of that first day, Judith's clothing was heavy with perspiration. She did not wash at the sink as the others did, but carried a basin of cold water up to Lind's room where she knew no one else would enter. Then she stripped and bathed her entire body, her flesh rippling under the cold water. She hurriedly donned clean clothing from head to foot, and placed in her bosom a little bagful of lavender she had grown the summer before. Over her garments she pulled the greasy overalls she had worn all day, so that the others should not notice any change in her dress. Then she heard Amelia's call to supper.

After the meal, which the family ate in the silence of complete fatigue, Judith hurried out and got Prince from the corral. She hoped the cattle would be close at hand so that she might have more time with Sven. She felt no tenderness toward him, but a terrible need of contact with something apart from the life about her.

Sven was not at the spring when she arrived. She tied the horse to a tree near the edge of the clearing, beyond which she could see the cattle among the willows. Then she threw herself upon the moss under the birches, grasping the slender trunks of the trees in her hands and straining her body against the earth. She had taken off the heavy overalls and the coolness of the ground crept into her loose clothing. The light from the setting sun seemed to run down the smooth white bark of the birches like gilt. There was no movement, except the narrow trickle of the water from the spring, and the occasional flare of a bird above the brown depth of the pool. There was no sound save the tuning of the frogs in the marsh that seemed far away, and the infrequent call of a catbird on the wing. Here was clarity undreamed of, such clarity as the soul should have, in desire and fulfillment. Judith held her breasts in ecstasy.

Sven stepped down from the bank on the opposite side of the water hole, and she saw him for a moment in the light with the long shadow stripes of the birches falling upon him. In that moment he came as a god, out of space. Judith did not move and he came and looked down at her.

"Why don't you say something, Judie?" he finally asked querulously, "I never know what you're thinkin' about."

Judith flushed with disappointment. She sprang up.

"Oh—you," she said hotly. "Why do I always have

to *say* something? Isn't it enough for you that I'm here at all?"

Sven looked up, hurt.

"Oh—well. If that's how you feel about it—" he turned to go.

"Come here," Judith muttered, looking away from him. He came slowly and stood before her. "What?"

"I thought you might know—" Her breast rose quickly. She turned and threw her arms about him passionately. "I don't want you to go—you've got to learn to be like me. There's something in me you don't know. Nobody knows—in here. We're going off somewhere— far away, you and I. We're goin'—going—to be somebody else, great people, like you read about. I know I can be, and you *must* be, because you can hurt me. We're going to be different, not like people round here, Sven, or even in the town you worked in. We're going away, across the ocean, maybe. Aren't we, Sven?"

Sven patted her shoulder to quiet her. He strove to understand her. He wanted to be kind, but a man couldn't lie.

"We'll go places, Judie, after I've worked hard for a year or two. But we can't just get up and go on nothin', can we?"

They sat down at the edge of the water and Judith's mood became quiet again. Presently a cow lowed and they remembered that the sun had set. The girl hastily drew on her overalls and soiled shirt over her clean dress. Sven smiled a little ruefully as he watched her.

Judith untied Prince from the tree and sprang into the saddle. This time she looked back at Sven and waved to him until he was out of sight. She drove the cattle home rapidly to make up for the lost time. She felt recklessly happy for the first time in weeks.

Ellen and Charlie were waiting in the milk yard.

"Where have you been all this time?" Ellen complained. "*He's* in the kitchen calling her down, all on your account. You might think of somebody else besides yourself once in a while."

"Oh shut up!" Judith retorted. "If you did any thinkin' at all you'd be better off."

She ran toward the house, but Caleb had already gone out when she got there. Across the field she saw him, his lantern swinging along the earth. Amelia was preparing the separator. Her face betrayed the tongue-lashing she had just undergone.

"Jude," she said. "Charlie will get the cattle after this. It needn't have taken you an hour."

CHAPTER XIV

1

THERE was a sudden change in the weather and the haying had to be delayed. It became raw and wet, almost like early spring. Amelia had the girls in the house helping her with the canning of the early vegetables, and wild strawberries and green gooseberries which she had spent hours gathering in the meadows and the bush. Then followed a day of high wind, with great canvases of white cloud sailing across the blue.

It was on that day that the Klovacz family returned in the covered wagon which had taken them months before to the city in the south. Caleb had gone away for the day, and Amelia out of pity ran out to the road and bade them welcome home.

Anton Klovacz was emaciated out of recognition. But his face was bright with gratitude when Amelia urged him and the children to come in and rest for a while. They had traveled all that day from Nykerk, and were dusty and cramped from sitting still in the wagon. The two eldest boys were almost twenty, sturdy and good to look at. Anton would have left them at home to take care of the farm had it not been that he feared he might never·return. There were two girls, in their early 'teens, with Slavic eyes and gleaming white teeth. The three youngest children were boys, dusky and mischievous; their clothing was in tatters, and they were barefooted.

219

Amelia gave them hot water and soap with which to wash their hands, and spread the table with a hearty lunch. Anton sat by, watching her in silence, the tears coming to his eyes again and again. He twined his thin fingers about each other, almost as a woman might do. Amelia hurried about, talking and laughing with the children, a feeling of tremendous, free warmth coming over her. It seemed that this little act of kindness was making up for all the meanness of the past years. She found herself unable to look at Anton. His great, dark eyes with the hollows under them were like something within herself that she kept concealed. . . .

Finally, they were all seated about the table and Amelia was pouring milk into the cups for the younger children. She asked Anton whether he intended staying on the farm.

"Until God says, 'No more, Anton,'" he smiled, his voice husky. "I will try to make these improvements the government wish. Then it will be mine—the homestead. And my children will have a home. After—" he made a characteristic outward and upward motion of his hands, like brown leaves blowing in the wind.

When the children returned to the wagon, Anton lingered behind and thanked Amelia for her hospitality, grasping both her hands.

"I will remember it, Meese Gare," he told her. "I have only a small time to live, so he tell me, the great doctor. But I work now for to make these improvements, and the homestead will be for *them*. I thank you many times."

And the Klovacz family drove off in their white topped

wagon, the canvas curtain at the back flapping in the wind. The great boundless clouds of midsummer moved over them like a majestic fleet with sails as pure as snow.

2

It was earlier on that day, too, that Caleb drove in the cart to call on Mark Jordan. He drew his left hand across his mustache every now and then as if to wipe off a smile that came at the thought of the trip he was taking. As he drove past the hayfields he measured the height of the grass with his eye and considered that the few days respite had perhaps been of value. Martin and the girls would have to get out again to-morrow—idleness bred mischief.

Mark's hammer was ringing on new lumber when Caleb drove into the barnyard of the Klovaczs. He got down from the short ladder on which he had been standing against the wall of a low shed and came to meet Caleb as soon as he saw him. He wondered what the old man's mission could be.

"Good morning, neighbor," Caleb greeted him heartily, getting down from the dog cart. "I'm Caleb Gare, from over near the school. Thought as how you might be gettin' a mite lonesome here."

Mark shook hands with him. "A man does get rather lonesome," he said. "Have to keep busy on jobs like this—" he indicated the repair work on the shed "—to make the time go. Anton Klovacz will be coming home soon, and as I hear won't be able to do much. So I'm just trying to put the place in shape for him."

"He'll be gettin' in his fodder soon's he's back, eh?" Caleb suggested. His eyes ran over the well set shoulders and the fine, narrow thighs of Mark, and covertly took in the clean lines of his face. Amelia must not see him, he reiterated to himself.

"That'll be the first thing, I guess. Come over here and sit down, Mr Gare—" Mark turned toward a bench outside the milk shed. Caleb followed him, his head bent forward as if there were a weight on his neck, his feet half dragging. Both men seated themselves on the bench.

"How'll he manage with just the two boys?" Caleb resumed easily.

"Oh, I'll stay on and see him through that," Mark told him. He threw Caleb a close scrutiny while the old man's eyes were on the distant fields.

"Yes, yes, of course," Caleb said, as if in afterthought. "But what brings you out here, among these heathens? A young fellow like you——"

Mark laughed. "Doctor's orders. I had a little nervous trouble that came from overwork—nothing much, but the doctor thought he ought to nip it in the bud. He happened to hear of Klovacz who wanted to come in for examination, and the doctor, whom I know very well, thought I would fit in here while Klovacz was away. So the two patients changed places. I'm afraid poor Klovacz has lost on the proposition, as far as his own health goes. The doctor writes me he's too far gone even for hope."

Caleb made a clucking sound of commiseration. He

drew his hand over his mustache, shaping his next remark adroitly. "What'll you do when you leave here? Wouldn't like to come over and work for me, would you?"

"No—I guess I'll be through with farming when Klovacz gets settled again. I'll pull out before the cold weather starts."

"Your folks likely want you back, eh?"

"Folks?" Mark smiled. "My folks are all dead, Mr Gare. So I can come and go much as I please."

"Well—" Caleb spoke softly. "Perhaps it's best so—perhaps it's best. Folks er lot o' trouble sometimes —lot o' trouble. Your people was farmers, now, like as not?"

"No—as much as I know of my father, he was a scholarly sort."

"A scholar, eh? And a gentleman, I suppose—yes, yes," Caleb repeated, delighted with the irony of the situation. "Us farmers are not so fine, like, but we know what education is wuth. Nothin' like it—nothin' like it, eh? Your father perhaps gave you your first lesson? A B C's like, eh?"

"No. I don't remember him at all. He died just before I was born."

Caleb took out his pipe and filled it thoughtfully.

"You don't say! And your mother left alone with you? That was bad—that was bad!"

Mark glanced at Caleb and thought what a whimsical old man he was, after all. A character, indeed. Sitting there sentimentalizing over a near-stranger. Mark smiled.

"Mother died soon after. She had very little money and I was brought up by some priests in a mission," he explained, thinking to humor the old fellow.

"Well—well. But you must have folks somewhere?" Caleb seemed incredulous. Inwardly he applauded his cunning. How Mark Jordan unfolded himself before him! What a story for Amelia!

"Perhaps, in England. My parents came over together, and as far as I know, my father was the last of a very old family. I intend to look up my ancestry some day, and perhaps I'll locate some relatives. But I don't miss them, Mr Gare." Mark grinned as he saw Caleb shake his head as if in sympathy. "I couldn't very well find any of my mother's people, because I don't know her maiden name. The priests forgot it, on purpose, I think, because they hoped by keeping me away from any possible relatives they would be able to train me for the priesthood."

Caleb passed his left hand gently over his mustache. He could scarcely keep from smiling at this complete show of confidence. It would repeat itself well to Amelia —very well indeed. He almost squirmed with pleasure.

"The little teacher at our place is a mighty fine girl, eh?" he observed presently, with a side long glance at Mark.

Mark crossed one knee over the over and folded his arms. He would have to head the old fellow into another direction. "Yes, she's a very fine young woman," he remarked, looking out toward the fields. "How long ago was that school house built, Mr Gare?"

"Eh?—Oh, let me see . . . it must be close on to

twenty year ago. Solid old cabin that—stand forever.
I was in my prime when I built that, my boy—in my
prime. All my kids got their learnin' there . . . maybe
they ought o' had a little more, but I'm a poor man,
Jordan, I'm a poor man, and I give 'em all I can afford.
Don't grudge 'em anything—give 'em all they need of
everything. Like to have 'em around, you know. It
doesn't do no good for 'em to be scallywaggin' off to
towns where they get high ideas. The simple life's the
best, eh? Best for soul and body. That's what I say."

"Well, you can certainly get too much of the other,"
Mark agreed. "But it wouldn't hurt them to get out for
awhile. They might do better at something other than
farming, if they got a chance."

Caleb's face seemed to close in upon itself like a folding door. "No—no. Not my children. They're too
close to the land," he said. "The Gares are farmers,
from way back. No Gare ever did good at anything
else. No—they'll not leave—they'll not leave."

Mark glanced at him, curiously. The old man's voice
was soft, intent, as if he were repeating to himself the
words of a charm.

"Looks as if those beasts are breaking down that fence
back there," Mark said, getting to his feet and shading
his eyes with his hands as he looked east. "They're
trying to get into the clover. Guess I'd better go down
and stop them, Mr Gare."

A temptation came to Caleb to get a last grain of
amusement out of his call. He held up his hand.

"Just a minute—just a minute. Did you ever run
across a horse dealer in town by the name of Bart Nu-

gent? Him and I used to be right friendly." He raised his eyebrows and put his hands behind his back.

"Bart Nugent? Why, sure, I've rented riding horses from him right along. He had a farm near the mission when I was only a kid, and he used to let me ride then. He's a fine scout." Mark smiled with pleasure. "But he's not been well lately, I think."

"No," said Caleb. "He's dead."

Mark was shocked. Bart Nugent, in his homely way, had been a good friend. A greater lover of horses he had never known.

Caleb climbed into the cart. "Come again, Mr Gare," Mark called to him, saluting with his hand.

"That I will," Caleb assured him, smiling grimly to himself.

"Funny old codger," Mark mused as he went down to the field. "Fancy him having known Bart Nugent. But I can see the tyrant in him."

3

On the road home Caleb saw approaching him the clumsy, gray-white bulk of a covered wagon. The Klovaczs were returning, he thought to himself. It would be well to stop and talk with Anton—perhaps he might learn from him just how long Mark Jordan would be staying on.

Two teams with gay trappings drew the covered wagon. The scarlet tassels at the horses' ears tossed about in the wind like the decorations on circus horses. On the high seat behind them Anton Klovacz held the reins, sitting straight as a reed. The boys had driven over the miles that had gone before, but on the home stretch Anton himself would drive. It might be the last time. . . .

Caleb drew his horse to the side of the road as the Klovaczs approached. "Hullo—hullo!" he called out when he saw Anton's face. "Back again, eh? How are ye—how are ye, Anton?"

Anton leaned out from the wagon seat and smiled his strange foreign smile at Caleb. "Very good, we are all," he replied. "And how go these things with you, neighbor?"

"Everything fine—just like when you left," Caleb returned. "I've just come from your place—been talkin' with your hired man. Fine fellow, that, Anton. Think you'll keep him on?"

"Eef he stay, yes. He write me maybe on-til freeze up. I hear these crops they are good, yes? But you have always the good crops, Mr Gare. You have the fine wife to help you, too. I will thank you for her great kindness to me and these children, Mr Gare. We have just been in to your house, a great kindness she gave, thanks. A very good woman your wife is, my friend."

Caleb's eyes narrowed. "Yes—yes, you stopped in? That's fine, that's fine. The children got something to eat, and you too, I hope, Anton? And maybe some little thing to take home?"

"The good food, that was plenty. We should not take more," Anton said. Then he held his hand to his dusty, flat-brimmed hat and bade Caleb a good journey home, after the manner of the Hungarian.

And Caleb, leaving him, thought with satisfaction of

the accident of meeting him. Here would be a choice morsel of discovery for Amelia. He took the road north, which led around the long stretch of bush and met the west road, so that he could approach his own farm from the west and make it appear that he had been, perhaps, calling on the Thorvaldsons. In which case it would have been impossible for him to have met Anton Klovacz in the covered wagon. These little tricks gave a dash of variety to life, besides being mighty useful.

He drove slowly along the west road home, in order to give Amelia ample time to see him coming from that direction. As he had hoped, she was in the garden bending over her tomato vines when he drove into the yard.

"Thorvaldson feels pretty good over the sale of that half section," he told her when she came out of the garden to met him. "The money came in pretty handy— pretty handy."

"Yes," she said, and he noticed the light tone of her voice. She thought he did not know about the visit of the Klovaczs. Well, he'd give her a little time to tell the truth about it.

"Have to start mowin' again to-morrow," he went on as they both entered the house. "Martin get the bolts for that old machine?"

"Yes—he went to Yellow Post and got them," she said.

"Where are the girls and Charlie?"

"They went berrying."

"Been alone all day, then, eh?"

Amelia bent down and dragged some milk pans out from under the table, lifting them with a clatter to the sink. He noticed narrowly that her face was red when she straightened up. "Yes—I've been busy all day," she said. "The tomatoes are starting to get ripe."

Caleb grinned under his mustache. She'd try to get out of the lie, then, eh? Well, that made the skirmish more interesting.

"Guess people are beginning to be too busy for visitin'," he continued, puttering about his tool cabinet that was nailed on the kitchen wall.

"Likely," Amelia said. He could not have known the Klovaczs had stopped in. To tell him would only bring on trouble.

"Think I'll take a little trip out to the Klovaczs' after supper. Heard in Yellow Post that they're gettin' home soon. Perhaps they're come, already."

Amelia drew in her lip. He might not go, after the trip he'd taken to-day. She would chance it. . . .

He went out to the barn and Amelia breathed a sigh of relief. Then she heard voices outside and realized that the girls and Charlie had returned from the bush. The Teacher was with them. They would have a bushel of berries among them. She should have asked Martin to buy more sugar at Yellow Post. There were a hundred things to think of. Thank God for that.

The girls came in with two great baskets full of blueberries. Their hands and faces were stained with the ripe fruit, and they were laughing and arguing as to which one had picked the most during the afternoon.

"I'm sure Teacher did," Amelia observed eagerly, to get into the conversation. "Her face is bluest."

"I'm afraid I did eat more than I put into the basket," Lind laughed. "But there's lots here, anyway."

They heard Caleb calling to Charlie immediately outside the door, and their mirth subsided. Lind carried water to her room, and Ellen and Judith went about washing at the sink. Afterwards Judith came up to Lind in the loft and sat down on the bed, watching the Teacher wash her face and neck and long smooth arms with a fragrant soap. Lind turned and surprised a peculiar look in the girl's eyes. Judith grew red and leaned back on the pillows.

"It makes my mouth water to watch you do that," she said. "It's so—oh, I don't know what it is—just as if somebody's stroking my skin."

"Why don't you use this soap, Judith? I have lots of it. I've told you so many times to use anything of mine you like. Next time you expect to meet Sven—" Lind lowered her voice and smiled roguishly at Jude—"let me fix you all up, will you? Nice smelling powder and a tiny drop of perfume in your hair. He'll die of delight, Judie! Just die."

Judith chuckled and ran her hands over her round breasts.

"It doesn't take perfume to kill him," she murmured.

Lind looked at her, stretched full length across the bed. What a beautiful, challenging body she had! With a terrible beginning of consciousness, like a splendid she-animal, nearly grown.

"Let me comb your hair, Lind, will you?" Jude asked.

The Teacher sat down on the floor beside the bed and Judith loosened the long skeins of bronze hair that fell all about her shoulders. Judith loved to run her fingers through it, and to gather it up in a shining coil above the white nape of Lind's neck. Lind talked to her about things of the outer world, as she often did when they could be alone together. But presently Ellen's voice came up from below, the thin, usual protest. Judith fastened Lind's hair up with a single pin and left her. Lind thought that her step was a little lighter than it had been.

4

That evening, before Amelia was aware of his intent, Caleb had harnessed the mare to the dog cart and was driving eastward in the direction of the Klovaczs'. Amelia looked down across the sheep pasture and saw him go. He would find out, then, that she had evaded telling him the truth. Perhaps, somehow, the Klovaczs would not mention having been here. But they would. They would. And Caleb would advance upon her with a dreadful sneer and insinuate, and threaten, and probably insult her before the whole family, as he had done again and again, in his gentle way. She stood for many moments shuddering physically in anticipation of his return— staring after him to see if he would not, after all, change his mind and come back. But the cart became smaller and smaller along the bluish road, and finally vanished around the curve of the timber.

Caleb, reaching the road on the east where it went north, turned in the direction of Skuli Erickson.

Amelia washed the dinner dishes and declined Lind's offer to wipe them. Lind thought her face looked more drawn to-night than usual, and would have liked to help her with her work.

Ellen and Martin and Charlie milked, Judith fed the pigs and the calves that were no longer sucking. After the separating, Ellen carried the crocks of cream into the cellar. Then she, Amelia and Judith sat and picked over the blueberries until the flame in the lantern near the door became smoky and the smell of soot and rank oil stung the nostrils.

"I'd better fill the lantern," said Judith, rising to do so.

"Not to-night, child," said Amelia, brushing the bits of leaves and blueberry stems from her apron. "We've done enough. I'll wash the chimney and clean the wick to-morrow."

Ellen and Judith went up to bed where Martin and Charlie were already asleep. Lind, who was tired after her day in the bush, had also gone to the loft. She listened to Judith's step on the stair. It was again heavy as a man's.

In the kitchen below Amelia took the lantern down from its place near the door. Moving the sitting room lamp into the kitchen, she filled the lantern with oil, cut the wick, and rubbed the chimney with a piece of old wool till it shone. Then she lighted the lantern to see how it burned. Caleb would be coming in, and would notice if it were not ready for his use should he want it.

Amelia returned the lamp to the sitting room table. It had a long, white glass pedestal, and a ruby colored, round body, within which the wick floated like a red, swollen tongue. Amelia stood looking into the rosy globe as if it held some strange significance. It was half full of kerosene. But under the ruby colored glass the kerosene looked like thin silver.

The outer door opened slowly. Amelia heard Caleb's step but did not turn. She could hear him taking off his hat and coat, hanging them on the wall; turning down the wick of the lantern; walking across the floor, like a large turtle dragging its shell.

"Everybody gone to bed?" he asked pleasantly, sitting down to unloosen his shoes.

"Yes—they're all tired out," Amelia said cheerfully.

"Hm. Why haven't you gone? You must be more'n tired, after a hard day like this. Heh, heh! Yeah— you must be more'n tired, Amelia."

Amelia did not answer. She sat prepared for the next.

"But you're a fine woman, Amelia. Least as I know, Anton Klovacz says so. And *he* ought to know," Caleb said gently, drawing his hand across his mustache and leaning back in his chair.

"Well—what could I do but ask them in?" Amelia said suddenly. She was startled at herself. She felt no desire to placate Caleb.

Caleb turned his head slowly, not moving his body. He tilted his head back and regarded her through half closed eyes. Then a sneer spread over his face like a mask. The look terrified Amelia. She knew a sort of insanity had him when he looked like that. An insanity for power over her, at any cost. Her hands moved up and down over her apron in her lap. Then she caught hold of the edge of the checked table cloth and began to roll it up tightly.

"So—you'd lie, too, eh? What else have you done, tell me that, can you? Anton Klovacz—the infidel—in my house! He'd say you're a *fine woman*, he'd say it, heh, heh! And with a reason, perhaps, eh? Him and his lice—your kind, eh? Tch–ch! Mark Jordan and Anton Klovacz—pah!"

He thrust his face out toward her, snapping his fingers under her nose. Amelia recoiled as if he had struck her. He laughed softly, in his throat. "Ha! That beautiful son of yours—he's a fine boy, he is. I've talked to him, *I* have—" he tapped his chest with a knotted forefinger. "—the likes of me. And he told me what his father was—heh! heh! A scholar and a gentleman. And his mother, a lady, like as not. Tch–ch! How would you like me to tell him, eh? Perhaps I'm not *good* enough to tell him. Perhaps Anton Klovacz should tell him—or maybe yourself—" a little light appeared in his eyes— "Heh, heh! That's good—*you* tell him, Amelia, *you* tell him, the pretty boy!"

Amelia stood upright. Her eyelids were drawn back beyond the iris of her eyes.

"Do it!" she whispered. "Do it! See what'll happen!"

Again her own voice alarmed her. It seemed to come from some other person. She sank weakly back into her chair. Caleb laughed. He saw that she was overcome.

Slowly he undressed and went to bed, turning the lamp low so that Amelia sat almost in the dark. She sat so for a long time, stroking her apron over her knees. She would have to go to bed soon—lie beside Caleb, lie awake, far into the night.

CHAPTER XV

1

CALEB's instructions, through Amelia, were that Charlie should go for the cattle every evening. And a few days later Charlie was appointed to take Judith's place in going for the mail and provisions at Yellow Post. So that now Judith's freedom was narrowed down to the space within her own thoughts as she moved up and down the hayfield on the mowing machine. Following the rains, the heat was not so intense, and the dust had been washed from the sweet hay. There was something almost soothing in the whirr of the mowing machine. It enclosed one's thoughts from every other sound.

But Sven would be wondering why she didn't come to the meeting place. She would look for him to-day on the way out of the field and try to tell him that Caleb was watching her. That he would have to wait for a few evenings until her father made a trip somewhere so that they could meet at the spring without danger of discovery. While she thought about Sven, her eyes fell alongside the mower where the depth of the hay stirred under the wind like something alive. A sudden gust flattened the tops of the growth into a gray sheet, as if an enormous invisible hand had brushed across it. A dark understanding had come upon Judith and now every living thing caressed, or was caressed.

She looked behind her at Charlie and across into the

235

other field where Martin and Ellen were working. She knew Ellen had wanted to go away with Malcolm. That Ellen had denied the greatest impulse of her life Judith could not forgive. She hated Ellen, and found it in her heart to hope that she would have to remain forever regretting and waiting for a thing that did not come.

Jude's thoughts turning toward Lind. She had found herself stepping softly in her presence, had found herself looking into the mirror for some resemblance to Lind. These things Sven would not understand. He would have to learn to understand them, in the other world where they were going together after the haying. Amelia's suffering eyes came before Judith's mind, but she brushed them away. It would have to be sometime, it might as well be now. Perhaps with the going of Lind the dream would go—and there would be nothing but another winter of frozen manure and hungry cattle. . . .

On the last day of the mowing, Caleb declared his intention of going that evening to see Bjorn Aronson about the purchase of a bell for the church at Yellow Post. He told Martin about it at the dinner table, and Judith pretended not to hear him by turning abruptly to Lind and asking her something about the school. Caleb went on to tell Martin that he might get Bjorn for the threshing.

"He'll not ask more than the breeds, and he'll work harder," Caleb added.

Returning to the field with the horses after the others, Judith stood in the hollow near the road where the willows hid her, and whistled for Sven. He would be moving about in the Sandbo farmyard if he had not yet returned to his own field lying to the north. Judith sounded a long sharp whistle and presently he came, running. He kissed her clumsily in his haste.

"Oh, Judie!" he cried, "I've got to have——"

"To-night," she said quickly, "and don't be late."

She slapped the reins across the backs of the horses and turned into the field. Her heart beat like a hammer under the greasy breast of her overalls. Sven had been clean and ruddy, and his shirt was open at the throat over his fresh skin.

They completed the mowing in the early afternoon, and took the machines home. Judith saw that Ellen's face was white, her eyelids red and swollen. But the feeling she had toward her was only one of contempt. There was nothing admirable in Ellen's suffering. Before the return of Malcolm Judith had pitied Ellen and would have done much to spare her from duties that were too heavy for her. Now she felt that anything that befell Ellen was her just due. She had had her choice.

Judith drove ahead of the others going home. She hurriedly unharnessed the horses and turned them into the pasture. Then she strode into the kitchen where Amelia was pickling tiny cucumbers.

"What are you going to do?" Amelia asked when she saw her take a basin full of hot water from the kettle.

"Wash my hair," said Judith shortly.

Amelia looked at her curiously. It seemed an odd time of the week for doing such a thing. It was usually done on Sunday morning, when it did not interfere with the work. However, Caleb was far down the pasture examining some horses and he might not return until she was through.

Judith took the water into the sun outside the house and placed it on the ground. Then she knelt down and dipped her whole head into the basin, scrubbing the black mass of her hair with the soap that Lind had told her to use. Afterward she sat on the ground sunning it until it was dry. It had a lovely, unforgettable smell now, like Lind.

Then she went to Lind's room and bathed. It was delightful beyond words, the delicate soap. She had never before used any but Amelia's home-made soap. She made her whole body white now with lather, hating finally to wash it off.

Lind came in from school while she was dressing. The Teacher gave her a silk blouse to wear, but Judith was afraid that Caleb would notice it. She let Lind dress her hair, however, and promised that after Caleb had gone she would permit her to put a drop of perfume at the nape of her neck. Then they went downstairs, where Ellen was playing the organ.

Ellen still played *Red Wing*. Years ago somebody had stopped at the Gares' and had sung and played the song. No popular air had become familiar to her since then. It was a childhood memory that she never lost. Lind had offered to teach her other songs, but Ellen protested that she had no time to learn them. Lind suspected that she had resented the offer.

Ellen looked up when Judith came into the room, but made no comment on the fashion of her sister's hair. Judith marched outdoors.

In the corral stood a shining black stallion that had been brought from the farm of one of the Icelanders. The animal stood pawing the earth and arching his huge, glistening neck. Judith paused for a moment beside the corral gate, looking at the horse. He lifted his head and turned his flaring nostrils toward her. His eyes were hostile. Judith turned away, instinctively lifting her chest.

2

Immediately after Charlie had gone for the cattle, Caleb drove away in the cart. From the sheep pasture Jude got a glimpse of him turning off the wood road and going north. She was content that he had gone to Aronson's.

Sven was waiting for her at the spring when she got there. She stepped quietly down the bank and parted the birch trees, standing for a moment framed in the light as she remembered he had done on the last evening they had come together.

"Gosh, you're a picture, Judie," he exclaimed. She was pleased at that and came and sat beside him.

He noticed the fragrance about her. Noticed how fine and dusky her hair was, and how gratifying it was to touch her. Judith put her strong arms about him and felt the beating of his heart against her own. She pulled down her dress so that her skin would be bare against his breast, and she was glad that she had bathed with the fragrant soap.

"Judie . . ." Sven whispered, and put his lips to her ear.

"I'm a little bit afraid, to-night," she murmured.

He held her hungrily in his arms. Time drifted into a blissful eternity.

Behind a clump of willows north of the wood road, Caleb had stopped the mare and waited. He had sat patiently looking in the direction of the Sandbo homestead until to his satisfaction he had seen Sven ride out into the clearing and cut across the pasture westward. Then he had tied the mare to a tree and had slipped through the bush to the point where he had seen Sven enter.

He crept along slowly, taking care not to step on dry branches. As the light fell he could make out low voices that seemed to come from a hollow. Now he could look down and see them, seated together, their arms about each other on the bank above the pool. Caleb drew his hand slowly across the lower part of his face. He turned and went noiselessly back to the edge of the pasture, then north to where the mare was tied.

3

The next day was full of dreams for Judith. She stood getting chicken feed from the bag in the barn, thinking of Sven, and of the distant place where they would soon go together. Sven had been wonderful last night, had talked to her as he had never talked before. It had been almost impossible to get up and say good-by to him. Soon there would be no more good-bys. They would have a snug cottage in town, and Sven would go to his work every day, but at night they would be together again—all night. . . . It seemed that it was already true, that Caleb, and the cattle, and the land, and sweat, and hay dust, were gone forever. She glanced up and saw a shadow fall across the floor of the barn. Then Caleb stood in the doorway.

Judith stood erect. She saw his face, like a mask cut out of granite. He had seen them—she knew it instantly. Somehow he had discovered—spied on them. He stepped into the barn. Judith was dumb.

"Well—what've ye got to say for yourself, eh? What've ye got to say for yourself?" He descended upon her, his head thrust forward. Judith did not move. Her eyes swept the floor for the fraction of a second. A yard from her feet lay a small ax with a short handle. It had fallen from a strap on the wall behind her.

"What 'er you up to, out there in the bush, eh? With that Sandbo dog, heh, heh! A bitch like your mother, eh? Come here and I'll show ye it pays to be decent!" He took another step toward her. Judith's hand swept down and grasped the handle of the ax.

She straightened like a flash and flung it with all her strength at Caleb's head. Her eyes closed dizzily, and when she opened them again he was crouching before her, his hand moving across his mustache. The ax was buried in the rotten wall behind his head.

"So—that's your little trick, is it? Well!" He sprang forward and seized Judith by the wrists, throwing her to the floor. Then he snatched a coil of rope from the wall and tied her hand and foot to the base of the manger.

Judith was too stunned by the violence of her own act to struggle. She lay on her face, as he had left her, scarcely aware of the smell of manure from the floor of the stall. Presently she began to tremble uncontrollably. She knew he had gone out. She was not afraid of him on her own part. But he would go to Amelia. Amelia was powerless against him. He would be insane with rage. Murder, perhaps . . . everything going, now . . . everything closing in . . . only the land, and the cattle, and manure. . . . She lay until the diagonal shadow that fell within the door of the barn lay toward the west instead of the east; until the rope had chafed red circles about her wrists, and her hair was full of bits of dry manure.

4

"She's in the barn," said Caleb when the family had made an effort to eat supper and no mention had been made of Judith.

He need not have said that. Everyone knew where she was. Everyone had been told to keep out of the barn that day.

"Now, what shall we do with her, eh? What shall we do with her, mother?" he turned amiably to Amelia, who was white and speechless.

He leaned back in his chair and assumed the pose of a judge.

"There are no courts near enough by to do the right thing," he went on softly, as if he were talking to himself. "So we shall have to do the best we can by ourselves—by ourselves."

Martin, Ellen, Charlie and Amelia sat about the room, in the circle in which they listened to Caleb's sermons from Yellow Post. The Teacher, who had heard from Charlie what had happened, was completely unstrung. She had gone to the Sandbos in the afternoon in the hope of finding Mark there, and human warmth.

"There has been an attempt at murder on this farm," Caleb went on sonorously. "A crime has been committed. The responsibility of dealing with the criminal lies with us. Now, first of all, we must go out and see the evidence. Amelia, you will take the children with you to the barn. I will wait here."

Amelia, Martin, Ellen and Charlie went out without a word. They went into the barn and saw Judith lying on the floor of the stall. Amelia held herself stiff lest she should fly to her and release her. It was a terrible moment for her. Martin's face grew longer as he saw the ax with its head almost buried in the rotten log of the wall. Judith did not stir nor look up at them. Her clothes were twisted about her body and there were bits of chaff and manure in her hair.

"Jude," Ellen said, standing on the threshold.

Judith did not answer.

"Oh, well—" said Ellen. But her body shook.

They went back to the house. Caleb was sitting in exactly the same position as when they had left him. They resumed their chairs again.

"There are several ways of treatin' this case," he went on judiciously. "One I have mentioned—the city. The other, you saw for yourself—in the barn. But there is still another one—perhaps Amelia would like you to know what it is—" he glanced slowly at Amelia, the lower part of his face covered with his hand.

Amelia sat rigid. It was coming now, then. Mark Jordan would have to pay for Judith's insane act. No, as God lived, she would kill him first—no one would know the reason for that.

"However—I shall let Amelia choose—after all, Judith is her child. Heh, heh! Her child, indeed!" Caleb sat chuckling to himself, apparently having forgotten that he was waiting for Amelia to speak.

Amelia glanced at Ellen, then at Martin, then at Charlie. It might be a trick, after all. He might tell them even yet. She swallowed to control her breath.

"I think, Caleb, it would be better to keep her here."

Caleb regarded her with amusement. "Let her run amuck, you mean?"

"No—keep her in—for a while—until she quiets down. Talk to her—make her see her mistake."

Amelia had hit the right word—*make*. It flattered Caleb. He grew mellow. Perhaps this was not the opportune moment, after all. He would save the revelation. Mark Jordan would not leave for some time, yet. He rose amiably from his chair as though the discussion had been on a pleasant subject of general interest.

"I think you're right, Amelia, I think you're right. Now let's see about the milkin' and the separatin'. I'm goin' 'cross to look at the flax, mother. Got the lantern full?"

5

Lind ate a little supper at Sandbos' so that there should be no questions asked. But she took Sven aside and hurriedly told him what had happened.

Sven swore fiercely and became white. It was all Lind could do to keep him from leaving at once for the Gares'. But he made her promise that if Jude was not let out that night she would come and tell him. He tugged at his hair wretchedly and tears of rage and futility came into his eyes. Lind talked to him until he was calmer, and then he walked down the road with her toward the Klovaczs'. When he saw Mark coming he turned back.

Lind met Mark on the road beyond the cedars. He jumped down from his saddle and put his arm about her. She leaned against him shaking. He tightened his hold around her shoulders and put his hand under her chin to look at her face.

"What has happened?"

"Judith has tried to kill Caleb," she told him.

"My God—that kid?"

Lind gave him what she knew of it. They went on for a while in silence.

"Lindy, dear, you've got to get away from that place before the old boy goes crazy and kills you with the rest of them," Mark said finally. "Why don't you go to live at Sandbos'?"

Lind shook her head. "Judith won't be let off the place at all now. I think it would only be human for me to stay there and be as much of a comfort to her as I can. I told Sven what happened, and he's going to wait until a chance comes for him to take her away—forcibly. Then the old man will probably burst and it will be all over with him."

They went on through the deepening shadows between the cedars. The road lay like a blue ribbon ahead of them, and the evening was as pure as many that they had known. But over the earth hung a pall, as if there had come a halt in the process of growth.

"Mark—this place is sinister—can't you feel the *dread* in it?"

"But it doesn't touch us, Lind. We don't belong to it. We have each other."

Lind moved closer to him to assure herself that it was so.

CHAPTER XVI

1

It was an unusually dry August, and the stacking would begin early. Martin wondered whether Caleb would get a man to help now that Judith was confined to the house. Ellen and Charlie were scarcely skillful enough for the job. But Martin knew better than to ask any questions after what had happened. Conversation between Caleb and the rest of the family had practically ceased, and the only bond now was the work that went on without interruption and without question.

Amelia went about her tasks in the house and the garden from morning until night with almost rapt attention, as if they were something she was afraid to lose. When she came in from the glaring sun, the comparative darkness of the house would blind her, and she would have the feeling that Judith was not there, that she had gone. Then she would see her, sitting with her back bent, peeling potatoes for dinner, probably, or mending a bit of harness that Caleb had handed her without a word that morning. And Amelia would harden her heart again and repeat her resolve. Judith was Caleb's child. She did not speak to the girl, except to give her instructions about the cooking or the house work. Judith had become only a pair of hands that did what they were told. She spoke to no one, looked at no one.

To Lind her apathy was heart-breaking. For days the

Teacher did not approach her, knowing that it would do no good. When she came in from school she would hear her, perhaps, moving heavily about upstairs, scrubbing the pine floors, or would see her sitting stolidly absorbed over a pailful of vegetables that she was cleaning. Lind knew that it could not go on like this, that the fire in Judith would break out in some still more turbulent form the longer she was kept under control.

The ax was left in the barn wall where Judith had driven it. It was Caleb's wish that it should not be removed.

The days became languid and sonorous with the drone of bees over tawny meadows; white and yellow butterflies danced as thoughtlessly as ever over the pink remnant of the last wild rose; the bush was a flurry of wings and song, and every day the children brought to school deserted nests to make drawings of with charcoal or colored crayon. Lind felt a false mellowness in the air; growth had come to an end. But she went on with her work, grateful for the duties that kept her in the school house, away from the Gares.

Martin learned, to his mild consternation, that a man would not be hired for the stacking.

"Ellen and Charlie will start stacking with you to-morrow," Caleb said to him at the supper table.

Judith appeared not to have heard the statement, although everyone knew that she must have been looking forward to the stacking to release her from the house.

For the first few days Caleb was on hand to supervise the work. The hay was gathered from the field where it had been drying, in ricks. Ellen worked with

Martin on the stacks while Charlie handled the crane below. Martin saw that the work Judith should be doing was too heavy for Ellen, but he said nothing. Physical inability to do a set task was a thing that Caleb never recognized. It was set down as unwillingness.

Caleb sat in the cart patiently watching the growing stacks. Occasionally he gave an encouraging word to Charlie or rebuked Ellen for her carelessness. Ellen set her mouth in a straight line and her small red hands took a firmer grip on the handle of the hay fork. The stacks grew, large, smooth and rain-proof, gratifying to the eye of Caleb Gare. It was product of *his* land, result of *his* industry. As undeniably his as his right hand, testifying to the outer world that Caleb Gare was a successful owner and user of the soil.

He had ease for thinking, there in the field surrounded by the rich produce that was his. The case of Judith had been fortunate rather than otherwise. At first it had been a bit disturbing. The ax might have done more than graze his hair. As it was, the incident merely gave him greater control over affairs. It was another thing to hold over Amelia. And it gave him security in regard to Judith—it was a case for the police if he wished to make it one. The ax must remain where it was, in case he should ever have need to use the evidence. However, as long as Judith was managable, he would be lenient. Her work was more satisfactory than that of any hired help he could get. He would keep her indoors until the malevolent spirit was broken in her and then he would keep it broken with work in the fields during harvest.

Caleb lifted his eyes to the south, where the flax was

ripening, slowly, deliberately. The crew would have to return to thresh it on the first of October, after the other crops were in. A pang of regret struck him as he thought of the cutting of the flax. It had grown with such pride, such rich dignity. It was beautiful, stretching out and stirring with life, as though nothing could end its being. But there would be other years and other yields, he comforted himself. Next year he would plant more flax. Its delicacy was a challenge to the harsh conditions under which it grew—it was a challenge to Caleb himself to force from the soil all that it would withhold.

He glanced casually once more at the labor of Ellen and Martin and Charlie, then turned the mare out of the field. As he passed the timber he got from Fusi Aronson in exchange for the lake bottom and the muskeg he smiled to himself. This would be a dull life if one could not invent artifices of amusement. Still, in a year or two the lake bottom might become arable land, and the muskeg be dry enough for flax. Then he would have to buy it back again from Fusi. There was a joke for you! In the meantime, however, the timber would be of value for fire wood and for building. And what was there to stop him from cording it and selling it at the Siding? Judith and Martin would be idle after the harvest. . . .

As he drove home his mind turned to Amelia, and he speculated upon just what her thoughts might be these days. He would have to create conversation again, lest by too much silence he lose contact. Circling about in her own thoughts Amelia might even begin to think that unselfishness did not pay, and that Mark Jordan might as well know the truth about himself. That would bring about a sort of hiatus. Things would run along smoothly only as long as he kept a balance of contrariness. He would have to make conversation, and in a few days release Judith for work in the fields.

2

One day when the Teacher came in from school Judith was running the churn in the kitchen. Amelia was in the garden and there was no one else about. Lind sat down on the floor beside Jude, and watched her strong arm move around and around as steadily as a machine. Her eyes were on the floor, and she made no sign that she had seen Lind enter.

"Judie—Judie, why can't you talk to me?" Lind asked softly. She could scarcely keep the tears from her eyes as she watched this great dark girl, sitting absorbed in turning the handle of a churn as if nothing else mattered.

Judith lifted her eyes slowly. "Nothing to talk about, is there?" she asked. They were the first words Lind had heard her speak since the day of her commitment to the house.

"You must *not* let it affect you this way, Judith. I know why you did it—you just lost your temper, and it was an awful mistake. But it will blow over—he'll forget it. Why don't you begin to talk to them now, so that everything will become natural again? Sven is waiting to hear from you, too, Judith."

A flush came to Jude's cheeks, and Lind thought she saw tears in her eyes as she turned her head away.

"It won't do any good," Judith muttered. "If I see

Sven he'll find out and then he'll send me to the city.
I know—nothing good ever happens."

"Judie, your own life matters more than anything else.
If you stay here much longer you'll get to be like Ellen,
and you're too splendid to waste yourself like that.
What if he does send you to—to the city? The judge
would find out all about how he has been treating you
before they would do anything to you. People aren't
all like him, you know. Everything would be better in
the end, Judie, I'm sure."

Judith sat back in her chair and looked at her.

"You might just tell Sven not to worry about me, if
you see him," she said. "He can't keep me here forever,
anyway."

Lind was glad to find some response in Judith. "I'll
see him, perhaps to-morrow, Jude. I'm sure he's thinking about you all the time," she said cheerfully, putting
her arm about Judith's shoulder. "Do you know what
I'm going to do now? I'm going to make you something
pretty. Something you can wear without anyone else
seeing it. You just wait." Lind went into the other
room, smiling back at Jude, who half smiled in return.

Amelia came in then and Judith stood up and looked
into the churn at the butter.

"I'll have to be getting some new crocks from Johanneson," said Amelia.

"He has two of our old ones down there," Judith remarked.

Amelia looked at her quickly. It was the first volun-
tary word she had uttered for days. There was a change
in her. She wondered what would happen when Judith

came fully to herself again. But the girl kept within herself for the rest of that day and went to bed immediately after supper, so that Amelia had no way of knowing what was forming in her mind. Amelia herself would give her no reason to think that her mad act would bring her ultimate freedom. She had not spoken to Judith of the thing that had happened, thinking in this way to impress upon her the appalling aspect of it.

That night Judith lay awake. The suggestion the Teacher had made, that the authorities of peace and justice would perhaps not be so harsh as she had feared, if Caleb brought the thing to their notice, occupied her mind and crowded out sleep.

And yet, she could not be sure. She knew so little of such matters. Perhaps the Teacher was mistaken. A halfbreed girl from Yellow Post two or three years before had tried to kill her baby, and she had been sent to prison for it. Prison—a place where you were confined to a tiny cell and never saw the sky, or felt the wind on your face—a wretched place, worse perhaps, than this farm. Caleb would manage to send her there if he found any other reason to be dissatisfied with her. He had a special hatred for her, she knew it—had always known it. It was because she hated the things that were God to him—the crops, the raising of animals, the rough produce of the land.

She thought of Sven. When the opportunity came, she knew he would take her away. She knew he was waiting day and night for the moment to come, that he would at once defy Caleb if any good would come of it. But Caleb held the whip just now. They would get no farther than the Siding before he would be upon them—would notify the police. For the first time in her life, Judith felt a need of Sven that did not spring from passion. She no longer saw the powerful muscles of his throat, or the taut, narrow shape of his loins. What she did see was a certain wistfulness in his eyes, that had come there through her scorn of him. Lying in the darkness beside Ellen, she felt a great need just to sit near him and not say anything for a long time. She began to cry and covered her face with her pillow so that Ellen should not hear her.

3

After school the next day Lind walked home with the Sandbo children to convey Jude's message to Sven. At the side of the road the milk-weed stalks hung with heavy purple bloom, and dandelions stood a foot and a half high, fluffing their down in the wind. It was a year of lavish growth for Oeland. The children had found more varieties of birds and butterflies than ever before. The leaves of the trees were free from insects. Lind thought how the plan of nature for a perfect year had been carried out between her and Mark Jordan. She wished that this harmony could have extended to the Gares, and thought sadly of Judith.

Lind had seen Mark Jordan nearly every day since the return of the Klovaczs. He had managed to ride over and talk with her in the late afternoons while she was still at the school house, or they had walked together into the timber and had sat beside the little pool that

Lind had found long before. They began to make plans for the fall, when they would leave together for the "outside." The winters at Oeland were too bitter to keep school open when the children had so far to go.

"I'd rather like to spend a winter here," Mark had said once. "Particularly at the Gares'. What a chance to study human nature that would be."

"I'm afraid I'd emerge from it unable to study anything for the rest of my life," Lind had replied. "It's heart breaking enough under favorable weather conditions."

Sven was watering the horses when the Teacher and the children arrived. He came forward eagerly to meet her.

"Judith send any word?" he asked when the children were out of hearing.

Lind put her hand on his arm and walked with him back to the water trough.

"She's beginning to forget, Sven, and she wants you not to worry. He doesn't let her out of the house yet, but as soon as he does she'll try to see you. Perhaps you'd better try to be patient until after the hay is stacked. He'll have to let her out on the binder, and he won't be able to watch her all the time."

Sven scowled. "Damn him! I'd like to wring the old devil's neck," he said. "But he'd live to have me jailed for it."

"That's the trouble, Sven. He'd make a terrible fuss if you went away just now. Perhaps after the harvest he might be able to get over it. But Judith is as anxious to see you as you are to see her."

Mrs Sandbo came out of the house then, shooing the flies away from the door as she opened it. Sven went to the pasture with the horses.

"Vell, and how goes it vit' Gare and the haying?" she asked.

"Fine as can be," Lind smiled. She had not told Mrs Sandbo of the affair between Caleb and Judith.

Lind had told Mrs Sandbo that she and Mark were planning to be married at the end of the school term. Mrs Sandbo bore the information without too great a show of surprise. She had been expecting it all along. "T'ink tvice and jump vonce," she had warned Lind, reminding her of the disastrous marriage of her daughter Dora. But the confidence had pleased Mrs Sandbo's vanity, and she now treated Lind with a motherly solicitude.

Mark came a little later and Mrs Sandbo would not be denied the right to make coffee for them. After they were seated at the table she ostentatiously slipped out and left them alone.

The coffee was very good, and had a cheering effect on Lind. She discussed the situation at the Gares' with Mark, who decided that there was nothing that could be gained by outside interference.

"The kid ought to bolt, as soon as she's sure of getting clear. But that old rascal could catch the wind if he felt like it," Mark said.

"Yes, I know," Lind admitted. "But even if they got no farther than the Siding, something favorable might result. I scarcely think Caleb Gare would dare call in the authorities to stop them—I think his wife would stand up for Judith and tell them the abuse she has suffered.

And yet—" Lind thought suddenly of the rumors she had heard of the threat Caleb Gare held over his wife.

"It's a pity. If the girl ever gets to town I'll certainly do all I can for her," Mark declared. "But I guess if I went over to talk to the old man he'd throw me off the place. He was over dickering with us yesterday about the hay Anton has to sell even before it's mown to get cash. I told Anton to hang on for a better price, and the old man almost flew at me. He'd steal from the dead, I believe. Anyway, Anton is waiting until he calls again, because he's got to get rid of the hay in order to make 'these improvements' as he calls them, before the government inspector comes around."

"How is he, Mark? Do you think he'll——"

"The winter will do for him, I'm afraid. Of course you never can tell— But Lindy, come here. Let's talk about *us* for awhile. It's two whole days since I last saw you."

Lind glanced out of the window and saw Mrs Sandbo far down near the barn.

3

On the day that Caleb decided he would free Judith from her household duties to help Martin in the field, Martin slipped from a hay stack and dislocated his shoulder.

Now that it became imperative that he should release Judith, Caleb was reluctant to do so. He turned over in his mind every possibility of doing without her on the field. But that would mean hiring two men, no matter how he considered it, and the remainder of the hay wasn't worth it.

"You could o' watched where you stepped—always something—always something," Caleb complained softly, going to and fro from the kitchen to the sitting room where Amelia was bandaging Martin's shoulder so that he could go to the doctor at the Siding. There was no doctor at Yellow Post.

Martin made no reply. He knew why he had fallen from the stack. It was to catch Ellen, who was just about to step backward off the hay. Ellen might as well leave her eyes at home as try to use them on the field.

Caleb drove Martin himself to Nykerk. He would see to it that the doctor charged a fitting fee. A dislocated shoulder was, after all, not a broken one. It was a nuisance—a nuisance. Now the haying would be held up another day while they saw the doctor, since he could not let Jude off the farmstead into the field without proper surveillance. The weather was getting sultry again. There would be rain perhaps before they got it all stacked, if Martin did not get around quickly. So Caleb fretted to himself, all the way to the Siding. He did not speak to Martin. The boy had a feeling of having committed an offense, a feeling more keen than the hurt in his shoulder.

The doctor discovered that the dislocation was not a bad one, and that Martin would be able to work again in two or three weeks. Caleb paid the fee, and because he thought it a little high he did not speak to Martin on the way home.

That evening he told Judith to be ready to take

Martin's place on the stacks to-morrow. He resented the fact that an accident should have definitely set the course of events for him, even though he had decided previously that that was the course to take.

Lind did not get a chance to talk to Judith until they had both gone to the loft. As Ellen had not yet come upstairs, Lind slipped into the girls' curtain-partitioned bedroom, and whispered with her for a moment.

"Don't do anything reckless, Jude. Remember he spied on you once and he'll do it again," she cautioned her. "If I were you I would wait until I thought he had forgotten this, and then simply tell them all outright that you want to marry Sven."

Judith looked away. Her eyes were obstinate, with something of Caleb's own evasiveness when he wished to avoid an issue. Hot color came into her cheeks.

"I can't wait—longer than after the haying," she said shortly, then began to undress, turning her back half way to Lind.

Lind tried to fathom her expression. "Why not, Judie?"

"I have my own reasons."

Her underclothing slipped down off her breast and she quickly snatched it up to cover herself. A defiant look came into her eyes as she met Lind's. She blew out the lamp and crawled between the covers of her bed, leaving Lind standing in the dimness from the light that shone through from her own side of the curtain.

CHAPTER XVII

1

MARTIN's accident seemed to Amelia to be a direct move on the part of fate to hasten what was in store. Judith would have broken away eventually, but her release from the house now with the indignities she had suffered still fresh in her mind would surely be followed by an immediate effort to escape. On the night before Jude was to go to the field, Amelia put her mind to the problem and resolved to make clear to her the folly that would lie in further rebellion.

The morning broke heavy and gray, but there was sufficient wind to prevent rain. Judith came down before the others, washed at the sink, and then began to set the table for breakfast. Caleb was already outside, Amelia busy over the stove.

Before he had gone out Caleb had said to Amelia, "You'll tell her it's the city if she tries any more tricks."

Amelia had understood that. Judith would have to be kept on the farm at any cost.

"You know, Judith, you'll be worse off if you cross him in anything, now. The ax is still stuck in the barn wall,'" Amelia said while they were alone together in the kitchen. "He'll send you to the city—you're of an age now when they can keep you there for years for such a thing. Don't do anything foolish, child. It'll be worse for you if you do. He'll catch you anywhere you go."

Judith made no reply but her face grew hard. She knew what she had to do. She took the coffee pot in to the other room and set it on the table. Then she called upstairs to the others.

After breakfast Lind stood out near the fence of the sheep pasture and watched them leaving for the hayfield: Judith, Ellen, Charlie, and Caleb. Caleb was riding in the cart while the others, on foot, drove the horses ahead of them. Lind thought of prisoners being escorted to stone quarries by armed guards.

Amelia went about her work that day as if she were holding Judith mentally in leash. She kept reminding herself of the thing at stake, and strengthening her will against Judith's. All the possibilities of evil befalling Mark Jordan now resided in Judith.

Amelia's mind reeled under the weight of this knowledge. But she must maintain control. Judith must be broken. Judith was Caleb's child.

Caleb remained in the field all that day, casually watching the stacking from his seat in the cart. He had turned the mare loose, and the cart stood in the shade at the southern end of the bush. Once in a while he walked across the field to see how the girls and Charlie were faring. His mood was genial, his comments on their work encouraging.

Judith, pitching and pounding the hay tirelessly, refused either to hear or see him. She permitted nothing to enter her mind but one thought, that after the hay was stacked she would leave, no matter what the consequences. She knew now that there was no other thing to do. Somehow she would have to see Sven and tell him what had happened to her. She would wait a few days. She would close her ears to the warning of Amelia. They meant nothing—except that Amelia was afraid of Caleb. What if Caleb did send her to the city? They could prove nothing by the presence of the ax in the wall. She might even be able to break into the barn and take the ax out. Caleb had locked the door, but it was an easy matter to break a window. No, she would not take the ax out. That would be cowardly—as cowardly as Caleb's leaving it in. The ax could stay where it was. They could do anything they liked with her. But after the stacking she would go.

Judith looked over the flat country, colorless under the gray sky. To the north there was a whitish haze. Smoke. Bush fires. And there had been no rain for a long time. But now the wind was falling, and the air became thick and hot in the nostrils. The smell and the heat of the hay rose in gusts. The lips grew prickly from the little particles of chaff, and sweat fell in cold drops from the armpits to the hot skin below. The stack grew and grew, and finally was completed with a last forkful of hay. Judith looked at Ellen, saw her terrible, inflamed eyes, and turned away with the pitchfork gripped tightly in her hand. They both slid down from the stack and began a new one a distance away.

Judith saw Caleb walking to the cart in the bush, his top-heavy body forming an arc toward the earth. She considered what would have happened if she had not missed the mark with the ax. Martin would be building a house in the spring. Ellen would have new glasses. There would be a hired man or two. Amelia would have a new set of teeth. The neighbors would stop in on the way to and from Yellow Post. She herself would be taken away somewhere—there wouldn't be anything any more. Sven would marry someone else. Lind would marry Mark Jordan. Everything would go on, but not for her. Again she found herself growing cold at the thought of her own violence. It was a thing Lind would never have done, a thing no one else would do. That's why they wouldn't understand it—those people in the city before whom Caleb would take her. No—she could never face them. She could never make them understand. There would be no one to plead for her. The whole family would be against her, they were all afraid of Caleb. She would be closed in, forever, in a tiny space, no sky, no wind, nothing but her own thoughts, and that hot flood of feeling that came upon her sometimes when she thought of Sven, and always when she was with him.

In the listless heat that hung over the hayfields, Judith shivered. She caught Ellen looking at her, and took a firmer hold on the fork in her hand. She hated Ellen and her red eyes, and would gladly have struck her for that curious look. But she contained herself and went on working.

When they were driving the horses home at the end of that day, large rain drops began to pock the dust of the road. The sky was slow and heavy as if it were full of eternal rain. The stacking would be delayed now another while. But what did that matter? The end of the stacking would not bring freedom. Nothing would bring freedom. The land was here, they were all rooted to it, like the hay, and the grain, and the trees in

the bush. Departure from it would only mean an end
of growth, not a beginning of life. Judith's thoughts
turned over and over each other on the way home. She
lifted her hot face to the rain, but somehow this time there
was no coolness in its touch.

She looked ahead and saw Caleb stooped over on the
cart. Although he had his back to her, he was watching her. He would know it if she so much as glanced
in the direction of the Sandbos'. It was his way to go
ahead, as if he were not concerned with what she was
doing.

"If we'd had another day at it we would ' a' finished,"
Caleb said at the supper table. The rain had turned
to a steady drizzle, which promised to last several days.
"Always somethin'—always somethin'." It depended
upon his mood whether Caleb pronounced his "g's" or
not.

Martin who was lying on the couch, twitched uncomfortably. He knew what Caleb was hinting at. The
day that had been wasted was the day on which he had
gone to the doctor. Since that day Caleb had scarcely
spoken to him.

"Jude will help with the milking, mother," Caleb said
huskily just before they rose from the table. The red
crept into Judith's cheeks. This instruction was a reminder to them all that she was still a prisoner.

Ellen glanced at Judith. Judith saw her eyes, in which
there was something like satisfaction. Again there came
upon her the need of striking Ellen full in the face.

The milking was done in the cattle shed that evening.
After the others had gone out, Lind threw a coat over her

shoulders and went out to the shed, the door of which was open. The lantern was hanging from one of the rude, low beams, and the light fell directly on Judith and the black and white flanks of the cow she was milking. The heavy smell of the cattle with their wet hides steaming in the warm enclosure of the shed, struck Lind's nostrils as she stood in the doorway. Then she saw Judith's fine dark face. She stepped in without being seen by Ellen and Charlie, and bent down beside Judith. In the dim light she saw the vapor rising from the milk in the pail under the cow.

"Judith," she whispered. "I have just finished it, and I thought you'd like to see it right away."

Judith watched her take a folded silk undergarment out of her pocket. Lind spread it out over her knees.

"It's lovely," Judith murmured, tracing a lace insertion with her finger but not quite touching it. "Too pretty for me."

"Nonsense, Judie," Lind scolded. "You put it on to-morrow—you won't have to go to the field. Here—" she thrust it down into the front of Judith's blouse. "Keep it."

Lind was to have met Mark at Sandbos' to-night. She knew that he would be there regardless of the rain. Going to her room, she put on her heavy breeches and her short jacket, and set out down the trail. The sky and the earth were indistinguishable, blended like dark water. The timber poured away into the night, a black, liquid mass. Dimly Lind made out the fence posts along the road. Once she saw a gray shape dart across the trail ahead of her. It was perhaps a furtive coyote seeking shelter, and was harmless, but Lind started to run after she had seen the thing.

The Sandbos were separating the milk in the kitchen when she arrived there. She threw the door open without knocking, and stood in the doorway laughing at her own fright.

Sven was uneasy. He wanted to get Lind out at once where he could talk to her. He saddled two horses and they rode down the trail together toward Klovaczs'.

"She's been let out to work now, on the field," Lind told him. "But you had better not try to see her, because he is watching her all the time. Why don't you both wait until after the harvest, when he will have forgotten about the ax, and then tell him right out that you want to be married? He can surely have nothing against that, can he?"

Lind, like the others, had fallen into the habit of referring to Caleb as "he."

"Yeh—" Sven laughed bitterly. "He'd as soon let me marry Judith as cut off his nose. He just wants to keep her there to work. He'd shoot me if I came near the place. But there's something else I want to tell you. He's been talking at Yellow Post—about you and Mark Jordan."

"Talking—how?"

"Oh—braggin' about how he could put a stop to all that, quick enough. I heard him telling Johanneson and one of the Icelanders. He likes to show how he's got a hand on everybody. He didn't say it in just so many words, but he sort o' hinted that he could finish Mark

Jordan quick enough. Like he *had* something on him. Sneerin' about him. I stepped up and says, 'You better be careful what you're sayin' about Jordan, Caleb Gare.' He looks at me and sort o' smiles, and says, 'Who're you to be talkin' to me, eh? You take care o' yourself, and don't step in where you're not wanted.' Then he laughs and goes out o' the store. I would 'a' swung on him if he wasn't so old. But I knew what he meant—about me. I don't know what he meant about Mark, though. You be careful of him, Miss Archer. He'll go sneakin' around tryin' to find some way of hurtin' you and Mark if he gets any reason to think he ought. Perhaps he thinks right now you're tryin' to get Judie away."

Lind was silent for a while.

"Perhaps he will try to do some damage to Mark, but he can't really. Mark doesn't depend on this life for his living, you know, Sven, so you needn't worry. There isn't a thing he could do to him, and surely not to me, other than have me put out of the school, and that wouldn't matter a great deal."

"Well, you better tell Mark to look out, anyway."

"Oh, I will, Sven. Is there anything you want me to tell Judie?"

"You might just give her this—" Sven reached into his breast pocket and took out an envelope. "I been carryin' it round with me for a while. Perhaps she'll answer."

Lind smiled in the darkness at Sven's brusque attitude.

Mark rode up to them then and Sven turned back.

"It's so dark I can hardly see your face, Lind," Mark said, dismounting. "I want to be sure it's you."

He put his arms about her and she leaned down and kissed him. "Now, are you sure?" she whispered.

They rode toward the Gares' to take their favorite wood trail north. Just before they came to the Gares' Lind thought she saw a shadow cross the road toward the place where the wood trail branched off from it. It was too large to be a coyote.

"Mark," she said, moving closer to him, "I'm nervous to-night, I guess. I'm sure I saw something cross the road."

Mark peered into the darkness. "I can't see anything. Don't be nervous, dear. That's not like you. It's a wonderful night. There's nothing out but what ought to be here."

They turned their horses into the wood trail and heard the soughing of the rain through the branches that crossed overhead. It was so dark that they could not see the trees against the sky, but had only a mysterious knowledge of their presence. Lind kept close to Mark.

"Do you know that Caleb Gare has you blacklisted, for some reason?" she asked softly. "Sven said he had heard him talking about you in Yellow Post."

"About me?" Mark broke out. "What on earth—perhaps it's because I told him where to get off at in regard to the price he tried to make Anton take for the hay."

"Perhaps that was it—but I hope he doesn't do anything to upset poor Anton."

"I'll not let him. By the way, Anton has sent in his report to the government. Inspectors will be out soon,

I suppose. Poor devil, he certainly deserves that home-stead."

They had come to the end of the wood road, where it opened upon the clearing. Here there was no shelter whatever from the rain, and Lind turned back. When they rode again into the main trail she looked about to see whether there was any sign of the shape she had seen move through the dark. As she thought of it, it had appeared broad and bent over at the shoulders, like a bear. She glanced about without saying anything to Mark. But she saw nothing except the dense black blur that shut in the garden. There was no light visible in the farm yard at the Gares', and they could not see the house where they paused to say good night to each other on the road. Lind let Mark take the pony back to Sandbos'.

When Lind turned in at the gate after leaving Mark, she started at a sound that seemed to come out of the rain. It was like fir branches brushing together. The darkness was too closely knit for her to see anything except the sprawling bulk of the out-houses. The lantern was lit in the kitchen, and she ran toward the house.

Judith was inside washing the parts of the separator when she entered. She spoke to her quietly.

"Judie, don't say anything to the others, because I may be mistaken, but I thought I heard something in the hedge near the road. Is everybody in?"

"They've all gone to bed, except him and mother," Judith replied. Lind saw Amelia moving about in the other room. "I'll go take Pete out and have a look around when I'm through with this," Jude added.

Lind went upstairs and took off her wet coat. She stood for a moment in the dark, looking out of the window. As it was still darker outside, she could make out a shadowy, top-heavy figure coming from the direction of the front gate. It came within the light from the kitchen window, and she saw that it was Caleb Gare. At first she wanted to laugh from sheer relief. Then an unaccountable feeling of dread came over her. He must have been spying upon them, from within the hedge. It was he who had hurried across the road when they had turned into the wood trail. What was his motive in watching them?

Lind sat down on her bed without lighting the lamp. She heard him come in downstairs with his dragging step. There was something ominous in it. Lind shivered and undressed with weak fingers. She let her hair down and crawled between the blankets.

Judith came upstairs and lit the lamp on the other side of the curtain.

"Judie," Lind whispered.

Judith came around from behind the curtain. "What?" she asked.

"Did you go out and look?"

"Yes—there wasn't anything," said Jude, and then after a moment, "Thanks for the—the thing you gave me, but I can't wear it. Not yet, anyway."

Lind gave her the letter from Sven. Jude leaned toward the light that came through the curtain, and read the letter. She could not go back to her own bed to read it, because Ellen was there.

When she had gone, Lind lay trying to think clearly.

But she came back always to the baffling conviction that Caleb was trying to bring some evil upon Mark and herself.

She went to sleep finally from the monotony of the rain upon the roof of the log house.

CHAPTER XVIII

1

It rained steadily for two days. Ellen, Judith and Charlie took care of the animals, milked and churned, and prepared the cream and butter for shipment. Skuli Erickson came twice a week to take their produce to the Siding, in rain or shine, and Caleb would learn of it were they not ready for him. Martin still lay on the couch, asking no attention, no sympathy. Amelia began knitting heavy woolen stockings for the girls in preparation for the winter. And Caleb puttered about all day between the house and the barn and the tool shed, unlocking drawers and reading old, yellowed letters, examining bottles of medicine and matching the parts of broken tools and implements, deeply concerned with things of which no one knew the significance.

But Judith knew that under his preoccupation he was watching every step she took, hovering over her like a hawk. Until something happened to take him away from the farm there would not be a moment's respite for her. He still kept the door of that part of the barn where the ax was, locked, and went past it every hour or so to see that it was secure. Once or twice she had seen him unlock the door and go in, closing it fast behind him. She fancied him standing before the ax, gloating over it as a symbol of his control over her. Judith felt circumstances closing over her head like rushing water. She went about her work on the farm all day as helpless as when she had lain tied hand and foot on the floor of the stall in the barn. There would be no escape. Amelia was already knitting woolen stockings for the coming winter. This year there would be more calves than last, more manure to walk through, and more freezing water to carry from the pump to the barn. And Caleb's doubled hatred and his doubled power, and another thing now . . .

She had destroyed the letter Sven had sent her through Lind, after carrying it about inside her blouse all day. During the night after she had received it, she lay beside Ellen and said over and over to herself that she must go—after the hay was stacked. But in the morning when she had seen Caleb's face at the head of the breakfast table, and had heard him single her out with instructions for the day's work, her courage failed her again. He had not for a moment forgotten the ax. He would not for a moment let her forget it.

In the only secret place on the whole farm she composed a letter to Sven. The words came laboriously, without much meaning. But when she finally signed her name she thought he would understand. She carried it about with her all day, to give it to Lind when she came from school.

Judith avoided Ellen lest her pent-up emotion should take form in the injury she had considered inflicting upon her sister when they were together on the stack. Once, when she was churning, she watched Ellen out of the tail of her eye, saw her scrubbing the rough floor of the other room, moving on her hands and knees about the couch where Martin was lying. Ellen's mouth was drawn, her chin flat, and every now and then she cleared her throat and coughed from the fumes of lye that rose from the scrubbing pail. Judith hated her dolorous expression and could have choked her when she uttered that hard little cough. Then Ellen got a sliver in her hand. It was because she had not seen a particularly worn board over which she ran the scrubbing brush. From where she sat Judith saw a trickle of blood run down Ellen's wrist. Ellen sighed and rose to attend to it. Judith found herself viciously glad that it had happened. There was nothing admirable in Ellen's suffering. It had no purpose.

Amelia came in from the chicken house. Judith permitted herself to glance at her and saw for the first time the dark hollows under her eyes. What had happened that she should look so? It was not she who had thrown the ax. Uncomfortably, Judith turned again to the churn and applied all her attention to it.

In the evening she gave Lind the letter to take to Sven.

The two days of rain came to an end, and a wind rose at nightfall promising sun for the morrow.

2

The door of the barn remained locked, and Caleb was pleasant and genial about the house, talking cheerfully about the crops, the animals, and the weather. The softer his mood became, the more alert Amelia grew to the reactions of Judith.

"Remember now—nothing foolish," she said to her on

the morning of the day that was to complete the stacking. "You're better off here than locked up with a lot of thieves and what not." The words sounded terrible to Amelia as she uttered them.

Judith made no response. As she stalked down the road behind the horses she tried to believe that Amelia had her interests at heart when she warned her against Caleb. But somehow Amelia was too deliberate about it all. Judith could not understand what it was. Amelia appeared to feel no pity. Perhaps if she knew the truth she might . . . Judith's heart began to beat heavily under her overalls.

The haying would be finished to-day. After that they would be working on the binders in the fields to the south, out of reach of Sven entirely. A bitter feeling rose in Judith's throat as she thought of him. She could not bear the separation and the doubt and the unhappiness any longer. She was not an animal, to be driven, and tied, and tended for the value of her plodding strength. She knew what beauty was, and love, and things in no way connected with the rude growth of the land. She had something that Lind had, who was sweet and lovely, as wild honey . . . wild honey . . . who was she to be thinking this? She, Judith, who had hurled an ax with the intent to kill . . .

Lind would not have done that. Lind was fine, and controlled. She, Judith, was just an animal, with an animal's passions and sins, and stupid, body-strength. And now she held an animal's secret, too. She was coarse, brutal, with great beast-breasts protruding from her, and buttocks and thighs and shoulders of a beast.

What was she to be comparing herself with Lind? The tears rose to her eyes and ran unchecked down her face.

She glanced suddenly aside and saw that Ellen had come softly abreast of her. Ellen had not been ready to leave the house when Judith took the horses out. Judith saw her curious red-rimmed eyes peering at her from behind their glasses, and in an instant all her fury against Ellen broke upon her. She dropped the reins and whirled about.

"You get away—you bitch! Don't you look at me like that or I'll smash your face!" Judith shouted. Ellen darted back before a great swing of Judith's arm.

"Stop—Jude—" she gasped. "He'll see you!"

"I hope he does—let him! And you stop sneaking around looking at me, or you're going to get it worse than this!" She drove out with a terrific blow which caught Ellen on the cheek, knocking her to the ground. Then she marched off, catching the reins up from the road.

Ellen got to her feet in a moment or two, sobbing hysterically. But it was not like her to go back to the house. She followed Judith slowly, wiping the tears from her face and soothing her cheek with her hand.

Amelia had seen it all from the door of the chicken house. She glanced hurriedly about and thankfully saw no sign of Caleb. But Judith had broken out again. Nothing could stop her now. Caleb would never spare Amelia if Judith broke away. Mark Jordan would be told. Lind would learn of it. Caleb would play his "trump card" as he had called it. Illegitimacy was a stigma which would not be overlooked by the society to which Lind and Mark belonged. Amelia had given her whole life to preventing him from finding out. She felt suddenly tired and old beyond thought.

The stacking was completed without further trouble. Caleb was on hand all that day, smoothly encouraging the girl, joking with Charlie, or sitting quietly in the cart with his eyes out upon the land. The grain would be cut next week. And after that the threshers would come. And then the flax would be cut, and the crew would thresh it on their return trip. Everything was working out smoothly this year, at last, and as it would work out in the years to come. The completion of a perfect cycle: plowing, harrowing, planting, growing, reaping and threshing. In all life, where was there such harmony as could be found in the cultivation of the land? Caleb could well afford to be mellow and content before the wide testimony of his success as a farmer, as a tiller of the soil.

Ellen, Judith and Charlie walked home behind the horses that evening too tired to be aware of hunger, or thirst or heat. The haying was finished, and no extra man had been hired to help.

3

Caleb had business the next day at the Klovaczs'.

"You will come with me, Jude," he said amiably. "And put up a lunch, Mother. We'll not ask the heathen for a bite."

Amelia was glad that Judith was going with him. She would at least be relieved of worry for the day. She hurried about and got together a basket full of food, which she placed in the back of the cart. Then, while Caleb was harnessing the mare, she spoke to Jude.

"If you don't know it by this time, I'll have him tell you himself," she said coldly. "And what you did to Ellen yesterday isn't doing you any good, either. If he had seen you he wouldn't 'a' given you another chance. You best be careful, and watch what you're doing, Jude."

Judith sullenly drew on the heavy boots that Caleb had bought her that summer. They were still new, since she had refused to wear them.

Judith mounted the cart beside Caleb without saying a word to either him or Amelia, who came out to see them off.

"That's a fine crop o' hay out there—a mighty fine crop," Caleb commented, indicating the stacks in the field with his whip as they drove past them. "Not another like it among all the Icelanders—not even Bjarnasson himself, I'll warrant. We done mighty well—mighty well."

The rest of the trip was made in silence, Judith watching the sailing gossamer against the sun and noticing the streaks of red and yellow that were already tingeing the leaves. It was the end of summer—the end, perhaps of everything. She sank into a lethargy, her shoulders slumped forward and her hands hung listlessly between her knees. After her rage at Ellen yesterday, the thing that had risen within her had died a clumsy death. Her spirit was in thick sleep.

At the Klovaczs' they found Anton confined to his bed. His voice was almost inaudible when he spoke to them.

Judith withdrew after she had given him a greeting, and left him alone with Caleb. She sat and talked with the girls in the kitchen, and was impressed with their beauty and their somehow elegant manners. She had seen them only once before, at Yellow Post, and then it was at a distance. Because she did not know that the girls admired her equally, she felt extremely awkward and large. They began to prepare dinner, and Jude saw that they set the table with two extra plates. She blushed at the thought of the lunch basket out in the cart, and despised Caleb anew. She hastily told the girls not to set places for her and her father, that they had to be going at once.

In the room where Anton lay, Caleb sat beside the sick man for nearly an hour. Caleb Gare was not the man to advance upon an objective ungracefully. Even a dying man had to be treated with diplomacy.

"I have examined the hay, Anton," he began gently, "and it's half sow thistle. Besides any amount of stink weed. You've got to learn to cultivate it, Anton." Then he went into a long discourse on the growing of tame hay, advising Anton what to do next year. Anton moved from side to side, trying to escape the pain that racked his body.

"What I will do next year, it is not for you to say, my friend," he smiled at Caleb.

"Nonsense—nonsense, Anton. You'll be around again before you know it—before you know it. Remember now, clear that field soon's the hay's cut. There's no reason why you shouldn't have as clean a crop next year as I have. Your land is as good as mine, Anton—every bit as good. But you can't ask that for the stuff that's on it now. Why, it's scarcely worth the cutting—scarcely worth the cutting!" Caleb raised his eyebrows and leaned back in his chair, throwing out the palms of his hands in a deprecatory gesture.

Anton sighed and turned his face toward the open window, through which he could see the hayfield under discussion. His unfailing sense of humor kept him from calling Caleb a liar outright. True, there was a certain amount of weed in the field, but it was far from worthless. Caleb's berating of the hay was only another way of telling Anton that he would buy it for exactly the amount of money that Anton would have to pay to a threshing crew. He knew that Anton could not and would not sell for less. He might as well let it rot in the field.

"I am tired, my friend. Take the hay," said Anton, closing his eyes from the glare of the light through the window.

"You don't give me credit, Anton, for helping you out," said Caleb injuredly. "There's not another man this side of Nykerk who would 'a' bought you out, cash."

Anton laughed softly. "You are the good man, Caleb Gare, the very good man, God bless you! And may the hay feed your many cattle well!"

Caleb rose to go. "There's only about a day's cutting. I'll have it off right away. And you might's well as not take the money for it now." He reached into his pocket and drew out a shiny black wallet, frayed at the edges.

Anton did not even look at the roll of bills he handed to him. He stuck it under the pillow at his head and crossed his hands behind his thin neck. Then he turned his hollow eyes upon Caleb with amusement. He would force the man Gare to extend his hand in token of good feeling. Anton enjoyed the irony.

"Well—well," Caleb said mildly, replacing the wallet back in his inner pocket. "It has been a good day for us both, eh, Anton? And perhaps you'll sign a receipt for the money?" He drew a note book from his vest pocket, and a fountain pen, and after he had made out the receipt form he handed it to Anton. Anton signed it unsteadily and gave it back to Caleb. Then he replaced his hands behind his head.

Caleb cleared his throat. "Yes—yes," he said absently, picking his hat up from the table. "And how long will this Jordan fellow be with you, Anton? Kind o' hard on you keepin' hired help now, eh?"

"This Jordan—he is one of God's good fellows," Anton said. "He is cutting the grain with my boys—but not for money."

"Well, Anton, must get along—must get along. Lot o' work over on my place these days. Come over and have a look at my crops when you get around again," Caleb said from the doorway.

"I will come on these wings, Mr Gare," Anton smiled. Caleb had not offered his hand. It amused him a great deal. A farmer who did not offer his hand after a transaction. . . .

In the kitchen Caleb told Judith to wait for him. Then he went out and drove the mare down to the field where the Klovacz boys and Mark were already shocking the grain. In two or three weeks Anton would have the threshers here. He would have feed for the winter.

Then, too, he had a smaller hayfield farther away. But
he would have no hay to sell in the markets to the south.
He would have to sell some of his cattle soon, to get
money to live on. Anton was well known for his fine
cattle. They were all he had of any worth. How he
had come by them no one seemed to know—a poor homesteader like him. Probably in questionable ways, Caleb
thought—he was capable of anything, heathen that he
was.

Mark Jordan paused at the end of the field when he
saw him coming. What was the old rascal up to now, he
wondered.

Caleb got down from the cart.

"Thought you'd like to know that Anton and I closed
the deal," he said when he had come up to Mark. "So
Anton is fixed for the thrashin'." There was a sardonic
grin on his face as he spoke. He'd show this interfering
city fellow a thing or two.

Mark looked at him. How he was gloating, behind his
smooth, genial smile. "Got it for nothing, I suppose?"
Mark asked, his anger mounting.

"Nothing? Nothing? Heh, heh! A lot you know
about the value of hay! A lot you know, my boy!
There's not another man in the country would a' taken
that stuff off his hands for real *cash*. Nothing, indeed!"
Caleb laughed softly, a cold gleam appearing in his eyes.
He peered craftily at Mark.

"And what 'er *you* doin' round here, I'd like to know?"

Mark smiled tolerantly down at Caleb. After all,
he was a pathetic, meddling old man. Mark could afford

to keep his temper. "What am *I* doing? Oh, cooking, washing the babies——"

"None o' your smartness, young fella. You'll mind your business and not butt in between me and Anton, see? Or we'll soon find out who's the trustee of Oeland school." With that he turned on his heel and was about to jump into the cart. But Mark's curiosity was roused.

"Wait a minute, Mr Gare. I really didn't mean to be smart, as you say. I beg your pardon. But what do you mean about your being trustee—that has nothing to do with me, has it?"

Caleb turned about. "No? I kind o' thought it had," he observed, with a knowing lift of his eyebrows.

"If I were you I would not mix my doings up with Miss Archer," Mark told him quietly, "if that's what you're hinting at. We aren't all fools, you know, and I might make trouble for you if you did. You aren't trustee for life, remember."

"I'm not, eh? We'll see if I'm not. Heh, heh! What I want to be, I *am*. And the likes o' you won't stop me from bein' it."

Mark leaned his elbow upon a fence post and looked down at him. "Is there anything in the world you care for as much as for yourself, I wonder, Caleb Gare?" he asked curiously.

"Eh? What is there worth caring about? Nobody helps me except *myself*—what else should I care about? What do you care about, except yourself? What does anybody care about? Every man for himself, that's what I say. Nothing matters to me but myself. What do you think of that, eh?   What do you think of that, my boy?"

Caleb's shoulders shook with almost noiseless mirth as he got into the cart.   Mark watched him drive away, his feelings a mingling of pity and amusement and resentment.

Then he went back to the field, and wondered for the rest of the day if Caleb really might not create some mis‧ chief for Lind and himself before they got away.   The old fellow would stop at nothing to achieve some perverse object, or satisfy a groundless grudge.

CHAPTER XIX

1

On a Sunday morning, Lind and Mark walked to the farm of Fusi Aronson. It was very quiet on the wood trail, as if the trees were keeping the hour. Already many of the birds had gone south, and there was not so festive a singing. But the woods were gorgeous with color, and the swamps a scarlet maze of cranberry bushes. The sky was infinitely remote and blue, with scarcely a cloud sailing.

Mark and Lind walked slowly and talked over their plans for the coming year. He had a little money—they would go to the cities in the east and play around for a while.

"I'm beginning to be so impatient, Mark," Lind told him. "But I'm in honor bound to stay here till the end of the term."

They walked on past the slough with its little bright tufts of islands, and came finally to the farm of Fusi Aronson. The great Icelander strode down to meet them before they were well within the gate of the barn yard.

He ushered them hospitably into the rude cabin where he and his brother Bjorn lived alone. Bjorn had gone to church in Yellow Post. The brothers took turns in attending, since one of them had to be about to look after the place.

"Anton Klovacz will not live, they say at Yellow Post," Fusi said slowly, looking questioningly at Mark.

"I'm afraid not, Fusi," Mark replied. "I wish you had been able to buy his hay, instead of Caleb Gare. He forced him to sell it for almost nothing."

Fusi scowled. "One day I shall do for Caleb Gare. He should not live," he declared. "Mees Archer—she say it would do no good. But I think it is bad for the world that he lives."

Lind shook her head. "It would only bring you trouble, Fusi, to try to get even with him," she warned. "He is too sly for honest people. If you did anything to make him angry at you, he would hound you out of the country."

The great Icelander smiled. "A small girl like you are afraid, but I am not afraid of Caleb Gare. I will take my time, but I will get him. I cannot forgive what he did to my brothers. He shall suffer for that, Mees Archer."

He took them out then to his barn and showed them the new addition he had built to it, and told them of the house he hoped to build in the spring. Then he showed them the stone cyclone cellar he had dug in the earth, where he kept cream and eggs before he took them to the Siding.

"You need a wife, Fusi," Lind smiled at him.

Fusi laughed his great, deep laugh.

"When I have a house—then maybe, a wife," he answered.

Mark and Lind intended walking back across the ridge

and dropping in upon Joel Brund and his wife, so they left Fusi before Bjorn returned.

"And don't get mixed up with Caleb Gare," Lind advised him again.

Fusi's face hardened. "Do not fear, Mees Archer," he said, "when I shall make Caleb Gare pay for what he have done, he will go where he can do nothing back."

He walked with them to the beginning of the ridge, then turned back. Lind looked after him, a tremendous hulk of a man, with long, powerful arms that could crush out human life in an instant.

"Do you suppose he ever will, Mark?" she asked uneasily.

"Kill Caleb? If he gets more reason to, I shouldn't be surprised," Mark observed.

They walked across the ridge and from the top of it could see the morning light lying like a pale sheet all over the earth below them. This was the highest elevation of land at Oeland. From it, they could look southward across the slough to Sandbos' pastures, and beyond that to the fields of Caleb Gare. They could barely make out the southern ridge where Caleb was used to going with his lantern. The two ridges might at one time have been the steep margins of a lake. It gave Lind a very lofty feeling to stand here in the clear morning, with the serene world lying below.

"It's hard to imagine that people are concerned with anything ignoble when you look out on the world like this, isn't it?" she said.

They walked on across the ridge and down the north

road past Ericksons' toward the homestead of Joel Brund, discussing as they went the possibility of Caleb Gare's making mischief for either or both of them. Mark had been inclined to scoff at Lind's suspicion that he had been spying on them from the hedge on the night when they had ridden in the rain. But he promised her that he would do nothing to incite the old man's rancor.

At the fork in the road where it took three new directions, one to Yellow Post, one to the Klovaczs', and one to Sandbos', they met Joel Brund driving two work horses. He was sitting on the high seat of a sparkling new green lumber wagon.

"Hello, Mr Brund," Lind called out. He had been about to drive past without looking at them. He drew in the horses and glanced down.

"How do?" he said. He reached down and shook hands with them both, Lind introducing Mark.

"It's such a lovely morning, we've already been out for a walk," Lind told him. "Where have you been, Mr Brund?"

"To Yellow Post. I bought this wagon this morning from Johanneson."

"It's a fine wagon," Mark said.

"Pretty good. Johanneson sells cheap on Sunday," Joel said shortly. "How is Anton Klovacz coming?"

"Not very well, I'm afraid," Mark said. "He's a sick man."

Joel shifted about on his seat. He seemed to have nothing more to say, and his heavy body stirred awk-wardly. He looked away.

Lind and Mark said good-by to him, and he clumsily re-

moved his wide straw hat and picked up the reins. Then
the wagon rumbled on down the road.

"Poor Joel," Lind murmured. "Think of all that must
be going on in his soul that he can't get out, Mark."

"He'll get it out—somehow."

"In work."

"Perhaps."

2

The days went by, and Martin was able to use his arm
again. Caleb continued his soft chiding whenever he
came into the house.

"Could 'a' got that wagon from Johanneson for half
price if I'd 'a' had somebody to send down for it," he
said in the presence of the entire family at the dinner
table. "Always losin' on somethin'—I'm no business
man, or I'd 'a' had somebody down. I'll have to get you
to go for me next time, Charlie. You're dependable."

Martin's face grew red, but he said nothing. During the days of inactivity he had been thinking. He had
found himself, and with the finding had come a sense of
shame. He resolved to assert himself as a man should
as soon as he had all his strength back. There would be
a new house in the spring. But he would wait—until
after the harvest.

One day was spent in mowing the hay at the Klovaczs'
and carrying it to Caleb's land, where it would be stacked
after a period of drying. Then they turned to the grain.

Judith and Charlie began the cutting and binding.
Martin would be strong enough to go to the fields the

next week. The work began on a raw, windy day, from which the last vestige of summer seemed to have departed. Judith had been inert and dull since the day when she had vented herself upon Ellen, and Caleb was confident concerning her, but he remained on the place nevertheless, occupying himself with mysterious tasks that kept him in full view of the field in which Judith was binding barley.

She came home to meals every day with apparently no change in her mood. Her eyes were heavy and shadowed, and Amelia was almost unable to wake her in the mornings. Lind tried in vain to speak to her once or twice. She remembered the peculiar expression in the girl's eyes the last night Lind had talked with her in her room, when she had covered her body quickly with her clothing. A thought had come into Lind's mind then that she had later dismissed. Now it returned to her.

Ellen elaborately paid no attention to Judith, but the girl was too heavy in spirit even to know that she was being ignored. The only thing she was conscious of was the eternal vigilance of Caleb, and the hostile reminding Amelia gave her every time she came into the house. She was become so inured to misery that nothing else seemed to exist in the world.

The weather cleared again, and now came the bright, dry heat of late summer. Lind went down one day to stand outside the fence and watch Jude where she drove up and down the field on the binder. The grain stood like stiff brown gold, and over it the heat moved in dazzling waves. Judith went on and on monotonously, not once turning to look at Lind. Not once, even, did she lift her hand to wipe the moisture from her face.

Her spirit was gone, and all that remained was her great, lasting body, that went on working like a machine.

Lind was startled at the change in her. She hoped that when Martin was ready to help with the grain, there would be a lift in her mood. She saw Sven one evening and told him that she feared Caleb was breaking Judith by his ceaseless watchfulness. Sven sprang up at once on the impulse to go to Caleb and handle him as he saw fit, but Lind persuaded him to wait. Something must surely come up soon to take Caleb away from the farm.

Martin was finally able to go to the field. His shoulder was still sensitive and stiff, but he could no longer remain idle and see Judith going out each morning and coming in each night. Then, too, Caleb's oblique complaints were becoming intolerable. So he went to the field, and his shoulder, so lately out of its tight bandage, smarted under the sun. But he doubled his industry to make up for the time he had lost. Caleb, watching from the outside of the fence, drew his hand across his mustache and smiled. Martin knew his place.

Judith's mood did not change with the coming of Martin into the field. Amelia watched her narrowly, and felt that there was something unnatural about her attitude that did not grow out of the surveillance under which she was kept. She did not question her, however, fearing to rouse her from her stupor to greater tempestuousness than she had yet shown. It might be, too, that her terror of Caleb's threat had had a lasting effect. Amelia did not forget to remind her of it every day.

One evening Ellen, driving home from Yellow Post, saw an Indian on a pony riding south on the road that led past the Brunds' and Ericksons' northward into the wild bush country and beyond that to the land of myriad lakes and rivers where men went to lose themselves from the world. She recognized the Indian. He was the son of John Tobacco, and he had been spending the summer in that region. On his way home he must have met Malcolm, and talked with him. She turned her head and watched him until he was out of sight.

When she could no longer see him her throat tightened and her lids winked rapidly behind her glasses. For a moment she had been near someone who had seen and talked with Malcolm. Now even that moment was gone.

She raised her eyes and could see dimly the white clothes fluttering on the line in the yard at home. She would take them in when she got there, and dampen and roll them up for ironing.

3

On a night of high wind, Anton Klovacz died. Mark went the next day to Yellow Post to arrange with Johanneson about the burial, and Caleb Gare was notified in a message sent by a halfbreed to come to a meeting in the church. The question to be discussed was whether it was ethical to bury a Catholic in a Protestant cemetery.

Mark happened to be on hand when Johanneson sent the message with the halfbreed. He waited at Yellow Post until the man returned with the answer. Caleb had promised to be at the church on the morrow, when the weighty question would be gone into. Johanneson assured Mark that he would do his best to bring about a favorable decision, but reminded him that Caleb Gare was a hard man, and a "Christian."

Mark returned to a scene of desolation. Mrs Sandbo and Lind were there with the children, who were sitting about the kitchen in great-eyed terror. The door to the other room was closed. Behind it lay the body of Anton Klovacz. Mrs Sandbo had washed and dressed him, telling Lind between her sobs that it was the tenth time that she had "laid out" since she had come to Oeland.

Anton had died in peace. The inspector had come the day before and had gone over the place, and papers were signed which made him sole owner of the land to which he had given the last glow of his spirit. He had satisfactorily "proved up" his homestead.

Lind and Mark went out to talk alone when the latter returned from Yellow Post. "If Caleb Gare holds out, by God, I'll throttle him!" Mark muttered after he had told her of the meeting that was to be held.

"Surely he can't," Lind protested. "He hasn't the power, has he?"

"Well, the church has, I suppose, and *he's* the church, here."

Lind was thoughtful for a moment. "He'll be gone most of the day to-morrow, I should think?"

Mark thought he probably would.

"It'll be a chance for Sven to see Judith," Lind observed. "I had better take the children and the girls over to Sandbos' now, hadn't I? And you intend to go to Yellow Post to-morrow afternoon?"

"Yes, I'll see to that. If Caleb won't give his consent,

it'll have to be the Indian cemetery at the mission. That's far away, but it'll have to be."

"They—they wouldn't let him be buried on the place, I suppose?"

"These people are superstitious as the devil. No—but I'll certainly make a few facts plain to old Gare if he refuses."

Amelia signaled to Judith three times that evening before she finally turned the horses toward home. Lind met her at the door of the kitchen and saw her face grimed with dust and sweat. She did not so much as glance at the teacher when she went to the sink to wash.

As Amelia was outside, Lind ventured to speak to Judith.

"Come up to my room and wash, Judy," she said.

Judith looked at her heavily. "It's no use," she replied, "no use for you to try to fix me up."

"But I have something to tell you," Lind went on in a low tone. "Come on, bring the hot water and use my basin."

Judith picked up the kettle of water and followed Lind. In the room above, Lind helped her undress and found her unreluctant this time to having her body exposed. When she was thoroughly bathed, Judith relaxed back upon Lind's bed, and closed her eyes.

"What do you want to tell me?" she asked. "Oh Lind, I feel so nice now, I guess I must be going to die." She sighed heavily and stroked her smooth sides with both hands.

"Wait a minute—where's that silk thing I made you?"

Judith had put it preciously away, but Lind found it and made her slip it on. Jude took a deep breath. "Now tell me it," she said.

"You are going to meet Sven to-morrow."

"How?" Judith looked at her with startled eyes.

"Don't be frightened, child. Your father will be away all day to-morrow. Or at least most of the day. Anton Klovacz has died, and he has to go to a meeting about the funeral at Yellow Post. I told Sven to watch and notice just when he leaves. Then he'll ride around south and meet you at the end of the field, where Amelia won't be able to see you. How's that?"

Judith sat up doubtfully. "Are you *sure* he's goin'— going—and that it isn't just a trick?"

Lind assured her that it was no trick.

"Well—but nothing comes out right, somehow. It was nice of you, though, Lind—to think of it," she said slowly, her eyes upon the floor. Lind put her arm about her and kissed her cheek.

"Things *will* come out right, I know it. Now where are your clean clothes?"

4

The next day, while the air was still fresh and cool, Caleb left for Yellow Post. Sven, watching covertly, saw him leave, and immediately saddled his horse and rode south, skirting the acres of Caleb Gare until he came to the rough timber land beyond the dried lake bottom.

He saw Judith in the southern field, within hailing distance from the fence. When he realized that she had sighted him, he jumped from his horse and lay in the long grass looking up at the clouds.

She drove the binder to the fence, tied the horses, and crawled under the barbed wire. She knew Sven was hiding somewhere. Before she had time to look around he grabbed her by the ankles and she fell forward upon him. They both laughed boisterously at his little prank, and then Judith burst into tears. He drew her down into his arms, where she lay flat, crying bitterly and unable to speak.

"Judie, Judie, don't cry so," he urged softly, rocking her back and forth as though she were a child. "What's the matter, anyway, with her? Here I come galloping to see her the first chance I get, and she cries all over me. That's thanks for you! Listen, dear Judie, I love you, and I'm goin' to take you away from here real soon. I don't care what happens, you're comin' away. What do you think of that?"

Judith sat up and wiped her eyes. Sven got to his knees and looked at her. Then he put his arms about her, felt her shoulders, her arms, and breast. "Judie, you're gettin' thin!" he exclaimed. "Why, you're nothin' but a little girl! What's the matter?"

"I just can't stand it any longer, Sven. I'll die," she whispered, her lips quivering.

"Will you come away right now, Judie?"

She looked across the field. Her heart leaped at the thought of going away with Sven, of having him with her all the time, out in that lovely, gentle world where Lind came from. She felt that another day under the silent persecution of Caleb Gare would drive her mad.

Then, too, there was that other thing, that even Sven did not know, yet. She must tell him. She must tell him now. He would force her to come away at once if she told him. Perhaps it would be better to wait—until after the harvest. By then Caleb might have forgotten the ax. At least she would have spared him the expense of a hired man. Judith decided not to tell Sven—just yet.

"Wait until the thrashin' is over, Sven," she replied.

"Oh—thrashin'—damn the thrashin'," he exclaimed impatiently. "First it's the hayin' and now it's the thrashin'—what d'you s'pose I came back for, if it wasn't for you? I could 'a' sent ma money to hire a man for our work."

"But he'd only catch us, Sven, and put me in—in jail," Jude pleaded.

"Jail—shucks! They'd put *him* in, more like!"

But Jude's fear stayed, and they decided to wait until after the threshing.

She pressed close to him once more, and lay still for a while with a luxurious feeling of rest and comfort, then she slipped under the fence and mounted the binder. Sven sprang to his saddle and waved his hat at her until she was far down the field, the long path of cut grain unrolling behind her, smooth and yellow.

CHAPTER XX

1

MARK JORDAN was already at Johanneson's store when Caleb arrived there.

Anton Klovacz's horses were tied among the slender birches behind the church up the road, and in the back of the wagon there was a long box made of rough, split poplar logs and crossings of lath. In the box lay the body of Anton Klovacz.

Mark was smoking his pipe and leaning back with his elbows upon the counter when Caleb Gare entered. Caleb shot a quick glance at him from beneath his brows, then went over to talk with a small group of men who were waiting for the arrival of the other members of the church committee.

Presently he sauntered leisurely over to Mark and stood before him with his left thumb hooked in the pocket of his vest where he rubbed the secretary key against his silver watch. His other hand moved thoughtfully across his chin.

"So you're makin' this your business, too, eh?" he smiled up at Mark, his eyebrows raised.

Mark kept his temper. "As far as I am able to," he returned, his eyes hard. He was glad the Klovacz boy had remained out with the wagon.

"Hm—well, like as not—like as not," Caleb mused.

He gave vent to a deep sigh, and continued, "Of course—you understand how this is kind o' hard on us members of the church. The responsibility of conductin' affairs lies on us, and we can't shirk it, like. I'd be glad as the next one to do all I could, even for a heathen. But you ought to know, comin' from the city like you do, that the sanctity o' the church and its grounds has got to be considered. I'm willin' to do all I can, but you see how it is." He raised his eyebrows again and tossed his hands out on either side of him to indicate the rather hopeless aspect of the matter.

Mark's teeth came together in spite of himself. The man's smooth arrogance was maddening. "You'll take care what you say about Anton Klovacz's religion, Caleb Gare," he said evenly. "Make your decision and have it over with. And remember that even now Anton Klovacz isn't begging for anything from you—not even a grave."

Caleb Gare's eyes narrowed to veiled points.

"You take it upon yourself, young man—you take it upon yourself. I can show you, for all your city smartness, that Anton Klovacz might still be beggin' from me. His land ain't so far from mine but what I could link it up——"

Mark drew himself up, his anger going out of bounds at last. "So that's what you've got your eye on, is it? Well, just take it off. You'll not get an acre of Anton Klovacz's land so long as there is justice in this country!"

The group in the corner of the store were looking toward them. They were most of them easy-going farmers who would not have thought twice about permitting Anton

Klovacz's body to be buried in the cemetery. But they had fallen into the habit of looking to Caleb for leadership in any issue, great or small. Now Mark Jordan's evident animosity toward Caleb amused and gratified many of them.

Caleb glared up at Mark, his head jutting out menacingly. He lifted his hand and snapped his fingers under Mark's nose.

"You get out o' here before I make it hot for ye, hear me? Before I tell the whole place what I know about ye —ye slick alick. You and that little chit of a school marm—yeah——"

Mark's arm had shot out. His right hand circled Caleb's throat and lifted him almost clear of the floor. Then, grasping him by the lapels of his coat, Mark fairly hurled him into the group of staring farmers, where he fell sprawling.

White with fury, Mark stood above him. "Take every word of that back, damn you, or I'll break your neck!" he shouted.

The farmers had cleared a space for him, and Caleb pulled himself together. He stood up and carefully dusted and straightened the tails and the lapels of his treasured broadcloth coat, which he had worn for the occasion.

"Don't know as I said anything to take back," he said with a bland smile. "I think the little school marm is too good for any man. Heh, heh!" While Mark stood before him with his lips twitching, Caleb took his silver watch from his pocket.

"Time for the meetin' to commence, gentlemen," he

said. "Everybody ready? If so, we'll repair to the church."

The amazed farmers looked at one another. Mark strode grimly to the doorway. He looked back.

"Never mind the meeting. Anton Klovacz wouldn't rest in ground that Caleb Gare squeezed him into," he said, and was gone.

Caleb looked after him, his eyes glinting under their heavy brows. "Hm. You'll be sorry for that, my boy! You'll be sorry for that," he muttered to himself.

The farmers, as one man, felt heavily abashed.

Mark saw that the Klovacz boy was still sitting on the seat of the wagon.

"We'll ride to the mission, son," he said to him kindly. "They have more room there."

So the two of them rode on the seat of the wagon over the twenty miles to the Catholic mission that lay to the south. It was a long, rough road, seldom frequented and for that reason neglected. A great stretch of it lay through timber, where the air was mellow with the scent of drying leaves. Cranberry bushes hung in red cascades along the trail, and the thorn apple trees were heavy with clusters of waxy fruit, already tinged with pink. The day was still save for sudden little gusts of wind that lifted a whirl of dry leaves now and then in the road before them. Mark had never in his life known such a mood of loneliness. The boy sat beside him in heavy silence all the way, glancing back once or twice toward the box in the wagon. Under the canvas, the rough boards of the box rattled against the floor of the wagon with a monotonous sort of rhythm over the endless miles to the mission. The sun rose to noon, the heat beat down and made little shining disks on the black flanks of the horses, and Mark and the boy knew it was time to stop at some settler's home for food.

The afternoon led them through marsh country, flat and dun-colored with dying reeds. The Klovacz boy sat beside Mark without uttering a word. Occasionally he adjusted the canvas more securely over the box, as the heat became more intense and the way led on without shade. Once they saw a giant hawk swoop down over the marsh and keep low to the earth until it rose suddenly almost straight into the air. Then it vanished against the sky with some little animal fast in its claws. The Klovacz boy saw it but made no comment. The unusual sight scarcely started an expression of surprise on his brooding face.

There was only a narrow sheaf of color in the western sky when they drove the horses up to the front of the mission house. Mark got down and knocked at the door. An aged priest opened it and peered out upon the strangers.

When Mark had told him his story he bade them come in. Then he vanished to another part of the building, and returned with a younger priest, who greeted Mark with great kindliness.

"It is very sad," he said softly. "We shall have mass for the poor soul in the morning. I will have my men take in the casket. Now you will come with me."

He led them into a warmly lighted room where there was a table set with simple food. "I always have it in readiness for wayfarers," he said, indicating chairs for them to be seated in.

On the morrow, which was the third day after his death, Anton Klovacz was buried, in a grave among the Indians. It was a simple ceremony. Mark and Anton's eldest son stood bareheaded beside the grave while the priest chanted the requiem. Then a crude wooden cross with name and date was erected, and Anton Klovacz was left alone. The wind blew with a little dry sound through the long yellow grass among the graves. It was the end of the season of growth.

2

At the Gares' things went on just the same. Judith, Martin and Charlie finished the binding, then began to shock the grain. Caleb watched them confidently from the house.

So that Caleb would not increase his vigilance, Judith tried to hide the change in her mood after her meeting with Sven. She had come home at the end of that day with the same heavy face, and had eaten her supper without looking at anyone. But Lind, watching her shrewdly, and knowing what the others did not know, saw the buoyant change in her.

Something had happened to Caleb. He had come home after the meeting at Yellow Post surly and uncommunicative, and Amelia, giving him a sidelong glance, wondered just how she would be made aware of what had happened. That what had happened had been unflattering to Caleb she knew. She could see by his face that something was rankling bitterly in his mind. He would stand for long periods with one foot up on the lowest wire of the sheep pasture, his arms crossed and leaning on the fence before him, his eyes brooding out toward the wide fields where the new haystack stood. Then he would come into the kitchen and tinker about absently with broken bits of harness or boxes of rusty nails and screws. Amelia prepared herself for an avalanche of abuse: these were the signals for its approach.

Two days after Caleb's trip to Yellow Post it came. The children and the Teacher had gone to the loft. Amelia was preparing the oatmeal for the next morning's breakfast. Caleb had come in from the field, closed the door gently behind him, shaken the lantern and hung it on its hook near the door.

"Your son is a gentleman, Amelia. A *fine* gentleman," he said almost in a whisper, going past her into the inner room.

Amelia sighed. She felt suddenly very tired, as if she had worked a long time for nothing. In spite of everything she had done, it was coming. Her mind grew dull under the certainty. She made no reply to Caleb's remark.

"Well? Thought you might like to know it," Caleb went on in an injured tone. "Got nothin' to say?"

"No—nothing," Amelia said.

Caleb returned to the kitchen and stood before her, his head thrust out. "You'll probably have somethin' to say when I tell you what the pretty boy done to *me*," he sneered, tapping his chest with his hand. "And perhaps

you won't blame me for doing what I'm going to do—
when I get good and ready."

Amelia looked at him. She paled before his eyes.
"What did he do?" she asked faintly.

"Yeah—heh, heh! What did he do?" he laughed
gently. "You'd like to know, eh? Well—keep on guess-
in'."

With that he returned to the other room and began to
undress, dropping each of his shoes with a thump to the
floor. Amelia heard him laughing softly to himself.

She stood over the stove in the kitchen for a long time,
trying to think what it could possibly be that had roused
Caleb's direct spite toward Mark. Whatever it was, it
would simply add weight to that greater grievance he held
against him. For Amelia believed that Caleb considered
Mark's existence in the light of a personal offense, which
would be vindicated only in one way. Amelia cast about
in her mind for some straw of hope. The thought had
occurred to her many times that she might go to Mark
Jordan and beseech him to leave before any ill befell him
through Caleb. But each time she had realized that this
would only hasten his discovery of the truth, for Mark
Jordan would never be induced to run away without
sound reason. She knew that she was helpless. The
only thing to do was to wait and pray that something
unforeseen would preclude his ever finding out the thing
that haunted her. She would have given anything to
know whether Bart Nugent was alive or dead. Caleb
spoke casually now and then of having heard from him,
but Amelia knew that signified nothing.

Finally she set the pot of porridge on the back of the

stove, blew out the lantern in the kitchen and went into the other room. Caleb had let down the folding bed and was already asleep. Amelia looked at his rough hair standing up at the edge of the quilt. He had his face to the wall, and was snoring heavily. A wave of disgust came over her. She could not bring herself to undress and lie down beside him. Softly she blew out the lamp, picked up the fur rug that lay on the floor, groped in the dark for her shawl, and went outside.

Amelia went to the more recently built section of the stable, which was not locked, and through the dark found her way to a pile of clean straw in a corner. Caleb was a sound sleeper, and she was always the first up in the morning. He would not miss her. She wrapped the shawl about her and lay down on the straw, covering herself with the fur rug. All night through her sleep, fear beat on her heart like the wings of some ominous bird.

3

Ellen joined the others in the fields to shock the grain. They worked tremendously, to get it up in time to be dried for the threshing.

It was in Martin's mind a number of times to go to Yellow Post and hire a half-breed to help, without asking Caleb's permission. But before he actually got started, his will fell, and long habit kept him under Caleb's dominance.

Judith's body failed a little now under the heavy work. But she strove to conceal the falling off in her strength by being the first up in the mornings and by making a great show of swift industry in the fields. Ellen regarded her skeptically, but avoided any further collision with her. Caleb was secretly pleased with her and was convinced that her spirit was broken. But Amelia watched her with growing anxiety, undeceived.

Lind contrived to talk with Judith whenever it was propitious. She kept reminding her that escape lay ahead, and that she must keep up her courage and take advantage of the opportunity when it came. Judith clung to Lind desperately, thinking of her all day when she was in the field, seeking to be near her for the sake of the physical sweetness of her when the others were not about.

Finally the grain was all in russet gold shocks, drying on the field. Caleb wound his way among them, examining the wheat and the rye and the barley with minute attention, and deciding upon what land should lie fallow next season. Judith had no way of telling beforehand how long he would be away on these tours, so she dared not go beyond the school house if she left the farm gate at all. In any case, Amelia kept close watch on her, and Amelia was becoming a more severe task master, in a way, than Caleb.

Ellen, Judith and Amelia went into the bush that had been bought of Fusi Aronson and gathered the wild grapes that grew there. The vines weighed down the branches of the slippery elms over which they had grown like a net. They were a blue mass of tiny, pungently sweet clusters. The women carried home several flour sacks full, the blue stain oozing through the white cotton

of the sacks. Then there were the jelly and preserves
to make and wine for Caleb. So that every day was full,
and every evening came with sleep for mind and body.

Lind, observing the unbelievable amount of work that
was done by the women in the Gare household, wondered
what would happen to them if they were suddenly bereft
of these endless duties. She realized that it was only oc-
cupation that kept them sane beneath the sneering vigilance of Caleb Gare, and saw that somehow things bal-
anced themselves under the most appalling conditions.
But her pity for Judith grew with the passing of every
day. She saw that Caleb was by no means releasing his
hold on her, and wondered how it was going to be possible for her to free herself. The door of the barn remained locked, and Caleb examined it now and then to
make sure that it had not been tampered with. Had it
not been for her affection for Judith, Lind would not
have been able to bear the rigid atmosphere at the Gares'.
When she saw Mark in the evenings, it seemed as if
she was relieved of a physical burden.

The time during which the grain dried on the fields
was a trying one for Judith. She did not once see Sven,
and the messages that Lind brought from him only served
to make her impatience more pointed. Even after the
heaviest day she would lie awake for hours thinking of
him, feeling the dark pressing down upon her like a
weight. She avoided Amelia and her detecting eyes, and
went out of her way in order not to encounter Ellen,
whose triumphant passivity was galling to her. Ellen's
face had taken on a perpetual, self-righteous smirk. It
seemed to Judith that it gave her sister some satisfaction

to witness her debasement—as if she were congratulating herself on having given up what would have ultimately brought her the same misery that she, Judith, was enduring.

Martin, somehow, lost sight of the dream that had come back to him during his days of convalescence. Every hour that brought him back to the land and its exactions took him farther away from the vision that had stirred him while he had time for dreaming. His shoulders resumed their tired slope, as if nothing had happened to set them straight. And when he finally looked out over the fields dotted with their cone-shaped shocks, it was only with the relieved feeling that Caleb would have no fault to find with his work.

4

The threshing machine came, with its crew of three men, great coarse farmers from north of Latt's Slough. They were housed in the newer part of the barn, where Amelia and Martin had built beds for them on the floor of cedar branches and straw. But they ate with the family, and Lind, after making an heroic effort to ignore them at the table, finally gave it up and had her meals, except breakfast, at Sandbos' during the three days of their stay.

Judith worked with the men and Martin. Caleb had not hired an extra man.

At the end of the first day, Lind, coming from school, saw her lithe young body standing against the sun on the top of a load of grain. She was rapidly pitching

great forkfuls of grain down into the feeder of the threshing machine. Martin worked with her.

Lind walked past the load of grain to where the men
were working at the other end of the machine. The
grain was brought in huge rackfuls from the fields by
Judith, Ellen, Martin and Charlie, and was being threshed
a short distance from the stable. Lind sat down on the
ground and watched the yellow chaff shooting in a great
arc out of the funnel of the threshing machine. Against
the late sun it was a volley of gold particles. The
Teacher wondered whether Judith, from her height on the
rack, saw any beauty in the scene. She glanced back at
the girl and noted that her face was expressionless, her
arms moving swiftly and easily as pendulums over the
pitchfork. While Lind was watching her, she looked up,
as if she had suddenly become aware of her regard. Lind
pointed at the yellow cascade of chaff that was being
thrown out by the machine. Judith nodded and half
smiled, then went on pitching as steadily as ever.

On the last day of the threshing, Caleb went out across
the stubble to the standing flax, the only grain left now.
A slow-growing, deliberate, delicate thing it was, and a
pride to any man who could successfully raise it. As he
had done when it was in blue flower, he slipped between
the wires of the fence and stood in the midst of it, almost
furtively running his hand over the rough, fully seeded
tops. Then, stepping with care, he waded far into it,
touching it now and then, his eyes roving over it hungrily.

When he had had his fill of delight in looking at the
flax, he turned toward home across the empty fields. A

thing lay on his mind which discolored his satisfaction with his crops. Mark Jordan had inflicted upon him bodily injury, in the presence of the most dignified members of the church. It was a thing that he could never forgive nor forget. He had hidden his humiliation, had brushed the affair lightly away, but he knew the tongues of the country-side would wag forever with the episode. At church hereafter he would be pointed at and there would be stifled snickers. He who had been unapproachable, revered, had been picked up and tossed like a puppy into a group of the church's most prominent personages. That he was helpless to retaliate save in one way was not gratifying to him. He desired that the moment of his revelation to Mark Jordan should be one of his own choosing. He felt that he should keep his "trump card" for some overwhelming offense against himself, that also involved Amelia. So he forced himself to lie idle until something occurred which would justify his revealing to Mark Jordan his true identity, and so forever clear the score. He would see that such a consequential thing came about before Mark left for the city.

In a few weeks' time, the flax would be taken off, threshed, and the seed sold to the markets in the south for a fine sum. Yes, yes, things were going along very smoothly indeed, very smoothly indeed.

CHAPTER XXI

1

Two announcements were posted in Johanneson's store. One was to the effect that fishing was now open in Bjarnasson's lake. Everyone read it with a mingling of awe and fear, knowing what it meant. The other gave the particulars of a harvest jubilee that was to be held in Latt's School, and was to take the form of a masquerade.

Charlie brought the news home to the Gares. Caleb took no notice of the harvest jubilee announcement, but his face soured when he heard that the Bjarnassons had at last found what they had sought for a year.

"Could 'a' had fish the year round if I'd 'a' had somebody with a mite o' spunk to send for it," he complained.

When the children were all in bed that night, Caleb sat reading his farm journal under the lamp. Amelia, busy with her knitting, thought of the jubilee and resolved that none of the children should go, since she could not with fairness single Judith out to remain at home.

Caleb looked up. "Figgerin' on sendin' to the mail order for stuff for this masquerade, eh?" he asked genially.

"No," Amelia answered. "They'll not be going."

Caleb looked at her narrowly. Then a smile relaxed his face. He raised his eyebrows. "Not goin'? Why not?"

Amelia looked at him and saw his amusement. She realized at once that she had made a mistake. "Oh, well— if you'll let them. I just thought maybe we couldn't afford it."

She dropped her eyes to her work so that he should not see her anxiety. Had he seen through her excuse, she wondered? Or did he think she was as confident concerning Judith as he was himself? She waited almost without breathing to hear what he would say next.

"Well—" he yawned comfortably, "—we'll see. We'll see. Plenty of time yet, eh? And let's go to bed. I'm gettin' old, I guess—gettin' old."

Amelia went to bed and prayed that he would refuse to let them go. She knew in her heart that Judith could not be trusted. There was something beneath her quiet these days that baffled and harassed Amelia. She was constantly on the alert for a change in her mood, and relentlessly reminding her of what lay in store if she crossed Caleb again. But Judith would not think twice if the opportunity came for her to get away free. She prayed Caleb would forbid them to go.

Caleb, turning his face to the wall, laughed to himself. This was one of the little strategies that made life interesting.

In the loft above, Judith and Lind talked, quietly so that Ellen should not hear. They had turned the lamp low, and were sitting on Lind's bed. Judith was combing the Teacher's long, fine hair.

"You must keep on working, Judie, and don't let them suspect for a moment," Lind whispered. "If they let you go to the masquerade you must keep on the road until

you get to the Siding. I'll see Sven to-morrow and tell
him about it. When it's all over, they'll forgive you.
What else can they do, unless what *he* threatens? And
I don't think he'll dare do that, Judie. He knows that I
would be a witness against him. Anyway, you must risk
it, dear."

Lind looked up at Judith and could have cried at the
change in her. Her defiant beauty was gone. She was
pale and listless, and the only indication that any of her
old spirit remained was a certain dogged look in her
eyes.

"You are tired, Judie. Go to bed now, and to-morrow
I'll talk to Sven," Lind said gently.

Judith rose from the bed. "He'll not let us go to the
dance," she murmured indifferently. "It'll have to be
some other way."

Then she went to bed with heavy thoughts and fears
moving to and fro in her mind. They would have to go
before the end of the month. She could not bear the
secret knowledge of her body any longer than that.

3

Caleb said nothing more about the masquerade than
when he winked at Ellen at breakfast the following day
and chuckled, "Ellen'll be findin' herself a beau at the
jubilee, like as not, eh?"

But everybody was waiting his final word. Amelia
most of all. She dared not broach the subject to him,
lest he should see her perturbation. She knew that he
would keep them all in suspense until the very day of the

affair. It was his way. They would have no time for making costumes. Amelia Gare created work for herself about the place; it blunted her feelings somewhat, and kept her thoughts occupied.

Dismissing school early, Lind rode to Yellow Post on the Sandbos' pony and bought gaudy cottons and ribbons. She and Mark made it an occasion to be together, as he had to make a trip there for provisions. They went to old John Tobacco and got an outfit of doeskin and feathers for Mark, and a costume for Lind ornate with beads and feathers.

Riding home in the soft fall evening they discussed the situation of Judith and Sven.

"It's criminal of him to keep that girl here as he does," Lind asserted. "And I see nothing wrong in urging her to get away. Even if he does follow them, it will lead to something better for her in the end."

Mark agreed with her that at least no worse condition could result. Then they talked of the Klovaczs', and Mark told her that a woman relative of Anton's was coming out to spend the winter with the children. Mark was surprised that Caleb had not already tried some vindictive trick to mollify his injured vanity. But Lind was uneasily anticipating some catastrophe that would sweep away all that she had found in Mark. It was a fear that was somehow bound about Caleb Gare. She looked at Mark's reassuring profile against the light, and tried to shake herself free from the oppressive dread.

They rode on toward the Sandbos'. Along the horizon were knots of scarlet and gold; here an isolated bush or a single fiery-leafed tree stood out and took the sun, and here the water of a swamp shone, already a cold, metallic blue.

Sven met them at the gate. Lind quickly told him to prepare for the masquerade on the chance that Caleb would permit Judith to go. Sven was almost beside himself with impatience and indignation at Caleb Gare. He had planned advancing upon him and taking Judith masterfully away if no opportunity came soon for their escape. He had heard from his former employer in the city and had had an offer of work. He was ready to go at once. He looked toward the Gare farm as Lind stood in the road talking with him, and his wholesome face twisted into a scowl. He finally agreed to wait until she brought him further news. Then he went back to the house, his step a little lighter.

Lind looked quickly up at Mark, who stood holding her hands in his own. "It makes me—impatient, too," she whispered to him. Although Mark knew Mrs Sandbo was looking out of the window, he stooped quickly and kissed her hair. Then he mounted his horse and rode back to the Klovaczs'.

Judith was pouring a mixture of buttermilk and feed into the pig trough when Lind returned. Caleb was in sight beyond the granary so Lind merely waved to Judith and went on into the house. She hurried upstairs and hid the things she had bought at Yellow Post under the bed in her room. When she returned to the kitchen Ellen threw her a curious glance.

"Ellen," said Lind, "aren't you a bit anxious to go to the party?"

Ellen shrugged and continued washing out the milk

can at her feet. "Why should I be? I'll go if he says," she returned. "Can't see as it'll be a lot of fun, anyhow."

Martin came in then. "Don't *you* want to go to the masquerade, Martin?" Lind asked him.

Martin smiled slowly. "Well—I can't dance," he replied, "but I guess we won't be goin', anyhow. Ain't nothin' been said about it, eh, Ellen?"

"No," said Ellen shortly, scrubbing away at the can. "Well, if you were given permission, you'd go, wouldn't you?"

"Guess so," Martin said.

Lind turned away disheartened. So well did they know their place that their imaginations had not been stirred in the least by the coming of this novel event.

Amelia took up the remainder of her vegetables. Her tomatoes had ripened beautifully, and there was a great crop. She would preserve them in various ways, and they would do the family for the whole winter. Yes, the winter was coming. Presently there would be frost. Then there would be the old months again of housing and bedding the cattle, the horses, the sheep, and the hogs. And sod would soon have to be placed on the roof of the chicken house, and manure spread over the garden. Then the snow would come like a white presence, and enclose them all in the log house. Caleb would be watchful as ever, and would receive letters now and then from Bart Nugent, keeping him informed of the movements of Mark Jordan, who would have gone back to the city. Judith would rebel occasionally and would have to be quelled with threats and reminders. Another winter of life under Caleb Gare. No, no . . . anything but that. But in another moment she would have resigned herself to the prospect.

She knew what satisfaction it was giving Caleb to withhold his decision about the jubilee. In the end he would probably let them go. That would be the end. . . .

On the following day Ellen and Martin were sent to Nykerk with a drove of cattle. They went while the morning was still dim and gray and heavy with dew, and drove the spotted heifers and steers before them like fantastic figures in a dream. Ellen slumped forward in her saddle half asleep, and was dully startled now and then by the crack of Martin's whip upon the flanks of the cattle. When she opened her eyes the animals looked unreal and incredible in the road before her. She wished again that Judith were more trustworthy and could be sent in her place. Judith was always thinking of herself. A lot she would get for it in the end! She would be tied more closely to the farm than any of them. Perhaps it would have been delightful to have gone away with Malcolm. The northern lakes would have been deep and blue, and there would have been infinite rest beside them at night, under the stars.

Ellen found herself nodding again over the pommel of her saddle. Her feet were asleep and full of needles in the stirrups. She shook herself and sat upright, stretching her red-rimmed eyes. They were going through the timber, and the gray glamour of early morning still obscured the brilliance of the foliage. It seemed to Ellen that they had been going for hours through sleep.

There was a telegrapher at Nykerk who kept the farm-

ers informed concerning the prices of grains and live-
stock. From him Martin learned that flax had taken a
tremendous leap upward. It was the news that Caleb
had been waiting to hear.

When Martin announced it to him on the return home,
he drew his hand across his mustache and wiped off the
smile of satisfaction that appeared upon his face. There
was still time for something to happen to the flax. No
need of rejoicing too soon.

"Gone up, eh? Well—lots of time for it to go down—
lots of time," he said.

But the news was sufficient cause for him to go out to
the flax field that evening with his lantern to look out
on the broad wealth of it. A short time now, and it
would be taken off. And there would not be a farmer in
all the country around so rich as Caleb Gare. It was
well that even Amelia did not know the extent of his fortune. It might make her avaricious, or turn her head.

Caleb thought of the Bjarnassons. They were well
supplied with this world's goods, too. But they could
not raise flax like this. They did not go much beyond
cattle and horses, that bred in the flesh. There was a
spirit in the flax—the growing of it was a challenge to
a man's will in this gaunt land. It took Caleb Gare to
raise flax.

The Bjarnassons—they had at last found the precious
remains for which they had dragged the lake a whole year.
A great deal of satisfaction that gave Caleb Gare—a
great deal! And Martin, that poor weakling, had not
dared take what was his just due. There had been
twelve months during which the Bjarnassons had arro-

gantly set their will against that of Caleb Gare for the
sake of so puny a thing as sentiment, and kept it set. An
annoying thought. But it was Martin's fault. He
should have compelled Martin to fish. What was the
matter with him, was he losing his grip on the family at
last? No—no, Amelia was still in her place, and there
was a tremendous change for the better in Judith. He
had no cause for apprehension. It occurred to him that
to taunt Bjarnasson, the family would do without fish
that winter.

Mark Jordan. Yes, there was something in store for
him. Caleb turned back across the stubble with his
lantern swinging low along the earth. He chuckled with
confidence in his power. It was all a huge joke, so simple
was this living and ruling. And to make the season complete, the price of flax had shot up like a rocket.

4

Secretly, in every spare moment that week, Lind and
Judith worked on the costumes in the privacy of the
Teacher's room. Judith stitched half-heartedly, dubious
as to whether there would ever be any use for the gaudy
apparel. Lind was generous enough to make a gown
for Ellen without saying a word about it to her. She
took Martin into her confidence, however, and fitted a
clown suit over his awkward body. He grinned bashfully, and she had the gratification of seeing his face light
up with amusement when he beheld himself in the bulky
garment.

Judith's somber demeanor did not lift, however,

throughout the week of hopeful planning. Lind began
to fear that she was losing courage, that Caleb's vigilance
and the plied warnings of Amelia were achieving their
end.

During the week Thorvald Thorvaldson drove up on
his way from Yellow Post, stopped in and stayed until
Amelia could do nothing but ask him to have dinner, at
Caleb's prompting. Otherwise nothing unusual happened all week. Amelia thought it would never come to
an end. No mention was made of the jubilee, and everyone on the place went about his accustomed tasks as if
the entire community were not alive with preparations
for merriment.

Judith plodded about, from the pig pen to the sheep
pasture, from the sheep pasture to the wood pile, where
she stood splitting kindling wood for Amelia as if that
were the thing she wanted most to do.

One day she and Martin and Charlie went to the bush
for more wood, and on the way her heart quickened with
the hope that somehow she might see Sven, since the
neck of timber bought of Fusi Aronson led past the
Sandbo farm. But she did not see him, and on the way
home her body felt heavy and lifeless. Lind was unable
to rouse her or to get any confidence from her.

The door of the stable remained locked. On Friday,
the day before the masquerade at Latt's School, Caleb
went past the stable and smiled to himself. The incident
of the ax had been a piece of good luck, after all. It was
time that he should try Judith out, to further convince
himself that she was permanently subdued. It was well
to know where he stood. Moreover, Amelia was set

against Judith's going to the masquerade—he could see that. And it would be well to show Amelia that her will in the matter bore no weight.

Caleb was confident that Judith would not dare go beyond Latt's School. And if she did—the responsibility was Amelia's. It might bring a settlement of that little score he had against Mark Jordan.

On Friday evening he announced to the family that the children would go to the jubilee at Latt's School. There was a general start around the table. But Caleb kept his eyes on Amelia, his hand stealthily moving across his chin and mustache. Amelia did not flinch. She smiled across at Martin and said, "You'll have to learn to dance before then, Martin."

Her equanimity disturbed Caleb. He took his lantern out and started across the stubble before darkness set in. The feeling had come upon him suddenly that somehow he was losing his grip. Perhaps after all he had made a mistake. Perhaps it had been Amelia's wish that Judith should go—should have this chance to escape with Sven Sandbo. Perhaps the woman had been adroit enough to conceal her real design from him. Perhaps she was even now plotting to get Judith away. Well, let her plot! She would remember in due time who was master. He still had control of the secret of Mark Jordan. Let Amelia try her tricks!

6

Lind rode that evening toward the Klovaczs' and met Mark in the hollow of the wood trail. He dismounted and put both arms about her where she sat in her saddle, as he liked to do.

"Dear little Lind," he whispered, lifting his face to hers, "every day seems a year."

Lind held him close against her. "Do you know, Mark, I can't shake this feeling that something fearful is about to happen. A loon passed right over the house last night," she told him, and he felt her body shiver against him.

Mark laughed. "It's your worry about Judith that's doing it, dear. We'll be away in a few weeks, now, and this life will seem like a dream. Here—let me help you down. Let's walk. How'd you like to go around that dried lake bottom? It's a weird enough place for your thoughts."

There would be light enough for an hour to walk over the rough land. Lind agreed. "I've only seen it from the top of the south ridge. It looks like the land in the pictures you see of Noah's Ark standing on Mount Ararat after the flood, with the creeping vegetation down below."

They walked their horses through the dry timber, where the yellow drift of leaves rustled underfoot, and the branches overhead made a brittle sound. When they emerged from the timber they skirted the hayfield of the Gares', where the generous stacks were standing. Then they came to the muskeg beyond which lay the lake bottom, a drab, flat disk with enormous, ugly cracks crisscrossing upon its surface. Grotesque roots and stones still covered with a pale sediment stood out in the wan light. Lind and Mark made their way across the narrow strip of solid land between the lake bottom and the muskeg.

"You'd be swallowed up on either side, Lind," Mark observed, glancing across the treacherous, hair-like reeds of the muskeg and then across the gray lake bottom, that grew darker toward the center, where it was not so dry.

Southward, across the hollow where the lake had been, lay Caleb Gare's flax field. From where they stood, Lind and Mark could see him going away from the field, his squat body leaning forward toward the earth, and outlined against the amber sky.

"Mark," Lind murmured, taking his hand, "he frightens me."

CHAPTER XXII

1

In order to get all the work done before they left for the jubilee at Latt's School, everyone was up at dawn the next day.

When Caleb had gone to the barn after breakfast, Lind ventured to show Ellen the costume she had made for her. Ellen's comments on it were sparing.

"But will it fit?" she said, eyeing it askance.

But Lind could see that Ellen was pleased. She put her arm about her and said, "Try it on."

The dress was made to resemble a great sunflower, with a skirt of petals. It was very becoming to Ellen's figure. Ellen blushed when she looked down at herself.

Amelia and Judith went immediately to the potato patch where they began to dig up the potatoes. Martin was building a new bin for them in the cellar. It had been Caleb's request at breakfast that they should begin taking them up to-day. It was his way of reminding them that the duties on the farm must go on, jubilee or no jubilee.

Judith worked with Amelia in the potato patch until well toward noon, when Amelia left her to make dinner. Then Judith sat down among the dried stems of the plants and pressed her hands against her abdomen. The stooping she had done for five unbroken hours had brought a strange new pain there. She made a pretense of pulling at the potato vines so that no one from the house should notice that she was resting. Then, finally, she saw Amelia beckoning to her from the doorway.

In the afternoon they returned to the potato patch with bushel baskets. Judith doubled her energy so that Amelia should not become curious.

Occasionally Amelia glanced at her. From her resigned attitude she half believed that the girl had no intention of abusing the freedom she was to be given that evening. And yet it was folly to trust her. Before night came on she would have to give her another severe admonishment. It was the most she could do to keep everything from falling into ruin. For Caleb would be inexorable. He would not spare Mark Jordan for a moment if Jude got away.

During the afternoon Amelia worked incessantly to keep from collapsing under the strain of her thoughts. It seemed that the awful knowledge of the possible outcome of the approaching night had stretched her mind until it would contain nothing more without breaking. In countless ways she pictured the scene in which Mark Jordan would learn the truth about himself. She went over and over the images until they were a continuous scroll unfurling automatically in her mind. Her hands became gray and coated with dirt, her back stiff from bending, and she carried basket after basket of potatoes to the house, almost unaware of the physical effort she exerted.

At the end of the day Judith carried the last basketful of potatoes into the house and down to the bin in the cellar. Then she hurried upstairs before Amelia could talk to her, and threw herself on Lind's bed. The Teacher had gone to the Sandbos' to talk with Sven. Ellen was out gathering eggs, and the boys and Caleb were about tending to the animals.

Amelia came upstairs to talk with Judith. She found her on Lind's bed, half asleep. The girl sat up and brushed her hair back from her eyes.

"What's the matter with you?" Amelia asked sharply.

"Nothing," said Judith, starting to rise. She sat back again suddenly with a quick tightening of her lips. Amelia gave her a searching look.

"You don't look right to me. You better not go to this thing to-night if you feel bad."

"I don't feel bad. I'm just tired," Jude insisted, an obstinate look appearing in her eyes.

"Well—I just want to tell you this," Amelia went on, "if you go, you go to Latt's School and nowhere else. And you go with Martin and Ellen. And you come back with them. If I hear different to-morrow, you needn't look to me to save you from *him*. He has told me it's the city for you if anything goes on. And remember this, Judith, he can catch you no matter how far you go. It won't do you a bit of good to try to get away. Do you understand that?" Amelia's eyes were sharp and searching, her mouth firm.

When she got no response from her, she leaned down and shook Judith by the shoulder.

"What makes you so stupid, child?" she asked, a little anxiously.

Suddenly Judith sprang to her feet. Her face was white.

"Who're you to be talkin' to me?" she cried harshly.
"You don't know—anything—about me! I don't belong to you—or him. I don't belong here. And I'm
goin' away. Right now—to-night—" her voice came in
gasps, almost unintelligibly—"—and I don't care—what
happens! He can put me in jail—if he wants to. He
can kill me—or you—or everybody. I don't care, I'm
goin'! And you can't stop me! You can't stop me, do
you hear!" She flung her body forward and Amelia recoiled, aghast at her vehemence. Her eyes were terrible
to see. Then suddenly she shrank backward and sat
on the bed. Her head dropped and her arms hung limp
at her sides. She had become in an instant almost helpless.

Amelia stared at her. "You shan't go—you shan't go,
Judith! I forbid you to go! I'll tell him—I'll go out
and tell him now, if you don't take back those words," she
said evenly. "You are *not* going to leave this farm."

"Your talkin' doesn't do any good," Judith said dully.
"I've got to go."

Amelia's eyes fastened upon her. "What do you
mean—you've got to go?" she demanded.

Judith stood erect. Her eyes were cold and emotion-
less. "It's none of your business—what. I've said I've
got to go. That's enough. You don't care anything
about me—why should I tell you anything? Go away
and leave me alone."

The older woman's eyes swept over her. Amelia felt
suddenly as if cold water had been poured into her
veins. The inevitable knowledge had come to her.
Judith was going to have a child.

Without another word Amelia turned and walked carefully down the stairs. She felt as if a terrific, incog-
nizable world had opened upon her. She had need of
something familiar to cling to. As she crossed the dining room the floor seemed to swim up toward her. In
the kitchen she stirred the fire and put more water in
the tea kettle. Then she beat up a custard and began
to peel potatoes for supper. One by one the others
came in from the yard. The Teacher returned from the
Sandbos'. Ellen began to set the table in the other room.
The natural routine was, mercifully, still going on.

Caleb was in high spirits that evening. A group of
horse traders had passed by and he had made a profitable
deal with them. He discussed the trade with Martin at
some length.

"The fires up north have turned east. Swept out five
homesteads, they said. No danger of us gettin' it down
here—no danger at all. The rangers have checked it
on this side," he said comfortably. "It's been dry
though. Good thing they controlled it just when they
did. Couldn't of stopped it down this way, if it once got
a hold, eh, Martin?"

Martin agreed that it would have been a bad situation.

"Goin' to have a good time to-night, everybody?"
Caleb went on, including them all this time, magnan-
imously. "What 'er you goin' to wear, Ellen? You'll
be the belle of the ball, like as not, eh?" He winked
good-naturedly at Ellen, who contrived to half smile in
response.

Caleb let his eyes rest on Amelia with an amused
twinkle. Amelia was so transparent. It was almost no

trick to follow her thoughts. At this moment, for instance, she was joking with Martin and Charlie about not eating too much at supper lest they be unable to relish the jubilee feast. She was trying to hide her real feelings. Well, he would do her justice—she was not doing so badly—not so badly.

The girls went to the loft immediately after they had done the milking, and Lind helped them dress. Their brief comments on the costumes she had made them were pathetic to the Teacher. They were afraid to say too much lest they should seem ignorant of and unused to such frivolous array. But Lind understood them, and was unhurt by their seeming indifference.

When they were finally dressed she stood them both off at arm's length and exclaimed, "You'll be the prettiest girls at the party! Wait and see if I'm not right!"

"No, we won't, Lind—you'll be," Judith said. She looked down at herself and half sighed. Lind had made a flowing white Greek robe for her, of delicate material, which might with slight alterations be worn as a dress. Jude blushed slightly as she thought of the significant color. She felt ponderous in the garment. Her shoulders seemed too large for it, her arms too strong. It was the kind of thing more fitting for Lind.

"If I take a deep breath this will fall off me, Lind," she said doubtfully.

Lind laughed. "Oh, scarcely, Judie. You really look glorious in it, with your dark hair and shining eyes. And so does Ellen in hers."

Downstairs Amelia ran the separator. Her mind was stumbling about among confused objects that seemed to have no relation to each other, but the old familiar tasks came easily to hand. Jude, then, must go away. That was what she had meant. There could be no doubt of it. She had read it in her face. She remembered the look in her own face, years ago, when she had confronted herself in the glass.

Judith would have to go away. With Sven. Caleb would hold her responsible. He had promised he would hold her responsible. It was a thing like this that he had been waiting for. What would happen now? What would happen? Would Mark Jordan believe the story? Would Lind Archer believe it? Who was she, a poor down-trodden woman of the land, to be the mother of Mark Jordan? It would be a dreadful blow to find him unable to believe it—unwilling to believe it. And yet Caleb had proof. He would have to accept it. What then? Would Lind Archer change toward him—or he toward her, feeling himself unworthy? What would become of them all? What would become of Mark Jordan, who had grown to manhood in the belief that he was well-born? How would he adjust himself to the truth? No—no, he must not know—he must not know. Somehow she must outwit Caleb. She must match his cuning with her own. She must pit her whole soul against his will. Somehow . . . somehow. Even if it came to . . . Judith had not been sure enough with the ax. What did life mean, anyway, for her, Amelia?

She watched the last drop of cream enter the container under the separator, then she lifted it from the floor and poured the cream into a large can beside her. The can would be full to send with Skuli Erickson on

Monday. She must remember to have Martin paint the name on the outside of it more plainly before Skuli took it away. Lately old cans had been sent back because the name was not clearly written on them. The cans belonged to Skuli, anyway, and it was only right that he should get his own property back.

She heard Judith and Ellen come down the stairs with Lind Archer. Immediately after them came the boys. They all appeared in the kitchen to show themselves to Amelia. She managed a smile of pleased surprise as they stood before her.

"Where on earth—is this your work, Teacher?" she exclaimed to Lind. "That was nice of you, I declare! My, don't they look fine!"

She turned the boys around admiringly. Martin grinned and was apparently enjoying the novelty. Charlie regarded his high pointed cap in the glass on the wall, and cocked it a little more to one side.

Judith returned to the inner room while the others still stood and talked with Amelia. She suddenly felt faint from the suppressed excitement of getting ready. And the knowledge that Amelia had guessed the truth about her bored dully into her brain. She had wanted none of them to know. They were not fine enough to know. They would denounce her for the thing she regarded with pride. She belonged to another, clear, brave world of true instincts, she told herself. They were muddled, confused souls, not daring to live honestly. Living only for the earth, and the product of the soil, they were meager and warped. She had not wanted them to know. Well—now that Amelia knew she would not stop her from going away—she could not stop her. Judith looked from the window. In the corral Caleb was bringing out the team, Prince and Lady. He would harness them, probably. He was in a very good-natured, playful mood.

The sun was dropping behind the poplar grove, and the trees stood before it like long black bars. Sven would be ready to leave soon. He had sent word through Lind that he would meet her at Latt's School, to avoid any trouble with Caleb. It was safer that way. From there they would leave for Nykerk. He would arrange with somebody at the Siding to take his team back home. There was a train that stopped there for a few minutes on Saturday nights. Judith had never seen a train. Neither had Ellen, or Martin, although they had been at the Siding many times. They had seen flat cars standing on the tracks. But never a train. It must be marvelously free riding on a train. Like the Magic Carpet she remembered about when she was a child at school. Going somewhere—away to another place. Just away—that was enough. But with Sven, that was heaven. Tears sprang into her eyes. It could not be that the night had at last come. She could scarcely control her excitement.

She sat down on a chair near the window, got up again and walked across the floor to the organ, where she picked out a few notes of Ellen's favorite song, *Ben Bolt*. Then she jumped up again and went out of doors, passing Amelia and the others in the kitchen. She saw that Caleb was, indeed, harnessing the horses. She returned to the kitchen and told the others that it was time they were getting into their coats. Her hands trembled so that she had difficulty in putting on her own things.

Amelia placed a cloth and paper over the basket of food they were bringing as a contribution to the feast. Her thoughts bounded about uncontrolled in her mind. Judith—Judith. Herself over again. Judith must go. Enough to have one life ruined. Not Judith's, too. "History repeating itself," Caleb would mock at her. Judith was her child, all right, with all of her virtues, hah! Amelia could hear his sneering laugh. It took more than one generation to wipe out bad blood, he would say. Judith's indiscretion would ring in her ears forever. She could not stand it—she could not stand it. Her brain reeled. She straightened up and placed her hand to her head.

"What is it, Mrs Gare?" Lind asked softly. She had come up to the table where Amelia was preparing the basket. "Headache?"

Amelia smiled at her. "Just a little—worked hard to-day getting the potatoes in," she said.

Ellen, Martin and Charlie, ready to go, said good-by to Amelia. Judith stood before her when the others had gone out with Lind. "Good-by," she muttered, "I'll write to you—if you want."

Amelia's hands moved spasmodically toward the girl, then fell stiffly to her sides. "Yes—write, Judie," Amelia whispered, her mouth dry. "Good-by, Jude." Then Judith was gone. She had not stopped her.

She had not stopped her. Amelia stared at the vacant doorway through which she had gone, as if she expected to see her return. Her fingers opened and closed over her hot, moist palms. Judith was gone. She had had to go. She, Amelia, had let her go. There was a ringing tumult in her ears. Mark Jordan would know now . . . but another young life would not be ruined as hers had been . . . the room seemed to grow dark and intolerably warm . . .

Amelia went and leaned against the side of the doorway, looking out. Caleb was hustling the children jovially into the wagon. Lind stood smiling up at them. Now they were off—driving through the gate. Caleb was waving after them. There—he closed the gate. There was only a narrow streak of gold threading through the poplars. Caleb entered the barn. Lind returned to the house, and Amelia withdrew into the other room.

Lind went upstairs to her room, and Amelia looked about for something to do. She dreaded being alone and unoccupied. All her pent-up emotion would break out if she did not get to work at something at once. She decided to start a new pair of socks for Martin. Then she could find only four of her knitting needles. She kept new ones in a drawer of the secretary. She went to it and found that somehow the lock of the drawer had got caught and she could not open it. She gave the handle of it a jerk, and when it flew open the front of the drawer above it fell out. It was the drawer in which Caleb kept all his correspondence and papers safely locked away. Amelia straightened up, frightened. She tried to put the front of the drawer back in place, but it would not fit. She hurried to the window and looked out. There was no sign of Caleb.

For fully a minute she stood before the secretary, undecidedly hovering over it. Then she dropped to her knees and snatched out the handful of papers and letters it contained. Most of them were yellow and ragged with age. No one wrote to Caleb now, or had any dealings with him, except at the bank. There were one or two documents and land deeds, newer in color. But there was one envelope addressed in a cramped hand. Amelia knew the writing. It was Bart Nugent's. Nervously she drew out the letter. It was brief and almost impossible to decipher. But Amelia made out from it that Bart Nugent was dying at the time it was written. The date was obscure. With numb hands she fumbled through the other papers and found a letter sent from a hospital in the city. It apprised Caleb Gare of the death of Bart Nugent, stating that it was the dying man's last request that the enclosed letter should be sent to him. The letter was dated nearly six months before. Bart had lived just long enough to let Caleb know that Mark Jordan was coming to Oeland.

Amelia sank to the floor and leaned against the secretary. Hysteria seized her. She was still sitting there with the litter of yellow papers and envelopes about her when Lind came down stairs. The Teacher had heard her sobbing while she was in the loft above. She knelt down beside Amelia and put her arm about her heaving shoulders.

"What is it—what is it, Mrs Gare?" she cried.

Amelia drew herself up with a tremendous effort. "Never—never mind. It's nothing," she said breathlessly. "Help me fix this, will you—quick."

Lind gathered the papers hastily together, and put them

back in the drawer. Then she inserted the front of the drawer while Amelia tapped it lightly with a small hammer she got from the kitchen. It was finally in its place again.

They were no more than away from the secretary when Caleb came in. Lind's heart was beating nervously.

"They have a fine evenin' for it—a fine evenin'," Caleb declared in a pleasant voice. "I'm going to take one of the nags I bought out for a trial. Wouldn't like to come, eh, mother?"

"No—not to-night, Caleb. I'm starting a new pair of socks for Martin," Amelia said calmly.

"All right—all right. You women sure like work," he observed in a mild tone. Then he went out once more.

Lind sat down and breathed freely again. Whatever it was, a catastrophe had been averted. Amelia's face had been for a moment distorted with fear.

The Teacher returned to her room, where she was going over some school work. She and Mark had planned not to go to the affair at Latt's School until late in the evening, as it would last all night and they would have had enough of it even though they weren't among the first arrivals.

A wind was coming up, and whistled thinly under the eaves of the log house. It made its way into Lind's mood and haunted her. Again there came to her the feeling that something evil was in store.

She waited uneasily for the hours to pass so that she might go out to meet Mark on the road. The Sandbos' pony was already in the barn for her to ride. She would go out soon and lead the animal to the watering trough.

It would be something to do. And then she decided that she would not water him until just before she would leave.

The house was heavy with mystery. What was the reason for Amelia's breaking into the drawer of the secretary? And why had she acted so strangely? Lind felt herself the victim of a bewildering fear. From somewhere out on the marshes she heard the call of a loon. And the wind whined under the eaves. Lind wanted Mark near her. His presence was reassuring, always. But was it? It was he who needed her. He needed her to keep him from himself, to keep him from his isolation. Lind felt warmed by the thought.

2

The school house beyond Latt's Slough was festooned with sheaves of wheat and yellow corn husks and colored paper lanterns hung from the ceiling. The great Mathias Bjarnasson played the fiddle on a low stool in the corner, and an accordeon and an organ were keeping pace with him. The shuffle of heavy feet could be heard above the music, and against the colored light of the lanterns the dust rose in a gray sheet. But there was no limit to the merriment among the dancers.

Ellen was carried out of herself by the attention the young Icelanders showed her. She felt giddy from the noise and the music. But beneath the ripple of excitement, there was a flat, hard ache. Malcolm had loved to dance. It was he who had taught her the few steps she knew.

Suddenly she realized that she had not seen Judith for some time. She went out to the porch of the school house and glanced about. There were a number of people seated on the railings and the steps to get fresher air between dances. But she could not see Judith. She returned indoors and sought out Martin and Charlie. Neither of them had seen Judith for over an hour.

Ellen's eyes drew into a straight, narrow line.

"She's gone," she said to herself. Tears sprang into her eyes. They were tears of vexation and something akin to envy.

The trail to Nykerk led for a considerable distance through timber and then broke upon the bare prairie. Judith and Sven rode in the latter's buggy over the long miles through the bush without meeting a soul. Everyone was at the jubilee. Judith kept urging the horse on and looking back now and then to see that they were not being followed.

"Say—cut that out," Sven commanded at last, seizing her roughly about the shoulders and kissing her. "If you look back once again, I'll——"

It was starlight now and a wind had risen. The dry-leafed branches along the road rubbed each other and made an uncanny sound. Judith moved closer to Sven.

"We'll have to hurry if we're going to make the train," he said, spanking the horses with the reins.

Ahead of them a team rumbled over a small wooden bridge. Someone was coming. Judith raised her head defiantly.

"Wa–al! Who's this?" a voice called out. Judith

recognized it as that of Thorvald Thorvaldson. They had come upon the prairie road, and had met him on the forks that led south.

Sven exchanged a brief hello with him and passed on. But Thorvald had seen Judith. They knew that by the chuckle that sounded after him.

"Well—he'll not be seeing *him* until to-morrow at the earliest. And by that time we'll be in town," Sven commented, and squeezed Jude's hand. She returned a quick, nervous pressure.

The touch of her hand excited Sven. He quickly forgot all the misfortune that threatened their journey, and drew Judith over upon his knees. She clung to him and felt deliciously small and helpless. His arms surrounding her, he held the reins and drove all the way to Nykerk without changing his position.

3

Thorvald thought it a good joke. Too good to keep. It wasn't so late but what he might find Caleb up if he drove to his farm. So when he reached the road upon which his own farm was situated, he continued eastward to the Gares'.

Caleb was going the rounds to see that everything was safe for the night when Thorvald drove up to the gate.

"I will not stop," he told Caleb, keeping his seat in the cart. "Thought you should like to know somet'ings."

Caleb peered at him. "Well—out with it, man—out with it!" He was losing his patience with this Thorvaldson.

"Wa–al, now, you maybe wait," the Icelander said, enjoying his advantage for once. "Why, perhaps, is your purty daughter on the way to Nykerk when all others they are at the jubilee, eh?"

Caleb was silent for only a moment. "Oh!" he laughed. "You fool yourself, Thorvald. You fool yourself! She's not goin' to Nykerk. She's goin' to fetch one of the Teacher's friends from up west way. No—no, Thorvald."

Thorvald threw back his head. "Not so smart, Caleb Gare, are you. Who wass with her then, but this young feller, Sven Sandbo? Hah, hah!" He turned the horse about and drove off down the road, laughing as he went.

Caleb stood in the road and looked after him, his heavy head drooping forward. "She's gone—she's gone!" he muttered to himself. Then a bedeviling fury broke loose within him.

He rushed to the barn and threw open the door. He struck a match and looked at the wall where the ax had been buried. There was a hole in the wall where the rotted wood had dropped out with the weight of the ax. The ax lay on the floor, still deep in the wood that had fallen with it. Caleb backed out of the barn and the match was blown out by the wind.

4

Fusi Aronson had been burning out a stretch of willows that day, intending to clear the land for planting next year. The willows grew in soggy ground, where the

grass was matted deep. Darkness came down upon him
before he had finished the job, and he carefully stamped
out every glow of the fire he had been watching. He
had started burning the willows out at a short distance
from the edge of Caleb Gare's timber—the timber that
used to be his own. He was confident that not a spark
of the fire remained at that end of the burned stretch.
But the day had been calm and treacherous. With nightfall came the wind.

Smouldering cinders under the thick black web of burnt
grass grew to a red glow. The glow quickened in the
bits of dry grass that remained—spread underground
through the roots of the willows, and was caught in the
wind that lifted it into the timber. Because there had
been a smell of smoke abroad all day from Fusi's willows,
those who remained at Sandbos' thought nothing of it.
And the wind was directly south, so it did not penetrate
immediately westward to the Gares'. But within an
amazingly short time the fire rose like a flaming feather
fan against the sky, and hurtled southward.

5

Caleb stepped softly into the kitchen. He could see
Amelia sitting in the other room, her head bent over her
knitting. Carefully he closed the door behind him.

"Done it at last, eh?" he chuckled. Amelia looked up.
She stepped forward and laid her knitting on the table.
Something was wrong. But he could not possibly have
found out about Jude already.

Caleb stood before her, his hands behind his back.

"You tell him, Amelia," he said softly. "You'll tell him—to-night."

"What—tell who?" Amelia stuttered.

"You know well enough what I mean. Heh! Had your nerve, eh, sending her off when you knew what was comin'? You're goin' to Klovaczs' *now* and tell him—tell him all about it, your pretty son! Are you gettin' ready?"

Amelia looked him squarely in the face. "No," she said between her teeth. "I am not."

"You're not, eh? Well—we'll see if you're not!" He drew his hands from behind his back and Amelia saw the huge cattle whip he held.

"Have your choice, Amelia—have your choice! He'll find out anyway, but I'd rather you'd tell him. He insulted me one day, and I'd like him to see that I'm *above* retaliatin'!" He raised his eyebrows at her and smiled.

"I tell you, I'll *not!*" Amelia cried. He advanced upon her a step, confident that he could, as usual, frighten her into submission with a look. But Amelia faced him without cringing.

He stooped and looked into her eyes. There was no fear in them. For the first time in her life Amelia was not afraid of Caleb Gare.

Caleb raised the whip and struck. His face was livid with wrath—wrath at her resistance. What had become of his power over her? She recoiled when the whip bit into her flesh, but she did not cry out.

"Not a whimper, eh? Like it, maybe. Are you comin'? No? Then I'll show you who you're answerin' to round here—I'll show you!"

His voice was rising to a thin, high pitch. He was beside himself now, baffled and furious at her endurance. Amelia cowered in the corner between the organ and the wall. She kept her eyes unwaveringly upon him. Steadily in her mind, like a balance of fine weights, she kept the thought that all depended upon her will now. Bart Nugent was gone. Once Mark Jordan got away from Oeland no harm could reach him.

Caleb reached out his long arm and caught her by the hand, throwing her into the middle of the room.

Lind, who had been listening in paralyzed horror above, now came running down the stairs. Caleb had his back to her. She saw the whip and flung herself upon him. "I did it—I sent her away!" she cried wildly. "Leave her alone—I did it!"

Caleb turned slowly and looked at her, a curious smile on his face.

"Heh! *You* did! No, you didn't. Don't try to lie to me, Miss. It wouldn't give me any satisfaction to know that *you* did it. *She* did it." He pointed with the butt of the whip at Amelia, on the floor. Then he turned again to Lind. "Get out!" he shouted hoarsely. "Get out before I throw you out!"

Lind shot a glance at Amelia and ran out of the house. She stumbled over the ruts of the cattle yard until she came to the gate. Sobbing and trembling from head to foot, she climbed over it and kept on running blindly down the trail toward the Sandbos'. Surely Mark must be coming! She raised her head to see if he were in sight. Then an astounding spectacle met her eyes, and at once she perceived that the air was thick with smoke.

North of the trail the timber had become a blazing spume that was being thrown southward by the wind. Even at this distance she could hear the roar of the flames. For many seconds she was unable to move. Where was Mark? Had he passed the neck of timber? Were the Sandbos safe? What would happen to Amelia, indoors with Caleb? She ran down the road a bit, scarcely thinking of what she was doing. Then she made out a horse coming along the trail, and heard the swift hoof-beats. In another moment Mark reined in beside her, and dismounted.

"Lind!" he cried, throwing his arm about her, "we're in for it!"

Lind broke away. "Mark—hurry—Caleb is killing Amelia!"

Amelia still had consciousness. Caleb leaned forward over her. His face was twisted with disbelief. He could not bring himself to admit that she had beaten him —beaten him in the very crisis of her life. The moment he had waited for had come. And she had cheated him. He would be forced to tell Mark Jordan himself now if he wanted it told. Little satisfaction in that—little indeed—a clumsy business. He stepped back from her prostrate body. Cold realization came upon him suddenly. He had spent all his will on her—with no effect. She had broken him. Broken him in the crisis. Something crumbled within him, like an old wall, leaving bare his spirit. His sanity came back to him, the cold clear sanity that had been gone from him during the years of his hatred. It was like sudden, clarifying sobriety after a drunken brawl. Shame and self-loathing broke upon him over-poweringly. He lunged aside and made for the door, feeling his way as if he had gone suddenly blind—blind with sight. His eyes were half closed.

Outside he lifted his face to the air. A pungent odor struck his nostrils. Then, his eyes opening, he saw the east sky.

"God!" he shouted. He felt his brain splitting. He ran down the sheep pasture to see more clearly the extent to which the fire had spread. The wind was due south.

Caleb rushed to the tool shed and dragged out a small plow. Then he got one of the work horses out of the corral and hitched it to the plow. He let down the bars of the sheep pasture and lashed the horse furiously, driving him toward the southern point of the timber he had bought of Fusi Aronson. He would have to plow a fire-guard around it so that the flames would not jump to the bush on the east. Once into the bush, it would have a clean sweep to the edge of the flax field. There had been no fires here for years. He had thought a fire guard between the bush and the flax would be a waste of land. . . .

Back at the house Lind and Mark came in upon Amelia. She had dragged herself to the couch and was lying there motionless. Mark stood in the doorway while Lind bent over her.

"Dear Mrs Gare," Lind whispered, "has he gone?"

Amelia nodded. She was unable to speak.

"Let me get you some water," the Teacher said. "Mark Jordan is here. If he comes back he won't dare to do anything."

Lind put her hand under Amelia's head. She appeared to have fainted. "Mark—get me some water," Lind said quickly.

Presently Amelia sat up and half smiled at them. She brushed the disordered hair back from her face, and drew her collar over a great red welt on her neck.

"If I had known he would carry on like that, I should have done everything I could to prevent Judith from going," Lind said regretfully. "Although I am sure she would have gone anyway."

"Yes—she would have gone," Amelia said in a weak voice. "I wanted her to go."

Lind hid her surprise.

"We'll have to tell Mrs Gare, I'm afraid, Lind," Mark said then. "She may have to be prepared to leave." He glanced at the woman pityingly, and with rage in his heart for Caleb Gare. If he had only come a little sooner——

Amelia looked up quickly. "What is it?" she asked.

"The bush is burning," Mark told her. "Making south—it will be almost at the trail by this time. And there's a strong wind. I'll have to ride to Yellow Post and get help."

Amelia straightened up. "Where has he gone?" she asked. "He must have taken the plow out—" She got to her feet unsteadily and ran to the door. When she saw the burning timber she made an exclamation of dismay. Mark hurried after her.

"I'll go to Yellow Post," he said. "Lind, you'd better stay here with Mrs Gare. I'll come back by way of the west road. We can't do anything alone with that gale."

"Wait, Mark," Lind kissed him quickly. "Take care
of yourself." Amelia opened the door for him and he ran
out.

It was a matter of minutes before the fire would reach
the road leading to Yellow Post on the east. Mark rode
as he had never ridden before in his life. He passed
safely through the neck of timber and left the roar of
the flames behind him, heading south. Then he looked
back, and could make out against the glare the figure
of a man stooping forward over a plow, driving a horse
before him. It was Caleb Gare, trying to cut off the fire
at the southern extremity of the timber he had bought of
Fusi Aronson. Mark knew it was futile work. The
wind would launch flaming torches into the bush a short
distance from the place where Caleb was plowing, long
before it got to the stubble of the hayfield at the edge
of the timber. Because of the direction of the wind,
Caleb might with great good luck save the hay. But the
bush south of Fusi's timber was doomed. And adjacent
to it stood Caleb's flax field, dry and rich with oil. . . .

Caleb faced the lurid column of flame and smoke on
the north and beat the horse, pressing down with all
his strength on the plow share. Presently the heat advanced, and with it tiny sharp sparks that stung the face
and hands like buck-shot. But Caleb did not feel it.
He had only one thought—to confine the fire to the neck
of timber. He cursed himself for having permitted Martin to go to the jubilee. With Martin here the thing
would be simple. He looked up and saw great bright
flakes sailing through the air, accompanied by darker
flakes. He coughed and sputtered from the smoke and

once or twice the horse stumbled. But he would not yield, although the heat was becoming terrific. The horse would probably bolt—there was that danger. He must get the most out of him before he became unmanageable. To and fro he plowed, across the whole end of the neck of timber. The roar from the north seemed to shake the sky and the earth. When Caleb had finally plowed the entire stretch between the two pieces of timber, the trees on the north were glowing just a short distance inward from the edge of the stubble he had turned up. He whipped the horse and turned him toward home. The exhausted animal used his last bit of strength in a gallop across the field toward the sheep pasture. Caleb ran after him to escape the intense heat.

In the farm yard he looked back. A single tree at the end of the bush south of the strip he had plowed was waving like a plume of fire. Caleb stood staring at it stupidly. Then he groaned. His work had been all for nothing. He ran toward the house. There was only one thing to do. Plow a division through the flax and burn the part nearest the bush. From old habit, he lit the lantern, ignoring Amelia and Lind who were waiting in terror in the other room.

When Caleb started across the fields southward, with a fresh horse, he saw that the fire had got well into the bush and was sweeping everything before it. He drove the horse like a madman. There was a remote chance of making it. He must have that chance. The flax must be saved, the beautiful flax, rich and strong . . . acres and acres of it. . . . He looked back and saw that the fire was gaining on him. It was swell-

ing against the sky in great blown clouds of flame and
smoke.   If it weren't for the wind he could get ahead of
it.   He saw presently that it was of no use trying to plow
a fire-guard.   He would have to burn the flax a distance
inward from the bush without plowing.   He would be
careful to stamp it out as he went along.   It would not
have to spread.

He let the horse go, left the plow on the field and ran
on alone.   In the bush the flames were leaping from tree
to tree like grotesque, golden animals.   Even alone he
could never cover all the distance around the muskeg.
Damn that muskeg!   And yet—the autumn had been
extremely dry.   Perhaps it would hold the weight of a
man.   No—no, this was madness.   The muskeg had not
been dry for years.   All summer it had been full of water
holes.   He hurried on, panting from his exertion.   He
would have to get around the muskeg and the dried lake
bottom.   It was a mile out of his way, but he would have
to make it.   The flax must be saved.   He might have
ridden the horse.   But the animal would have gone wild.
From the tail of his eye he could see the fire now, without turning his head.

Caleb stumbled over a rut in the field and lay for a
moment without being able to breathe.   The earth
seemed to be playing him a trick.   He got to his hands
and knees and looked toward the burning timber.   It
seemed to have jumped forward half a mile while he lay
on the ground.   He picked up the lantern which was still
lighted, and rushed toward the muskeg.   A shattering
rage at the fire seized him.   It seemed to be taunting him
with human ingenuity.   He would beat it with all its

tricks. The earth under him became black and began to give beneath his feet like cushions. He ran on blindly, conscious only of the direction in which the flax field lay. The fire was gaining with every moment. The wind kept up its velocity. Now silky reeds were beginning to tangle themselves about Caleb's legs. They impeded his progress. He stepped higher so as to crush them under foot. The earth seemed to billow like water. But Caleb paid no heed. He clung to the lantern and rushed on, his head leaning far forward, his shoulders high. Then suddenly, something seemed to be tugging at his feet. He could not release them. Water was oozing into his shoes and pushing up about his ankles. He was close to the timber now, so that he could feel the gusty heat from the fire, but the water about his legs was colder than ice. He bent down and pulled at the reeds in an effort to jerk his feet free. But the strength in the earth was irresistible. His arms were those of a feeble puppet fanning at the air. He stood upright again and strained with all his might. But the insidious force in the earth drew him in deeper. He raised the lantern as far as he could stretch and signaled toward the farm house. He shouted but his voice was carried away in the wind and lost in the roar from the burning timber. He reached his arms outward toward the flax, as if in supplication to its generous breadth. The fire had now got past the point where he was sinking in the black mud. He turned away so that he should not see it. But he knew that his position would force him to look upon it to the end . . . unless he closed his eyes. He bent down and pulled frantically at the reeds, but they gave way at the roots and came up in slippery clods. He fell back upon his hands and clutched fistfuls of the wet sod, straining at his legs. His hat fell off and his pointed locks of hair tossed about uncouthly with the twisting and heaving of his body.

Disconnected images began to pass before him. He closed his eyes but they continued to come. Thorvaldson, rejoicing when he heard what had happened to him. Fusi Aronson, on whose land he was about to die. Amelia . . . he had failed there, bitterly . . . and Mark Jordan, who was not his son . . . the ax buried in the rotten wood of the barn wall. . . .

The fire was racing ahead. Only a little while now, and it would have the flax . . . a fine, abundant growth it was . . . only a little while . . . ah, the over-strong embrace of the earth . . . Caleb closed his eyes. He felt tired, too tired to struggle any more. He had given his soul to the flax . . . well, it would go with him. He could see it shimmering still, gray-silver, where the light of the fire fell upon it. The earth was closing ice-cold, tight, tight, about his body . . . but the flax would go with him . . . the flax . . .

From the door of the log house Amelia spoke to Lind. "Look—his lantern is standing still—low down. Teacher, isn't that where the muskeg ought to be?"

Lind came to the doorway and looked out, her eyes following the older woman's. She felt a long shudder pass through Amelia's body.

"Yes," she replied in a whisper.

CHAPTER XXIII

1

Octuber came, and the languid peace of Indian summer. In the early morning a milky scud hid the horizon, but by noon the entire sky was clear and blue as a harebell. And over everything was a profound silence, as if somewhere a hand had been raised commanding reverence. It was a time of rest on the Gare farm.

Amelia was quiet and serene, and went about her work as before. But she did not do it hurriedly now, crowding her day full of unnecessary tasks.

Martin journeyed to the city, and there saw Jude and Sven. He found them very happy, and carried this news, together with a plan for the New House, back to the farm with him. Ellen received both items of information morosely, with secret indignation.

Young Erik Bjarnasson came to the Gares' one day.

"There is good fishing now, in the lake," he said to Martin. "We want you should come over any time you will."

Martin thanked him and told the others about it at supper.

"I don't think you ought," said Ellen. "He didn't invite father to."

"Well—" said Martin slowly. He was thinking of a humiliating day in midsummer, when Erik had seen the fish-pole in the back of the wagon. "Well—I'm not goin' to look like a fool by *not*. And I'm not goin' to insult Erik by not."

On another day, Mrs Sandbo came. Amelia Gare made her at home and served her with excellent coffee, bought in the city. Mrs Sandbo noticed that the coffee was not the brand obtainable at Johanneson's, but contained her curiosity. Privately, she thought it almost indecent of Amelia to put on airs so soon. Buying town coffee so immediately after— Well, she, for one, wouldn't say anything. . . .

The first hoar frost came, and Lind woke one morning to find the earth covered with white, powdered glass. The sun took its glitter within a few minutes, but the land was not the same after it had gone. It seemed to have left a shadow over the stubble and over the short brown grass of the pastures to the west, and over the black corpses of the trees that had been ravished by the fire. The days that followed were as full of mellow radiance as those that had gone before, the wind was as soft and the sky as intimate a blue, but there had come a change in the mood of the earth.

Then Lind heard the honking of the first wild goose, high overhead. On a night that was cold with moonlight she heard it, a full, clear trumpeting, in a sky that was vacant of clouds. The wild geese were passing over —passing over the haunts of man in their remote seeking toward the swamps of the south. They marked the beginning and the end of the period of growth. Next year they would fill the sky with their cold, lonely clamor at sowing time, and again when the earth would have closed in upon itself after yielding its growth. But next year Caleb Gare would not be here to note their coming or their going.

Lind felt humble as she heard the wild geese go over. There was an infinite cold passion in their flight, like the passion of the universe, a proud mystery never to be solved. She knew in her heart that Mark Jordan was like them—that he stood inevitably alone. But because of the human need in him, he had come to her. It warmed her to dwell on the thought.

The day came when Lind locked the door of the school house and watched the children she had taught scatter to the three roads that led east and west and north.

On the following day she and Mark left Oeland, promising Amelia that they would return some time. But Amelia knew that they would never come back again, and in her heart she was glad.

They drove by night to Nykerk, to take the train from the Siding to the city. They would leave the team in the livery stable there, and the Klovacz boys would get them the following day.

"I wonder just what the mystery was at the Gares'," Lind mused as they rumbled along in the buggy over the hard road. "It seemed to vanish with Caleb."

"Strange the way it worked out—the only thing he really cared for claimed him in the end," Mark observed.

Lind shivered a little and he put his arm about her, drawing her bare head down beneath his lips.

Far overhead in the night sky sounded the honking of the wild geese, going south now . . . a remote, trailing shadow . . . a magnificent seeking through solitude . . . an endless quest . . .

THE END